girls write now

GIRLS WRITE

THE 2011

ANTHOLOGY

OPENING LINES

girls write

GIRLS WRITE NOW, INC., NEW YORK CITY

Opening Lines: The 2011 Girls Write Now Anthology

Girls Write Now would like to thank Amazon.com, which provided the
charitable contribution that made possible this year's anthology.

Girls Write Now, Inc.
247 West 37th Street, Suite 1800
New York, NY 10018

www.girlswritenow.org

Co-Edited by Kirthana Ramisetti and Léna Roy
Graphic design by Deb Tremper
Photography by Jennifer Chu
Copyediting by Karen Schader

Anthology Editorial Committee:
Lee Clifford
Rachel Cohen
Naima Coster
Kristen Demaline
Nora Gross
Emily Grotheer
Jessica Jorge
Vani Kannan
Jennifer McDonald
Meghan McNamara
Christina Morgan
Maya Nussbaum
Elaine Stuart-Shah
Jessica Wells-Hasan
Rhonda Zangwill

ISBN 978-0-615-48397-9

CONTENTS

By Nana Brew-Hammond

It was a Sunday afternoon in 2004, and a weird time in my life. I was three years out of a wrenching break up and four years into a job I loved that wasn't paying me enough to live on. I was also a writer, taking my aspirations out on overly written emails and press kits at work; hustling on my lunch breaks, nights, and weekends to build a portfolio of writing clips; applying to every writing contest I could find.

In those days, if I wasn't obsessing over the circumstances surrounding my break-up, I was handwringing about how much I ~~wanted~~ needed to write. It was in that confused time in my life, upon the forwarded email recommendation of a friend I have since lost touch with, that I wandered into Housing Works Bookstore on Crosby Street for the Girls Write Now Spring Reading.

I joined the audience, my eyes taking in the walls of books, the patrons, the presumed "girls" of Girls Write Now, and the baked goods for sale; and waited somewhat restlessly for the program to begin. I was not prepared for what was to come.

Tears surprised my eyes as I watched girl after girl approach the microphone, some with shaking hands, a few with trembling delivery—all courageous voices. I saw in those girls my 13, 14, 15, and sixteen-year-old selves; sure that they had something to say, but still figuring out how best to say it. How I wished I had a program like this growing up. How I wanted to be a part of it.

I identified the GWN leadership and I lobbied to become a mentor. I filled out the extensive application, and with more anxiety than I've ever had on a job interview, tried to keep my cool as I answered the thoughtful, probing questions a duo of GWN staffers posed at my in-person interview.

It was nerve wracking, the wait to find out if I had made it, and when I learned I would become a mentor, I felt the bubbles of validation and anticipation—coupled with the hangover of apprehension and insecurity. Who was I to be mentoring anybody, let alone a young girl?

In the weeks, then months, then years that followed, Girls Write Now would prepare me to answer that question again and again.

Because the organization is committed to arming the mentees with the right tools to articulate themselves in written and spoken word, we mentors were rigorously trained in daylong workshops accompanied by a thick, pages long handbook. Just as the girls were expected to come to Girls Write Now focused and ready to learn and write; the mentors were required to hold the girls' attention and capture their imaginations with carefully thought-out lesson plans complete with Ice Breaker exercises and what we used to call "Warm Fuzzy" prompts.

I say this all to point out that whoever wrote the rules of airplane emergency procedure knew what she was talking about. You can't fit an oxygen mask on another person if you're gasping for air yourself; and as we mentors were being equipped to lead and serve, we, in turn, equipped our mentees as writers and young women. Together, we created a community committed to empowering a generation of female voices; voices that are too often silenced or dismissed, voices that wouldn't necessarily be heard outside the Girls Write Now meeting space.

Class, race, culture, religion, sexuality, family drama, career goals, college prep, time and money management… nothing was off limits, as guest editors and educators, guidance counselors and girls' rights advocates, actresses and authors, filmmakers and financial experts exposed the girls to their respective disciplines and led meaningful, focused discussions. In every workshop, the girls—knowing they were safe and respected—expressed their thoughts with candor and bravery, logging them in lyrics, poems, and powerful prose.

And with each workshop, I saw girls who started the year whispering, hiding behind hair, or literally shrinking into themselves with hunched shoulders and bowed heads project a little more clearly, push strands from their face so they could see and be seen, and stand tall as they spoke.

If I had space and time, I would write a cheesy poem about the mentees I saw flower in the program, including my own, Farida, Patrice, Lauren, and Tina; about how much they challenged and inspired me. We learn in school about the metamorphosis that turns caterpillars into butterflies, and understand that seeds planted in the right soil sprout into buds and fragrant blossoms, but to see it happen up close was something to behold.

Farida, my first mentee, a Nigerian-American girl with endless talent, sharp business acumen, and a sharper sense of self, was the girl I wished I had been as a kid—a leader. She directed and acted in school plays, and continued to carve out creative opportunities for herself when she went to college, interning for a production company in LA one summer, at CNN another.

Ebullient Patrice was and is a light, so open, so full, and it showed in her candid, collar-grabbing, cheek-caressing poetry. Patrice was enterprising too, fearlessly pitching herself to work on high profile projects at school and various print and online publications, yielding hard won clips on some of the most prestigious style blogs, nabbing coveted styling assistantships, and a shout-out in *Teen Vogue* along the way.

I remember Saturdays in the Queens Public Library with Lauren. An avid dancer and a brilliant poet, Lauren could make a poem out of vapor—quickly. I'm still floored by how fast she came up with the poem she wrote and submitted one afternoon to a poetry contest, that was ultimately published on the contest's website.

Tina was a deeeelight. She had recently emigrated from China to Brooklyn, NY when we were matched, and every line she wrote seemed infused with perfume of her childhood, as she gracefully transcended the language barrier, working so hard, so patiently, so admirably. Just about to complete her first year at SUNY Stony Brook, her work ethic continues to amaze me.

It has been seven years since that Sunday afternoon I wandered into Housing Works with no clue what to expect, and yet every expectation I had was fulfilled. Inspired in no small part by the bravery of the girls and women in the program, it was during my time at Girls Write Now that I finished my debut coming-of-age novel *Powder Necklace,* which Simon & Schuster released in April, 2010. As you turn the page to read the works of the girls for whom this program was started over a dozen years ago, I have every confidence you'll be moved to pursue that thing you've been aching to do, too.

We see an opening line as an invitation to another world, to a new perspective. "*Will you come with me?*" the line asks. This is what we ask of you—share our journey. The 2011 curriculum at Girls Write Now was organized around the idea of *Opening Lines*, and each chapter of this volume welcomes us with the first line of a mentee's piece written this season.

Inspired by this concept as both mentors and editors, the members of the Anthology Committee challenged each other to reconsider the genre-based structure of our annual book, to open up the possibility of understanding our community in an entirely new way. What emerges in our weekly pair sessions, our monthly group workshops, and our public reading series? We discovered an organic set of themes exploring who we are alone and with each other, at home and abroad, and how these identities define us as women and as writers.

Playing with *Opening Lines*, we encouraged mentors to borrow an intriguing sentence from their mentees as their own opening lines—an exercise illustrating the intimate relationship forged between writers and their readers, mentees and mentors, and how the line of communication between us is continuous, mutually reinforcing, wildly diverse, and always surprising. You'll find these shared lines indicated in **bold** throughout the book.

When we sat down to organize the writers' pieces into a cohesive whole, we often found that the opening lines of these works also opened a dialogue between us about writing, creating, and sharing stories, and about the passion and discipline that transform an idea into a polished piece. The same pieces that made us laugh made us emotional, and made us so happy and proud to be part of this organization.

With the spirit and innovation of our Committee and the tireless support of staff, it has been immensely gratifying and truly an honor to edit this year's anthology. Now we open these lines to you.

—Kirthana Ramisetti and Léna Roy, Anthology Co-Editors

I. GROWTH

"It all started in September..."

Personal development is a common literary theme, but it's particularly salient to the Girls Write Now community. Musings on growth inevitably appear in our work because we are experiencing it firsthand. In the most literal sense, these teenage girls are growing up—shedding their childhood selves and blossoming into smart, strong young women. At the same time, over the course of the year, mentees and mentors progress as writers. And then there's the remarkable evolution of pair relationships. The first chapter of our 2010–11 anthology celebrates growth in these and many more forms. Like change itself, the entries are sometimes painful, often poignant, and always powerful.

—Elaine Stuart-Shah, mentor

Hollow

By Jennifer Fuster

The sea wind felt warm on my skin. It was a gloomy day, the clouds thick, promising a storm. I didn't feel like myself. I wasn't myself. I felt hollow but knew that inside, there was life. But I didn't want it.

I breathed in the salty air. My steps followed no rhythmic pattern. I walked aimlessly around in the sand, feeling as though the seemingly boundless beach was purgatory. Without realizing where my steps had taken me, I had wandered into the chilling water, each wave whipping my body. The water was now neck high. I stood, one foot raised, ready to take another step. Ready to wash away my sin, wishing I had gone through with the abortion.

■ ■ ■

A warm hand rocked my left shoulder, prodding me awake. I didn't know where I was. My sore eyes widened, only to quickly seal again, blinded by a strong overhead light.

"It's okay. You should, like, get up now."

I listened to the soft voice and opened my eyes again, realizing I was lying on an itchy couch with a large towel wrapped around me. Across from me sat a boy, no younger than I, possibly older. His face familiar. The room was small, intimate. Wooden walls and floorboards formed the small space. Knickknacks were strung generously around the stacks of shelves and various tables. Two large windows revealed an ocean view. I instantly remembered what had happened.

"Was I drowning?" I asked, my voice faint, throat burning.

"You sure were. I wasn't even on duty today so you're lucky I caught you in time."

"You're a lifeguard?"

"Only during the summer. I think we go to school together, by the way."

"I think so, too," I said. I adjusted my position on the couch. A sharp pain surged through my body.

"Are you all right? Do you want some water or something?" The boy stood up.

"No, I think I've had enough water today. I'd just like to go home."

"Okay. I can drive you."

"No, I live on the beach. I can walk."

"Walk? After a near-death experience? I don't think so."

"Thanks for saving me and all but I think I can walk myself home. It's not like the water paralyzed my legs."

"Your legs may not be paralyzed but they are pretty banged up. Take a look."

I examined my legs and sure enough there were a few bruises and marks.

"Hey, let me get you some bandages," the boy said.

He walked out of the room and returned with a large first aid kit. I watched him rummage through the bandages until he found the right size. He surprised me by whipping out some rubbing alcohol.

"It'll burn a bit but that just means it's working," he said. Then he laughed at himself. "Like you don't already know that. Sorry, I'm just used to giving that speech to young kids when I have to apply medicine to them."

"It's okay. I'll do it."

"Don't be so guarded. I'm trained to help people, you know."

"I'm used to doing things by myself."

"And why is that?"

"After my parents split up a few years ago, I learned to do things myself. I live with my mother and she focuses so much on working that I barely see her around the house."

"I can sort of relate because my mom died a few years ago and my father moved to Burbank for a job recently so I live here with my uncle in his beach house."

"Why didn't you move to Burbank too?"

"I didn't want to have to abandon my whole life and start anew. I'm gonna be a senior this year." Our small talk helped deter the pain I felt after spreading alcohol over my wounds.

"There's a shitload of Band-Aids there if you want to take some home. I have a ton of those first aid kits."

"Thanks," I said. "And I'm sorry for putting you through this trouble." I stood up.

"It's no trouble. Are you sure I can't drive you home?"

I gazed out the windows. A light storm had erupted. It wouldn't be smart to walk home. "Actually..."

■ ■ ■

School was approaching. My last year. I could not arrive pregnant. When my mother left for work, I hopped onto my bicycle and headed toward the free clinic a couple of miles away. I've passed it before but never thought I'd have to actually use its services.

The building was small, perfectly square; the white exterior paint had faded, and dirt specks decorated each side. Weeds consumed the cracks on the sidewalk, which gave me an unsettled feeling in my stomach. The inside wasn't much better.

A loud ding sounded after I crossed the threshold. The tired eyes in the waiting room studied me as I entered. If I didn't go through with the abortion, I would have to get used to the judging eyes.

All the Things Left Unsaid: A Personal Reflection
By Katherine Nero[*]

What is it about all the things left unsaid that haunt me more than words actually spoken—even more than thoughtless comments and spontaneous outbursts? Maybe it's the "what if" factor, that unsettling feeling that a given situation would be different—perhaps better—if something, anything, had been said. Those "what if" questions mercilessly linger and continuously taunt me: *What if I had been honest and tried to discuss the problem? Would we be friends today? What if I had asked for more money? Would the job have been more satisfying? What if he knew that I loved him? Would he have still married her?* No matter how hard I try to rationalize, justify, and imagine, the answer to those nagging questions remains the same—*I'll never know.* So I choose to learn from those regrets and move on.

And what have I learned? Life is an unpredictable, exciting cycle of twists, turns, reversals of fortune, laughter, and tears. Pain and discomfort cannot and should not be avoided. Often I hid my feelings to avoid imagined unpleasantries and the perception of vulnerability. While the relief was temporary, the sense of loss was and is long term. Unknowingly, to my detriment, I missed opportunities for personal growth, enlightenment, and intimacy—the rewards of stretching one's comfort zone.

Sharing your feelings—revealing yourself to others—is risky. So far, my own efforts have met with mixed results. Two relationships deepened and two relationships ended. One job was lost and several career options are emerging. Yes, there's still some pain and discomfort to opening up, but now my healing is no longer interrupted by "what if."

[*] Katherine's mentee's piece on page 61 shares this title.

3

A Four-Year Journey: My High School Reflection About Friendships, School, and Life

By Daelina Lockhart

It all started in September of 2007,
the beginning of a new journey,
one that would last for four years.
The creation of new bonds and some endings occurred,
but for the most part we all held it together.
Year by year
we have grown.
Freshman year
we began our family bond
growing and understanding one another.
Fundraisers, contests, relays in history class outside on the lawn,
our school days were a maze. Having our school move was no fun,
but it gave the second part of our journey together a chance to begin again.
Closing the door to a year of exploration,
opening the door to a year of challenges,
this new part of the journey was challenging both socially and academically.
Friendships were torn and some were mended,[*]
but everything happened for a reason and that's just how it ended.
Papers and tests started to pile up,
but we had to learn how to handle the bundle of work given to us.
On many of our minds,
after taking certain tests,
many could agree
that they had the thought in their heads,
"man are you kidding me?"
Stressful nights of AP Euro,
and loads of homework from other subjects
were thrown our way out of the blue,
many of us would complain
that we just simply
didn't know what to do.
Trying to comprehend geometry became our lives,
but guess what, guys?
We survived.
As we closed the door on challenges we opened the door to a year of acceptance.
This year is a year of acceptance because
we have learned how to be successful.
We have accepted our challenges,
conquered them one by one
and in the middle we had some fun.
Better prepared for
the real world
we are today,

---

[*] Daelina's mentor's piece on page 20 shares this line.

comparing our knowledge and experiences
to when we first began this journey in September of '07.
Guys, I can't believe it is almost June of 2011! We are almost at the end of our four-year journey, but
    as our journey ends,
we must not forget,
to hold on to the shared ideas, thoughts, and charitable memories of the years that passed.
Our futures are right ahead of us
on the other side of that last door,
with dreams and opportunities
available for us to strive toward.

A new beginning is occurring in our lives,
where we will be able
to apply the skills
we have learned during our journey
for a prosperous future.
But it will be up to us
to take full responsibility for the choices we make
as we go through new doors and
new beginnings in life.

Intern
By Samantha Henig

Crowded trains. Morning commutes. Tourists. Crappy coffee. It was all so exhilarating. Walking down Thirty-Fourth Street, dodging men who clearly worked in law firms, women who clearly worked in fashion, and out-of-towners who clearly should be exploring less shopping mall–esque parts of the city, if they really wanted the trip to be worthwhile. What did they think of me, in my work-appropriate clothes culled from my mother's closet: boxy sweaters meant to flatter someone else's frame and shoes far too sensible for a rising college sophomore? Could I don this costume of an actual magazine reporter, as our models donned whatever swimsuits or rompers we laid out before them, and convince the world, or at least the people walking on Thirty-Fourth Street between Seventh and Fifth Avenues, that I was anything but a poser?

Rayne
By Lashanda Anakwah

I stood up to take a good look at the place. There was green everywhere. Green growing past my knees, touching the sky. The sky—the sky was blue! Not the sad gray on the other side of the wall. And the air seemed lighter here. The sun was shining just the right amount. It wasn't blistering or cold, as I had feared. There were purples, blues, and pinks growing out of the green. I remembered the name for them from my vegetation textbook: flowers. I had proudly memorized the parts of trees and other flora; now my knowledge would come of use. The flowers seemed to be reaching across the green. Excitement with a lacing of fear fueled my ambition to reach the settlement or whatever it was. The more ground I covered, the more confident I got; the trees seemed to be hovering, watching over me. I felt at peace here, just me and the green.

. . .

I woke up the next morning on the side of the enormous tree. My clothes were dirty, my hair disheveled; as soon as I woke up I realized things were only going to get harder.

The sun blinded me temporarily. The first thing I felt was a stabbing hunger that made me weak. I rose to my feet unsteadily, contemplating what to do next. One thing was certain—I had to eat. I looked up at the tree that I had slept under. Streaks of sunlight were pouring through the branches and leaves. This place was still beautiful even though I was suffering. Life goes on. I shook my head, breaking the abstract thoughts of my daydream. What was edible around here? I pulled out my map; there were drawings of points I had to reach. The first point was a gigantic tree. This place was one huge tree, as far as I was concerned. I shoved the map back into my pocket. I felt my face; it was still a little sore. The little cuts were starting to scab over. I walked around looking for something, anything; there was no one to help me and I had no idea what to do. I walked back to the tree feeling defeated. I sat on one of the roots—probably the one that had tripped me, I thought. With my back leaning on the tree trunk and eyes closed, I wondered if I had made the right choice crossing over to the other side. I was going to starve to death and no one would even know or care. There was no way I could go back. I was trapped, and realizing that was enough to make me cry.

I looked up and realized for the first time what a grand tree it was. The branches were growing from the trunk; the leaves were growing from the branches. I gazed up at the tree and wondered what it was like to grow outward from yourself. What was the tree trying to reach? I blinked myself back to reality. And that's when I saw it, a little shadow caused by a sudden flutter. I got a closer look at it: It seemed to be made entirely of just wings, the inner wings blue with black outlining them. The most amazing thing about the creature was that it could fit in my palm. The creature rose from one of the branches. It stayed at the same spot for a few seconds and then started to fly toward me. I turned around and ran. My heart was racing. I broke out into a cold sweat. **What if it was poisonous?**[*] There was no way I was going to take that chance. I ducked and weaved, running through the close-knit trees. I stopped and hid behind a tree, trying to catch my breath. I felt faint; I still hadn't eaten and I had just used up most of my energy. I sunk down to the ground, leaning on the tree for support. I was still breathing heavily, so I tucked my head in my lap just in case the creature could hear me. After what seemed like forever, my curiosity got the best of me. I picked up my head slowly, searching for any signs of the creature. I sat there for a while, too afraid to move, until I saw something moving out of the corner of my eye. I turned hesitantly, afraid to look…It was the creature. I held my breath but I soon realized it wasn't concerned with me. It hadn't even noticed me. I watched it fly away; it seemed to be cutting through the forest. I could feel the trees and flowers turn and gaze at it. It did not exist in time at that moment. I exhaled, unaware that I had been holding my breath the whole time. I realized I had left my RNS back at the tree; even though it wasn't working, it was the only familiar thing I had. I had to go back. While I was going back to the tree it suddenly dawned on me—the tree I had slept beside was the first point. I had accomplished something. Now if I could only find something to eat.

---

[*] Lashanda's mentor's piece on page 9 shares this line.

How Dark Is the Light?
By Tatyana Alexander

A world in the dark will be filled with passionate crimes and unsolved murders.
Apples will not be red and plants will not be green.
Blood will be tar and there will be no grief. Tears will not exist.
                                        The beauty of the morning is no longer.
Love will be truly blinded, in a lifetime of solitary confinement.
With no light to keep warm, earth will be a cold place.
A world with no diversity will bring us to peace or slowly create a war of its own.
We will stay, live, and breathe in the past.
                                        Without light no one can advance.
A world with light will be so shiny and bright. We will lose countless hours of sleep
Because night will never fall.
Winter, spring, nor fall will be among our seasons.
                        The heat of the light will create madness inside the minds of all.
                    Broad daylight brings bloody horrors and scares the children and mothers.
Light will never stop the crooked minds of the wicked.
Light will shed on the racist and prejudiced people.
                                        But neither light nor dark can stop inequality.
John Locke believed that every human is born with a blank mind, and it is the
Environment that surrounds you that makes you good or evil.
But it does not matter if you're born into the light or dark.
If you're born into the light, darkness will find you. If you're born into the dark, you can be shown
the light.

Tattoo
By Jenny Sherman

Mr. Manley, my high school speech teacher,
Would prop his bare foot
On top of his desk,
Clipping his thick yellowed toenails as I
Sweated and stammered through a
not-so-persuasive piece.
He snipped and I saw
A murky blue anchor peeking from his sleeve;
An indigo shark swimming beneath the
Surface of his white shirt.
I saw the flesh held taut between practiced fingers,
Heard the needle buzz
In some filthy shop tucked between a
Noodle bar and the waterfront.
How faded now, this indelible totem;
How clear, the oratory a cipher can sing,
A constant cobalt sounding of his days in the navy

His heady young-man days, those
Ribald stories and lady-luck nights
Blazed in an inky trail on
Age-spotted skin.

Waiting to Run

By Josleen Wilson

Every weekday morning at 8:00 a.m. I walk from our two-room apartment down at the end of Virginia Street, on what they called the Flats, all the way up to Judy Zuker's house so we can walk another few blocks together to Garfield Jr. High School where we are in the seventh grade. She lives in a two-story white house set a little ways back from the sidewalk. You walked through the front door straight into a small, dark living room with a television set, the first I had ever seen (this was back when Uncle Miltie was the only show on TV), then straight through to a square kitchen filled with sunlight. A Formica table stands just inside the kitchen door on the right. Judy is sitting at the table finishing her breakfast. She seems to do this on purpose every morning, waiting until I arrive before she finishes eating. She knows that I do not get breakfast before school. My mother works a split shift, lunch and dinner, then usually goes out with her girlfriends to the dance halls. I close my eyes but don't sleep until I hear her come home in the wee hours. Mornings, let alone breakfast, are something we both despise.

Mr. Zuker is sitting at the table, too, reading the newspaper, his empty plate pushed away. He is plain and pudgy, just like Mrs. Zuker, who is standing at the kitchen sink in the far corner on the other side of the room. Two rows of little curtains, one above the other, hang across the window above the sink, allowing the sun to stream in, all the way over to the table where Judy is methodically eating a single egg, its sunny-side-up yolk glistening when the sun hits it.

I watch as she carefully cuts away the white skirt of the egg and eats it bit by bit, leaving the yolk intact. This is how she is, precise in all things. White Peter Pan collar tucked around the neck of her blue sweater, gold hair wavy as pleats pinned back on each side of her face. She tells me that she sets her hair in pin curls every single night.

Judy looks up from her egg and sees me standing in the doorway. "Hi," she says. Mrs. Zuker turns and says, "Good morning." This is all she ever says to me. I say "good morning" back to her. I don't call her by name. Everyone calls my young, flamboyant mother Jeannie. Timid as I am, I would have stood in front of a speeding truck before I would call anyone else's mother "Mrs." Mr. Zuker never says anything to me; he just reads his newspaper.

Judy finishes nibbling at the white part of the egg and maneuvers its slimy yolk onto her folk without breaking it. She puts the yolk in her mouth and swallows it whole. This act is both mesmerizing and disgusting. My stomach lurches just as it does every morning. This is only the beginning of my day, another in which I count each hour, waiting to escape.

Ipetac, Ilecac, Ipecat

By Rachel Cohen

What if it was poisonous?[*] I scooped up Tucker, slinging him over my forearm like a purse, and scurried up the stairs as quickly as I could weighed down with a squirming seventeen-month-old. For once I was oblivious to the jagged shriek of his crying. I sat at the computer, trying to hold him on my lap with one hand while mousing and typing with the other and looking down every few seconds to see if he was turning green or blue or yellow.

"Vasleine piosonous?" I entered, and then hit return before noticing the typos. Blessed Google replied: "Showing results for Vaseline poisonous?" What was that stuff called we always had in the house when I was a kid? That made you throw up if you swallowed something poisonous, that my mom always pointed out to the babysitter? Ipetac? Ilecac?

Why didn't the baby books remind me I needed to buy it? Where do you even buy it?

Maybe I was imagining things but Tucker did look slightly purple. I glanced back up at the screen. Couldn't focus enough to read completely through any of the entries, but I saw enough. No. Nontoxic. Safe. OK.

Tucker's shrieks were slowing to hiccups—the cry of being startled by my yelp of terror and knocking the jar out of his chubby hand, and now he'd tired himself out and didn't even remember why he was upset. "I'm so sorry, baby," I said, as if he could understand. Lightheaded, I needed a few moments before I could stand up.

I snuck a peek out the window as I carried Tucker, his head now resting on my shoulder, toward his room. Like I was worried somebody was peering in, seeing what a terrible mother I was, even though nobody was ever on the sidewalks of this new subdivision.

I wondered, as I seemed to about once a week for the last seventeen months, if there was some class I missed, or some switch that had failed to fire in my brain. How does everybody else somehow manage to become a parent? Not in the technical sense, of course—having a child made you a parent. But a Parent. Someone who instinctively knows you need to buy ipecat and where to find it. Someone who doesn't get distracted by a meaningless text message long enough for her toddler to pull down a jar of Vaseline, open it, and eat a scoop.

Or maybe Grown-up is really what I mean. How to apply for a mortgage. How to hang shelves. How to decorate a birthday cake. How to clean strained-squash stains.

Things my parents just…knew.

My mom could watch three kids at the playground and notice when I swallowed dirt in the sandbox and my brother went too high on the swings at the same time. She would never eat some of her kid's Cheerios off his high chair, causing him to bawl, because the box was empty and she was hungry. Or pout because her family wasn't invited to the first birthday party of a co-worker's twins.

I couldn't fathom calling my mom and asking, "When you had me, did you feel like you were still the kid even though you were a mother?" Because that's the kind of question only one Grown-up asks another.

---

[*] Rachel's mentee's piece on page 6 shares this line.

Becoming Tooth Fairy

By LaToya Jordan

She drops the small
dull white tooth into my hand,
a baton passed from mother
to daughter. Weightless bounty,
the tooth's ridges tickle the lines
inside my palm. I hold tight
to the nugget, clenched fist
falls to my side from the pressure
of filling mother's wings.

I drop the small
dull white tooth into my little
brother's hand while whispering
secrets of the Tooth Fairy.
Later, the rumble of his snores
masks my footsteps into the room.
I watch his mouth open and close
in sleep as I slip my warm hand
against the cool of his pillowcase
reaching for the fallen tooth. It comes
to me, electric against my fingertips.
I replace it with the sparkle
of a silver dollar.

I show my mother the small
dull white tooth. She covers
my hand with hers. Our wings
light up the dark of our apartment.

Planting

By Linda Corman

I pull the carrots out of the ground and pop them
Into my mouth as if they were salty taco chips.
But, they're sweet and crunchy and
There is no guilt in eating them. The only trouble is
I am so proud of my tiny, green feathery children
That I dread thinning them.
So, every year, my candy grows less tasty.

By Kristasiah Daniels

Have you ever stood in the dark and felt so cold, but seemed so warm? I have. It started with a dream… if it even was a dream. It seemed so real, but felt impossible.

It was cold, so cold. The darkness took over me and we became one. My heart raced with power every second as if waiting for something. Something was coming. I could feel the rush in my veins passing through with such excitement. The night was still, yet time seemed to move. I still wasn't prepared for what was coming.

My heart still racing at a fierce beat, the temperature was dropping. I could only think of the moon and its glow as it rose in front of me, amazing me with its glow.

Then there it was; it stood in the light of the moon stealing my gaze. The silent night had come alive. Its eyes pierced me with such rage. Its aura gave off immense energy. In the blink of an eye, the beast stood before me, its skin a raging red, its fangs sharp, just enough to penetrate the hardest of shields. Yet I was not afraid. Because what stood in front of me was the most beautiful creature I had ever laid eyes on. It was a man. I did not wonder why he seemed so beast-like, but I was too caught in his gaze. His breath slowly breezed through my skin as he wrapped his arms around me, his muscles taking over my entire being. My heart fluttered and skipped a beat, yet I withstood the pain in my face with lust as every drop of blood drained from my neck. His scent was overwhelming! His claws sunk deeper into my back. My teeth sunk into his neck, his fangs began to grow and his strength increased as I licked the blood from his shoulder and he licked mine. The moon had finally risen to the sky and I saw that he was a chocolate brown and drenched with danger. His eyes said evil, but invited you in as if offering protection, his grip leaving you breathless. As I looked into his eyes, everything had changed. The black werewolf had stolen my heart. He used all his strength to throw me against a tree; it seemed as if he kissed me. Every second getting hotter. The pain had begun to seep in and I called upon it, for I was a vampire! Every drop of his poisonous touch filled me with lust. My only love was spurred by my only hate. That was the day I yearned for danger. The adventure had only begun.

We sat there in the forest. It was snowing. We looked up at the moon in silence. Curled up in his arms, I was seated between his legs. My red eyes fixed on the moon. He held me tight, his every breath slowly caressing my ear. My moon glistened in the light as my black hair flowed in the wind. My mind was spinning in circles. My kind was never to associate with a filthy beast such as a werewolf. Yet I lay my head on his chest, consuming his warmth. My attraction to him almost couldn't contain itself. Time was so still, yet my mind was running rapidly.

He finally spoke and said my name: "Crystal." His voice rang like the purest bell, or a bird's song, but it was so stern.

"Yes, Jay."

He turned me toward him. "We're from different worlds," he said. "My father would kill me if he ever knew about us."

No fear stuck in my heart like those words. I could feel his claws run up my skin. He knew the cost of us being together would be him having to leave his pack.

"And my father would be out for blood."

We stood up, alarmed. The cries of a nearby animal took the silence of the forest.

"My brother," Jay said, with fear. "He's coming. He caught my scent." He hissed one more time, and was gone. The next second I was already down the mountain. As I ran, I had no thoughts, only to get back to the destination. In a matter of seconds I was back in my house. My dad was still asleep. I lay in my bed thinking of Jay and what he might be doing and if he missed me. It seemed like only with him could I feel normal.

Being a vampire can be cool, but it can also be a burden. I remember the day like it was yesterday. The day I was turned, the day I was attacked. The day when everything started.

Black-Eyed Ferocious
By Yolandri Vargas

I heard that she was dangerous
Black-eyed ferocious

Her smile told me stories I struggled to comprehend
Her eyes made me feel what she never wanted to feel
I could see her bones under her skin
Her lips had difficulties remaining silent

I asked her what her story was
"If I told you, I would have to kill you"
She responded

They told me that she was dangerous
Black-eyed ferocious
But I doubted these stories

I was satisfied with the fact that her favorite color changed every day
The amount of mascara that volumized and curved her eyelashes
The perfection in the twists of her braids
Her lips full of undesired kisses
I was satisfied with the way her curves could never be tracked on GPS
systems

She promised me
That I was her good luck
To find more good luck
To carry good luck
And feel good luck
So I embraced my good luck

But her voice
Sugar-coated in high notes
And melodious rhythm
Sang for me a cry for help
A cry for change
To free her from methamphetamines
To embrace her with affection and a new future
She needed me

But she sang me into silence
And I fell
Compliant and dependent
Into cruel rejection
Into the voice of officials in foreign countries
Into the ignorance women faced

I felt sex-trafficked myself
Unvalued
Uneducated
Unequal
Incapable of standing up for myself

She said
"Walk on me naked
Barefoot
With ambiguous intentions
Tie clear plastic bags over every foot
Protection
Protect me from feeling your fears on every shoulder blade
Be careful where you plant every foot
I'm a light sleeper
I'm also afraid of feeling your voice
Your intentions with me
I'm afraid of feeling the color power ranger you desired to be when you were
younger
I never wanted to feel the young you
I wanted to feel
Let the grown man in you touch me
I'm stepping, can you feel me now?
I'm a light sleeper
But I'll deep sleep with the real you
Let you rule me
Rule my penmanship
My signature
The rest of this poem from here on now
Till the end
Till my eyes let go
Own the rest of this poem
Like it's April
Like it'll always be poem in your pocket day
But you keep heartbeats in your pocket for plan B
I want you to finish walking
Just find your destination"

And I believed her
But I still said please
She enslaved me in silence
Hung me from my dreams

Fed me poisonous expectations
She refused to unmute me

My body reacted to the beat of rebellion in her music
Danced to tell her story
But I was a comedian
So officials laughed
She refused to unmute me
Never out of fear but out of shame

They told me that she was dangerous
Black-eyed ferocious
But I doubted these stories

I was right
There was nothing dangerous
Ferocious
Or black-eyed about this woman

She never let me unstitch her cut
To stitch
To stitch
To stitch
To re-stitch her cut properly

She never rose

It's Not Easy Being Green
By Nathalie Gomez

In the powerful words of Kermit the Frog I say, "It's not easy being green." It really isn't. But we've made it, somehow. Let's go back a few years to clarify exactly what "It" is.

"It" is the friendship. Our friendship.

Jazmin's and mine.

It hasn't been easy keeping our friendship alive, but we've never given up.

We met in the fourth grade. She was the new girl. Of course we would eventually become friends, because there was a desk available at Table 4 and she ended up sitting next to me. One day, for an activity, we had to cut a piece of paper into the shape of a shirt, and then design it with drawings or words that expressed who we were. And while we were working on it, I noticed that our paper shirts had similar stuff on them. Then we started talking about them, and we saw that we had a lot of stuff in common. We both love to draw and make art. We both had dogs. We were both part Colombian, so we knew Spanish well, too. And we loved to bake. Now those might not seem like big similarities but if I tried to list all of them, they wouldn't fit in an 850-word limit.

So after that, we instantly became best friends. She lived, like, only two blocks away so we were at each other's houses almost all the time—hers more than mine, since I always forgot my house keys. But we would spend time with each other a lot, like true friends.

But then around April, things took a turn. I had only known her for half a year and then she moved to Pennsylvania. When she left, I didn't really feel anything, like how you're supposed to feel when you lose your best friend. I guess it was because we didn't have much time to be the best friends we are now. But sometimes it's not how long you've known one another, it's how short the time feels when you are together. And as I'm reading this in my head, I know it sounds a little lovey-dovey, but it kind of is. She's my best friend. I love her like a sister.

So she left. We exchanged screen-names and phone numbers, but it didn't really work out, seeing as I ended up losing the piece of paper on which her information was written. But then, almost two and a half years later, I received an IM from Blondiechixz3ooo. I was a little skeptical about opening it, but it looked familiar and what do you know? It's Jazmin! She wasn't lost anymore—I was so happy. (She wasn't really lost but she was missing for a while. Not literally, just in my life.) After a few back-and-forth messages, our friendship snapped back into place. It was like she never moved. We began reminiscing about us before she moved. A funny thing we always end up bringing up is how we got pretty much the same presents for Christmas.

When we were on the bus going to school the morning after the break, everybody was talking about what they got. I got an Xbox, and she got a Playstation 2, and we both had gotten a Dance Dance Revolution game. We then started talking about how we are now—how the family is and little things like that. And then she casually said she might be moving back. Might. This was epic news. I was ecstatic.

I had my best friend back, for real. She did live way farther away than before, but nothing a half-hour ride on the bus couldn't handle. This time I was going to make our time together count. We went on adventures, where we would get lost in SoHo, the Village, and Chinatown. We'd make plans to do something and then end up just staying home watching movies and baking. We'd speak in our Kermit the Frog and K-Stew (Kristen Stewart) dialect in the trains, looking like crazy people. And anytime anything would get tough, like we felt we couldn't do something, we would just think of those five powerful words of Kermit the Frog.

The first time she left wasn't a big deal for me. The second, well now it was. See, she moved again. Farther. Twenty-seven hundred miles farther, to be exact. All the way to Colombia. I don't want us to be separated again because before I met her, I didn't have a best friend. I had a lot of friends, but not someone who I felt I could trust with anything and know they'll be there for me.

And this time, I'm going to be there for her. It may sound like a bit much to travel to Colombia just to see my best friend, but it's far from it.

"It's not easy being green," but if I have the ticket already, then it's doable, right?

Open Your Eyes, Scarlett
By Cindy Caban

I doze off into a deep sleep.

I see myself running through the woods in complete darkness. I can't see where I'm going. It looks like a maze and I keep ending up in the same dead end each time. I'm heaving and sweat is dripping down my forehead.

"Why am I here?" I scream out.

"To understand," says Emily.

My body stands still. Hearing Emily's voice so near makes my thoughts set loose all at once.

"Emily? Where are you?" I shout.

"I'm everywhere. Don't you see. I'm in your brain, your spirit, and in your sleep."

"What do you mean?"

All of a sudden all the trees and jungle atmosphere gets ripped off, like a person tearing out a page from a book and an empty park gets drawn in. I see Emily twenty feet away near a seesaw and run after her. I start to hug her and begin frantically to cry. Tears are pushing themselves out of my eyes like a waterfall releasing into the air.

"I'm so sorry. God dammit I didn't know, Emily. I didn't know. Just please tell me why? Why did you—"

"Scarlett, I love you dearly, but I can't stay for long. So just listen. The day I took my life had nothing to do with you. It was a deed that had to be done. Death was seeking me and I didn't say no and he led me here. You won't understand now, but it was my only way to seek happiness, to become part of nature and to be free from my treacherous body. Don't ever feel guilty. You did everything you could and you're my best friend and always will be, but you have grieved enough. You have to let go and accept the truth. I'm better now. And I hate to see you behave with such remorse. You need to come alive again and do all the things that make you happy. But you have to open your eyes, Scarlett. Open your eyes!"

I wake up startled as sweat is dripping down my forehead and I close my eyes to make sense of what just happened. The dream felt like reality. Even though I didn't get to talk to Emily as much as I would have liked to, I feel content that I got to hear her voice. It gives me a sense of closure and a sense of relief that she's all right. And I think to myself that, yeah, nothing is what it seems and can't work out perfectly. But, deep inside I know everything is going to be okay, which is weird since I hate hearing this from others. Then a quote enters my mind: "I shut my eyes and all the world drops dead. I lift my eyes and all is born again."[1]

I Say Good-bye to My Mother
By Temma Ehrenfeld

These days we watch your chest rise and fall
You are your breath now

Alone with you, I lay my chest on yours
and make our beats one

Once as I was becoming inside you
your heartbeat was all time
so, now, I lay my chest on yours
and make our beats one

As if we are lovers, war torn
and one day the war might be over
I believe one day I will be with you again
in peace
as I lay my chest on yours
and you breathe

hoarse breath for days
gently for a time
and your family jokes, waiting

---

1 From Sylvia Plath's "Mad Girl's Love Song"

Sip

By Jennifer McDonald

Breathe.
Breathe in… breathe out. [*]

The instructor moved his hands as if in benediction, a liquid grace: toward his chest, and away… toward his chest, and away…

Amelia knelt on the floor of the sea, trying not to panic.

Breathe in… breathe out. Breathe in… breathe out.

She was training to dive, learning all the ways in which things might go wrong. She could lose her mask. Lose a fin. Run out of air. She could watch her one connection to breath float out of her grasp on a wave.

This was her especial nightmare: The regulator—a mouthpiece attached to a hose attached to a tank of compressed air, the device that controlled changes in pressure and the release of breathable gas—could flow free. Compressed oxygen would erupt from the mouthpiece, bubbles exploding as if at a roiling boil. And then? And then?

Breathe in…breathe out. Breathe in…breathe out.

She was training, then, to prevent panic.

She was learning to be calm.

If it happens, the instructor said, *tilt your head.* Just so. Keep hold of the regulator even as it tries to jiggle and dance away. The gas escapes with such power that it displaces the water, creating an air pocket. Ease the regulator from your mouth, position your face, and *sip.*

It is within the pocket of air that the difference between drowning and living exists. Amelia knew that to dive was to court uncertainty. You sink, you plummet, the world goes strange, you go to a darker place. You drink, you drug, you dance, you create, you cry, you write, you love—all involve a tempting of danger, all require a letting-go.

The key to survival existed in the safe spots, those places from which she must not forget to sip at the air. The point was to go deep, yes, but also to ascend—to emerge into the open and survey the depths from which she had risen. Only then would she be able to say: Okay. I can breathe. I am here.

And now?

Obscured by the Gloom

By Samantha Young Chan

Adriana ran down the vacant streets, her heart thumping a fast, frenzied beat. Her feet pounded against the cobblestones and her hair whipped about her face, the corset binding her breathing. The full moon was the only source of light. She glanced over her shoulder, her eyes searching. They widened, and she began to run even faster. Her thoughts were racing and she tripped over the uneven terrain. A shadow approached and loomed over her. She yelped, her fingers clawing frantically against the cobblestones. Her hands were bloodied and throbbing, but she managed to stand upright. To keep herself from falling again, she gathered the skirt of her dress and sprinted away. She passed many taverns and houses, but all were empty and desolate.

Adriana. Adriana. The voice that whispered her name was low and dangerous, almost threatening, and the repetition was hypnotizing.

"Leave me alone!" she shrieked, covering her ears. She trembled and slowly walked forward. Her gaze landed on a tall man in a trench coat who was hunched in the shadows. She approached

[*]   Jennifer's mentee's piece on page 55 shares this line.

him and grabbed his arm. "Please, sir, help me!" she begged. "I'm being—" Her voice faltered and dropped when he tilted his top hat up to look at her. Her heart drummed even faster, the noise flooding her ears. She screamed and let go of his arm, pushing herself away. He grasped her wrist, but she wrenched away from his grip and fled. Even as she turned several corners and felt the distance between them widening, she could still feel his eyes on her. She imagined him grabbing her, his mouth curving up into a wicked smile, his hands and clothes drenched in blood.

"No, go away!" she mumbled to herself. Her voice was barely audible, and she was breathing heavily. The moonlight had grown intense and bathed everything in a cool, white light. She stumbled forward, all of her energy drained. Her head was pounding to the rhythm of her heart. She felt the coolness of the shadows envelop her and welcomed their calming darkness. She closed her eyes and leaned against the side of an alley building. She touched the rough, grimy bricks, causing pain to shoot through her hands. They began to feel warm and sticky, and when she looked down, they were coated with a fresh layer of blood.

Adriana. Adriana, I found you. You can't hide from me forever, Adriana. You knew I would find you. Her eyes snapped open and her pupils grew wide. She pushed herself away from the wall and began to run again. She heard heavy breathing. *Oh, Adriana, why do you run? I'm always going to find you. No matter where you go, I shall follow.* She shook her head and pushed herself to go faster, but slowed when she saw the tall brick wall blocking the end of the alley. She watched in horror as the outline of a person crawled up the wall.

"Why can't you leave me alone?!" she cried.

Adriana, you don't understand, do you? I will never leave you alone. Never. The shadow grew and she heard approaching footsteps. Dark spindly fingers reached a hand out toward her, and she felt dizzy. Her heart was beating so fast that she thought it would burst out of her chest.

"No," she whispered in a barely audible voice. She squeezed her eyes shut and whirled around. "No!" she yelled. "Leave me alone!" Her hands were clenched by her sides and her whole body trembled. As her eyes flew open, a look of confusion flitted across her face. No one was there.

The Hitchhikers
By Christina Morgan

They were fourteen years old; I didn't know why they just didn't take the bus. Instead, they chose to hitchhike home that evening. Maybe they were short of bus fare, and the bus drivers that evening had all been unsympathetic? Anyway. They'll never have the chance to tell me what really happened. Missing is worse than dead. At least with death, comes closure.

Beneath the Orange Globes
By Sharline Dominguez

Beneath the orange globes,
Lining the unpaved streets,
There stands a child, alone.
Adorned in Christmas lights, she stares.

Beneath the orange globes,
Deluged by wet trash, where no one can see,
Her dignity lies

Obscured and broken.
A chair she turns to for support,
One of its brown, filthy legs missing.

Beneath the orange globes,
In the depths of the winter coldness,
A child alone rummages for a Bible,
Screaming salvation, guidance.

Cornered in the end of a forgotten street,
How to excite her taste buds, she mumbles hopelessly.
Traces of forced entry, dry blood,
Still line the flesh between her thin legs,
All of it marked by lost innocence.

Cornered in the end of a forgotten street,
Inexplicably tracing the edges of a boundless sky,
Following the ticks of the clock within,
She awaits the presence of her shadow.

Cornered in the end of a forgotten street,
A child in need, impossibly in love
With her knotted brown hair, is warm in the blackened snow.
Heartily embraced by little things.

Befriended by stray cats and dogs,
The smell of urine welcomes her,
Underneath the eyes of the well-to-do,
A nobody, another victim to society she remains.

Befriended by stray cats and dogs,
They read her chapped lips,
Consume her thoughts,
And
Caress her feeble frame.

Children taint filthy sidewalks with life,
Befriended by stray cats and dogs,
Cornered in the end of a forgotten street,
Beneath the orange globes.

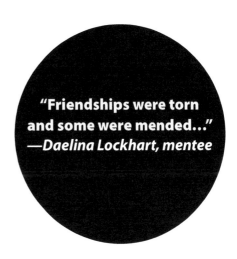

"Friendships were torn
and some were mended..."
—Daelina Lockhart, mentee

Before We Were Here
By Heather Graham

The slow climb into adulthood changed us.
Walking separate ways, finding an identity carved from new places, new faces,
friendships were torn and some were mended,*
some never to be spoken of again.

Walking alone was strange, exhilarating, frightening;
stepping unsteadily, unsure, stumbling through grown-up problems for the first time,
often without grace.
Standing in the kitchen talking two languages,
stories so different it felt miles away. It *was* miles away.

I was off the reservation, far afield from where I'd come from,
living a separate ideal, unhealthy, unclean.
Somewhere I righted my path and later we found each other,
sitting in a car curbside, clandestine secrets once again,
there it was, the thing we'd had all those years.
It hovered there, between our shoulders,
starting up our two-woman conspiracy with revelations, heavy sighs,
burdens finally lifted from sagging shoulders.

Letters,
cards,
commiserations.
Shared space and heartbreaks.
Sad good-byes exchanged for happy beginnings,
but something remained constant: You and me.
Me and you.
"I'll never turn my back on you."
No, we never will.

Song for a Pilgrim
By Allison Adair Alberts

Having walked through all the stages of dawn, through a hot, shimmery pink and glowing sunrise, through distant hills, through a forest, past your airport, your industrial parks, your secret outlying places, you caught my eye as I crowned the top of the incline whose decline led me to you. I wandered through your cobbled streets, following the same yellow arrows which began my journey more than two hundred kilometers east. I reached you, Compostella, field of starry skies, on a brilliantly blue morning in June. It may have been a Tuesday. I met some other *pereringos*, who, starting in the west, were planning to walk east: *it will not have the same effect*, I thought, *beginning at the cathedral instead of ending there.* I sat in your square, Santiago, pilgrim passport clasped in a blistered palm. I ate some chocolate, given to me by a stranger. I took off my shoes. I left them there

* Heather's mentee's piece on page 4 shares this line.

20

for another pair of soles to begin anew. I waited my turn for your pilgrim mass, entering through your archway, as thousands have done before me: I caught my breath as the massive censer flung laterally through your church's crossed arm. In the pew, clouds of incense lulled me to sleep after a long journey.

I've kept your scallop
shell safe in the top pocket
of my yellow pack.

Days of Our Lives
By Evelyn Berrones

It was Saturday around 3:00 a.m., maybe. I was lying on my bed ready to go to sleep when I heard a gunshot outside. Nothing out of the ordinary, though, so I tried going to sleep, which didn't work out because people outside were making so much noise screaming. I got up from bed, and when I looked out the window, I saw ambulance lights coming from Cromwell Avenue, right down the block from me. I used to hang out there all the time until a few months ago. I was worried and hoped that nobody I knew was involved, but a few minutes later my friend sent me a text saying that Alexis Abreu was the one who'd gotten shot, and that's all anyone knew. So I went to sleep with that information, just hoping he would recover and be fine. But I woke up to a text saying that he'd died.

Alexis and I went from middle school buddies to saying hi and bye in the streets, then to just looking at each other, and now to my never seeing him again. It's been two months since his death, and I really miss seeing him around, but all that's left are the memories we shared. I met Alexis through my friend Donald. Donald, Alexis, and a few other kids would sneak into my gym period to hang out. Alexis would play basketball unless the gym teacher brought out the baseball equipment; everybody knew Alexis had a passion for baseball and wanted to be in the major leagues when he grew up. He was about my height, 5 foot 3, or maybe a little taller, dark skin, Dominican, with long black hair. And he always wore a baseball cap. Donald and Alexis would throw balls "accidentally" toward me, and I would chase them. Alexis had a ponytail, and that made him an easy catch. That was what we did—bother each other for fun. But after he graduated, we grew apart. I was still in middle school and he was going to high school.

On the morning I learned that Alexis had died, I was still in shock about Juandy Paredes' murder three months earlier. He was stabbed seven times, and unlike Alexis, he didn't make it to the hospital but collapsed on a concrete floor. He was the first person I knew from my neighborhood to die violently and young. I didn't expect any more deaths like this, but then three months later another friend was taken away.

Before these deaths I never really thought about dying, but now I'm worried about it. I knew that Alexis and Juandy spent more time with their friends than their families, and I knew that like all families, theirs argued, and I knew that they had dropped out of school, causing disappointment. At both funerals, though, the families' crying really broke my heart. At some point tears couldn't come out their eyes, and neither mother could even stand up to see her son in his coffin, lifeless.

When people die, they leave a lot of other people heartbroken and destroyed. And I can't help but think what if I died, or what if someone I truly love passed away. If that happened, I would rather have memories of our good times together than regrets about bad moments. Having friends pass away really made an impact on me and my behavior. I appreciate the people I love more than before, and I try to give fewer headaches because nobody lives forever.

Have Faith in Me

By Octavia Lowrie

You say go to school, don't be no fool and I do as you please
I not only go for you, but myself.
When I get older, I don't want to be poor
Just right.
Not full of wealth
At seventeen I can proudly say I achieved more than the woman who birthed me
But for some reason you just can't see
Instead you accuse me
You accuse me of not being good enough
Why do you let your fears underestimate my strengths?
This hurts!
You say I think I'm better than you
But that ain't true
I'm just trying to break this cycle.
The cycle of young mothers in a deep struggle trying to make it
The cycle of depending on the government instead of getting my own
The cycle that carries on from generation to generation.
I would love to have your support and care
Instead you carry the burden full of fear.
It won't change me!
I am who I am
I have dreams and they're going to be fulfilled
If I have nothing in my pocket but a dime
If I have to stand from line to line
If the only sleep I get is within a blink of an eye
I'm going to try.
If I have to work as hard as a slave
If my path gets deep as a grave
If I have to stand like Martin and Malcolm
Trust me, I'm going to overcome.
I understand you want better for me
You want to see me exceed
Go beyond my dreams
You care too much of what others think
But not I
I'm going to stretch my wings and fly
And wave to those who doubt me good-bye.

"I heard that she was dangerous
Black-eyed ferocious"
—Yolandri Vargas, mentee

Past vs. Present: Wake-Up Call to the Next Generation!

By Idamaris Perez

If we teleport back in time and look at the glass of the past, we see the gap of differences. We see kids happily, eagerly walking to school ready to learn. And today we see kids complaining and whining about school. Back then our parents and grandparents depended on libraries to get their schoolwork done. Today we, teens and kids, have the Internet, Google, etc. We retrieve all the information of the world with just a click of the mouse. But what we like to do is be brainwashed and brain-wasted by Facebook, Twitter, and all those social networks. Our education gradually is being flushed like shit in the toilet. It sounds sad how our ancestors who had fewer resources cared more about knowledge and now this generation who has almost everything takes all this for granted.

Before, there was more respect for authority. Before, people paid attention to what was going on in the government. Before, people were more appreciative and humble. Yes, today we serve more of our community and care about others and have immense knowledge and technological advances. But the flaws of today in some ways outweigh the accomplishments. Let's be real, what is the use of all this untamed knowledge and technology if we don't put them to good use?

What happened to opportunity? Opportunity didn't reveal herself that much when our ancestors, great-grandparents, grandparents, and even parents were young. She was behind closed doors waiting to be opened. Now our past generation has unlocked her for us. Instead we just ignore her. Now that we have in our hands opportunity, why don't we use her as often as we should? She is granting us a treasure that she did not give to our past generations. Irony is laughing before our eyes. How thoughtless and immature can we be?

No! We can't be stagnant like rocks. We should continue to improve what our ancestors left us. We should fix the fragments of the past, not worsen it. We can't afford to disappoint our past generations' sacrifices. Their "swimming against the currents" and innovative minds paved the world of today. Look at the women of the past. Their hoarse voices fighting for suffrage and education. Thanks to those women we receive these privileges. But now, why are we women tossing a great future away with the wind at such a young age?

Does Eve's vulnerability to temptation still run in our veins? Think smart about sex. That is why we have birth control pills and condoms. If that is not helping, then the best option is abstinence. It is hard, but rewarding. But we need measures to take to ensure a better future for us, women, in order to save one for our children.

Men of today, don't stay behind. You're definitely the first on the line. Men of today, don't be cowards, share the burdens and responsibilities of your women. Stop tripping over your lusty or selfish desires. Be the men of integrity that God sent you guys to be. We, "the next generation," have to change our ways. Just because we have more does not mean that we are entitled to do whatever, like spoiled, ungrateful brats. Also, people on the other side of the world (Asia) can't be the only ones to at least do a little bit more of the work. There must a dynamic equilibrium in both worlds. We have to balance our efforts to the future like the seesaw. This is the Wake-Up Call for the Next Generation: Let us stop being lazy, fix our mistakes, and expand our innovations, resources, and minds to the high, new horizons of the future. Let us not let our past generations' efforts die in vain.

Moving On

By Shannon Talley and Jen McFann

Clothes

Jen: I'm going to have to dress for the cold. I'm told Russians are annoyed when people assume the entire country has a Siberian climate, yet I assume it won't endear me to my new Russian hosts to dress as if I'm wintering in Tampa. I own a Soviet-era fur hat with the Red Army star on front, but that may prove even less endearing. I will need clothes, but I will probably buy most of them there so I can fit in with the cool kids.

Shannon: Because I actually want to look nice sometimes and not parade around in the campus sweats and sweatshirt 24/7. Don't get me wrong, I love being comfortable as much as the next person, but it doesn't kill to look nice sometimes. Not too nice, though; I don't want my roommates asking to borrow any of my clothes.

Textbooks

Jen: The main point of going to live in Russia is to learn Russian, which means buying textbooks. I haven't looked twice at a textbook in five years. I vaguely recall that they are expensive and that the school bookstore will try to buy them back for 0.1 percent of their actual value (which I have warned Shannon about). I wish I were like Antonio Banderas in *The 13th Warrior* and could sit around listening to Russians speak until the language imprints itself onto my brain, but the sheer amount of Russian pop music I've listened to and subsequent lack of fluency suggests that I cannot. I will need textbooks, and their pages upon pages of conjugation exercises.

Shannon: I'm sure everybody counts down till the day they graduate from high school and can get away from all the nagging teachers and especially lugging around heavy textbooks to study and do homework from. But when we stop to think, we realize that unfortunately the books are still part of the learning process in college.

Money

Jen: I guess I'd need money even if I stayed in New York. I will need rubles. I've applied for fellowships to make a dent in the tuition expense. I have no idea how eighteen-year-old me thought $45K/year was a reasonable expense; $18K now seems obscene to me. I imagine it has to do with the way twenty-six-year-old me pours paycheck after paycheck into the black hole that is Sallie Mae and yet my loan debt holds steady as I row against the current. Well, you know what? Screw you, Sallie Mae, if you think I'm gonna crawl to you for a dime of my tuition this time around! But I still need money—an obscene amount of money.

Shannon: A scholarship would be nice. I don't want to be in debt and I don't want work-study. It's a tease to know that you're making money and you can't use it for your own personal entertainment. You have to put all of it toward your tuition debts. What fun is that? If I work it'll be because I want to be able to afford a life and not be stuck on campus every weekend. My parents? Yeah, right; I think my weekly allowance will stop as soon as I take a step out the door with my suitcase. I think they're secretly counting down the days. But come on. Have they never heard of mail? E-checks?

Jen: This is the longest I've lived in one place since high school. I thought this mobility was a skill to maintain at the expense of happiness. I thought it was my obligation to move frequently and to keep myself from getting sucked into a social circle, putting down roots, settling in, hunkering down. In the twenty-third hour before I moved to Pittsburgh last April, my friend Lisa saved me from myself, saying, "You don't move away from a place; you move to one." As usual, she was right. I'm not moving away from New York because I'm afraid I'll like it too much. I'm moving to Russia because it sounds exciting. This extra one and a half years Lisa gave me was priceless; I needed to make the Dorothy Gale realization that you can learn about yourself in Astoria as easily as in the Republic of Georgia. The biggest surprise was that I got to fall in love like an adult, and even though I didn't get the guy I wanted, it was a relief to know that I, too, could go batshit insane over someone attainable. When I go to Russia, I need to remember that.

Shannon: New people and new places mean having to say good-bye to old things. This will be my first time being away from my parents for more than a week, and I have to admit that I don't really know what to expect. I don't know whether I'll be excited or if I'll be homesick within the first hour, but it's a new experience that I'll have to live at some point. All the new kids I'll be surrounded by may be overwhelming and exciting, but I'll never forget my closest friends. The ones who got me through the crazy, hell-bent years of high school. I can't imagine being away from them, but I know we have to move on to our individual lives. I think this is why man created Facebook.

"In the powerful words of Kermit the Frog I say, 'It's not easy being green.'"
—*Nathalie Gomez, mentee*

II. FAMILY

"'How was your day?' Ma asks."

First, we have to acknowledge that we wouldn't be here without them. After that, things get much more complicated. At their best, they love us—they bring us up without bringing us down. They take care of us, and later, we take care of them. They're the people we're closest to, though inevitably, they also become the people we can't wait to get far, far away from. Yet no matter how far we travel, they haunt us. They're always with us. And still we miss them. As writers, we pour our hearts out to them in words. They inspire us—so much material!—but they also annoy us, hurt us, misunderstand us. And so we write: to understand them, and to be understood. We fear what they might think. We want to make them proud. If we're lucky, they'll get us. They'll laugh right along with us. But we know, too, that they might censure us, be shocked by us, push us away. That's okay. We write about family as we write about anything else: we seek truth. Even when the only truth we may ever know is that they're a part of us, like it or not, flowing through our veins and onto the page.

—Jennifer McDonald, mentor

FAMILY

A Taste of Duck and Family

By Priscilla Guo

Outside, the sidewalk is a little crooked. The little pond in the gutter reflects the glow of the restaurant. Laughing oranges hug the bright yellows in the crowd while dark clothing melts away with the gleam of crabs and the flesh of ducks. Foreign sounds pound the air with the hammer of a foreign tongue. Two tin teapots find a place at the center of our table. I like to be the one to pour tea into everyone's cups. *Dou Zhu*. Pouring tea. It's not without drips on the tablecloth but it's become my responsibility to make sure everyone's cup is full. Grandma drinks like a turtle while Grandpa swallows gulps of tea down like an ox. We all drink zhu while we wait, cracking peanuts in a bowl at the middle of the table. I take only a few, saving the emptiness in me to be filled with the main courses. When the food comes, steaming in the air, everyone at the table shares the universal language of taste. The first dish for my family has always been jellyfish. Cold and slithery. It's hard to chew. It is the beginning. We slurp it up and chew a little but then we swallow. All the day's problems burrow themselves down our throats and there is no taste. *Ke yi wang ji*. Forgettable. Chatter hums around the table filling the air. Our stomachs are empty but our mouths are full of the latest gossip and jokes. Waiting is a big part of the dinner. We all wait together for the next course: Mayonnaise Shrimp with Broccoli, Crab Rice, Fried Tofu, and Peking Pork Chops all at once. In English, the names inspire nothing in me. They are as evocative as dust, dry and meaningless. In Chinese, ah. It is in Chinese that succulent tastes strike my tongue. It is in Chinese that my belly feels warm in the coldest times. The string of sounds in Chinese brings me to the table, where my family sits. They all laugh as they chew the tendons of pork chops or dip the tofu in soy sauce. They are all there, waiting for me.

Glowing puddles laugh.
While jellyfish slide away.
Tasting. Family.

The College Essay that Worked: My Grandmother

By Quanasia Wheeler

I could sit here and tell you all about how I'm committed to Girls Write Now, which is a nonprofit writing mentoring program. Maybe I could even tell you about how I spent a summer running a youth market that provided underserved neighborhoods with fresh fruit and vegetables. While both were great experiences, I don't think either one would really say anything about who I am or why I am the way that I am. I come from a single-parent home, where my mom has spent all her time working to pay the bills rather than spending time with me; and my father moved down to Florida when I was ten years old. I also never spent a lot of time with my grandparents. Therefore I've never felt a strong sense of family; however, I have always felt responsible to and for them.

A year ago my grandfather had to take a job in Arizona. He wanted to take my grandmother but her care wouldn't be covered if she moved with him. Shortly before he got the job, my grandmother was diagnosed with lupus on top of her many other existing health issues consisting of dementia, arthritis, heart problems, ulcers, and depression. After the diagnosis, she became bedridden so there was no other choice but for her to stay. He wasn't sure how long he would be gone so he tried to find someone to take care of my grandmother in his absence. To help out, I offered to take care of her while he was gone. It simply made sense to me as I already knew what her diet was like and when she had to take her medicines.

Before my grandfather left, I would visit on the weekends and he would teach me new recipes that my grandmother liked. From casseroles to poached salmon to cheesecakes, I learned about it all. I also learned the ingredients I had to avoid, like Lowry's seasoning and Adobo because of the high amount of salt. I never pieced it together till now, but it was like he was prepping me then because he knew I would need to take care of her, but he wanted me to do it on my own terms.

It would be a lie if I said it's been easy, but I don't believe any of it compared to having to watch my grandmother cry every day because she felt like a burden to everyone around her. She had always been an independent woman. So when her doctor told her she was not going to be able to leave the house or move around a lot, I saw every bit of confidence she ever had vanish. I felt helpless when it came to her depression. It seemed no amount of cooking or errand running was going to make her feel better.

As much as my grandmother hated it, she needed me and had to listen to me when I would say things like "keep your feet up" or "you need to just sit down because your legs are going to hurt later." She would often get cranky and cry when she made a request and I told her I had to do something later or in a few minutes because I was doing my schoolwork. Even though I tried to do what she asked as fast as possible, I always felt bad having to make her wait. Sometimes she would send me to the store for candy. For a while I fought her on whether she should even be eating candy, but I soon realized it was never about the candy. She just wanted to have a few minutes where she could walk around and feel like she was doing something on her own. Even if it was only for five minutes, I felt as if I owed her that bit of dignity.

I believe taking care of my grandmother has benefited me in more ways than I would have ever imagined. Although I wish it would have been under better circumstances, I know that taking care of her has made our relationship better. I've been able to make up for all of those years I only saw her on the holidays. Most of all, I learned that a strong sense of family is not about being in touch with one another, it is about taking the time to be there when they need it most. Although I never thought I had that, I was wrong because my grandmother and mother were always there for me and they taught me to do the same.

As a result of my commitment to my grandmother's health and well-being, I've come to realize that I want to help people with mental disorders. The best way I can think to do that is by getting a degree in psychology and pursuing a career as a psychiatrist. I will then be able to provide underserved minority communities with the same quality of counseling that predominately Caucasian communities receive.

Mah Pitom
By Amy Feldman

He was six foot tall, with blond hair and blue eyes. Not Jewish looking at all, definitely not Jewish. In line at the movies, Israelis would speak Hebrew in front of him—and he liked to surprise them by interrupting. *Mah pitom?* I always loved that story that my grandfather would tell about himself, laughing. I loved the element of surprise, of things not being as they seemed.

Everyone else in our family looks exactly like who they are.

His father had come to this country from Lithuania, from a town called Rasseini, which had been a center of Jewish life in the late 1800s and early 1900s, until it was wiped off the map midcentury. I researched the family history with vigor and for quite some time, thanks to an online genealogy site and a bunch of old Lithuanian census records translated into English—the Lithuanians, being extremely anti-Semitic then, kept very good records. As it turned out, the story I'd always believed, that our family emigrated before the violence began, was false. My grandfather's grandfather, Eliahu Rubinshteyn, I discovered, had been shot by Lithuanian soldiers, when he was in his seventies, along with a number of my great-grandfather's siblings.

Their names had been dutifully recorded at Yad Vashem.

Thanks to a cousin I'd never previously met, I now have digital photos of this Eliahu and his family, posed, sepia-toned. He is a harsh-looking man with a large beard, but maybe he just looks harsh because in formal photographs of that era no one smiled. They were learning Russian, another cousin told me. They had money. No one talked about them.

And why do I care? you might ask. To what extent does the place we come from generations ago determine who we are, the lives we lead? That question has been asked so many times, with much better answers than I can possibly give you. And, anyway, I simply meant to tell you about my grandfather.

He's gone now, but I can still hear his voice, singing, holiday songs, cantorial, in my head. He and my grandmother would fight over which tune to use, and end up singing two or three versions of the same song. "Not like that," she'd say, and start humming. And they'd be off, on a different tune, a different melody, a different memory.

If I had any musical ability, I would sing for you now. We could all stand and sing together, and blot out our harsher histories with our voices. We could sing, and sing, and the room would shake with happiness and power and joy and history. We could sing, not just in Hebrew, as my grandparents would, but in English, Spanish, Hindi, and Arabic, a veritable tower of song. We could bring down the house with our singing.

But I don't have any singing talent, having to my great chagrin inherited the unmusical genes from the other side of the family, so you will have to imagine the singing. As I do.

The Two Cousins
By Ilana Schiller-Weiss

Big Cousin

She is nine years old, has dark black hair cut as if she had a bowl on her head, and she is Chinese. She lives in New York City, so I see her fairly often, and also had to spend the entire Christmas break with her and the family, because we all go out to Long Island to spend Christmas together.

She loves to draw and thinks she is a regular Picasso. I must admit, she is a very good artist, but she always flaunts her talent and tries to criticize anyone else who likes to draw by saying that she could draw it a whole lot better.

She constantly tries to get me in trouble. For example, if I'm sitting down next to her and I hug her or nudge her accidentally (or even poke her if I'm really bored), she screams a piercing cry, and a family member comes in and yells at me saying that I need to stop "torturing and harassing" her.

She also has a passion for ancient Greece and Greek mythology, so for Christmas I got her that book, *The Odyssey*, which I thought would maybe smarten her up a bit and also be something she would enjoy. But when I gave it to her while the whole family was around the Christmas tree, I got a disapproving look and a protest from both her mother, who is my aunt, and my grandmother, for giving her a book that was too challenging.

She can be very fun to be around sometimes, and she tells me all about the gossip from her school. As much as I would not like to admit this, I think we will probably be lifelong friends.

She pinches and pokes me, pulls me and pains me. Here I am, just minding my own business, and she comes from behind! I don't know why I bug her so much. I just want to be with her. I like to do what she does. If she makes a face out of her crumbs on a plate, then I need to do the exact same thing! I do tell her a lot about my life in school. She listens and tries to give me advice.

I hate it when she ignores me, though. I always get really annoyed by that! She often reads a book when she decides to ignore me. So I try turning up the volume of the TV. That doesn't work, so I try raising my voice. She puts down the book and rolls her eyes. Then she tries tickling me. Here's my cue! I yell and scream until my mom or grandmother comes in to yell at her. It's very funny, and at least it's not me getting in trouble, but then my mom says that I shouldn't provoke her. I'm not "provoking" her! I just wanted her attention, that's all. If being annoying or irritating is a way to get attention, then so be it.

I also like watching what she does. For example, if she is on the computer or writing something, I like standing behind her to see what she's doing. She gets a little annoyed, though, when I just stand behind her, unmoving. But it is a way to at least be closer to her, right?

She makes me feel sort of stupid, sometimes. I told my aunt that she did and my aunt told me that I shouldn't feel that way. But I do. It's okay, though, not a big deal.

But I didn't mention, I am an artist. I love to paint, draw, sketch, and everything related to art. And also, I am very good at it. She sometimes draws with me, but I do believe I am a lot better. I try and tell her this sometimes, but when I do, she puts down the pencil or just walks away.

Just telling her the facts, that's all. Well, I suppose our relationship is just a little complicated, but I expect it will clear up a bit later in life.

Drawers
By Ilana Manaster

My sister's drawers looked not that different from my own, I'm sure. They were filled with things we kept away from each other. Our twin drawers in two rooms on two floors, our twin drawers heavy with our lives apart, our struggles with getting along, the glimpses we got of what happiness might look like.

In my drawers there were cigarettes. In my sister's...Sex? Love? Fear? I kept fear in a drawer, too, next to the bras she'd given me when she heard the mockery of the other girls. I whispered to my dog and not my sister because I didn't want anyone to understand too well.

Familiar Strangers
By Syeda Showkat

His legs began to tingle, like a thousand tiny black ants scurrying between the dark hairs on his calf. That image always bothered him. He wasn't fond of ants, or any small creature for that matter. They crawled between the sugar crystals in the aluminum tin on the kitchen floor. They slowly drowned in his afternoon chai, lying on their hidden stomachs. He picked them up with an old silver spoon; it took them several seconds to die. Aakash flexed his toes now, thinking of their tiny bodies on the saucer. He looked out at the rippling of the muddy waters from the ferry, wondering how long it would take them to drown here. Calculating the cups of tea it would take to fill up the Pauda Nodi. Thirty thousand, he guessed. Thirty thousand cups of ant chai to fill up that river.

"Do you have a light?"

"Pardon?"

"A light, a match? Come on *bhai*, I've lost all the flames from my matches to this goddamn wind, and this ferry stinks. I think I'm getting seasick. Light me up, will you."

"Um… sure."

Aakash had his old lighter. The one his *abba* gave him when he left. He didn't smoke really. Like the ants, that too made him queasy. Abba had said that he'd get over that once he moved out to take that government post in Calcutta, a job his father had won him soon after his twentieth birthday, the most practical gift. His queasiness, his inability to deal with even the most minute creatures, his fear of being a real man. Abba believed Aakash would get over all of that once he left the house. Once he stopped hiding behind his *amma's achol*. Abba was sure of it, for he was the family oracle. History and their lives usually followed the path his father predicted. Now Aakash wasn't so sure of Abba's abilities. He wasn't sure that he could stop craving the smell of his mother's sun-dried saris or the taste of unripe guavas from his *dadi's* garden eaten after a summer shower on the old cement roof. He wasn't sure leaving would make him a man. He feared it would only transform him into a lonely boy.

"So do you have a name?" The voice was speaking again. Aakash hadn't gotten a look at him before. The man was tall with a thin moustache over his lip and rough stubble lining his cheeks. He was middle-aged, with wisps of graying hair above his forehead and a softening stomach poking out about his belt. His eyes shone, a bright hazel that contrasted with his dark creased skin. His left brow lifted, wondering whether or not Aakash heard him. A silent question mark was sketched on his forehead.

He reminded Aakash of his father. The same unwavering voice, the furrowed brows, the confident stance. He was a younger man, rough around the edges, but stern. Aakash thought it best not to speak. He lowered his eyes instead and took two steps back before turning around completely and walking away. He held his arms straight and lifted his shoulders uncomfortably up to his earlobes; an overgrown porpoise stumbling through the sweat-stained crowd. This was his special retreat, a retreat he only used in dire circumstances, saved for the harsh crack of his father's orders or his presence in the bodies of strangers. When he got to the other end of the ferry he realized he felt seasick. Maybe the sweat and urine smell was getting to him, or maybe it was just the fear. The aftermath of thinking of his father. He found a quiet corner on the other side; incidentally, it smelled worse.

Aakash had believed, only momentarily, that leaving would be the best. Not to become the man that Abba wanted, but to be rid of the life he dreaded. To be free of the father who transformed him into a shivering porpoise every time he walked into the same room; but now he knew he was wrong. Aakash could never lose Abba because Abba was more than a man. He was a memory; one that would never leave, stored away in the folds of his mind. Abba would be everywhere; on the ferry disguised as a stranger or in the ant chai river, forming the waves that churned his stomach.

My Favorite (Gay) Uncle: And Other Things I'm Not Supposed to Know
By Cynara Charles-Pierre

My uncle Stevie was such a force in my life. Outside of my mother, he was probably the only family member that I had a special relationship with. I admired and adored him. He was easily the best-looking member of my family (other than my grandfather when he was younger, at least based on a photo I saw of him in his twenties—is it weird to consider your grandfather as a hottie?). Anyway, it seemed like my uncle Stevie could do any and everything too. He was a model, a cook, a singer (what a voice!) and probably one of the funniest people I knew. His humor was pure snark; the kind of humor where you knew you shouldn't laugh, but you just couldn't help yourself. I also always felt more alive around my uncle…jokes were funnier, food was tastier, and a simple drive around town seemed more like an adventure. I looked forward to his visits like a starving man would look forward to a buffet…because it was like all-you-could-have fun with my uncle. He drove most of my family nuts, but not me. He was everything I so desperately wanted to grow up to be: charming, attractive, talented…basically the total package. To me he was as perfect as a person could be. Getting a compliment from my uncle was like winning the lottery (and about as likely) because he wasn't very generous with them. So when you got one, you held on to it tight. To this day I remember the day he saw a picture of me and noted that he never realized what pretty eyes I had. It's been almost twenty years since he said that to me and it still warms my heart. My mother often accused her little brother of being too cocky and particular for his own good. I just thought Stevie was confident and discerning…nothing wrong with that. So what if he quit every job he ever had…I'm sure they weren't right for him.

Dinner Time
By Joanne Lin

The summer air wraps tight against the room. "How was your day?" Ma asks. Her voice drifts into the air and collides with the smell of rice. Chopsticks bang into one another. Soft words said as a battle for the last piece of broccoli emerges. Taste buds, they sway and dance. Stomachs dissolve into happiness, smiles erupt.

This love,
rare as it is, stumbles and falls
into an everyday routine.

The Inheritance of Food
By Wendy Lee

When I was growing up, my mother was not like other Chinese mothers. Normal Chinese mothers knew how to make traditional dishes like soy-sauce chicken, lion's head meatballs, and winter melon soup. My mother, on the other hand, was very much into health food. Instead of making white rice for every meal, she'd make brown rice. She rolled her own dough for *jiaozi* (dumplings) but using whole-wheat flour. She called these "Indian dumplings" because of the color of their skins. My mother was not the most politically correct person.

So, cooking duties fell to my father, who actually had a lot of practice at it. When he first came to America from mainland China, he worked as a dishwasher at his uncle's restaurant in New York City. Later, he became a line cook, working for minimum wage as he put himself through engineering school. This is in direct contrast to my mother, who around the same time arrived in New York from Taiwan to take classes at Columbia University. Having grown up with maids her entire life, she had no idea what to do with her dirty dishes, so she stuffed them into a cupboard. Later, her landlady shamed her by opening the cupboard door to expose stacks of unwashed plates and cups. "What, did you think they would wash themselves?" she exclaimed. (My mother loved telling this story to my sister and me when were growing up, citing it as the reason she made us wash the dishes.)

Many of the foods my father made were the kind you can find in Chinese takeout places: chow mein, Kung Pao chicken, sweet and sour pork. He would try to use up all the leftovers in the fridge, from the last stalk of broccoli to the final wilted bok choy leaf. He also tried to sneak mung bean sprouts into everything, so that I grew to hate the unexpected crunch of bean sprouts in my food. Perhaps because it was cheap and easy to make, his go-to dish was egg foo yung, which is basically a fried egg patty stuffed with vegetables (including the despised bean sprouts).

These were the dishes of my childhood. But it makes me wonder what food my father ate when he was growing up. Certainly it wasn't the heavily fried, culturally confused dishes he learned to make while working in his uncle's Chinese restaurant. Maybe when people emigrate to another country, they leave behind the knowledge that isn't useful to them, certain foods that they'll never be able to get or replicate in their adopted country. As I myself am starting to cook for my own family (strangely enough, mostly Indian food), I wonder what kind of legacy I will be passing down with the dishes I make. I suspect it'll be a mixture of my mother's health-nuttiness, and my father's adaptability to the cuisine of a new culture.

How to Cook for Yourself
By Anita Perala

First, you have to cook the rice. Just use a regular long-grain rice. Basmati is too hard for *pulihara*. Make a lot, no? Because you can keep it a few days. It's a lot of work, so when you do it, you make a lot. Don't put too much water. You always put too much water. Then it comes out sticky, it's no good. Next make the sauce. You need tamarind—the dried kind, you know it comes in a block? Sometimes Wegman's has fresh tamarind here. You won't find that where you are, huh? Sometimes the tamarind is old, dried out, it's no good. It should be a little soft, so you can bend it. I use a whole block, but you aren't making so much, for only you, right? Use one quarter, one half of a block.

Boil some water and pour it into the bowl with the tamarind. Not too much. You used to put too much. Let it soak for ten–fifteen minutes. Then you squeeze the pulp out with your hands. Get it all out, otherwise it won't taste good. When you finish squeezing, put it through a sieve. Push it with a wooden spoon until all the pulp comes out. It should be thick, you know.

Heat a skillet and put some mustard seeds in. No oil, just a dry skillet. I don't know, maybe one–two teaspoons. Then add just a pinch of asafetida. Pinch of turmeric, dried chili peppers. A few, depends on how hot you want it. A pinch of fenugreek and some curry leaves. Do they have curry leaves there? If you can't find, you can leave them out. It won't taste the same, but it will be okay. Take ginger and grate it, and some coriander powder and salt, and mix that into the juice. Pour this tamarind mixture into the skillet and cook it. Twenty–thirty minutes, low heat, so it simmers.

When rice is cool, put it into a big bowl. In your hand, you mix a little turmeric and some oil. Then mix this into the rice. Not for flavor; it gives a nice color. Break up all the lumps when you do this. Now mix the tamarind sauce into the rice. Don't pour it all in, add little-little at a time. After it is mixed completely, you add the peanuts. You have to dry-roast them first in a skillet. Be careful! You don't want to burn them. Then you mix them into the rice. That's it. I put *chana dal*, but you don't have to if you can't find it there.

You can make it with lemon, too, you know? You always liked the tamarind one better. Some restaurants have it, in Toronto they have. It's okay, but homemade is better. We make this for all kinds of occasions in Andhra—any get-together, wedding, holiday. But I don't make it so much anymore. Your father likes simple food.

A Culinary Experiment
By Lee Clifford

I didn't want to eat the mysterious food put upon the table. Even at age seven, I knew the difference between a well-executed dish and a failed experiment. What I saw before me was most decidedly the latter.

My father, a normally excellent cook who unwound from work every evening by throwing together elaborate meals, had decided to try to recreate a dish he had sampled at a French restaurant. And so, to that end, on our table sat four gelatinous pink sponges that gave off an odor of seafood, jiggling ever so slightly when one of us moved.

Apparently, they were called "quenelles." And apparently, they were notoriously difficult to make properly. I would learn this as my father worked his way through quenelles that were too runny, quenelles that were too fishy, quenelles that were so unspeakably unpalatable that my seven-year-old self didn't have the vocabulary to even describe what was amiss.

Perhaps a normal child would have flat-out refused to even take a bite. But in my house there were strict rules when it came to food. Practically from the time my sister and I could eat solids, we knew the drill: we could each choose two foods that we didn't have to eat (mine were leeks and zucchini) but everything else was to be consumed.

And so, every time a new version of the horrific dish would appear on the table, I would squirm, I would gag, and I would consider the age-old question of whether it's less painful to consume something disgusting in several large bites or dozens of small ones.

But in the end, I would somehow manage to clean my plate.

All told, my father would attempt the dish five or six times, but a satisfactory result continued to elude him. My mother eventually intervened, informing him that he could no longer foist the results of his experimentation on us.

With time, the odious taste of quenelles was washed away by far more delicious flavors—late-summer pesto, hearty winter stews, farmer's market salads dressed with perfectly tangy vinaigrette.

In the end, my parents sent me off into adulthood with a wonderfully varied palate. And I suppose they also taught me an important lesson about life: sometimes a really bad dish comes your way. You may have to choke it down. But there's an upside: your next meal will taste extraordinarily good by comparison.

She Prays to You/I Pray to Her
By Deiona Monroe

You allowed mommy to understand you on June 30, 2008; mommy developed a smiling heart on June 30, 2008. Though she never knew what you were or why each section was named after a person, she clutched on tighter than ever before. The rigid marks aligned across your spine make her back ache less; you kissed her heart on the rough, cool side. She fell to her knees on purpose this time, whispering "God' every now and then between your lines; I love seeing mommy smile. And the smile you give her is a metamorphosis of some other type; she cries because it feels good to. I love the tears that mommy cries now. I don't quite get your rough text or hands touched tightly position with a bowed head; I stopped believing you on June 30, 2008. How could a being of so much power do something that extraordinarily heart-twisting with such a quickness? I can't open you up and read the words of John, Abraham or any other one of those irregular names because my heart can't see; veins are blind to anything outside the body. My veins don't see so according to you I can't pump such as mommy can; her heart is more open than mine. So open that sometimes when it rains, I hear you calling her name and the sun begins to outweigh clouds; mommy knows how to smile when there's a thunderstorm. Though I don't read you/praise you as I should, mommy does; I praise mommy. Praise to a point of no return because I read in between her lines; she aligns her life according to your hieroglyphics and though it seems as if you have betrayed me I align my life with her markings; I believe in mommy so it feels as if I believe in you. Mommy places her palms together, tightly; nothing can break her prayer. She bows down to you as if you pulled the bones out from her knees down; she gets speechless. Mommy's fingertips turn chilled when she aligns them along your scripture; your passages embark her onto a new trail, as if her soul is mimicking the gingerbread man; her spirit cannot be caught. Mommy's essence excavates the world and lights up the darkest edges; mysterious alleyways are skips through the clouds for her; I still fear alleyways. Repeating your name seems as though it is a battle for me; I hate participating in wars. I don't know what it means to aim weapons at heartbeats; mommy accepted you even after the bullets were fired. I didn't. I could read your word because I placed tears between lines. You burned my spirit in a way I didn't think was possible but then again who knew that gunshots would stain my family; mommy took the good side of you while I took the bad. Your beauty and pain is both memorable and unmatched, worthy of praise and makes me cry every once in a while. Mommy touches her palm, I make fists; we all share hugs. She has learned to pray to you and I have learned to pray to her.

An excerpt from *Dear Daddy*
By Gina DiFrisco

Dear Jamie,

First off, I miss you. Everyone has been asking how you are, and if you've written back yet. I always tell them no. I hope you write soon, though. I really miss my older brother.

You will never believe what happened at school today. I got to class late (I'm never on time), and everyone was making get well cards and putting money on the teacher's desk. The vice-principal, Ms. Rosario, was in the hospital. She had been beaten last night, almost killed. I hate her. She never has anything nice to say and is always on my case.

My friends said that the money was to get Ms. Rosario flowers and shit. I wasn't giving my money away, and I wasn't going to make her a card either. My friend Anthony made one in my name instead.

The day was going fine. Then the cops came into the building. One was a tall man with red hair. He walked in wearing sunglasses and his hands in his pockets like he owned the place. The other pig was a woman. Not as tall, but not too short. Everything about her was plain. It was about lunchtime when I saw them walking to the main office. I was heading back to class from the bathroom, and I had to walk past the office. When I did, one of the secretaries came out and called me. "Gabriella, come here please."

I couldn't say no 'cuz I would probably get in trouble so I went over. The cops that came in said that one of the secretaries overheard me yelling at Ms. Rosario yesterday and saying that I would kill her. I admit I didn't like the bitch, but I would never try to really kill her. I can't even cut through my own skin with a broken piece of glass before wimping out.

Anyway, I told those damn pigs that I had nothing to do with it and that I was at home all last night. When I was done, the office door opened and Annmarie, a friend of mine, walked in with the second vice-principal, Ms. Windromb. The room went dead.

Ms. Windromb told Annmarie to sit down. Before she even pulled out a chair, the cop with the red hair spoke. "What were you doing from 7:30 p.m. last night to 5 a.m. today?" he asked. Annmarie said the same thing I said: that she was at home the whole time. She sat down and the office door opened again. This time Marielys walked in with Mrs. Hewitt, the principal. I was shocked. Marielys would never do anything that would get her arrested.

The female cop said to Marielys, "Hello, Ms. Bearie. Take a seat." Annmarie asked what was going on. The red-haired cop said they were waiting for one more person.

I heard laughing outside the office door. It went on for a while. I asked Marielys what was going on. "I guess we're being questioned about Ms. Rosario's attack. They came to my house this morning to talk to me about it. Apparently there was evidence linking the attack to us."

It seemed like she was going to say more, but the door opened, and in came my friend Aliana. She was the one laughing, I'm sure. She came in with Mrs. Hewitt who had a sort of evil look on her face, gritting her teeth and glaring. Then again, I always think she looks evil.

Aliana looked at the cops. First she stared at the woman cop like she was trying to figure the woman out, to see if she could get the woman's backstory. Aliana loves to do that: to figure out what makes people tick—and use that against them if need be. Sometimes it's like she knows everything about a person just by the way they say "hi."

Aliana, however, got nothing from the woman. She quickly moved her eyes to the other policeman: the redhead. She smiled ear to ear as she sat down next to me and sounded so giddy as she spoke. "Ronald. Nice to see ya again!" Redhead Ronald. I wanted to laugh, but I couldn't out loud.

Aliana suddenly had a gun in her hand. I must have missed something because I had no idea where it came from. All I could do was look at the gun as Aliana took it apart and put it back together. I could hear people talking, but couldn't make out what they were saying—I was freaking out, the gun only inches away from me.

Aliana started yelling about some kid named Kevin. Something else about Hitler ruling the world. I also heard a phrase or two about power, "our power." Aliana was pissed beyond belief. Power this and that. It made me think of my power. The fire I can produce out of my own hands. The burning ability to heal my own wounds. You, brother, told me to never talk about it to anyone and I haven't.

From your favorite little sister,
Gabriella

Busking for Pie
By Heather Kristin

I'm sitting in the Automat on East Forty-Second Street with my mom and twin sister, age seven. Mom tells me to ask the guy at the next table for a quarter.

"But it costs seventy-five cents for key lime pie," my sister says.

I reach into my pocket and find a quarter from yesterday's busking on the street corner with my violin. I give the shiny coin to my sister.

Years later, she'll say I didn't give it to her, that she reached out and grabbed it from me.

But that's not how I remember it.

Death in a Family
By Erika Marte

There were no
words in response to
questions, just tears.

Amelia sat on the cold wooden floor of her bedroom. The windows were closed but the subtle December winds found mysterious hidden cracks to send chills to her entire body. The sun had decided to call in sick to work that day, leaving Amelia to fight the cold weather wrapped only in the darkness surrounding her. It was a darkness that slowly made her drift in and out of sleep. A darkness that stripped her naked and made her exposed to every sound and touch.

The entire house slept. The children were strangely fast asleep. The thought of Daniel and Pam sent a new wave of tears all the way from the gut of her stomach to her eyes. However, no tears strolled down Amelia's cheeks this time. Perhaps the wind had dried the tears. His death had dried up her heart and soul. He wasn't the only one who died and drifted away to the unknown that dark evening. Amelia tripped and stumbled right behind him, struggling to catch him.

Insanity is not
the inability to think coherently.
It is to love.

And to be
intertwined with emotions that one
could never explain.

A Time for Healing
By Marlyn Palomino

I have been avoiding this, but I found myself alone today and thought it was the perfect time to Get It Done. To cry as much as I can. To let all these buried feelings come out and to say the words and see them on paper. Mom—my first word, and my first loss. My memories of her have shaped me.

I look back and it feels like I'm paralyzed. My mind fights hard to send commands but I can't speak. Fear has sewn my lips together and cut out my tongue. I scream… I mumble… I purr. I want to rip all my hair off; I want to feel pain. Familiar voices are calling me. What do they want? Am I insane? The voices are getting louder, telling me that my mother has gone to heaven. The voices are the enemy, invisible but strong, squeezing and breaking me apart. I am flying at the speed of light. I can't stop. Is this a game? I'm not playing. I want to disappear.

Am I now the mommy? Fear knows me… knows my weakest point, what I'm scared of the most. Growing up, I always had a fear about the day she would be gone. Who would I be left with? My father?

I feel like throwing up right now, but I can still hear my mother's voice, singing by the moon: *Sana que sana colita de rana si no sanas hoy sanaras mañana.* "Heal, heal little tail of the frog. If you don't heal today, you'll heal tomorrow."

When my mother died of cancer in 2008, I lost my way. Everything turned dark because my shining light had shut down. I would wake up every morning and call her name, but it was too late. I wondered if it was my fault. I had no reason to go on, no direction, nothing—just a deadbeat father, a cold-blooded snake, silent, always hiding and stalking his prey, ready to inject his venom to kill a hope. Fear defeated me; it was so mean.

But a force kept pushing me forward, dragging me against my will. It was a strength—a healing power—like the *sanaras* of my mother's song. Now I know that healing revives—it brings a new state, but never the original one. Healing recovers and extracts the pain. Healing moves on, but never forgets. My mother is gone, but only physically—she will always be alive in my mind and heart. My father was never a father figure. He's a blurry image fading away into ashes. He cannot hurt me now.

My healing feels slow, but I know it is always mending me, making me whole. Scars are still forming, but they give me strength, help me grow physically and mentally, and toughen me so that I am able to take risks, and take advantage of opportunities, and use my talents wisely. I am positive. I am resilient. I am a survivor.

It's Not Christmas Without You
By Emily Sarita

She only walked through the neighborhood during Christmas because it reminded her of her mother. Her mother's green eyes would shine every time they passed by a house that was overly decorated with ornaments, plastic reindeer, and multicolored lights. She would smile at the beauty of Christmas and close her eyes while faint snow hit her cheeks lightly. Then her mother would grab her hand, and they would dance through the neighborhood singing Christmas carols. She opened her eyes and smiled slightly at the memory of her mother.

She stomped her way through the snow, feeling her soggy socks in her boots. She shuddered and wiped her runny nose as the wind blew. She never liked going out during the winter. She felt like winter was the only season when people should stay in and relax. She'd rather be curled up in a ball in her room, drinking hot chocolate and reading novels. But today she had the urge to walk out in the neighborhood. She felt like she owed it to her mother. Christmas was her mother's favorite holiday, and it was their tradition to walk through the whole neighborhood together to see the houses decorated.

She stopped when she arrived in front of her house, and cringed. It was a two-story colonial with faded white paint. The screen door was broken with screws sticking out, the plants were overgrown, and there was no trace of Christmas. No trace of her mother. Since her mom had died, her father no longer seemed to care about the state of the house…or Eva, for that matter.

When she entered her house, everything seemed untouched, and that meant only one thing: she was left alone on Christmas, yet again. She swore in Spanish under her breath and couldn't believe her father left her alone once again.

Eva had never been close to her father. He was a strict man devoted to his career, and he was barely there while she was growing up. He was always in another country handling business. Once her mother died, her father devoted more time to his job than to Eva. She was taken care of by her aunts and uncles while she was growing up, and her father would send her postcards here and there. This aggravated Eva. She needed someone to console her since her mother couldn't. Her dad just walked away and dealt with his emotions by taking on more work. He barely thought about Eva. She thought he was selfish. He never thought of how she felt and never tried to be there for her. He wasn't the only one grieving. She needed someone. She needed her father, and he wasn't there. The phone suddenly rang and Eva went to pick it up.

"Hello?" she said. She heard loud breathing and the person began to speak.

"Hello, Eva," a deep voice said.

"Hello, Dad," she said coldly.

"I was calling to let you know that, um, I won't be able to be home for Christmas. I was called suddenly to go on a business trip to Tokyo," he said awkwardly. He could tell she was upset because of her tone.

"I already got the memo, Dad, since you weren't here at all. Once again, Christmas all by myself and you don't seem to care since you are heading to Tokyo and never considered me in the first place!" she said, her voice rising.

"Do not raise your voice at me, young lady! I am your father and I am sorry I won't be able to make it for Christmas. To make it up to you, I left presents in your room," he said in a calm voice.

"Presents are not going to make anything better, Dad. For once in your life, act like a real father and be there for me!" she said as she hung up the phone. She rubbed her temples and marched up to her room.

She opened the door to her room, revealing her light walls, white canopy bed, and white desk where her laptop was lying. **On her bed, there were five boxes of every color, shape, and size.**[*] She walked over to her bed, sat at the edge, and knocked over a small box. It opened and a small necklace slipped out. She jumped off her bed and picked up the necklace. She stood there stunned as she recognized the initials on the locket. M.S. Her mother's initials. She opened the locket and there was a picture of her, her mother, and her father. She simply fastened the locket around her neck and swore that she would never take it off. Then she walked over to her window and watched as the tree branches danced to the wind's rhythm. *It's not Christmas without you, Mom,* she thought.

Daddy's Heartbroken Girl
By Diamond Arriola

How can I devour the sympathy of your harsh spoken guilt when you haven't even swallowed your pride? Sorry—my soul slowly turns into ice with each cold breath wasted on your promises. I need room to forgive but my heart is consumed with memories of your consistent lies, unsung lullabies, and unused Father's Day ties.

I've learned to place a knight's shield in front of my tears; a sword guarded behind my back, I've suffered from all the emotions that you lack. I will never let you see me cry. The thought of a "bond" seems absurd to me, a foreign language to my covered ears. My heart is leaking—one of my greatest fears.

No one understands it but me. I accumulated this hurt while writing this enduring plea. I don't know why but confronting you seems uneasy—proven fact that this mentality is indeed unhealthy. I refuse to find the cure in you even though we share the same blood. This relationship between us is a mess, a nasty flood.

I could take the time to comprehend this view from your perspective, but I won't. The past is too reflective. To reminisce on these sad scenes of voids too empty to fill? These words are sharp; if you read them they will kill. Love is painful. Complex, too.

Perhaps I should refrain from letting myself down. I was forced to understand your motives, but I guess I am a big girl now. You never tucked me underneath the sheets, or read me a bedtime

[*] Emily's mentor's piece on page 49 shares this line.

story from your lips. I guess I'll swallow this in small little sips. Though most of your wisdom was spilled with an intoxicated tongue, I've intoxicated myself long enough with feelings of regret, no anxiety to fret, a lost lonely bet.

This is something I will never forget. They say to forgive. And I am strong. I saved myself from these dreams that will never come true. Our relationship is a little past due.

Corny
By Cherish Smith

Corny misses his mom. He misses her more than he misses warmth in the middle of the night. He misses her more than he misses a full stomach at dinner and he misses her more than the last bath he took and that was nearing a year ago. He didn't know what he was going to do. Cry? No, he had done that already and it didn't make him feel better. Punch something? Not today. He put a nice hole in the wall, his knuckles bled, his landlord was going to kill him and it didn't make him feel any better. Shout? It could work but he knows it won't bring his mother back.

Corny's mom is not dead, she's not sick, and she's not on drugs even though she should be. She's just missing. The poor woman went wherever the wind blew, wherever a dog ran and wherever the voices in her head told her to go, at least that's what she told Corny. Corny hated those voices.

When he was younger he loved them. They were why he and his mother rode the elevator up and down and up and down. They were why they drew pictures like cavemen on the wall of their apartment. But they were also why his mom begged on the street for money. They were why she poured his cereal out the window and he couldn't eat breakfast. They were also why she busted a car window and had to go to jail. So Corny grew to hate them. He tried lots of times to get her to stop listening to them but she never did. Not for long anyway.

Corny never had many friends. Actually he never had friends at all. He could remember when mothers would rush their kids away when Corny and his mother approached the park. He remembers how they would suddenly have to leave when he asked another child to play. He remembers when he told his mom it made him sad when others didn't want to play with him and he remembers what she told him. She said the people (which was what she called the voices in her head) said it doesn't matter that they don't want to play with him; he had her. But that wasn't always true.

Many times Corny would wake in the middle of the night and walk down the hallway to his mother's room when he had a nightmare, only to find the pallet where she slept empty. He would run into the living room to see if she was there; sometimes she would be and other times she wouldn't. When she wasn't he'd check the bathroom and push back the shower curtain in search of her. If she wasn't there he'd check all the closets because she'd hide there sometimes. She wouldn't be there either, sometimes, and that's when Corny would miss school. He'd wait at home, days, sometimes weeks so he wouldn't miss her when she came back. She always came back, but not this time.

The teachers hated when he missed school. He was smart. He could, and still can, answer any question a teacher threw at him, even if they hadn't gone over it yet in class. He never got into fights, though children did everything to challenge that. Corny was the sweetest boy. They always demanded to know where he was when he wasn't in school, and he would always tell them he was sick. They believed him every time. He was also a scrawny boy. He didn't eat regularly and that went the same for baths too. In the winter he was always underdressed and every piece of clothing he owned had belonged to someone else at some point and they were always too big or too small.

This is Corny's life, for now at least. But he has a plan.

Snowbird

By Nancy Hooper

Six a.m. So muggy, you could suffocate out there. In here, it's like a meat locker, the hum of central air reminding me that sunny Florida was my husband's idea. No more New York winters, he said. So here I am, trapped in a pastel condominium for six months and a day. I'm a goddamned snowbird, I say to the big bay window streaked with sweat. I take a drag from my cigarette and blow smoke at my reflection—a hazy little figure with long hair and skinny legs. Outside, an egret struts around a manmade pond that looks too blue. The bird pecks at the chalky sand and stares at gnats that float like dust above the water's edge. I wonder if a gnat tastes sweet or salty, and if it dies when swallowed, or squirms inside the stomach for a while.

■ ■ ■

Ten a.m. We sit on plastic chairs near a sign that says Triage. A nurse appears and leads us to a wall of rubber curtains. She shoves the curtains back so fast, they sing along the metal rod they hang on. The smell of rubbing alcohol and urine taints the air, then white coats and big machines fill up the room. The nurse escorts me out and says, These older gents, they sometimes overdo it. Probably just heart palpitations, she says. I should stay with him, but she says, No, it's just routine, we'll hook him up to EKGs and monitors, probably all day. Go on, Missus. Your hubby will be okay. We'll keep you posted.

■ ■ ■

Three p.m. Loud ringing wakes me. A voice says, He's fine but keeps asking for you, could you come early? And suddenly I'm there and some nurse grabs my arm and yells, We're doing everything we can to save him. They pull me into a small room where he's on a gurney and bright lights sting my eyes and a doctor bangs on his chest and his body jumps a little but his eyes look like steel marbles and everybody says they're sorry and then I'm alone with him, wondering what do they say in the movies or should I kiss him good-bye or say you were my hero or forgive me and shouldn't somebody close his eyes or call a priest or pull the sheet up over his head.

■ ■ ■

Morning again, I think. They tell me he's to be cremated at eleven. As guests squeeze in with chatter, fruit, and flowers, I glance outside and see the egret sitting in a tree. I close my eyes and suddenly, I'm riding the breeze. Then my talons clutch onto a branch, as I stop to gaze beyond the gray-green mist below. I take one last deep breath and push off, my wings opening and rising as I glide toward the horizon and some strange new world.

Half-Staff

By Jessica Benjamin

My stepbrother, Nick, and I just found unwrapped Christmas presents in the basement. We're getting everything we asked for: a Gameboy and Walkman and Mouse Trap. Now, we're pink faced and puffed in our snowsuits. I'm at my father's feet, scooping snow in my mouth while he raises the American flag up a pole in our front yard. My gloves are bulky and slick; snow slides off, leaving me with a mouthful of dirty, wet nylon.

I laugh as Nick tries throwing snowballs at me. They leave his fist and powder in the wind, blowing flakes that catch in my eyelashes. He finally figures out to pack them tighter and he hits me good, right in the gut. He runs away, cackling up chalky white clouds. I wrap my arms around a pile of snow and try to lift it.

"Hey! You kids know better," my father shouts. "Santa's watching." He widens his eyes, peering up toward the flag, the sky, and scanning the clouds. He nods, having found whatever he was looking for.

"We know Santa's not real!" Nick yells across the yard.

"What?" my father shouts back.

"Santa's made up!" Nick smiles.

My father marches toward him and slowly drops down to his knees. Nick's eyes dart from house to pole to street to fence. I stare at him, hoping his eyes find me and settle. He's stiff and I'm waiting for him to sprint. I squint, hoping to keep him still. Hoping he'll keep our secret so my father can keep his.

"You don't believe in Santa?" my father asks, as if just saying so would kill the jolly old man, bury him under piles of snow. Shiny buckled black shoes sticking out like the wicked witch in *The Wizard of Oz*. But we couldn't kill Santa. Santa isn't real. "How can you not believe?"

Nick searches for an answer in the laces of his boots.

"Of course Santa's real. Who brings the toys every year? Who leaves footprints in the chimney?" He puts a hand on Nick's shoulder. "Who eats the cookies and milk? Who does all that?"

Nick's cheeks sag. "Santa," he says.

My father turns to me. My eyes avoid him, lifting up toward the flag whipping in the sky, the flag that covered his father's coffin. The flag he taught me to fold properly—half-width, half-width, triangle all the way to the stars. The flag that can never touch the ground.

My father kneels in front of me and grips his hands around my upper arms, forcing me to perfect posture.

"Jessie," he says, "do you believe in Santa?"

His eyes are wide and desperate, as if my next words will be my first. If I don't believe, something will die, not Santa or my father, but a kind of faith that ties them together. Faith that ties me to them like the seams of the flag. If I let go we will all drop to the ground.

Home

By Maura Kutner

I remember everything about my grandparents. My grandma had a drawer of silk scarves that I dressed my little brothers in. My grandpa had hung a handmade wooden swing on the oak tree in their backyard that stayed up long after my brothers and I could fit in it.

Whenever we went to visit them, my grandma had a small present for me—a bag of gumdrops or a set of pencils: the gifts were never anything fancy, yet they always made me feel like the most loved girl in the world. My grandpa, who had endured a tough childhood and was haunted by Pearl Harbor 'til the day he died, somehow never tired of tea parties and make-believe.

As adults, do we ever feel the same love and sense of home that our grandparents gave us? Why are scents and songs from childhood more vivid than something we experienced yesterday?

You learn a lot about yourself and others as you make your way through life. The sweetest things are earned, not given. A small act usually means more than a big one. People's actions say more about them than they do about you. But if you have a good foundation, it's easier to grow. My grandparents gave me one.

After they were both gone, their house was sold, but we kept everything else. (I still have my grandma's scarves.) I learned that you have to leave one kind of love behind in order to receive a new one. Because of them, I am brave enough to do that.

Run Real
By Ingrid Skjong

Confidence is bruised
What I love isn't faked
My baby: light, sure steps

Singin' in the Rain
By Alissa Riccardelli

On nights in New Jersey, my grandfather would come home after work in the city, sit on the lid of the toilet, his sleeves rolled up to his elbows, and make sure that my cousin Emily and I didn't drown in the bathtub. We'd play with plastic china sets, pretending to sip soapy tea until our skin pruned and became cold. When our teeth started to click, he'd lift us out, one by one, wrapping us in towels and drying the pads of our feet so we wouldn't slip on the tile.

Downstairs our grandmother whipped onion flakes into a bowl of sour cream, creating a magic dip that always materialized when we were with her, much like broccoli on our plates or Cheerios in plastic bags on mornings we went rushing off to museums. She never slept but she was never tired. She was the kind of woman who never took off her heels, always commanding and refined and elegant. Even her house slippers were raised.

Later we'd gather on the bed with my older brother, Robert, the technologically advanced seven-year-old. He'd toy with the television, with the remote control, the VCR. He'd get everything ready. We'd eat pretzels and chips, Dixie cups, or apple slices, kicking our feet into the air, turning onto our bellies to face the television. Every night we watched *Singin' in the Rain*. Emily and I had hair down our backs, wetting the shoulders of our nightgowns. We opened bouquets of umbrellas in the bedroom, twirling them in our fingers, singing along in our grandfather's raincoats and fedoras. We kicked our feet into the plush carpet as though it were full of puddles. Our grandparents may have had sore ankles or sore backs, they may have been worn out or hungry, their bones may have ached at night, settling onto a bed full of bowls and baskets and apple cores, anything to please us with our crowded, toothy smiles. If it was work, we never knew it. I can still see their faces, smoothed and slightly weathered, cleansed and always calming. They clapped their hands together, watching, satisfied. No matter how late it was, they always laughed and rewound. They always hummed along with the tune.

A Piece of Me: A Memoir

By Joanne Lin

The buzz of the television glides into the air: Saturday night's usual background music. My mom's warm fingers wrap a string around the wobbly tooth. I don't know what she's doing; all I know is that this is going to hurt. My mouth is wide open, going dry instantly.

"Okay, I'm going to count to three," Mom says, her voice loud and strong. I close my eyes, surrounded by darkness. My ten-year-old hands are fists, nails digging deep in my skin. I have a theory that if I distract myself with another sensation of pain, I won't feel my tooth coming out. "One…" my mom starts; the string teases my tooth. "Two…" I dig deeper. "Three!" I instantly feel the absence of the tooth, and a sting comes after. A few tears form but I quickly push them away. A soft cotton ball is pressed against my gum, bringing a bit of an odd pain.

"Hold this in for a few minutes," my dad commands. "Good job!" he says after I hand him the cotton ball, covered in a teaspoon of blood. I feel accomplished as my brother looks up at me with amazement.

"Did it hurt? Did you cry? What did it feel like? Does it feel like this?" His seven-year-old voice is pestering. He pinches me hard on the arm: "Did it feel like that?" I call out in pain and my mom scowls at him.

"Jack, leave Joanne alone. Please," my mom says, obviously tired. I secretly smile, loving the feeling of being put up top. He begins whining but stops immediately when Mom reaches out for my hand. Her dangly bracelet bangs against her wrist, reflecting the light. She drops the small, dull white tooth into my hand. It is like a piece of my skin has just fallen off and been handed to me. The ridges of the tooth and the smoothness of the outer layer all seem so surreal. This is *my* tooth. I show Jack quickly, afraid he might steal it. I can't stop staring at it, fascinated by a tooth outside of its natural habitat. I place the tooth in my pocket, patting it every thirty seconds to check if it is still there. Soon enough, my ten-year-old attention span fades away and I forget about the tooth in my pocket.

Later that night, after brushing my teeth, I search my white pajama bottoms for the tooth. All I find is a candy wrapper. Alarmed, I drop to the floor pressing my face against the cold wooden boards. I search for anything white, pulling out socks and pieces of paper from underneath the bed. No luck. I crawl into bed. It's as if I have lost something forever. The longing for the tooth nearly crushes me. I think about the ten years it has been with me, regretting not taking care of it properly. I slip into sleep wondering if my tooth would have anywhere to sleep for the night.

"On her bed, there were five boxes of every color, shape, and size."
—Emily Sarita, mentee

III. RELATIONSHIPS

"I remember how it all began, but I can't clearly see how it will end."

Oh, how the immediacy of their writing triggers our own memories. Enter here to remember how romantic love feels when felt for the very first time. And how love hurts when it is lost.

In smiling similes and unexpected metaphors, in crackling humor and ruffled whimsy, it is all here:

Love questioned.
Love healing.
Love clinging.
Love longed for.
Friends who truly know the meaning of friendship, and
Friends unable to bridge the widening gap between them.
Tenderness and panic.
Hatred and forgiveness.
Aloneness and distance.

In poems, memoir, movie scripts, and txtlingo.
Enter here to revel and remember.

—Josleen Wilson, mentor

Crush

By Anna Poon

I think I'm in love with my tenth-grade biology teacher. And I tell him this. Frequently. Because he's the kind of teacher I can go to after class to say something like, "I really loved this lesson!"

To which he replies: "Biology is *amazing*," and raises his fist so we can pound.

To which I reply: "I really love the way you teach."

"Haha, thank you. I know. I'm amazing too."

"Mr. Caparelli, I love you."

"And I love you, Beverly," he'll say with a wink and click of his tongue before walking coolly out of the classroom, laptop and notes in hand. But I know he's joking. Because he thinks I'm joking. Mr. Joseph Caparelli—I like to call him Joseph—is one of the most popular teachers in the school. He's used to the fan worship.

I've also told my friends, my counselor, and I almost even told my mother. None of them think I'm serious. None of them think this love that I have for him could be legitimate. My friends think it's cute. Borderline creepy, yes, but mostly cute. A phase, they assume—everyone has a teacher crush at some point in her life. My counselor tries to understand. She has me "talk through the crush," explain "why *exactly*" I like him so much, and to try to think about "what possible future this relationship could have."

None, is obviously what she's thinking.

And my mother. My mother-who-doesn't-want-me-to-have-a-boyfriend-until-college came back from parent-teacher conferences with a detailed report but the only thing I really remember is when she said, "Your biology teacher is kind of cute, isn't he? He's much younger than I thought he'd be."

I almost burst out with the truth then and there because for a moment I thought that just *maybe*, she'd be all right with it. Thirteen years is not such a huge age difference, I would explain. After all, people have done worse. Except I doubt she'd have taken me seriously, either.

I, Beverly Francesca Ramirez, am in complete and utterly hopeless love with my biology teacher. How much more serious can I get? Yet I don't deny that I've had my doubts.

I've wondered, for example, if because I was raised by a single mother, I've developed a subconscious, psychological need for a strong and older male role model. Or, if because I'm secretly afraid of falling in love, I've chosen for a crush someone with whom a relationship would be so impossible that I would never even get the chance to fall in love at all.

Then sometimes I think it's curiosity. And that would make the reason I'm in love with Joseph something of an innocent one.

Because when he teaches, his body takes on a bouncing energy, a passion and genuine love for the subject of biology, which in turn inspires a similar passion for the subject in his students, and it makes me wonder. Is that the way he would love a girl? With the same burning desire to know, respect, and understand her? With the same ability to inspire her to love him back with an equal ferocity of passion and respect?

I only wish I could find that level of profundity in a relationship.

Because high school boys these days, they all want the same thing. They're all either CIA agents when it comes to wooing a girl, willing to say and do anything to gain access to the secrets of her body, or turtles, awkwardly shuffling around in their clunky shells, too afraid to ask even to hold hands for a minute.

No, Joseph has passed that stage of voice-cracking, hormonal one-dimensionality and reached the point in a man's life where there are multiple layers to his personality. Layers I wish I could unfold and explore with the soft of my fingertips the way we did when, as a class, we examined the anatomy of angiosperms. Flowering plants. The gentle crush of their petals against my palms as I rubbed them together, getting a feel for the texture.

But whatever it is I feel, this love or not-love I have for Mr. Joseph Caparelli, I don't think it is fair to say that it is not serious. Maybe it is a phase, maybe it doesn't have a future, but you can't say it is not serious or that it's not real.

Because you can't deny that I sometimes lurk outside the door to his office just to catch a glimpse of him working on his laptop. You can't deny that I participate as much as I can in his class if only to hold his gaze for a precious few seconds. And you can't deny that I'll always take the longer route to my sixth-period class on the off chance that I might bump into him as he's walking out for lunch.

You can't deny the subtle attraction that draws me to him every time, like bees to an angiosperm.

Over Cake and Pesto
By Jana Branson

On her bed, there were five boxes of every color, shape, and size. *

"I'm trying to get rid of stuff. I'm going to start bringing odds and ends to the country house, just in case Phillip gets laid off at the end of the school year," she said as she struggled to move a box off the bed, which I noticed was actually two twin beds pushed together to make a king-size bed. She pulled a moss-colored sweater out of one of the boxes and spread it across the white comforter.

"What do you think? It took me weeks to make. The wool is from Australia…expensive," she said, nodding to herself.

"Wow. It's absolutely beautiful…really beautiful," I said as I ran my hand down one of the soft sleeves.

"Well then! I'm glad you like it. I made it for myself. Shall we eat?"

It had become our tradition. She called those monthly pesto dinners "our thing." Her husband of thirty years, Phillip, played tennis every Wednesday, hated pesto, and didn't seem to have the same appreciation for white wine that Mabel did. Her apartment, an elevator building, was large by New York standards, and I could read the titles of movies that were playing at the Angelika Film Center a few blocks away through the expansive living room windows.

"Shall I cut the pasta recipe in half this time? I have four different types of cakes I need you to try, and I don't want you to get full." She slowly twisted the wine opener into the soft cork. "Look there," she motioned toward the large stainless steel counter she used for baking and testing her recipes.

She handed me a glass of wine and pushed her finger into one of the yellow cakes.

"This one is pretty spongy. This one—this one is a little more crumbly. This one is dense…and this one…this one is a chocolate hazelnut tart. Mmm…" She put a single chocolate crumb in her mouth and closed her eyes. "Try this one very last."

Mabel talks and I talk. But mostly I listen as she talks while slowly twirling the luscious pesto pasta wrapped around her fork onto a large spoon. In between bites she tells me stories, and she is oddly candidly honest about everything. And I listen and I learn once a month, and always on a Wednesday.

---

*   Jana's mentee's piece on page 40 shares this line.

49

Aja and Julius
By Demetria Irwin

Aja shielded her eyes from the afternoon sun as she leaned up against the peeling bleachers. Her best friend, Taylor, had two more laps to finish before she could leave track practice and they could walk back to their neighborhood together. Aja exhaled deeply from exasperation and the heat.

"What's all the heavy breathing for? You ain't out there running."

The familiar voice belonged to Julius Rockford Jr., the most perfect human specimen created in several millennia according to Kennedy Middle School girls. Aja turned and found herself within inches of Julius' face. His lips crept into his trademark half grin, showcasing the dimple in his left cheek. She could barely see his brown eyes hidden beneath what seemed like miles of lush eyelashes.

Aja was trying to figure out what would be the most appropriate thing to say to the cutest boy in the school when Julius leaned in. His warm, Twinkie-tinged breath glided onto her lips.

"Aja, get up! We gone be late!"

A wave of ice-cold air enveloped Aja as her little brother, Aiden, stripped her blanket off her. "How come you never hear the alarm clock no more? You supposed to wake me up. I had to come in here, turn off your alarm clock, and wake you up. Mama gone kick yo' butt if you make us late to school again."

"Aiden, leave me alone! I can run be ready in ten minutes. I press snooze on my alarm, you know!" Aja shoulder-checked him as she made her way to the bathroom. She made sure to be ready in about eight minutes.

On the way to school in the warm rays of a May sun, Aja walked in front of her little brother, her burgundy backpack knocking uncomfortably against her back as she made sure to stay a few paces ahead of her bothersome sibling.

As she squinted against the morning sun, none other than Julius Rockford Jr. appeared on the other side of the street with his usual string of followers/fans of both genders. Aja was pretty sure he saw her, but he didn't break his stride or hold her gaze. Like every other day that she saw him on that walk, he totally ignored her.

Wide-eyed and heart-racing at the sight of him, but playing it cool, Aja smirked as she walked to school, thinking about how later that night she could get back to her dream Julius—much better than the real thing.

Spring Grass
By Sharline Dominguez

Spring Grass, I couldn't decide which was better—lying on my back or on my belly. So I stood up and asked Chris.

He said I should lie on my belly so I did. My body was cradled against Mother Nature's breast—her skin smooth against my bent elbows.

I inched a little closer to him, then I wiggled back to my place. It went unnoticed, so I looked into the branches above us floating in the air. A wind of uncertainty blew through my black hair.

His nails were jagged, so I told him to take better care of them before his mother noticed. [*]

The sun shined right in our youthful faces, and we saw that its lips were delicately painted pink. Its eyelids shadowed by multicolored glitter.

The cars sped by on the Brooklyn-Queens Expressway making *"whoosh"* sounds. I questioned the dangerously short distance between the highway and where we were.

Teenagers kicked a soccer ball around, careful not to disturb a boy and a girl talking senseless things. But then again, they couldn't quite hear, so they played their game.

I paused to think, and then stared at the boundless, blue sky. My thoughts were interrupted by the wild stomping of a nosy ant on my skull.

Furiously scratching my hair, I wanted to kill it. I wonder if Chris heard the crunch of its body when I caught it under my fingernails.

We talked about things we deeply disliked, loved with all our hearts, and even our troubled families. I hated divorces.

He said, "But why don't you get to know your father better? He probably cares more about you than you actually think."

I replied, "Forget about it. Maybe I just need to be a better daughter. You don't even have a father by your side anymore, but you willingly listen to me complain about my life all the time…"

I made direct eye contact with the sun again, hoping that in doing so, I could erase the unwanted memories of my father.

He mentioned something about his girlfriend, but I didn't listen.

It smelled of spring and the green, wet grass giggled under our bellies.

The clouds were swollen with warm milk, their cheeks full and fat. I smiled my illustrious, red-lipped smile, and he smiled in return, so the space between us widened.

I thought about the homework that I still had to do—Ms. Fisher's English paper killed the moment.

The smell of the ocean's water hung over the gate in front of us. It listened to our conversation and crept its way into our noses when the wind permitted.

I looked at my battered iPhone with a critical eye. He looked into his, and I wondered why. One day, technology will fail us all, but I didn't express the thought.

Somewhere in the distance, a joyous dog barked at its owner, demanding more play time and a loose collar.

[*]   Sharline's mentor's piece on page 53 shares this line.

The leaves blew all around, danced on my brown sweater, and signaled to him that it was time to touch me. But he didn't do more than just wipe the leaves off my hair—carefully.

"Hey, you have a little hair on your back, Sharline. That's so cute."

Chuckling, I replied, "It runs in the family."

I struggled to hold back my lips several times. Temptation surged through every vein in my body, but restraint triumphed.

The temperature slowly dropped, so I quietly shivered. Taking note of it, he offered his sweater and I said no.

I saw a jumbo plane in the sky. At one point, I was made to believe that people, like airplanes, can lift others off the ground, too.

Suddenly tracing the lines in his palms, I wished for something more than just friends. My eyelids voluntarily closed in conjunction with my heart's steady beats.

Silence struck a chord, so I opened my eyes again.

I thought of how to fill a heart with happiness, but quickly dismissed it when my mother texted me to come home.

I couldn't decide which was better—lying on my back or on my belly. So I stood up and asked Chris.

More Than a Crush
By Yvetha Jean

Dedicated to my fantasy soul mate.

Some people think that loving someone is easy. But my experience demonstrated that it is not. If I had known the real meaning of love, I wouldn't be trapped in its talons.

It felt special when Joshua told me how nice I was, how cool I was. In my mind, I thought everything was going to be exactly the way I dreamed…

I had liked Joshua for about three years, from the very first day I looked into his eyes. Right away I felt an incomparable connection. Liking Joshua made me realize certain things about myself because, before I met him, I never would have imagined dating someone like him. I liked Joshua less because of who he was and more because of how he made me feel. Joshua is the kind of person who manages to make others laugh and feel happy in sad moments. Whenever you need him, he is always there.

I tried many times to tell him how I felt about him, but I couldn't find the right words to say. One day I finally convinced myself. I opened the computer. I could feel my heart pumping out of my chest. Even though I knew it might be a mistake, it was my last chance: I had to do it.

I questioned myself: What if he says he does not like me back?

Are you there? I pressed enter.

Yeah I am here, weren't you supposed to be sleeping now? he replied.

Yeah. But I have something I want to tell you. My heart skipped a beat of terror. I clicked enter. *I know it might sound stupid but I think it's time to let it out.* I clicked timidly and shakily.

Ok, he said.

This was when I felt most terrified because I didn't expect him to answer the way he did. I kept going; I told myself that I wanted to know how he really felt. But I couldn't know it unless I probed for answers.

I like you. I quickly hit enter. In my mind I could picture his reaction. It took him about two minutes to reply back.

Wow really? :-o I could envision his shocked expression.

Yeah, and didn't you know that? I said, still shaking because I thought he knew.

No, I didn't, and for some reason I thought you liked Jerry though, he responded.

Lol, no I don't, and what makes you think that? I laughed awkwardly just to play it cool.

Because you're always asking for him, he said; for some reason he thought I liked his friend because I was close to him and always asking for him.

No I don't, I told him. *Now I feel relieved by the fact that I let it out. I want to know what you think and if you feel the same way too.*

I was so nervous, like a balloon about to burst. There was no response for a while and in my mind I could see him hesitating.

Well, all I can say is that I am not into this thing anymore because I want to focus on school and my music.

So do I, I abruptly typed, and I was okay with that because I respected his decision.

Ok, to be honest I used to like you, but not anymore.

Ok, I see, I wrote back. I could barely look at the screen, I was speechless.

That day I felt blank. My heart was tearing apart. It beat with a magnitude of agony. I saw my soul crying day and night in despair and grief. **But I fought my own soul to defeat its unkindness.*** Since then, there have been times when I tried to let the feelings go, but my heart wouldn't let me. I have these two sides: reality and my heart. Reality is telling me to let him go, but my heart still believes and it draws me closer to him every day.

The Missed Opportunity
By Sarv Taghavian

His nails were jagged, so I told him to take better care of them before his mother noticed.**

He wasn't listening to me. He was staring at me the way only a seventeen-year-old boy can stare at you—with that ephemeral mix of fear, curiosity, and undisguised lust. He thought I was beautiful; I could tell.

But I was only sixteen myself. I wonder what smoke signals my face was conveying to him. Did he know that I wanted to be kissed?

My guess is, no. As much as I was imagining the feel of his lips on mine, what his tongue might taste like, how exactly his hand would fit around my waist, I was staring at his nails and giving him manicuring advice. Not exactly screaming "Kiss me!" to your average teenage boy.

He muttered something and quickly hid his fingertips from my sight. And then he moved on to talking about the test we'd taken two periods ago.

---

* Yvetha's mentor's piece on page 154 shares this line.
** Sarv's mentee's piece on page 50 shares this line.

And like that, my moment was gone. He glanced at my house through the passenger window and it felt like the right thing to do was to open the car door, thank him for the ride, and head up to my bedroom, where I could imagine the scene ended differently.

The only problem was, as I was laying in my bed—my shoes dangling off of the end so that I wouldn't get yelled at for mussing up my grandmother's quilt—the first image that ran through my head wasn't of his lips or eyes or slightly too-long hair. It was of his gnarled fingertips resting chastely on the steering wheel. Perhaps I knew, even then, that they were destined to never graze my own.

"Do I Hear $50?"
By Jen McFann

"You were worth so much more!"* Katie cried.

I shrugged and descended from the stage. "The people have spoken."

She didn't hear me, or she did but her face was too busy signaling distress to agree or disagree. She tried on a series of disbelieving stances, moving her hands from her hips to her hair to her lips as we returned to our table. The auctioneer was already well into his next rambling set of dollar amounts, rising in fifty-dollar increments. I stopped listening and dropped into my chair, determined to watch ice melt in my highball glass for the rest of the night.

"Sold!" the auctioneer belted. "$650 for dinner with lovely Tara."

Had he called me lovely when bidding ended on me? It didn't really matter; I had only agreed to subject myself to this meat-market indignity because Katie begged me to be a sport. Supposedly the proceeds would purchase malaria nets for Uganda, though I doubted my contribution to that would cover the postage on the Ugandan thank-you letters.

"Her? She pulled $650?" Katie balked. "It's just because she's got huge boobs. Does that guy think he gets to grab them just because it's charity?" She shook her head. I looked down at my neckline. Surely my boobs were not such as would send suitors and pocketbooks screaming in retreat. "That dress must've cost her twice what she pulled in the auction," she continued. I folded the hem of my gray pencil skirt with my fingers; it sure sounded like she'd said I was dressed like a K-Mart model.

I was too busy parsing her subtextual insults to notice the dark-haired essence of male beauty who'd pulled up a spare seat at my right elbow. His eyes were striking, I saw when I cared to notice, not just for their golden hazel sparkle but because they were trained on me and not the well-dressed, boobtastic aid worker on stage.

"Thank God you were cheap," he said. I glowered at him with all the strength of indignation I could muster; I was inclined to be more offended, but he was too damn pretty. He noticed my theatrics. "That came out wrong," he apologized. "I meant that I'm glad you stayed in my price range."

For the sake of his tousled black hair, I allowed that slavery may not have been his intended connotation. "Why's that?" I asked, stirring the ice in my glass that melted without supervision.

He smiled sheepishly. "Well, it's one of two things," he began. "Either I assumed from your bio and picture that I'd have to take out a second mortgage to get you—"

At this I gasped and he paused politely. I hadn't meant to gasp, certainly, but at least I could never truly come undone by such platitudes. Any man so serious in his flattery was good for self-esteem, but not for engaging with my all-consuming sarcasm.

"Or," he continued, "I'm with the pro-malaria lobby."

"Sold," I sighed.

---

*   Jen's mentee's piece on page 80 shares this line.

Physical Things Meant to Be Choked On: A True Story

By Becky Chao

I love you.

That's it. So simple. Short and sweet.

But why's it so hard to say?

My throat closes up, like that feeling I get whenever I'm about to cry. Only this isn't something that I'm supposed to be sad about—I should be happy! Happy that I feel this way, but do I really…? I start avoiding eye contact, and my heart starts beating really fast, faster than it's supposed to, and I start wondering if I'm gonna die if I don't say it, or maybe I'll die if I do say it, and it's just like…

Breathe.

Breathe in…breathe out.*

Focus on the air entering my lungs through my nostrils, and hold it there, and then feel it leave, taking all the stress with it.

That's what a yoga instructor would probably tell me.

I don't do yoga.

I just proceed to freak out some more.

Love is…how do you know what love is? It's abstract, something that you just *know* (or so I'm told). You recognize it, love, when a baby is born and you see the way his mother looks at him, cradling him gently toward her breast, a soft smile on her face as she proclaims, "Oh, he's so beautiful!"

When really, that baby is ugly as fuck.

I know I was an ugly baby. We all were.

And that same mother will admit three, four, eight months later that as a newborn, her baby was ugly. But it doesn't matter because now her baby is beautiful, truly. And you can see her smile, so full of joy and pride and…love?

But none of this gets me any closer to understanding what love is.

Shit's complicated, man.

I mean, it's hard enough just figuring out one definition, but apparently there's a whole bunch of separate categories for the thing: familial love, sisterly love, brotherly love, incestuous love, friendly love, puppy love, true love, scholarly love—okay, so maybe now I'm making shit up.

Love! It's a word that's tossed around too much, like in middle school when a boy's all, "Hey, so you wanna go out?" to a girl, and the girl says yes, and then the next day she's all, "I love him sooooo much!"

Yeah, I never really liked that.

And then it's a word that some people, like me, rarely use. Heck, I don't even tell my own parents that I love them. Like, I've thought about it, and it's something that I've accepted as truth. I know I love them even when they get me so damned frustrated, when they yell at me and make me wonder if I hate them—though I don't like using the word "hate," either, because it's such an extreme word, and it's a word I don't really mean (does the same apply to "love"?[2]).

I read somewhere that 80 percent of songs are about love. That's *a lot.*

And I wonder if these singers who sing about love, do they sing with conviction, with feeling, with *love*? Or is it faked, a different sort of feeling mustered up and passed off as this *thing* called "love"?

I've been to many a concert with all those tweeny-boppy bands of late-twenty-somethings crooning about the love they let get away when they were seventeen or whatever, and I'm like, "Hey, *I'm* seventeen."

* Becky's mentor's piece on page 17 share this line.

2 Although, Happy Bunny does have that thing where "Hate is a special kind of love I reserve for people like you." Or something like that.

Maybe it's just that I'm a skeptic, but I'd like to think of myself as a romantic, too—someone who believes in fairy tales, Prince Charmings and Happily Ever Afters.

But when a girlfriend asks, "Do you love him?"—so matter-of-factly, too—I'm the person who finds herself unable to speak, unable to get the words out of her throat, so they're not even given the chance to hang in the air, but instead remain in her throat, blocking her airways, making her choke, choke on her words, like the cliché that, before, she'd always dismissed as simply impossible, because really, words aren't physical things meant to be choked on.

I love[3] my friend very much and all, but still. Why'd she have to go and put me in a situation like this, huh?

And then she'd had the nerve to add a, "Well?"

I love him. I'd be lying if I said it. Right? I obviously don't feel that way—i.e., in love—because I can't even define it, can't even figure out what the goddamned word means, and I can't think of any concrete reasons why I could possibly, even remotely, feel that way about him.

She presses. "Do you?"

For the sake of an Almost Happily Ever After, I'm going to say, "Not yet."

Maybe I will one day.

And if/when I say it, I'll be sure.

I'll be happy.

Maybe.

Hopefully.

Yeah.

Senses

By Marlyn Palomino

An obscure shape moves toward me in the darkness.
Would you dance with me? His tone is sly.
No, I'm tired, I say back, like a challenge.
He fades into the crowd, displeased,
Leaving a trail of attraction, untamable curiosity, and
A lingering, bittersweet mixture of cologne and sweat;
My milky complexion turns bright pink.

A whisper
Slides off his gentle lips:
You're so beautiful.
Are his words pure and sincere?
Ugh, I feel my braces!
His soft melody travels through my veins;
Suddenly, I feel limitless.

He is beautiful,
Sweet caramel, dulce de leche.
His fractured nose is flawless!
Beneath those bushy eyebrows
I catch a glimpse of dark brown sunflowers

---

3 Oh, there I go, throwing that word around when I'm not even sure what it freakin' means.

That surround the deep black pupils of his eyes.
Awestruck, I see a refuge and the missing jigsaw to my life.

I am simple, but hard to find.
His tender touch is the key to my lock.
Powerful arms wrap around my back,
Hold tight to my strengths and let failures crash against rocks.
Our feet are buried in sand, but
From the beach on our fantasy island
We stand tall.

When we finally kiss,
His lips are like cherry Jell-O.
We're both laughing—and
I don't care about his past.
This is our juicy story, a new beginning.
My taste buds tingle at the thought:
What's to come?

Outside of Myself
By Brittany Barker

1. Uninvited

There is nothing more awkward than the sight of us seated together
We sit like we are uninvited
Like there is nothing awkward about being awkward
Like standing out

Lately,
We've been so tired of standing out
That we've been sitting in

They look at us as if they've never seen an embrace so odd
How we sit body and body in each others' arms
Just holding like hands,
Talking like mind and mind,
Kissing like tongue and tongue

Look at how they look at us,
As if we are speaking in tongues
But ask any linguist,
The tongue doesn't speak unless it has another tongue to be spoken to
No one understands us
But we
We understand each other

There is no listening
Everyone just talks
They talk about us as if we aren't worth appraisal

But we praise each other every day
For the awkwardness of our compatibility
How we stand out
Our courage
Our strength to invite ourselves
Even though we are never invited

Who is ever invited to live their life as they want to?
The world isn't embracing enough to accept us with open arms
So we dwindle
Inside of each other
Is the only place that is welcoming

2. Break

Sometimes
You must praise the ones who attempt to break you
The ones with the hands that break
The ones that succeed at breaking you

Yesterday
My pockets made me feel what rock bottom felt like
I've been digging for some time now
On a succulent hunt for togetherness and conjoin-ness
A parade of oneness
A chorus of cusped hands

When alone,
I can't help but break with every hour

These days,
Breaking is all that I know
I break *from* and *over* the most fragile things
So much that breaking doesn't even feel broken to me

In fact,
Everything breaks.
Observe

Watch the day break
How an insomniac uncontrollably breaks night

Watch your boss give you a break
At a Jewish wedding, watch the groom break the glass
Watch your love life crumble after a heartbreak

How windstorms grapple with roots to make the trees break

Watch how money makes family ties break
How a dollar bill breaks

Ask a broker what he does
Read about what a condom sometimes does
Watch what infidelity does to a marital bond
What pressure and stress does to the human soul

How light breaks darkness
How salt water breaks evil

Observe
Believe
That sometimes breaking is a blessing

It is hard to understand yourself when you are one whole.
Breaking allows you to see just where
And exactly how you crack
What ushers it
We can't know ourselves until
We see the pieces that make us one

Praise breaking
Praise the ones with hands that break
Praise the ones who attempt to break you,
The ones that succeed at breaking
Praise the broken
Praise that moment when you realize that
No one is more capable of breaking
You than yourself

3. Mother's Carrier

I know my mother's footsteps when I hear them
The melodic drag of her slippers
She drags, but never drops

My mother is a carrier
One of religion
Another of family
And the last of the world

I get my shoulders from her
Broad
But ask anyone in my family and they'll tell you
That they are roaring beauties of strength
We know strength like the back of our hands

Like breath
And breathing

I carry like my mother
The moan of my slippers do not yet harmonize
The beauty of walking
But I am sure that it is close to it

She tells me
That age will deliver a strength like hers
This is the only reason in the world why I'd want to get older

My mother is muscle and escape route
At the times when I want to unravel from my own skin
She folds me back into myself

Fixer of puzzles
Filler of creases
Mender of the broken parts before they even think of breaking

Someday I will be her carrier
Carry her like she now carries me
And maybe,
Carry my own family

Treading Water
By Katherine Jacobs

When I was eight years old, my best friend failed our swim class. Every Saturday morning we went to the local college pool, and a college student taught us how to tread water and float and swim different strokes. We had graduated to the deep end of the pool that year. I remember clinging to the side; Kristin and I were gripping that space where the water is sucked back into the filter system and pressing our toes against the wall since we couldn't touch the bottom. Together we slowly let go and floated out to the middle of the pool, moving our arms in big circular motions just beneath the surface. Our teacher told us to imagine frosting a giant cake with our hands.

"My aunt Chris' wedding cake," I told Kristin. My aunt was getting married that summer, and I was delighted at the thought of making her a giant round wedding cake with heaps of white frosting that I smoothed out as I gently stroked the water.

I was surprised when my mom told me that Kristin needed to repeat our class. Athletic activities always came naturally to Kristin—it was me who struggled with our T-ball team games and archery class at camp and rope-climbing in gym class at school. But Kristin and I always did everything together so I was happy to take the class again. We continued going to the pool on Saturday mornings and venturing out into the deep end, practicing staying afloat.

Four, Five, Six

By Robin Henig

I'm starting to think she'll die lonely. Worse than that, really; I think she might die alone. No matter how much I want to keep her safe, befriended, nothing I do at the end will make much difference. We're all alone, of course, at the moment that we die, but what about the moments leading up to it? I don't want those moments to frighten her. I know that they do. Every morning I call her at 9:15 a.m. and listen to the phone ring, counting four, five, six, seven. As I count, I imagine her in bed, all still, all alone, never again to greet me with good morning.

All the Things Left Unsaid: An Original Screenplay

By Anaís Figueroa*

INT. NEW YORK PUBLIC LIBRARY - 66TH STREET—DAY

SIENNA, 17, and CATHY, 18, enter and look through the aisles. They find GREY, 17, focused as she shelves books. Cathy sneaks up behind Grey, surprising her with a light push. Cathy and Sienna laugh.

GREY

Shhh. Don't get me in trouble.

SIENNA

We were at the pizzeria and decided to
see you since the library's your bat cave.

GREY

(annoyed)

It's my job.

CATHY

I like your shirt. Where'd you get it?

Grey glances at her blue T-shirt and shrugs.

GREY

H&M.

Sienna looks at Cathy.

SIENNA

I've been too broke to go shopping.

CATHY

Same here. I definitely need to get a job.

* Anais' mentor's piece on page 3 shares this title.

                    SIENNA
              (nervous laugh)
         We should try working here.

Grey continues to shelve the books.

                    CATHY
               (to Grey)
         You could probably talk to your boss.

Cathy and Sienna stare at Grey. She stops shelving.

                    GREY
         Well, I tried getting a job for my
         cousin and my boss wasn't thrilled
         about it.

                    CATHY
         Maybe with us he'll change his mind.

                    GREY
               (exasperated)
         I'll see what I can do.

                    SIENNA
         It would be fun working with you.

Grey rolls her eyes as she continues putting away books.

                    CATHY
         You should have gone with us to
         Central Park on Monday. It was really
         fun.

                    GREY
         I had to work.

                    CATHY
         You could've taken the day off.

Grey slams a book onto the shelf. Cathy and Sienna look at
each other.

                    SIENNA
         What's wrong?

                    GREY
         Nothing.

                    CATHY
                  (louder)
              You're obviously upset.

Grey's boss, MR. WHITMORE, fifty-ish, tall and stern, walks over
to the girls.

                 MR. WHITMORE
             This is your first warning. Keep it
             down or you'll have to leave.

As Mr. Whitmore walks away, Grey gives Sienna and Cathy an
angry look.

                    CATHY
                 (whispering)
              Just tell us; we're supposed to be
              best friends.

                    GREY
                 (sarcastically)
              Of course we are.

                    SIENNA
              What's that supposed to mean?

                    GREY
              Exactly what I said.

                    SIENNA
              You've been acting weird around us
              for the past couple of months. If
              you feel a certain way then say it.

                    GREY
              If there were something wrong I
              would say so.

Grey keeps calm, but Cathy and Sienna get louder. PEOPLE
nearby stare.

                    CATHY
              Do you expect us to read your mind
              and know why you're pissed off?

                    GREY
              Stop yelling.

                    CATHY
Why would you say that if we're
supposed to be best friends?

                    GREY
Because we aren't.

              CATHY & SIENNA
              (shocked)
What?

                    GREY
              (pauses)
You only talk to me when it's
convenient for you. The only reason
you guys came here today was to get
a job, not to hang out with me. So
how could I possibly consider you
guys to be my best friends?

                    CATHY
If you had even the slightest clue
of the type of friends we are, you
would know that we've been worried
about you.

Grey looks at Cathy and Sienna, confused. She then looks down.

Mr. Whitmore rushes into the aisle and angrily stands over
the girls.

                 MR. WHITMORE
This is a library. There is no
talking in the library. Especially
no yelling.
              (to Grey)
You and your friends have caused
enough trouble here. The three of
you must leave now.

                    GREY
I'm sorry, Mr. Whitmore. They're
about to go.

                 MR. WHITMORE
Grey, finish shelving these books.
Then I want to talk to you.

                    GREY
Okay.

Mr. Whitmore stomps away.

                    GREY (CONT'D)
Are you guys happy now?

                    SIENNA
We just wanted the truth.

                    GREY
Well, you got it. The both of you
are best friends and maybe, at one
point, the three of us were; but it
hasn't been that way in a long time.
You don't know anything about me.

                    SIENNA
You don't let us in. We know nothing
about you because you made it that
way.
                    CATHY
Sienna and me got closer because
you stopped being there. One minute
things were fine and the next you
disappeared.

                    GREY
You guys don't need me. You have
each other. That's why I'm not around
anymore.
                    SIENNA
You came to that conclusion on your
own. Did you ever consider how we
felt when you stopped talking to us?

                    GREY
I didn't know what else to do.

                    CATHY
But this is our fault?

                    SIENNA
Everything's messed up and maybe
we're all to blame for what happened.
But you gave up on our friendship
before we could even try to make
things better.

CATHY
You threw out years of friendship
without even giving us a chance to
fight for it. How is that fair?

Grey doesn't respond.

Sienna begins to cry. Cathy puts her arm around Sienna as they
walk away.

Sienna stops and turns to face Grey.

SIENNA
(tearfully)
The only reason we wanted a job here
was to be closer to you.

Sienna and Cathy wait for a response. Grey opens her mouth
to speak but doesn't.

CATHY
This is pathetic.
(to Sienna)
Let's go.

Cathy and Sienna turn and walk away. Grey watches regretfully
as they exit the library.

THE END

Happy Birthday, Celia!
By Syeda Showkat and Kirthana Ramisetti

Sally: Ohmigod it's so freaking cold out here. She hasn't come out yet! Annie told me that Celia would be outside by 8 and it's already 8:07 a.m. Hello, Celia, we're on a schedule here! Does she think it's easy to wake up at 5:00 a.m. and bake two batches of red velvet cupcakes? Sure we could have bought them from Magnolia's like Annie suggested. But if Annie was a real friend she would have remembered that on March 13 Celia wrote on Facebook that Magnolia cupcakes were SO played out and that she wanted to try baking her own. So I did it for her. How thoughtful is that? Even though I've never baked before, I'm sure my cupcakes are a more kick-ass gift than whatever Annie has planned. She's been wearing that stupid smile all morning, so I know she's excited by whatever she's giving her.

Annie: (*Sally's sitting there, shivering theatrically.*) Ugh, she's such a drama queen sometimes. Where's Celia? Oh well, she's probably just putting on her coat. Let her take her time. We're not running late or anything. I just saw Mom circle the block again with that ugly green sedan. She doesn't know that I know she's following us. Stalking us is more like it! That's how she is. A stalker. A grade-A stalker like the ones they write front-page articles about in the *Daily News*, with pictures and statements from family and friends. What would I say if they found out about our Mom the Stalker? "She's always been this way and it's been so (*sniff, sniff*) hard. I've had to live with her through this nightmare." Oh, that's good. But it's something Sally would say. (*Turns to look at Sally.*) Man, Sally, calm down. She'll be here!

Sally: Celia's still not out yet. How long does it take to get ready? But it's her birthday so I'll have to be patient. I mean, how can I complain about Celia? And on her birthday, too? Even though it kinda sucks to be sitting in the cold outside Celia's building, so we can surprise her for her birthday. Of course this was all Annie's idea. If it had been up to me, we would have greeted her in homeroom. But noooo. Annie wanted this to be "special." I just think that whatever she has planned for Celia, she doesn't want anyone else to see. What could it possibly be? (*Beeping noise; checks phone.*) Ooh, Celia just wrote on Facebook that she's running late for school because she can't decide whether to wear her Louboutins or Jimmy Choos. Look alive, Annie, she's on her way!

Annie: Sally seriously needs to chill out. She's so uptight, just like Mom. Sometimes I feel like I'm Sally's pretend twin. We don't have anything in common! Never have, never will ... until Celia. Ever since she started being our peer-group leader, Sally and I had something we could both love. Celia is amazing! Really truly amazing! Like the funniest, prettiest, awesomest person I've ever met. She listens. Just listens. And she's so cool. Has like a million friends. Guy friends too! She was telling us the other day how she was popular in freshman year, too! Had older friends inside and outside school. I mean, who wouldn't want to be Celia? We wanna be like her. Have a chill and trusting mom, be super pretty, have a gazillion guy friends, be artsy and athletic, have a coolness aura around our heads! Celia has it all! So we're standing out here in the cold, hoping Mom will leave us alone and praying Celia comes out of her apartment soon so we can surprise her with cupcakes and birthday wishes, and our—scratch that—*my* song. She'll be stoked. She'll be grateful.

Sally: Okay, this is it. Here she comes. I see her talking to her doorman. Holy crap, did he just give her a cupcake? I'm screwed. I'm so totally screwed! Now what do I do? What else can I give her? My scarf? She'll hate it. My earrings? She'll just laugh at me. Oh no, here she is…

Annie: She'll love us and that's what matters. She'll take us under her wing. Love us enough to give us her secrets. Mold us into what she is so we can be happy too. She'll take us from boring Sally and Annie and turn us into two Celias. It'll happen, I'm fucking positive. It'll happen, but for now we'll need to be here to do our end of the deal and wait for her. Ohmigod I see her now. Come on, Sally, it's show time!

(*Both girls stand up straight and give big smiles.*)

Sally: (*sings tentatively*) Happy birthday…

Annie: (*breaks out into her own song, set to Jason Mraz's "I'm Yours"*)
We won't hesitate no more no more
It cannot wait
Happy Bir-er-er-thday day day day day dayday daydaydayday dayday day daday daday…

(*Sally is flummoxed, at some point tries to join in, can't, so just stands there with a big fake smile. Annie trails off 20 to 30 seconds into her song. Sally and Annie both turn their heads to the left.*)

Sally and Annie: Bye, Celia! Happy birthday! See you at school! We have cupcakes…no? Okay. Bye!

The Two of Us
By Rollie Hochstein

Sixteen is too young.

Sunny is a seventies woman. An ardent supporter of the sixties revolution, she marched, she met. She stood on the side of youth, fighting the age of inflexible authority. Now she stands for women's rights. Equal pay. Equal everything. Boys will be boys, she readily concedes. Sunny wants girls to have the same chance to explore their sexuality.

But Jessica is her *daughter*.

They're talking about summer vacation and Jessica wants to go away with her boyfriend, the magnificent Todd.

In theory Sunny gives them her blessing. In real life, she wants Jessica to wait another year. Sunny is not happy with the suburban seventies. Privileged kids home alone while swinging parents tour and sail and fly high in city or country clubs. Kids with cars and keys to the liquor cabinet and God-knows-what in the medicine chest. Sunny hears things, sometimes from Jessica. High-school kids—getting drunk, getting high, getting laid.

Jessica, thanks be, is not one of those kids. She is a flower child. Jessica glows in the dark. In her mother's mind, she's a Renaissance portrait, an annunciation—her wafting fair hair, her clear domed forehead, lemon-colored eyebrows, languishing long-fingered hands. Sunny admits it's an idealized vision, but in fact Jessica is a kind of Renaissance girl. Former infielder on the town's first unisex Little League team. Current stalwart of the sophomore class debating team. Plus a sometimes A student whose service project is playing piano (more breath-of-youth than virtuoso) at a local nursing home. Last year, after a raucous bus ride to Washington, DC, Jessica marched down the Mall beside her mother, waving a banner with the word CHOICE under a picture of a broken wire coat hanger.

"Why can't me and Todd have a week together?"

"You *can* be together. At the lake. You and Todd and your father and me."

Pastoral eyes look heavenward. "It's not the same. We want to be on vacation, just the two of us."

Untitled
By Sacha Phillip

The school year was as new as the bright blue running shoes on my feet. The blurry sun spilled over the cloudless sky, its power stilled by the veil of early-September pollen. The air was fecund, fragrant. I clutched a finger painting of my family with my right hand, and Emily held on to my left.

She lived across the road from my parents and me and, because she was two years older (or was it three?), she walked me to and from school every day. She had long, dark-gold hair and a cherubic physique, and was perpetually clad in my then-favorite color: baby pink. I thought she was the best, but the boys in the neighborhood disagreed.

They regularly taunted Emily about everything from her toque to her shoes and everything in between, but that day, their teasing turned sinister.

The boys substituted sticks and stones for cruel taunts and, as we ran, they pursued ardently. Emily never let go of my hand, even though it was obvious that I slowed her down terribly.

■ ■ ■

I stood on the bridge watching as she descended the hill toward the creek, picked up her school bag, and tried to retain her dignity while the boys blocked her return path. Eventually, one of the boys called the other two away, and after a few brief whispers they were gone.

I held Emily's hand tighter as we resumed the walk home. After a few silent minutes spent avoiding shadows, walking on sunshine, we finally exhaled. And then, it happened. Just as our heart rates returned to normal, we heard the first low growl. The second was followed by a guttural, angry bark. Startled, we turned around to see the three boys crouched around two large Huskies. Laughing, they shouted commands, and the dogs lunged, hungrily, toward us.

By-Products of a Broken Society
By Kathryn Jagai and Therese Cox

Part One: Ducking Around
By Kathryn

Fri, May24
hey. u sick?
3:30PM

Sat, May25
where r u? @theatre. jamies asking abt u.
7:13PM

AERON. CALL ME
11:33PM

Sun, May26
@downtown morgue. long story. pick me up. bring coffee.
3:14AM

WHAT? rite now? srsly?
3:20AM

stepdad. crash. SERIOUSLY.
3:23AM

?!leaving in 10
3:40AM

Mon, Jun3
lol txt from jamie: "sry 4 ur loss. want 2 talk?" like i'm going to "talk" to someone i've known for 2 weeks.
2:16PM

LMAO whatd u say
2:18PM

haha. me: "stepdad a jerk who crashed hot rod into farm animal and died. lost house to funeral expenses. nbd."
2:21PM

LOL SRSLY
2:25PM

no! lmao u make a spare key?
2:25PM

mm. ur going 2 unpack @some point rite? u dont xctly fit my clothes.
2:27PM

yeah, yeah. see u tonight.
2:25PM

Fri, Jul5
U BROKE THE LAMP!?
where r u btw?
12:16PM

no way. @jamie's. hungover. ttyl.
12:20PM

no, fuck u. that was my fav lamp. got it @a stoop sale. they don't even sell gargoyle lamps n u owe me 50 4 my headphones 2. stop breaking my shit!
12:32PM

DON'T IGNORE ME
12:45PM

relax. lamps r cheap. also, jamie's got a tattoo.
12:50PM

srsly? where?
12:53PM

and btw this is not abt the fucking lamp this is abt u leaving dishes n clogging the sink n bringn random ppl in when im sleepin n walkn around w/out pants when my lil bros in town!
1:03PM

STOP IGNORING MY TXTS
1:24PM

does jamie know abt the blonde from 2am on wed? cuz ill tell if you dont TXT ME BACK RIGHT NOW
1:37PM

thts it if ur not gone by tm morning i will burn all ur shit so srs right now
1:49PM

u wouldn't. where would i sleep?
3:18PM

u were kidding, right?
3:23PM

hey i'm sorry. call me back.
4:17PM

i bought a new lamp. i couldn't find gargoyle but i found rubber duck. it's in the kitchen w/ the receipt. brought most of my shit to jamie's JIC. call me back.
6:32PM

you cannot be this mad @me over a gargoyle lamp. txt me back.
10:18PM

jordan?
10:30PM

Tues, Jul9
thnx 4 the lamp
11:04PM

i didn't actually burn ur stuff u no obv i wouldn't
11:07PM

plus ud probs need gasoline n shit. idk where id burn it.
11:09PM

n u can move back iyw most of ur stuff is here
11:13PM

also the engravers left a msg on the landline. they fucked up ur dads last name.
11: 14PM

hey txt me back im over it
11:26PM

what r u even mad abt? ur the one who fucked up, fucking around with random ppl and leaving dirty clothes around.
11:35PM

u no whut fine u and lot lizard can go 2 hell u deserve each other
11:47PM

Fri, Jul12
i wasn't mad. i lost my phone charger 'til this morning.
1:03PM

shit srsly?
1:19PM

lol i was pretty drunk anyway so nbd n ignore it
1:20PM

lol. did u mean it? i can move back?
1:25PM

yeah def
1:30PM

good. because "lot lizard" and i broke up.
1:33PM

sry i didnt mean that
1:34PM

wait LOL srsly? how do u fail so hard?
1:34PM

u wanna know the trick?
1:37PM

and what does who i'm sleeping with have to do with living with u?
1:40PM

whats the trick
1:45PM

u didn't answer my q.
1:46PM

n u nvr told me where jamie's tat was
1:48PM

Whatever. see you tonight.
2:17PM

Tues, Sep11
i am the by-product of a broken society.*
10:56PM

u drunk? where r u? ill come pick u up
10:57PM

who needs to be picked up? nobody needs to be picked up.
10:59PM

today should be a national holiday. it was supposed to be such a big fxing deal but nobody even cares anymore.
10:59PM

i care tell me where u are
11:01PM

of course u care.
11:05PM

whats wrong w/ u? i do care stop bein a dumbass n tell me where u are
11:08PM

its 11:11. r u making a wish?
11:11PM

no im not makin a wish. im sittin in the apt worryin abt u drunk n alone n avoidin my calls on the anivrsry of ur mom's death.
11:12PM

u missed it. u know what i wished for?
11:20PM

i'm comin to get u stay there
11:23PM

if u knew where i was why'd u ask?
11:34PM

u no y I asked u idiot. n if u make me come all the way to astoria n ur not there ima kick ur ass. real classy breakin n2 ur moms cemetery. shed b rlly proud.
11:39PM

fxck u.
11:41PM

thnx.
11:54PM

* Katherine's mentor's piece on page 75 shares this line.

73

Wed, Sep12

u get that the whole one night stand thing only works when ur not livin w/ the other person
1:16PM

i had work. unlike some ppl who freelance… did u just wake up?
1:23PM

we didnt sleep til like 5am so yeah just got up
1:26PM

aeron
1:26PM

relax! i didn't even get ur first text. look, we can grab dinner or something and talk later ok? and not just take out. real food. promise.
1:27PM

u left small ducks in toaster?!
1:27PM

… I was trying to make s'mores with peeps yesterday?
1:30PM

o come on. i was drunk and distraught.
1:37PM

i'm sorry
1:40PM

i'll pick up a toaster on the way home. meet you at 7pm?
2:19PM

jordan?
2:45PM

"Breathe.
Breathe in … breathe out."
—Becky Chao, mentee

Part Two: Glasgow Juvenile Detention Center Wilderness Trek
By Therese

It's a bullshit walk, but they all have to do it.

"You wanna know the trick?" Tommy says. "Don't look at anything but the ground under your feet. Next ten paces. Don't even think past the next kilometer."

It's the first time since Tommy was ten that he can smell something other than nicotine on his fingers. He's licking raspberry jam from them, toast crumbs stuck to his chin, ass propped up on a rock. There's no shrink up here, there's no yellow pills.

Tommy's figured it out but Adele is saying it again.

"I am the by-product of a broken society." *

The convenience store stick-up was a bust. The cop just happens to be waddling in for donut duty when Adele (skinny as a greyhound but don't cross her) is rounding the corner in a balaclava, a water pistol hidden under her trackie top, trigger finger trembling. The cop tackles her, twists her arms behind her back like two ends of a twist tie.

Mostly they walk in silence, wheezing and out of shape, nauseous from nicotine withdrawal, the winds of Inverness biting, all the rations for the ten-day trek rolled on their backs. Runt, nearly left for dead in a Glasgow boxing neighborhood, isn't connecting with any of this nature stuff, pitched his tent last night on a bog and the damp seeped through and soaked his socks. He wishes he was in the city, breathing its carcinogenic air and sleeping on mattresses in alleys he knows, on streets with names.

Northern Lights are out tonight but all Emma can think about is crisps. Packets and packets of crisps. Salt and Vinegar crisps. Cheese and Onion crisps. Curry-flavored crisps. She can taste the salt on her tongue, feel the hard crunch between her back teeth, the ones not rotted after three straight years of injecting. A bruised yellow apple and trail mix is what she gets, but crisps are what she wants. She's dreaming of every flavor, even the bacon-flavored ones that probably taste like licking a week-old skillet.

Trish is storming about like a politician in a tantrum. She's had it in for Emma since day one when she found Emma brushing her teeth with Trish's toothbrush.

"If you're not gone by morning, I will burn all of your shit," Trish is shouting, storming up the muddy slope, but Emma doesn't care anyway because she's busy dreaming about crisps.

Her muscles hurt. Nothing to numb it.

The things you think up here. Here where air is thin.

Here on this trek, they are stuck only with themselves, and gazing inward—that thing they're supposed to be doing, away from the justice system—just happens to sour them to all the Highlands have to offer. Rolling hills of yellowed moss and brown bracken, mist and haze, after two days they can't remember what an apartment block looks like.

A thin layer of frost covers the bog, crunching under their feet. They stop to set up camp.

---

* Therese's mentee's piece on page 69 shares this line.

Rivals
By Linda Corman

I did sprints in the clear, blue, palm-frond shaped pool
You dove deep and exchanged jets of water with the frog statues perched on the edge
I challenged you to a race; you accepted
I worried you would beat me, and worried more I would beat you

A lifetime later
Winning has been
My luck and loss

Springing
By Kristen Demaline

It is the beginning. Cool wood floor beneath my bare feet. I arrange my worn blue yoga mat and eagerly recline on a foam block. I unwrap my shoulders and back like a gift for the tin ceiling. Air whirs through the fans, carrying invisible drops of perspiration, inspiration, and chanting to come. I imagine what I will eat after class. My eyes closed, I picture the farmers market with tables of new spring vegetables, first tender spinach, bitter ramps, stalks of rosy rhubarb for pies with ice cream. Honey and lavender and flowers and the lemon cupcakes I crave will be there—but my mouth becomes dry as I begin to move and build a slow-banked fire in my torso. Strange soreness hugs me. I want my back to arch open as I put my hands beside my head on the floor, like when I practice yoga at home and my cat tiptoes beneath me, stretching and settling down with a purr underneath my uplifted body. I ease back down, jump forward. I fly. A bead of sweat splashes down on the mat; I taste salt. Crouching, I let the pain undulate through my muscles like a sudden ocean wave that releases their energy. I muse that I will not cook for anyone later, be welcomed home with a kiss. I do not have someone who would walk twenty miles to see if I was safe. Thud! I fall out of starfish pose. There will be another welt along my leg. I squeeze out my body like a sponge, the wasted, old, dead cells flow out, and in their place come fresh air and water. I am grounded in earth. My own spring. At home, the angry purple patch roars back but, gently, my magic fingers do their work. The bruises will fade. In a dream, I can feel you next to me as though you've been there all along. I wait. You mull over vegetables. I laugh and stir, chop, gaze, and heal the wounded places.

I alight, my stem
Unfurls, pushes through cold soil.
A summer flower.

Friends with Money
By Hannah Morrill

Rob was short, but he was also rich. Both of which were reasons—though, looking back on it, not necessarily *good* reasons—why Rachel had agreed to marry him in the first place. They'd met her senior year at Georgetown, in an econ class, which, looking back on it, is as good a place as any to meet someone. (She hadn't done everything wrong…) She was right off her breakup with Colin—tall, beautiful, long-lashed, unfaithful Colin—and it wouldn't be quite right to say that she was heartbroken. In a way, she was feeling emboldened and freed, even though she was the broken-up-with, not the breaker-upper, spending extra time blowing her long, dark hair dry, feeling like a sexy feminist as she ordered black coffee at the Bean Scene. Being single agreed with her.

Rachel had hooked up with Colin on a rowboat at a grad party the summer before college started, simultaneously stunning herself and the entire graduating class in a single salty, not entirely unpleasant romp. She was small, skinny, and newly pretty; he was built, stunning, and going to Colgate to play lacrosse.

She'd spent the next three years basically marveling at her own good luck that someone like Colin liked someone like her, putting up with his emotionally vacant IMs, and figuring out the near impossible logistics of an Eastern Seaboard romance. To be fair, they'd had some good times. He liked hiking, she learned to, they looked good on a dance floor together, and he did earnestly seem to care for her. It had been a treat to taste-test the Cool and Normal lifestyle, to pose for congenial group pictures at sporting events, to love Dave Matthews, to wear Lily Pulitzer in the summer and North Face in the winter. They weren't unsuited for each other, they just weren't exactly the most natural pairing. Like, chocolate and orange, or bacon-wrapped figs. Something was a little off. So it wasn't such a surprise when he told her, over piping hot pad Thai in Georgetown on an inappropriately balmy fall night, that he'd started seeing someone else, and the distance was too much and he'd never forget her but he was in love. (Although evoking the L-word was uncalled for, she thought both then and now.)

She wouldn't miss Colin too much, but it haunted her a little that she couldn't keep up the charade. It had become a challenge: Could she continue holding the interest of someone whose affections had been such an unearned, but welcome surprise? She never fully understood why she'd gotten Colin in the first place, so it was fitting that she never really understood why he'd left, either.

But this was about Rob, not about Colin. Per Facebook, Colin was happily married in a Chicago suburb with a little baby named Charlie, whom his athletic, ponytailed wife dressed in mini baseball pants and teensy Colgate hoodies. Rachel, on the other hand, was babyless in New York City, and she wanted to divorce Rob.

"His nails were jagged, so I told him to take better care of them before his mother noticed."
— *Sharline Dominguez, mentee*

Better You Than Me
By Shyanne Melendez

Two decisions
Split understandings
A relationship
Ripping at the seams
The indescribable feeling with trust
Feeling irreplaceable is hard
When every day you need to heal
From new scars
A discussion then a fight
Tears falling onto paper
With every new word I write
I don't remember who you are
Or who we are together
The picture has been hiding from thought
As if it were a forgotten letter
I wish trust wasn't broken
Now tears continue to fall
No longer mine now yours
I suppose karma really does come back around
Because now I'm hurting you
Better you than me I think
Better you than me.

When You're Blind
By Olivia Carew

I used to be like you…you know…so free…Naive is the word that the old birds threw at me when I was too deep to see…Ray Charles blind to the fact that trust is not some thing you throw into anybody's lap just because they can catch. Naive to the thought that any guy with a smooth demeanor is a rock but only meaner…He's a stone out to break my bones…and then my heart since I threw it under the bus…I loved being with you and it was just us but it wasn't you it was me cuz I was love struck. Stuck like I'm a car on Route 66 but honey you were getting your kicks…I was sick and believed in what didn't exist you were a stick in my tire and I was getting sick and tired. So I accepted, felt so disconnected unwired…like I didn't regret it…saying those words that drew up some imaginary contract in my mind isn't it hard to find yourself when you're blind? Isn't it hard to find Section 4 Lines 3 to 9 that you would never hurt me…throw me in the dirt, bury then desert me in the cold desert of your mind when I forgot this is a contract you never signed…so violated like the contact I went back to knowing the truth…opened my eyes to finally see you…and me… separated by spaces and punctuation dot dot dots and sentences texted lookin so hectic cuz they r formed with aggravation…I have had it with hesitation cause I learned that game too well…picking up my dignity feeling pity on my reputation as that can-do attitude I can do anything you can do…You know I used to be like you…looking in the mirror you're unique just like everyone else… you're not me you're yourself…you're the dusty diary on my shelf. It goes dear diary you know the rest. This time fate really put me to the test.

Unintended Consequences

By Evelyn Berrones

I remember how it all began, but I can't clearly see how it will end.

He said she saw me kiss Anthony in the front of the pizza shop. It wouldn't have been serious if I hadn't had a boyfriend for two years. Maybe I sound like the bad "guy" in the story, but it's like Usher's song "What's a Man to Do" in a girl version, and I'm confused because I love both Anthony and Leonardo. My official relationship since sophomore year is with Leonardo. This is the relationship any high school girl would wish for—I'm the head cheerleader, and he is the star quarterback on the school's football team. Besides, he is sweet and respectful toward my friends and me; he is funny and has a nice smile, deep blue eyes, dirty blonde hair, and a nice body; and my family loves him. Our relationship was rocky in the beginning, but now he is perfect.

Anthony came into the picture a year ago when he transferred to our school after moving from California. We had every class together, and since I was the best student in the class, Mr. Kurry, the school counselor, chose me to guide him around the school. I accepted the responsibility, though I was annoyed at having to take time out from my social life to help out a student I didn't know. Those were my thoughts *before* seeing him. When I finally met him, I became 65 percent interested. He was tall, around 6'1", with caramel skin, amber eyes and nice long eyelashes, and a blazing smile.

I was intrigued even though he didn't seem interested at all. He had his hoodie on his head and headphones blasting music, completely ignoring me. While we were walking, everyone in the hallways said hi to me, which made him take off his headphones and actually look at me, but just a look. It didn't take long, though, for him to start talking to me to ask lots of little questions. We had a project for anatomy class, so we exchanged numbers to work on the project during the weekend. That started us texting and talking on the phone. We became good, good friends. I told Leonardo that Anthony was my best friend because I could talk to him about anything and feel comfortable. Of course this pissed Leonardo off, but he didn't oppose our friendship because Leonardo had girl friends of his own, and we decided it was fair.

L: "I think we need to talk."

P: "About what?"

L: "Michael told me his girlfriend saw you kiss Anthony in front of a pizza shop, and I want to know if it's true, from you."

P: "What? Are you kidding me? Why would she say such a thing? She knows how much I love you and that I wouldn't cheat on you."

L: "She knows how much we love each other and how much I love you, and that's why I find it hard to understand why would she even say that."

P: "So what are you saying?"

L: "I don't know."

P: "What is there not to know? You know I love you, and I would never cheat on you and I will talk to Karoline about this personally, and she better have a good explanation."

L: "I know, I know, but why would she say that, Pandora? She is your friend, too. We hang out all the time, all of us."

P: "What are you saying, baby?"

L: "I'm saying I truthfully don't know what to believe."

P: "Wow, how can you not trust me after all you've done with me? What about your affairs, which were actually true, after I only cheated on you once when we first started going out? You know I love you, and I know you know because I make sure I show you my love, but now you know what? Bye! I can't believe you don't trust me."

I'm regretting this whole mess. I did kiss Anthony, and the pizza shop kiss wasn't the first one. He and I have been talking for eight months, and for eight months it's been lie after lie after lie with Leonardo to find ways to see Anthony. It was supposed to be just between us, with nobody else finding out, but someone did. Karoline is Michael's girlfriend, and Michael is Leonardo's best friend, which makes it hard for me to deny the kiss because, of course, Michael trusts his girlfriend, and Leonardo definitely trusts his best friend, and I'm in the middle. But I'm wondering why Leonardo wouldn't trust the girlfriend he has had for two years because I've had no cheating history in our relationship. Leonardo *did* cheat on me plenty of times before he actually took our relationship seriously and didn't want to lose me. I never want to lose Leonardo, but neither do I want to lose Anthony. My intentions were not to cheat but to spend time with someone I liked, but my feelings started to grow, and now I'm stuck.

When They Came
By Shannon Talley

As the world came into focus around me I realized that it was soon coming to its end. He grabbed my hand and yanked me forward. I could barely tell what was going on. Everything was happening so fast. I could see things shattering and shaking around me. I remember getting scraped very lightly by things that fell to the ground a little too close to my skin. My hearing was fading in and out as I tried to take it all in. I tried to keep up with him as best as I could. His hand was clamped so tightly around my wrist I had to shake my arm a little to get him to loosen up his grip. At the pace we were running though, it was kind of hard.

The ground shook violently and I felt myself hit the floor, hard. He never let go of my wrist. I felt myself dragging against the concrete. I felt skin peeling from my arms as they scraped against rocks and twigs. "Get up" he screamed. I tried to help myself up as thunder rolled through the sky. "They're coming!!" As I picked myself up I tried to rack my brain for what had led up to us running; running for our lives.

"Who's coming?" I screamed so that he could hear me over all of the destruction. There was a hole in a wall that he was running toward. He dove inside. I stood there for a second, wondering if I should follow. As I heard more thunder sound behind me, I decided to follow him.

The dark eeriness of the hole made me sort of wish that I was still outside where all of the destruction was happening. I hated the dark. "Where are you?" I whispered. I felt his hand once again on my wrist gently tugging me.

"This way," he said quietly. I couldn't see but I held on to his hand tightly as he led me down a tiny tunnel that suddenly opened into a well-lit space. I could see a little better. His already pale skin looked ghostly and the hazel eyes that shone so bright now looked dead.

"What's going on? What's happening?" I asked. I was frightened and I demanded answers.

"They're here, Sarya. They've come to take me back with them." I studied his face carefully. I was a little confused by what he meant.

"The aliens?" I asked. "Why? Why are they coming back for you? I thought they abandoned you."

"I ran away. You knew that, you knew the day would come where they would come for me… now it's here." I swallowed hard. This couldn't be possible. It was a couple of months ago that I had found him almost dead in the desert. I had taken him home and helped him back to health. He lived with me for a while…we fell in love. He told me he was from another planet and that he had run away from his family. He said the possibilities of them coming back for him were small…but now they were causing mass chaos throughout the town, looking for him.

"You're leaving?" I felt the tears as they formed in my eyes. I squeezed them shut tight to try to prevent the tears from flowing but they came anyway. "Can't we just stay in here? They'll never find you."

"You saw what they're doing. They'll destroy this whole town to try to find me. Am I really worth it?" He started to backtrack toward the tunnel.

"You're worth a lot more," I said quietly. I felt my whole body shake as we stared at each other for a while. Finally he walked over to me and cupped my face in his hands.

"You've shown me something that no one on my planet knew how to do." I stared into his eyes, unable to respond. I could feel him searching me for a response. "You've shown me how to love, Sarya, and even though they're here to take me back, they can't take back how I feel. I will never forget you."

The floor shook violently. He let me go as he looked around to try to make sense of the damage. "This is where I leave you." The floor shook again. We gave each other one last long glance before he turned on his heel and ran down the tunnel. It all happened so fast. I ran down after him calling his name, trying to catch him before he gave himself to them. Something inside of me knew it was too late…and I was right. He was gone when I reached the opening of the hole. I fell to my knees searching the skies for him but they had erased all evidence that they had been there when they found him. He was gone and as I wept I couldn't help but think:

You were worth so much more…*

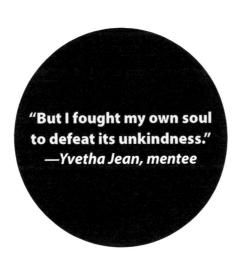

"But I fought my own soul
to defeat its unkindness."
—*Yvetha Jean, mentee*

---

* Shannon's mentor's piece on page 54 shares this line.

IV. WORKSHOPS

"A string of women writers slowly shuffle into the room…"

Halfway through this year, the Curriculum team (Maria, Mary, Meghan, Jess and myself) met to discuss the workshops that had happened so far and those that were still to come. One of my favorite things about Girls Write Now is that we are always trying to be a better organization, a more supportive community, just as we are all individually striving to improve as writers. For the curriculum team, that means a constant push to make our workshops even more fabulous than they already are. And at that meeting in January of 2011, we began with a discussion of what the ideal Girls Write Now workshop should accomplish.

Our six workshops are the place where we come together as a group, where we remember that we are all in this together, that when we are alone, gazing in terror at that blank white page, we are not actually alone because here is a room full of people who know exactly how that terror feels. Our workshops are the place where we get to hear each other's work and be inspired by our witty, unique, and wonderful takes on the world. And when we leave our workshops, it is with the satisfied fatigue of a fruitful day of effort and the beginnings of a new piece of writing—something surprising that we didn't know was inside of us when we arrived at the workshop but is now scribbled onto that white piece of paper—filling it so that it is no longer blank.

What we realized at that mid-year curriculum meeting was that the most important part of the Girls Write Now workshops is the feeling they create in the participants. And the leftover glow is what keeps us striving to pull the unexpected out of our subconscious long after the workshop is over.

—Maya Frank-Levine, Curriculum Co-Chair

THE FICTION WORKSHOP: FANTASY
October

By Allison Adair Alberts, mentor and workshop co-leader

Sun poured through the towering windows on the eighteenth floor of the Girls Write Now offices. A stretch of savagely blue sky was interrupted only by the dark silhouettes of buildings, which stood in a jumbled layer across the Manhattan skyline. The loft-like headquarters of GWN baked in the sunshine as girls and mentors began to fill the room. They sought out one another with open arms—it was the first workshop of the new year, and the room was alive with greetings and laughter.

Suddenly the windows fell dark. The temperature, previously (and uncomfortably) warm, dropped twenty degrees. White plastic folding chairs shuddered against the concrete floor, and the screens of iMacs frantically flashed with static. Girls screamed; mentors, too. To everyone's horror, the concrete in the middle of the room liquefied and swirled. A girl wearing a pointed, diamond-studded helmet and a heavy violet cloak pushed her way to the middle of the crowd. She stood beside the patch of swirling concrete, which had begun to descend as if it were soft-serve ice cream filling up a waffle cone. She raised her pencil and bellowed above the cacophony of the room: "Let us go forth into the portal!"

Just kidding—none of that portal business happened, but we did have an electrifying fiction workshop. The topic of fantasy literature set loose all kinds of creative juices. Drawing our inspiration from books like the Harry Potter series, *A Wrinkle in Time,* the Earthsea cycle, and *Twilight*, we wrestled with a definition for this shape-shifting genre. What makes fantasy *fantastic?* A creature? A feeling? A time-traveling portal? We concluded that fantasy replaces the familiar with the unfamiliar; its use is as various as its form, but it is just as likely to comment on the "real" world as it is to help us escape it.

For our Opening Lines exercise, the girls created their own fantastic heroines, complete with superpowers and other extraordinary skills. We'd already entered the world of dragons, vampires, talking trees, mirror-dwellers, and faeries by the time our guest authors, Sarah Beth Durst and Libba Bray, arrived to read from their new novels, *Enchanted Ivy* and *Going Bovine,* respectively, and later Caragh M. O'Brien who read from the first book in her new trilogy, *Birthmarked*. The authors told us about where they find their inspiration and how they edit a first draft into a polished novel.

The editing discussion prepared us for our Reimagining exercise, in which we returned to our heroines from Opening Lines and pitted them against their nemeses. Crafting our villains prompted us to consider our heroines' strengths and weaknesses, so by the end of the workshop, all our characters had developed into full, rounded beings. I was impressed by the sheer magnitude of the girls' and mentors' imaginations. Their Closing Lines promised to open doors to ethereal new worlds. I couldn't wait to see how these developed throughout the coming year.

Special Guest Authors: Fantasy Fiction

Libba Bray is *The New York Times* best-selling author of the *Gemma Doyle Trilogy* and the Michael L. Printz Award–winning novel *Going Bovine*. She lives in Brooklyn with her husband and son and two cats.

Sarah Beth Durst is the author of young adult novels *Enchanted Ivy* and *Ice*, as well as middle grade novels *Into the Wild* and *Out of the Wild*. She has twice been a finalist for SFWA's Andre Norton Award, for both *Ice* and *Into the Wild*. She is a graduate of Princeton University. Sarah lives in Stony Brook, New York, with her husband and children.

Caragh M. O'Brien is the author of *Birthmarked*, a YA dystopian novel published by Roaring Brook Press in March, 2010. Born in St. Paul, Minnesota, Caragh was educated at Williams College and earned her MA from Johns Hopkins University.

From the Workshop: Exercises and Excerpts

- Fantasy starts the same way any fiction does, sometimes with a character, sometimes with a situation or a setting. Imagine a character: What is her name? Her age? What language does she speak? Does she have any defining physical characteristics? Now imagine that your character has a single characteristic or has had one experience that makes her extraordinary.

- Imagine the scene where your character discovers her special ability for the first time. OR, imagine the scene of your character's first encounter with a magical object or new world. This is the strange, exciting, and probably overwhelming moment when your protagonist first realizes everything's not quite normal.

- There's nothing like a good enemy to bring out the best (or worst) in a character. Who or what could defeat your character. Is it a person? An organization? A monster? A force of nature? The loss of her own powers? Use your knowledge of your protagonist and her nemesis to imagine an encounter between them. It can be their first encounter, or their last.

> Have you ever tried to fit a tail into a size 2? Well, honey, get back to me when you have. While you're at it, maybe you'll discover the meaning of life.
>
> Oh, but I haven't introduced myself. I'm Anna, the one with the butt-ugly mermaid tail. No pun intended. In all seriousness, my tail feels like that guy who never took baths in your class times 1,000, plus your period, and yuck, you do the math. It equals nasty.

—*Priscilla Guo, mentee*

By Shannon Talley and Jen McFann, mentee-mentor pair

A Magical Gathering

In the light of the triple-moon glow, thirty elders and thirty apprentices gathered in the elven glade. They had come together on the fourth Saturday of the month of harvest to explore Fantasy Writing, but before they could even unroll their Papyrus of Wisdom, they were split into pairs—mentor and mentee—through the whimsy of a magical sorting hat.

The guest authors, Sarah Beth Durst and Libba Bray, two witches from nearby towns, enchanted the pairs with their craft and stories. They were very different yet similar in the way that they spun their tales. Both Sarah and Libba chose interesting excerpts from their books to read aloud. Their magical and emotional way of reading cast a spell over the audience and was enough to keep everyone engaged with what they had to say. Their reading, which was so strong and full of life, would have convinced anyone to want to read their books; some suspect a hex was involved.

Within the passing of one spin of the hourglass, the pairs were enjoined to conjure their own supernatural characters. Taking up their quills, they crafted creatures of many a magical variety and even summoned a fantastical world to house each one.

Mentor and mentee alike left the coven gathering with a greater knowledge of the mysteries of fantasy writing in all its forms. They honed their powers of perception regarding the distinct features of fantasy, while at the same time remembering that the ancient magics of storytelling—plot, character, and conflict—form the core of even the most fantastical of tales.

THE POETRY WORKSHOP: SHORT POETRY
November

From Our Workshop Leaders
By Mayuri Amuluru Chandra, mentor and workshop co-leader

Poetry, we said,
Is expressive and simple writing.
Perfect for you.

Short poetry examples:
Acrostics, haiku, lunes, bean biographies (!).
Less is more.

Freeing and personal,
But also challenging in form.
Imagine, but *specify*.

Lively Kristin Prevallet
Wrapped her poems in boxes,
Gifts for us.

She showed us
To find that thoughtful line,
To choose wisely.

With Khadija Queen,
we made up poem languages,
Opened our ears.

The haibun: new.
Long, emotive passage, diary-like,
Haiku to follow.

And how exciting to hear the poems carved from their everyday—the houses that house them,
the mouths that speak them, the beaches they remember.

Short poems for already long-lived lives.

Special Guest Authors: Short Poetry

Kristin Prevallet is a poet, essayist, performer, and educator. She holds an MA in Poetics and Media Studies from the University of Buffalo. Kristin has taught at NYU, The New School, Bard College, and Naropa University's online MFA program, and is currently teaching at the Institute for Writing Studies at St. John's University in Jamaica, Queens. She has received a 2007 New York Foundation for the Arts fellowship in Poetry and a 2004 PEN Translation Fund award. Her book, *A Helen Adam Reader* was published by the National Poetry Foundation in 2007.

Khadijah Queen holds an MFA in creative writing from Antioch University, Los Angeles and a BA in English from the University of Maryland. She is the author of the poetry collection *Conduit* (Black Goat/Akashic 2008), and recent work appears or is forthcoming in *jubilat; Fire and Ink: An Anthology of Social Action Writing* (University of Arizona Press 2009); and *Best American Nonrequired Reading* (Houghton Mifflin 2010), among many other publications. Her second poetry manuscript, *Black Peculiar*, won the 2010 Noemi Book Award for Poetry and will appear in fall 2011.

From the Workshop: Exercises and Excerpts

- Acrostics are poems in which the first letters of each line, when read downward, form a word, phrase, or sentence. Lunes are three-line poems in which you count the words in each line: 3-5-3. Try an acrostic or lune of your own.

- Imagine you are holding a bean. Imagine that it is alive, with its own personality, hopes and dreams, likes and dislikes. Write a bean poem!

- Make a list of places that have some kind of meaning for you—places that you recently visited, places that you remember from your childhood, a place where something important happened to you. Choose one place from your list and write a poem that fleshes it out. Use all five senses in your prose poem, and try to concentrate on the ones that we often forget, like smell and taste.

- Now, write the haiku ending to your haibun.

**Part of a
billion yet above
them all**

—Monica Chin, mentee

A Review of the Short Poetry Workshop, from the Girls Write Blog

By Priscilla Guo, mentee

The Marvelous Adventures of Our Beans

A string of women writers slowly shuffle into the room as they catch sight of the bright yellow packets lying on the seats. It is only poetic justice that we await meeting a bean, discovering the metamorphosis of haiku to haibun, and finding ourselves hypnotized by the contents of a box.

Of course, all things begin with breakfast. Soon, after our tummies had stopped talking to us, our mentor co-leaders Mayuri, Marisa, and Nancy started discussing three kinds of poetry. We began with acrostic, then lunes, and finally wrote about the personality of a bean…A BEAN? It was certainly a shock to my imagination to imbue a kidney bean with a personality, but it was really fun. We shared the marvelous adventures of our beans, and they started to resemble little people rather than seeds that give the gift of musical flatulence. After breaking down the concept of poetry, a poet came up to speak to us!

Kristin Prevallet brought her poems and her boxes, the latter of which she gave us to tuck away our little piece of poetry. We practiced getting our words onto paper no matter how terrible they sounded, and then going back and picking out the bits of "honey" in there. The girls who shared had the most delectable bits of poems.

I think what most people took from this workshop was that not everyone sounds like e.e. cummings or Maya Angelou coming out of the writing womb. There are different ways to cultivate writing and develop it. Kristin taught us her way of doing it, and seeing how many Japanese monks changed a haiku to a haibun showed us that we too can put a twist on tradition. We are the next generation of women poets.

THE JOURNALISM WORKSHOP: INVESTIGATIVE REPORTING

December

From Our Workshop Leaders

By Amy Feldman, mentor and workshop co-leader

We had a surprise in store for the girls at the Journalism Workshop this year: as soon as they walked in, they would be immersed in a newsroom, trying to figure out what had caused a fire at a school, and who was telling them the truth. In character—as the principal, the teenage smoker, the maintenance worker, etc.—we answered their questions. Why didn't the smoke alarm go off? What was the principal's relative doing on the payroll? Who was lying? In teams, the girls came up with questions, and then they wrote stories based on what they had learned.

No matter how much you plan out a scenario—and we had planned and planned, creating names and biographies for each of the people at the school that afternoon—the unexpected will happen. And it was those unexpected moments (the pair who made up a name for one of the characters because they'd forgotten to ask, the questions about the inappropriate behavior of another character that we'd never anticipated) that still stick with me four months later. This is, in fact, how most reporting goes, with false starts and unanticipated breakthroughs that ultimately result in a story. Since many of the girls and women in Girls Write Now are writers of fiction and poetry, not nonfiction, this was an especially fun exercise that brought them into a different universe.

Throughout the exercises and discussion that afternoon, the workshop participants got a flavor of what constitutes investigative reporting, and how investigative techniques can be used in all types of nonfiction writing.

Jo Becker, a Pulitzer Prize–winning investigative reporter for *The New York Times*, spoke about stories she had done, and how she would get difficult-to-interview subjects (like Dick Cheney, the former Vice President) to open up to her. Since we met as Wikileaks was dumping secret government cables, and Jo was part of the team working on that story, the workshop also got an inside peek into how the *Times* determined what to publish, and what not to publish, and how it verified the accuracy of the leaked information. In the morning workshop session, Marian Wang of ProPublica, shared her recent articles on the oil spill in the Gulf.

By the end of the day, the room was buzzing with energy. For the final exercise, everyone came up with pitches for stories they wanted to write for magazines, newspapers, or websites. Some girls looked to unfairness in their schools; others wanted to research their own families' histories. The trepidation about reporting at the start of the workshop was gone, and the room was filled with excitement about the possibilities of asking questions and uncovering the truth.

Special Guest Authors: Investigative Reporting

Jo Becker is an award-winning journalist, currently an investigative reporter for *The New York Times*. Formerly with *The Washington Post*, she won, with Barton Gellman, the 2008 Pulitzer Prize for National Reporting.

Marian Wang is an investigative journalist living in New York. She is currently a reporter-blogger for ProPublica, a nonprofit investigative newsroom that produces journalism in the public interest. She previously worked for *Mother Jones* in San Francisco and freelanced in Chicago for the *Chicago Reporter*, the *Chi-Town Daily News* and *ChicagoNow*.

From the Workshop: Exercises and Excerpts

- Investigative reporting usually starts with a big question—a mystery or an injustice or something that makes you think: "How could that happen?" Come up with a big question that has to do with your friends and family, school, neighborhood, city, or country.
- Choose one question that you would want to investigate and write about. Come up with ten words that are absolutely essential to your story.
- Starting with these ten words, construct a twenty-five-word pitch to sell your story to a news source.

> The 19th Amendment was passed in 1920. Still, women are fighting for the remaining rights they deserve. Women are struggling to pay the bills, mortgage, rent, etc. with the $.81 they earn for every dollar a man earns. This is not equality. Women never truly gained their equality. The Constitution says, "All men are created equal." Women were never addressed.

—Yolandri Vargas, mentee

A Review of the Investigative Reporting Workshop, from the Girls Write Blog

By Lashanda Anakwah and Rachel Cohen, mentee-mentor pair

Uncovering the Truth

NEW YORK - A group of girls huddled together to practice the art of investigative reporting on Saturday, December 11, an inquiry by the *GWN News* has found. The first task was to interview six sources played by Girls Write Now members about a fake school fire. They split off into groups to interrogate each source. Quickly, they started to develop theories of what really happened.

Then the entire group of mentees and mentors came together and shared what they found with their editor. Immediately they discovered some contradictions. The interviewers did such a good job they even discovered some facts not planted by organizers.

The workshop included a talk by Jo Becker, Pulitzer Prize–winning reporter for *The New York Times*. Reuters reporter and GWN mentor Claudia Parsons also described the ethical dilemmas of journalism. The girls had time to reflect on the challenges journalists face.

As always, there were tasty snacks.

At the very end, everybody came up with her own investigative story idea.

"This workshop goes down as my absolute favorite GWN workshop ever!" mentor Cynara Charles-Pierre said. "I absolutely loved it and so did my mentee. It really demonstrated how natural curiosity and persistence can be turned into a fun and satisfying career."

THE MEMOIR WORKSHOP: CHILDHOOD MEMOIRS
March

From Our Workshop Leaders
By Wendy Lee, mentor and workshop co-leader

"How hard can this be?" I thought at the beginning of the Memoir Workshop, as mentees and mentors filed into the room one morning in March. "Everyone loves to write about themselves!" And write we did.

What's a secret that you kept? What was something that you believed wholeheartedly? What was a time that you were misunderstood? These opening lines required everyone to dig deep into their pasts (not so past for mentees, more so for mentors) and try to remember details, or to develop strategies when those details were not so forthcoming. We talked about the difference between fact and fiction, where memoir lay on the spectrum of nonfiction, and why people seemed to like memoir when it "read like a novel." Without realizing it, a lot of us had already been seeing our lives as a narrative. (I see mine as a science-fiction novel, but that's another story.)

The guest speaker for the morning session was Annie Choi, author of the memoir *Happy Birthday or Whatever: Track Suits, Kim Chee, and Other Family Disasters*, and also a Girls Write Now Craft Talk veteran. She treated us to a never-before-heard piece from a work in progress, a hilarious tale about how her father made her take piano lessons as a child. (I know that in my household, learning piano wasn't an elective, but a compulsory course.) In the afternoon workshop, Liz Welch talked about writing her compelling family memoir, *The Kids Are All Right*, along with her sister.

Okay, at this point the workshop gets a little hazy for me. Luckily, I remember some advice Annie Choi gave us: you don't necessarily have to recall everything that happened, just the "greatest hits." I believe she was talking about dialogue, but definitely one of the "greatest hits" of the workshop was the Reimagining Exercise. Workshop co-leader Samantha Henig shared a photo she'd taken as a child—her sister is pictured in the middle, and her parents' heads are cut off. Using the photo as inspiration, we took our free writes about a childhood memory and recast them from a present-day perspective.

So yes, in the end, the Memoir Workshop was filled with writing about ourselves. But in doing so we discovered the common threads that unite us: those awkward preteen moments, the importance of family and friends, the triumph over difficulties that at the time seemed insurmountable—and the realization that everyone's life is worth examining.

Special Guest Authors: Childhood Memoirs

Annie Choi was born and raised in Los Angeles' San Fernando Valley. A graduate of the University of California, Berkeley, and Columbia University, she lives in New York City. She is the author of the memoir *Happy Birthday or Whatever: Track Suits, Kim Chee, and Other Family Disasters*.

Liz Welch is an award-winning journalist who has been published in *Glamour*, *Marie Claire*, *Vogue*, *Self*, and *The New York Times Magazine* as well as many other publications. She is a contributor at *Inc. Magazine* and is the co-author of the memoir *The Kids Are All Right* (Harmony 2009) with her sister, Diana Welch. She lives in Brooklyn, New York, with her husband.

From the Workshop: Exercises and Excerpts

- Think back to your childhood and describe… A secret that you kept; something that you believed wholeheartedly; a food that you hated or loved; a family ritual; a time when you were misunderstood.
- Write the scene of one of those memories from the perspective of yourself as a child, at the age the memory took place.
- Rewrite this scene from the perspective of your current self. What can you see now that you couldn't see in the moment?

I'm sitting on the couch with my mother and father, who both just got out from their jobs. The front door opens and closes, and a bunch of my relatives come in, chattering in loud voices and wishing everyone a happy New Year. I'm curled on the couch in a red Chinese jacket, running my fingers over the silky material. The Chinese drama I watched every day was playing on the television and I'm watching it intently. Suddenly, my aunt and uncle come over, wishing me a happy New Year and handing me a red envelope with money. They ask me what drama I'm watching. My grandmother answers for me and informs them that I know every character in the drama and can sing the theme song to it, too. She goes over and rewinds the tape recording to the beginning, asking me to sing along with it. I shake my head. I didn't see my relatives often, other than my grandmother, and I was too shy to sing. My aunt and uncle urge me to sing to them, smiling at me encouragingly. I shake my head again and say, no, in my high voice, crossing my arms as I do so. My aunt and uncle laugh, saying it's okay that I don't want to. My grandmother explains I'm not usually shy. When they walk away, I'm relieved.

—*Samantha Young Chan, mentee*

By ChanTareya Paredes and Alissa Riccardelli, mentee-mentor pair

Now and Then

ChanTareya (TT)

I was early. That was the one thing that kept running through my head as I arrived at the Memoir Workshop and took my place next to the window. I could feel the cold seep through the glass but not enough for a chill to go through my bones. There were a few girls there who seemed comfortable in the big empty space, but they smiled sheepishly at me. I returned the kind gesture, waiting.

Around a quarter to two, my mentor, Alissa, arrived. She was as happy as ever, despite the cold weather outside. We got food and ate in pleasant chatter, watching the other girls and their mentors walk in. Then, promptly at 2:30 p.m., the day began with a writing exercise that forced us to think back to our childhood. Despite all the groans from the other girls about how they had no idea how to think back that far, I knew exactly what I was going to write about. I laughed to myself because I had been waiting for the Memoir Workshop all year.

Alissa

First of all, I was totally overheated in there. It may have been cold outside, but leave it to me to be a New Yorker and rush everywhere until I arrive in a panting stupor. I saw TT right away, and we immediately went to where the action was: the food table. There was honeydew and I never pass up honeydew. That must be why I was in good spirits. That and the whole genre, of course—I've never really written a memoir—I was excited! But then it actually started—all of the girls settled in—the workshop had begun. But wait—we had to write about our least favorite foods? Secrets we kept? A time when we were misunderstood? It seemed that everyone around me was happily diving into their notebooks, pouring out the memories. Why was I drawing a blank? Suddenly I felt old—surely something must have been wrong! Did I not keep secrets? Was I that boring? I sat there and stared at the water tower outside until something hit me. I wrote it down: "Zucchini. As a child I hated zucchini and refused to eat it, though I was made to, frequently." I was back in my kitchen in my childhood home on Lacey Court—I could feel the steaming, mushy vegetable, cleverly disguising itself as a tasty cucumber, resting under my tongue, sour, oily. Ah, yes. I was eight years old again and the workshop had indeed begun.

TT

"My father died when I was thirteen from a car accident, and three years later, my mother died from cancer."

Elizabeth (although I like to think of her as Liz) sat in front of us, the stunned writers of Girls Write Now, as she confessed this. I remember admiring the strong jut of her chin and her sloping shoulders that seemed slightly stiff. She was relaxed. Her voice betrayed no emotion as she read an excerpt from her book, focusing on her father's funeral. There was no sag to her spine, no misery etched in the lines of her face. There was no sign of hidden pain, not even in her eyes. There was just her story, her truth. The only stutter came in her practiced habit of reading her and her siblings' memories, but in spite of her experienced tone, there was also that deep edge of remembering something so painful. The very definition of memoir and the insight to a reality the past brings.

Alissa

I knew I wanted to hear from Liz as soon as I saw her—she looked like someone to learn from. I hadn't read much about her memoir, *The Kids Are All Right*; I only wondered if it was anything like that movie, which I had just seen the night before. The first words out of Liz's mouth definitely answered those questions. Her life was nothing like that movie or like any movie. It felt stranger than fiction. I sat stunned the whole time—feeling that all of us were still, enveloped. As I listened to Liz, the world fell away. I was so moved by her honesty that it started to hurt. I could have passed her any number of times on the street, never knowing that she carried such a burden—the loss of both parents. Even watching her speak, I would never know; she seemed so joyful, so clever and witty, so optimistic. I took the book from TT and looked at the photographs, listening, investigating. Days later, I couldn't stop thinking about it. And people say that memoirs are useless—like it's all about what our minds can invent. Here's a strong statement for the case of honesty, reflection.

TT

I am flying across the bridges of New York, across the roaring rhythm of the heights and across free and happy Harlem. I land on my grandmother's roof only to come back to earth as the writing exercise "Now and Then" concludes. We had to think of a childhood memory and write about it from a child's perspective and then from our present-day perspective, looking back. I raise my hand. This is the sole reason why I brought my memory back to life. The sole reason why I remembered how I fell in love with New York in the first place. I recite my memory, word for word, inviting my listeners to dive inside of my feelings with me. To hear and feel the things that I have heard and felt. To know the reasons behind my actions. To relate.

Alissa

We were told to draw a memory, which sounds like an interesting exercise, except I can't draw. Like in grade school, I try to hide my paper from everyone around me—what if they see? I start with a window; I keep seeing my grandmother's bedroom window, the curtains, the shade, the heavy drapes. Soon my poor drawing skills don't really matter. I'm six years old again at that window; it's 1988. I'm with my cousins and we're dancing to *Singin' in the Rain*. I don't want to be pulled away and the following exercises don't disappoint. We all write furiously, intent, going backwards. I'm even smiling; others are smiling, too. After we write, some brave few share our experiences—even TT, reading a beautiful memory of being on a rooftop in New York City—girls telling stories that maybe they've never told anyone. When it's over, we take a collective deep breath, back on the Eighteenth Floor, back in New York City. We're all so different, but I realize that we're all so much closer now.

THE SCREENWRITING WORKSHOP: ADAPTATION
April

From Our Workshop Leaders
By Katherine Nero, mentor and workshop co-leader

INT. GIRLS WRITE NOW WORKSHOP ROOM- West 37TH Street

The room is filled with MENTORS and MENTEES who are seated. They wait eagerly for the screenwriting workshop to continue. The workshop co-leaders are CYNARA, CHRISTINA, THERESE, SARV, KATHERINE and TEMMA.

Cynara steps forward to address the audience.

> CYNARA
> Let's thank our guest authors for
> sharing invaluable tips and insights
> about adapting screenplays. Vicky
> Dann from New York University's Tisch
> School of the Arts...

The mentors and mentees applaud warmly.

> CYNARA (CONT'D)
> And Susan-Sojourna Collier, the
> executive producer of *Moment to
> Moment*, an Internet drama.

More warm applause.

As Cynara steps back, Christina walks forward. She stands next to the FLIP CHART.

> CHRISTINA
> Before we go, let's review what we
> learned today.

Christina reaches for a BLACK MAGIC MARKER. She writes "adaptation" on the flip chart.

> CHRISTINA (CONT'D)
> What is an adaptation?

Several girls raise their hands. Christina chooses WANDA (16).

> WANDA*
> That's when you turn something
> that has already been written into a
> screenplay.

> CHRISTINA
> What types of writing can be turned
> into a screenplay?

Hands fly up. Christina selects NICOLE (15).

> NICOLE*
> Books. Plays.

Christina hurriedly writes "books" and "plays" on the flip chart.

                            CHRISTINA
                    Yes! What else?

The girls look confused.

Therese steps toward the flip chart. Christina hands Therese the magic marker.

                            THERESE
                    Remember how you each chose one
                    of your portfolio pieces to adapt into
                    a screenplay?

Suddenly hands zoom up. Therese smiles and points to RENEE (17) for the
answer.

                            RENEE*
                    Fantasy fiction, poetry…

Therese writes the genres on the flip chart as Renee speaks.

                        RENEE (CONT'D)
                    Memoir and investigative journalism.

Sarv steps forward as Therese finishes writing.

                            SARV
                    What are some examples of books that
                    have been adapted into screenplays?

The girls raise their hands enthusiastically and shout out the answers.

                            MENTEES
                        (voices overlapping)
                    *Twilight…The Godfather…Harry
                    Potter…Hunger Games.*

                            SARV
                    Those are great examples. *Twilight*
                    and *Harry Potter* are also fantasy
                    fiction. What about examples of
                    investigative journalism?

                            MENTEES
                        (voices overlapping)
                    All the President's Men…Mean Girls.

                              SARV
                    Mean Girls was adapted from the
                    book *Queen Bees and Wannabees*.
                    What about poetry?

The girls look confused.

                          SARV (CONT'D)
                    Okay, I'll help you out this time. We
                    watched a clip of it earlier.

LISA (15) blurts out the answer.

                              LISA*
                    "For Colored Girls!"

                              SARV
                    Yes, that's right! As you can see there
                    are numerous sources for screenplay
                    adaptations. Books, plays, poems,
                    memoirs, articles, and even songs.

Katherine walks to the front as Sarv rejoins the other co-leaders.

                          KATHERINE
                    A story can also be adapted by
                    changing the time and location. Like
                    10 Things I Hate About You. What is
                    that an updated version of?

                          MENTEES
                    (voices overlapping)
                    Taming of the Shrew!

                          KATHERINE
                    What elements of the story had to be
                    changed to make *Taming of the Shrew*
                    contemporary?

Several girls raise their hands. Katherine points to Diane.

                          DIANE*
                    Language and clothes.

                          KATHERINE
                    Oh yes, there's a big difference
                    between clothes now and what they
                    wore in the sixteenth century. What
                    about technology?

                              DIANE
                    You would add cars, televisions…

                              BRENDA*
          iPods.

The audience laughs.

                              KATHERINE
                    Even though some story elements
                    may change, the core of the story—
                    what the character wants and the
                    conflict—remains the same.

Temma steps forward.

                              TEMMA
                    Let's pretend that we are in a scene
                    right now. Our objective is to learn
                    about screenplay adaptations.

The mentors and mentees look at Temma curiously.

                              TEMMA (CONT'D)
                    What would happen if instead of
                    being in New York, we were in the
                    Arctic? How would that affect our
                    objective?

No one answers.

                              TEMMA (CONT'D)
                    Looks like we'll have to find out for
                    ourselves. On the count of three, let's
                    all say "ch-ch-ch-changes" together.

Both mentors and mentees look confused. There are a few groans.

                              TEMMA (CONT'D)
                    Oh c'mon. Trust me. All together now.
                    One. Two. THREE!

                              ALL
                         (in unison)
                    CH-CH-CH-CHANGES!

EXT. THE ARCTIC — DAY

The mentors, mentees and co-leaders are seated on the ground. They wear thick, warm coats and snowshoes. There is ice as far as the eye can see. The temperature is 56 degrees below zero.

All of the mentors and mentees, with the exception of Temma, are stunned. They look at their new surroundings in disbelief.

> TEMMA
> So how does this environment affect
> our objective?

> NICOLE*
> I want to go home! Now!

> TEMMA
> Exactly! The weather here makes
> achieving your objective more
> difficult. Because now you also have
> to figure out how to stay warm.

Several of the girls begin shivering.

> TEMMA (CONT'D)
> This is an example of how changing
> one element can transform your story.

Temma looks at the audience warmly.

> TEMMA (CONT'D)
> Thank you for all of your wonderful
> work today. Enjoy the rest of your day!

No one moves.

> RENEE
> How do we get out of here?

> TEMMA
> (laughing)
> Oh, that's right. I totally forgot. Are
> you ready? One, two, three…

> ALL
> (in unison)
> CH-CH-CH-CHANGES!

FADE OUT.

*Names have been changed.

Special Guest Authors: Screenwriting Adaptation

With a background in playwriting, **Susan-Sojourna Collier** received an Emmy nomination for her writing on ABC's *All My Children*. A veteran television writer, Susan-Sojourna Collier has written for many daytime drama series, including *Port Charles*, *All My Children,* and *One Life to Live*. She has penned the screenplay *Get the Show On the Road*, an adaptation of a romance novel, which was a semifinalist in the Tribeca Film Festival Screenplay Series. Most recently, she was the story editor for the short film *Native New Yorker*, which was a recipient of Toyota Scion Short Film Funding. Ms. Collier is the author of four plays that have been produced throughout the East Coast. She is also the winner of the New York's New Professional Theatre's Writing Festival and Walt Disney Writing Fellowship. Currently, she is the writer and executive producer of the Internet dramatic series *Moment to Moment*.

Victoria Dann is a full-time faculty member at New York University's prestigious Tisch School of the Arts Department of Film and Television. She has published over fifteen books in numerous languages all over the world, and is a winner of a Writers Guild of America Award.

From the Workshop: Exercises and Excerpts

- Choose an excerpt from a book (*Persepolis*, *The Hunger Games*, *For Colored Girls Who Have Considered Suicide When the Rainbow Is Enuf, Queen Bees and Wannabes*) and convert it into a scene that uses only dialogue and action—no adjectives.
- Adapt one of your *own* pieces of writing from this year (fantasy fiction, short poetry, investigative reporting, or childhood memoir) into a scene. Remember, use only dialogue and action.
- Now take the scene you just wrote and adapt it to a new time and place. Think of how time period and location affect the scene: your characters' surroundings, how they speak, think, dress, and what they do.

INT. MENTAL ASYLUM — AFTERNOON

This is ANI'S third visit with the doctors/psychoanalysts. She is frustrated and tired of repeating the same thing to them: that she's not crazy and that she can read their thoughts.

> **NURSE**
> **(Directs ANI towards the hallway,**
> **where chairs are lined up.)**
> **This way.**

> **ANI**
> **(Sighs.)**
> **Whatever.**

> **NURSE**
> **Wait here until your name is called;**
> **don't make any noise.**

ANI
(Reads NURSE'S mind and sees
that she calls them all crazy brats)
I heard that.

NURSE
What?!

ANI
Nevermind.

Time passes until ANI'S name is called.

DOCTOR
Ani. Come sit. How are you feeling today?

ANI
Like everyday.

DOCTOR
I know you've been here before, but
we haven't been able to reach a more
specific diagnosis. Tell me again
what is going on.

ANI
(Reads the doctor's mind, *Yeah
right*, he says.)
Nothing, just that I can read minds.

DOCTOR
Is that so? And how did you come
to realize this?

ANI
I was by the river with my friends.
One of them threw stones at the other
one and blamed it on the boys. When
she turned around I heard a voice that
proved otherwise. Since then I've just
always heard them. People's thoughts.

ANI reads DOCTOR'S mind again.

DOCTOR
*Ugh, again with the same wack
story.*

ANI snorts.

DOCTOR

Anything funny?

ANI

**Nothing. I just heard what you
thought. Real professional.**

—*Emely Paulino, mentee*

A Review of the Screenwriting Adaptation Workshop, from the Girls Write Blog

By Cindy Caban and Juliet Packer, mentee-mentor pair

Script to Screen

(With apologies to the brilliant leaders for taking liberties with their voices—but this is an adaptation.)

FADE IN:

INT. GWN (*GIRLS WRITE NOW*) WORKSHOP ROOM — DAY

A group of about twenty TEENAGE GIRLS—MENTEES—and twenty WOMEN—MENTORS—are sitting on white folding chairs. On their laps are yellow-covered packets. There is a large TV screen at the front. Standing in front is a woman—LEADER #1

LEADER #1
Okay, what do we mean by an
adaptation?

A few hands shoot up. The leader points to various girls.

MENTEE #1
A translation.

MENTEE #2
Turning one thing into another.

MENTEE #3
Reworking material.

LEADER #1

Great. In our Opening Lines exercise
you'll see that any of the genres we've
worked with earlier this year can be
the basis of an adaptation.

DISSOLVE TO:

INT. GWN WORKSHOP ROOM — LATER

Everyone watches the TV, which shows a *Mean Girls* clip.

INSERT CLIP

The queen bees including Cady sit in the crowded cafeteria.

REGINA

Is butter a protein?

CADY

Sure.

O.S. Fellow mentees and mentors laugh.

DISSOLVE TO:

INT. GWN WORKSHOP ROOM — LATER

A WOMAN steps to the front of the room.

LEADER # 2

Who wants to share what they
noticed?

MENTOR # 1

In the book, it's written from the
perspective of the mother and in
the movie it shows the teenagers'
perspective.

LEADER #2

That's right. What else?

DISSOLVE TO:

INT. GWN WORKSHOP ROOM WITH ADJOINING SMALL CONFERENCE ROOM —
LATER

The small conference room is set up with a spread of food: bagels, cream cheese,
peanut butter, cookies, juice, fruit, pastries, etc. The girls and women dig in.

A STAFF MEMBER crosses to a mentor.

> STAFF MEMBER
> How was the guest speaker?

> MENTOR #1
> Terrific. She said voiceovers are addictive like Twinkies. And as a writer you never have to explain love. She also said the smartest advice she ever got about structure is: Act I, get your character up a tree. Act II, throw rocks at him. Act III, get him down from the tree.

> STAFF MEMBER
> Let's change that to putting a girl or a woman up a tree.

DISSOLVE TO:

INT. GWN WORKSHOP ROOM — LATER

The MENTEES and MENTORS are seated again. In progress.

> LEADER #3
> … Now you're going to pick one of your pieces from an earlier workshop and adapt it into a scene.

DISSOLVE TO:

INT. GWN WORKSHOP ROOM — LATER

SHOTS of MENTORS and MENTEES scribbling away, looking up for inspiration, silently rereading their work, etc.

> LEADER #3
> Time's up. Now for Pair Share: find someone other than your mentor or mentee and act out the scene.

> MENTEE #7
> I can't act!

> LEADER #3
> And don't worry about your acting. You're not out to get an Academy Award.

SHOTS of MENTORS and MENTEES as they break into groups.

DISSOLVE TO:

INT. GWN WORKSHOP ROOM — LATER

> LEADER #3
> Who would like to act out their piece
> for the group?

MENTEE #8 raises her hand. She and her partner cross to the front of the room. They are brave, but nervous.

> MENTEE #9 / SCARLETT
> Emily? Is that you? Where are you?

> MENTEE #8 / EMILY
> I'm everywhere. I'm in your brain and
> in your sleep.

> MENTEE #9 / SCARLETT
> (laughs nervously)
> Emily it's really you. I'm so sorry. I
> didn't know. I…but why?

> MENTEE #8 / EMILY
> It wasn't you, Scarlett. Don't blame
> yourself. Death was seeking me…

Mentee #8 stops reading and looks up.

> MENTEE #8 (CONT'D)
> That's as far as I got.

> LEADER #3
> That was great.

The other girls and women applaud.

DISSOLVE TO:

INT. GWN WORKSHOP ROOM — DAY — LATER

> LEADER #2
> As we finish up, what are some
> examples of works you'd like to adapt?

> MENTEE #13
> Sylvia Plath's poem "Widow."

                        MENTEE #14
            Twilight.

                        LEADER #2
            What part of it?

                        MENTEE #15
            Everything.

As the girls and women LAUGH…

                                                    FADE OUT.

THE WILDCARD WORKSHOP: SKETCH COMEDY
MAY

From Our Workshop Leaders
By Ilana Manaster, mentor and workshop co-leader

INT. ELEVATOR—DAY

A very tired MAN, 38, enters the elevator on the Nineteenth Floor after a long day's work. He sighs and presses the button for the lobby. The elevator descends one floor and stops on 18. A group of girls pile into the elevator, forcing him into the corner.

                        CYNTHIA
            Ohmigod. That was so amazing. I love
            sketch comedy! Making people laugh
            is so fun.

                        MAN
            Ooop!

He covers his mouth.

                        CYNTHIA
            Excuse me?

                        MAN
            No. I just—did you say sketch
            comedy?

                        ANNA
            Yeah. We just had a sketch comedy
            workshop.

                        106

MAN

Because I really really love sketch
comedy. I mean, I *love* it. You know?
It's so FUNNY! Ha ha ha!

The girls look at the man strangely, but decide it would be best to ignore him.

JASMINE

Anyway, I have a complete girl crush
on our guest speaker, Tara Copeland.

DENISE

She was hi-LAR-ious. And I heard that
Megan Neuringer from the morning
workshop was just as amazing.

MAN

Guest speakers! Like, professionals!
People who, you know, do sketch
comedy! All the time!

LYDIA

Uh, yeah. Sir.

She turns to her friends.

LYDIA (CONT'D)

My mentor was like, "You're a monkey
with a clown for a pet." And I had to
talk forever! I was like, "I take my pet
clown to the clown run so he can
practice getting into a tiny car with
other clowns."

The girls laugh. MAN bursts into hysterical laughter.

ANNA

It's a lot easier to make people laugh
than I thought. I mean, you only need
three things, right?

The man pulls out a notebook and a pen. He leans forward.

MAN

What? What are they? Well…? For
the love of…you have the secret!
You have the code! Share, won't you?
Share with those less fortunate!

LYDIA
Uh, well, you need something
unexpected.

MAN
Unexpected! Of course!

He writes furiously.

DENISE
And you need heightening.

MAN
Heightening! Right! It has to get
worse and worse every time. Just
bigger and bigger, until who knows?
Someone is just going CRAZY! Oh this
is good stuff. This is really good stuff.
What else? Please. You have to tell me.
Tell me.

ANNA
Uh, commitment?

MAN
Commitment! Oh! That's beautiful!

ANNA
Yeah. The characters have to really
fight for what they want.

The MAN begins to cry.

JASMINE
What's wrong?

MAN (CONT'D)
Oh my oh my. It's so simple. But does
it work? Can it really be this easy? To
do that greatest, that most ambitious
of all the arts—sketch comedy?

JASMINE
Well, yeah! We wrote sketches…

MAN
You! Sketches!

He sobs.

JASMINE
Yeah. In like, fifteen minutes…

His sobs increase.

JASMINE (CONT'D)
And they were super duper funny.

CYNTHIA
Ha. Yeah. Like when Barack Obama
showed up at the Starbucks.

MAN
(Crazed)
The president? At a coffee chain?
HOW RIDICULOUS!!

DENISE
Yeah. And the rapper at the Doctor's
office…

CYNTHIA
I laughed so hard at that one.

The elevator finally arrives at the lobby and the girls start to exit.

MAN
(Writing)
Barack Obama at a Starbucks. A
rapper in the doctor's office. Why
that's genius! Pure genius!

He notices that the girls are leaving.

MAN (CONT'D)
Wait! Don't go! I have so many
questions! Please, I have to know…
I'm so close. So very very close!

The MAN chases after the girls.

FADE OUT

Special Guest Authors: Sketch Comedy

Tara Copeland can currently be seen at the Upright Citizens Brigade Theater with the Harold team, The Scam. Tara is a member of the group Mother (2001 Cage Match Tournament Champions) and the group Ms. Jackson (2004 ECNY Best Improv Group). Tara has also appeared on *Late Night with Conan O'Brien*, *Best Week Ever*, and in the movie *College Road Trip*.

Megan Neuringer is a writer and actor and has been performing at the Upright Citizens Brigade Theater since 2004. She was a panelist on *Best Week Ever* and appears regularly on other VH1 shows. Megan has also appeared on HBO's *Flight Of The Conchords*, has written for VH1, Comedy Central, Bravo and more, and is currently freelance joke writing for *Late Night With Jimmy Fallon*.

From the Workshop: Exercises and Excerpts

- What would you expect to find in a doctor's office? How about in a Starbucks, at the prom, in a library, or at the GWN office? What would you expect to see, hear, smell, or do? Now, what would you NOT expect to find at these locations?
- Using the list of unexpected situations you just came up with, choose one, then build on that situation to come up with characters and a plot. Once you have the plot, take your action one, two, three steps higher!
- Turn that outline into a sketch for a team of comedians to perform.

Location:
Doctor's office

Characters:
Doctor's assistant, rapper, beat-boxer

Plot:
The rapper walks up to the doctor's assistant saying he has a cut from unwrapping his new Eminem CD. To get his point across he raps.

Step 1:
The rapper is rapping to the assistant while his friend creates the beats.

Step 2:
The assistant doesn't understand so the rapper brings in an actor to show how he's injured, he raps along.

Step 3:
The assistant still doesn't understand. The rapper brings in a marching band to do a song about his little cut.

—*Alicia Maldonado, mentee*

A Review of the Sketch Comedy Workshop, from the Girls Write Blog

By Joy Smith and Emma Straub, mentee-mentor pair

Top Five Things We Learned at the Sketch Comedy Workshop

1. Don't Try to Be Funny
Your life is funny already, so don't try to make jokes out of nowhere.

2. When Pushed, Both of Us Will Sing and Dance in Public
If you need tap-dance lessons, call Joy.

3. There Are Rules
If you escalate the ridiculous elements, bang! You have a sketch.

4. It's Good to be Embarrassed
Usually the most embarrassing things are also the funniest. Forget your ego—if you can't laugh at yourself, you're in trouble.

5. Some Words Are Just Plain Funny
Like squish. And cahoots. And goober. And uber. And uber goober.

V. HOME

"Across the river Manhattan
shines like a star..."

Home is the intersection of the buildings that house us and the
memories constructed in them. Its familiarity can be constricting or
comforting. The smells, the hues, the textures, the flavors. For the
women writers of Girls Write Now, home today is New York City. But
for many of us, a little part of our minds will always reside in the
homes of our past. Sometimes home is just the backdrop; often, it
is a character in the plots of our lives.

—Rachel Cohen, mentor

45-05, 159

By Emely Paulino

the magnolia tree
lived at the back of my house
and showered its pink petals over
our home,
which was attached on the left to its siamese twin
in a weathered red epidermis
laced with gray
rectangular veins,
the petals inviting lazy days
washed away by the spring months
desolate in the late months
blackouts and thunderstorms
the water infiltrating
the cracks inside,
my father always fixed them
when i was six years old
i needed a pink nightlight
that matched the hello kitty theme
because i was afraid of the dark,
the monsters under my bed
which always felt too big for me
and i needed a boost
until the age of ten
down to the day i wore heels for the first time
disregarding the quinceañera tradition,
i was thirteen
practicing on the polished wooden floor
the clack clack clack echoing, competing against the bark of the neighbor's dog,
who i rarely saw but always heard,
the arguments, buried in the cracks of the dehydrated soil,
beneath the magnolia tree
with the tulips and pet bunny
her hind legs would thump whenever a stray feline would stride by,
upsetting the birds that chirped and nested in the forsythia bush,
the yellow flowers sustaining the small robin home
as we settled into ours,
they were the first neighbors we met
i watched the blue eggs hatch, and babysat
while their mother was gone
returning with earthworms
until she pushed them off to fly
like the first time i stayed home alone
or was given my first set of keys

skipping breakfast as i walked down the paved steps in my school uniform
returning at five, my daily routine
was interrupted
the For Sale sign greeted me,
swaying to my right as the breeze rolled
just to make sure i saw it was there.

The Spin Cycle
By Rhonda Zangwill

Some women dream of shoes. Others rhapsodize over chocolate. Me? I'm all about washing machines—Amanas, Kenmores… Maytags. I dream of a nice Maytag. Off white and gently undulating in an unobtrusive corner of my kitchen. For me such a vision is pure poetry.

Also pure fantasy.

Blame it on my building. Six stories, twenty-three apartments, and home to many blended and extended families—families that constantly create laundry. We denizens of Manhattan's East Fifteenth Street share many things: a Croatian superintendent, an idiosyncratic buzzer system, the occasional mouse. What we do not share is a laundry room. The 1903 invention of electric washing machines, a miracle that coincides with the birth of my building, did not, apparently, have any effect on even one owner of this venerable building, then or since.

So, every Saturday my overflowing cart and I are off to the local Laundromat. That is if you call four long city blocks local. But before I even get there I have to summon up some serious navigational skills, especially on First Avenue. Half the block is shut up tight for Sabbath, while the other half is crowded with an army of street vendors offering everything from plastic wallets to mounds of mangoes. Add to this the hipsters still wobbly from the night before, refugees from the methadone clinic across the street, and confused tourists looking for the famous East Village. Negotiating this obstacle course comes only after I have banged the cart down the five flights of my walkup—if you're counting, that's seventy-two stairs.

Still, the Laundromat is almost worth the hike. First, it is air conditioned. This is revolutionary. No more sweat and swelter. Thanks to this modern touch, I no longer spend summers in the Laundromat dripping all over my still-warm-and-fluffy-from-the-dryer 100 percent Egyptian cotton sheets. What's more, this place has not one, but six televisions. Premium cable, too. And the night manager, a Japanese guy with a long braid, always lends me the remote. Sometimes I'll even put a few too many quarters in the dryer just to use that extra half hour to check out all the programs I'm too cheap to get at home.

Add to these amenities the constant people parade and you have entertainment to last the week: the tiny women from Guatemala who shoulder bulky nylon bags with the ease of bodybuilders; the mother/daughter combos who share a single set of headphones and shimmy with abandon while stacking towers of clean underwear; the old guys who check every machine for stray quarters and then devour a few McSandwiches while waiting out the spin cycle.

But mostly I like the feel of the place—open, airy, and equipped with dozens of gleaming machines arranged in descending size order. Honestly, there's nothing like a good front loader. Sometimes I just park myself in front of one of the MegaMachines for no other reason than to witness its many and varied cycles of cleanliness.

If only I were in my own home.

A View of Manhattan from Queens

By Ireen Hossain and Wendy Lee

Across the river
Manhattan shines like a star
Bright and sharp and cold.

Looks like a pretty snow globe.
Dear Manhattan, I love you.

I send you postcards
But you never write me back.
The mailbox is bare.

Please, don't choose to ignore me.
With all my heart I want you.

Manhattan, someday
You'll realize that even stars
Need a friend sometimes.

And when you do realize it
I hope it is not too late.

> "We walk from
> Broadway
> To Steinway
> To Thirty-Sixth Street
> As the sun disappears."
> —Meghan McCullough,
> mentee

Fontibón

By Naima Coster

The fastest way to get there is on bicycle. You have to be brave enough to ride down the cobbled streets. The stones will jolt you; the wheels will stutter over the remains of old railroad tracks. There is never enough room on the sidewalk. Everyone walks in the street. You will have to weave around them as well as the buses, trucks, and tiny battered cars. It will probably be raining and the way to *el centro* will smell like damp cement and stale laundry that cannot dry on the line. If you pedal fast enough, you can feel the blast of raindrops on your face. It is cooler than the exhaust from the *colectivos*, gray and reeking of gasoline. If you decide to keep going, pressing north, you'll reach *el centro*. You will know it by the vendors in the park, playing lilting *vallenato* and beckoning you to buy rings, cloth, a T-shirt of an American rock band.

You'll be panting and hot from the ride. Move to the cart that has what you want.

The woman will scoop crushed ice into a cone-shaped paper cup. She will squirt in red and blue sweet syrup, drench the ice in condensed milk and hand it to you. *Raspao—*

Bright, cold treasure: sweet.
Eat it all before you make
The long trip back home.

Sensory Impressions: The High Line and Chelsea Market
By Kristin Vuković

Lobsters lined up like soldiers at attention. French spoken so fast I can't understand. Safety deposit boxes unhinged and gaping from above the elevator. Wine Vault. Gravity-defying photographs: a man reflected in a mirror, prostrate and elevated. A mother rattles a paper bag and her baby smiles. Kids with pink and blue bobbing balloons. Chocolate made in Brooklyn. "It smells good in here." Bronze feet without legs aside torches illuminated with artificial light. Moroccan Bazaar, Going Out Of Business Sale, 70% off. Cucumber, 80 cents. *Dogs are not allowed on the High Line*. Skateboards raking against pavement. Dead grass blowing down onto Tenth Avenue. Squeaking cart wheels. People lazing on lounges on rails in the cold. A lady in a hairnet serves a taste of vanilla gelato. Humming conversation punctuated by footsteps. Heels clicking on metal grating. A little girl in a bright yellow skirt curtseys in the amphitheatre. A black man dressed in black walks with a limp. "Where are we going?" A poster of "la confiture." Fat Witch Bakery. Posing for photographs: Shoot. Click. A half wheel for a door handle. Marbles stacked in a glass case, different shades of blue. A looming clock framed by angry, jagged bricks. An army of strollers. Water running green from a large faucet into a large hole. People throw their wishes in with pennies and nickels and dimes.

Negative Space
By Anna Poon

I get on a train going into the city at two a.m. tonight because I can't fall asleep and I want to be where the other people who aren't asleep are.

It's easier to be with them, usually, because late at night, the feel of everybody and everything is different. Whether they're working or partying, drunk or high, tired or angry or sad or simply unable to fall asleep like me, everyone begins to reach out from their own worlds where strange things happen all the time. Then those worlds collide and even stranger happenings ensue.

Night does that to people and their worlds.

The thing that bothers me is that I wonder if this is a better way to live. It seems counterintuitive, unnatural even, because we're diurnal animals and everything feels unnatural when you're awake at night. We even begin to act unnatural. Afraid of each other and afraid of the dark, we paradoxically cling even tighter to the nearest human being. We are courageous suddenly, challenging the dark and challenging each other, often confusing the two and forcing collisions between shadows and multiple realities.

Intoxication helps this kaleidoscopic bleeding of worlds and colors. Our vision is smeared. We can't tell where things begin or end. In fact there is no beginning or end or passage of time at all, and personally, I've come to love the feeling.

But unlike most, I don't need the drugs or alcohol to achieve that effect.

Tonight's just the third night in a row I haven't slept.

And as the train lurches and leaps through the viscera of the underground, I recall the drunken walk from my apartment to the train station. The wind had carried the cold and neutral smells of my neighborhood through me and straight into the soul. Smells I know I will always identify with home and which I will crave again by the end of the night, though right then they were making me sick. I'd tilted my head back to keep from throwing up and drank instead the sight of the stars pinwheeling above. Was that Little Dipper I saw? If so, then why couldn't I find Big Dipper? Tree leaves whispered the answer among themselves in an undecipherable tongue. The rise and fall of a truck horn blaring in the distance reached me, resounding in my ears. And I marveled.

An overwhelming peace had settled over my feverish soul like a deep blanket of snow and I wondered if this is what I stayed awake for. Because I never felt that way when it was day.

During the day we are obsessed with ourselves. We're obsessed with each other and our complicated relationships and emotions and thoughts, obsessed with the endless task and subtasks of living. We make ourselves the subject of every portrait.

We never wonder what it'd be like to be the negative space. The landscape background, vast plains of white, the wind in the trees and the stars in the sky and the sounds of traffic. Anything and everything other than what we are.

It would be incredibly liberating, I imagine. To exist and exult in that simple existence. Outside of, yet irretrievably interwoven with, every other existence out there. But what would I know of that?

The train grinds to a halt before the doors pop open and I slip outside.

I don't get far before I accidentally kick an empty can of beer, bump into a homeless woman muttering to herself, check to see if my wallet is still there before I reach into my pocket for the tiny plastic pouch of some unidentified, ivory-colored, powdery substance which I'd stored there. I'd bought it off some kid on the street and never bothered to ask what it was.

As I walk, I undo the string holding the bag and once it's open, I dip my nose into the pouch for a sniff. I pocket the rest.

I don't really think about what I just did or how soon it'll be before it hits because I'm acting on impulse now. I see skyscraper lights now instead of stars, but through my blurry eyes they look the same to me.

Time passes. I feel cold.

I don't know where I am and I don't care. I am a dust mote floating invisible in the shadows of the sun. I am a whisper on the lips of leaves, a vast plain of white. I am Big Dipper. I am the smell of the wind, the sound of a horn on the night, not even the horn itself but the sound of it on the night. Exist and exult. Exist and exult.

I am powerless as a dust mote and as devoid of desire. Powerful, ultimately, because I am powerless.

I am home.

Wonders of the Universe
By Larissa Heron

From a rooftop, I saw a flare
Of moonlit wonder. Spread wings of night
In the universe's blinding light
Which traced my face above the sky.

Like bright silver,
The wandering stars soared through space,
A Milky Way galaxy to embrace.
The universe of planets fills the vastness of life.

The golden sun graces our solar system like a silken band.
Galaxies sweep through space like shattered coral.

Sailing fragments of wonder draw into my spiral
Of Van Gogh's starry night.

Our existing solar system, a spectacle
To sprinkle a moonlit sky
An enchanted garden beyond my eye.
A mystic sight so peaceful to behold.

Dino's Pizza
By Meghan McCullough

We walk from Broadway
To Steinway
To Thirty-Sixth Street
As the sun disappears.
The evening air is smoky blue
And the oil from the pizza seeps across my fingers,
Staining my sleeves.
It shines on her face.
The salt stays in my mouth.
We walk straight and fast
But the steps don't hurt enough
And the cheese is elastic on my insides.
"This is where he filmed *A Guide to Recognizing Your Saints*,"
She points to glass walls
And translucent chandeliers.
The chairs are smooth slippery leather and
I imagine him disappearing into them.
The buildings around us rise
From the white concrete floor beneath our feet.
We are lifted up where I can see that
Everything glitters
With the crisp lukewarm feel
Of the breeze in my nostrils.
Laughter from our throats
Bounces against the skies to stretch them to their limit,
And we are left with the powdery
Fading crust.
The stars will find us
Behind the scenes, creating
Lightning and thunder.

The Girl at the Next Desk

By Xiaoyu Li

"Everything happens for a reason, and I also believe light comes after the storm," says Nicole Garcia. Even though she is only seventeen, she has been through much: raised in a single-parent family in an impoverished city, kidnapped during a home visit, abandoned by her only relative in the United States, and most of all, the lonely separation from her beloved family. It is the bitterness, the strength, and the bravery she possesses that propels her forward.

The beginning:

Nicole is a Mexican-American who grew up in Mexico. She was born in Texas, where her mom and two half-siblings stayed with her aunt. Nicole's mom worked in a restaurant for a living. "Life is hard for a single mother, so when I was two, my mom moved back to Mexico and lived with my grandparents," Nicole explains. Her mother has been a model figure in her life—in her words, "a mother and father at the same time"—who showed her how to be a strong woman by raising three children without a man. When she speaks of her father, Nicole expresses a bit of unease. She lives with a melancholy feeling because she only met him once, at age eleven, and she doesn't have a picture of him as a father figure. However, she feels thankful that she had three beloved parental figures in her life: her mom and grandparents, who filled the empty space of the missing fatherly love.

The extraordinary new journey that took place with one ticket:

On December 17, Nicole arrived in New York City with her suitcases and guitar. For her fourteenth birthday, her aunt offered Nicole the opportunity to stay with her and go to school in the U.S. Consequently, she lived with her aunt's family in a tiny apartment in Crown Heights, Brooklyn. Nicole describes life with her aunt as "no privacy and no freedom," yet she conquered it as she shifted all her energy into schoolwork. Still, there were times when she got homesick. It is hard to be alone and leave family behind. When Nicole missed her mom, "I laid in bed and cried as hard as I could to get things out until no tear was left," she says. But she never thought of giving up and instead worked harder to be the best student in school, because she knew that was the only way she could achieve her dreams. Also, her mom's words, "You are the light I have left," pushed her forward.

The unforgettable summer:

Having not seen her mom for a year, Nicole felt ecstatic when she had the chance to go home. Within a week after she went back, two bandits abducted her on her way home from the grocery store. She is unbelievably calm while she describes this unbearable nightmare: "Two guys yelled at me to stop and pointed guns at me; then they dragged me into the van, hit my forehead with the gun, and taped my mouth shut." She did not try to run or struggle because she knew they would have shot her. The whole event lasted thirty minutes, and in that short period of time, she thought of every possible outcome. Fortunately, the bandits realized they got the wrong person. Before they released her they told her not to reveal a word; otherwise they would go after her family. Anger and hate were not something she felt when she reminisced about that horrible experience; instead she said she was lucky to be alive after all. The most painful moment of the summer was when her aunt told her that she couldn't come back to live with her. At that point, she questioned and cried a lot with her mother. As the summer passed by and she did not hear from her aunt, she worried that all her sacrifices were for nothing and she would never be able to fulfill her dreams.

The rainbow after the storm:

Fortunately, Nicole's mentor from the iMentor program heard of the news and offered her the shelter she needed. Her mom said to her, "We are blessed. We have found the way out of a maze." Currently, Nicole lives with her mentor and other roommates. They get along well and are happy to have each other. After all these phenomenal experiences, she realizes that life is unexpected and wonders why she had to suffer so much compared to her peers. Yet she values more of what she has and believes in second opportunities. She also expresses her hope that she can help others like her mentor has helped her.

The dreams:

Nicole's dream is to become a surgeon. In order to get there, she plans to finish high school with the best academic achievement, and then obtain a four-year degree and go to medical school. Her first dream prepares her for her second dream, which is also her mother's: she wants to reunite with her mom in the U.S. Nicole smiles very brightly as she expresses her dreams.

In this particular girl, I saw a story of hope, bravery, and strength that I hope others can share.

My Father's Office-World
By Julie Polk

If you're looking for a place to raise a kid, you could do a lot worse than an architect's office. My father's consumed the entire third floor of our Philadelphia home. It housed an array of treasures: glittering jewel-toned Windsor & Newton inkbottles with whimsical hand-drawn labels (gangly spider in top hat, tails and eight sets of spats for Black Indian Ink, vivid green solitaire ring with a woman's silhouette floating in the middle for Emerald); boxes of charcoal twigs still bearing the grain and occasional knotholes of the wood from which they'd been burned, crumbly little ghosts of trees; thick rolls of impossibly delicate yellow tracing paper; and, in a separate room under the sloping eave, a small herd of gallon jugs of ammonia leashed with rubber siphoning tubes to a machine that fed my father's drawings through a slot in the top, digested them in a loop around its back and regurgitated two sets of piercingly smelly blueprints. The variety of its contents and heft of its smells gave the place the feel of an old-fashioned emporium, like a butcher shop where nothing got killed.

Letter from Subway Hosts
By Ariana Nicoletta

Salutations, Passengers!

This is a message from your Metro-Voices, workers of the fifth busiest rapid transit rail system in the world, the New York City subway system. As always, we cordially welcome you and advise that you watch where you sit to avoid dirtying the bottom of your pants from the substance on the chairs that came from God-Knows-Where. We offer you subway service twenty-four hours a day, three hundred sixty-five days a year.

As the year has progressed, we, the Metro-Voices, have noticed that many passengers would like to get acquainted with us. Unfortunately, we are unable to converse with passengers due to our Voice-Passenger Motto: "There is no closer friend than a stranger's voice." Seeing us may ruin the pleasure of you, the passenger, enjoying our voices. However, we have all come to a unanimous agreement that you, the willing and paying passenger, deserve to know us a little.

I suppose I will start with my own voice. I am Alfred, named after my idol, Alfred Ely Beach, the creator of this marvelous underground transit system. I am, not to toot my own horn, the crème de la crème of this crop. I talk at a perfect pitch and enunciate every syllable so that my passengers know what stop they are at if the train is about to go local or express or if another train is approaching. I say, "Good morning," "Good afternoon," and "Good evening" with just the right amount of optimism to keep from seeming overzealous and never utter a single word to the passengers. I have been nominated for Metro-Voice of the year four times. However, I have only won three times.

I lost last year. I lost to a voice named Andy, or as I like to call him, Mr. And-I-Am-Not-Popular-Despite-That-The-Passengers-Adore-Me. I hate admitting this, but the passengers do like him. However, he does not do the job conventionally. Andy jokes with the passengers and flirts with the old lady passengers, telling them, "You know, darling. Your brooch and gray hair make my heart pound." At this, they blush and giggle, for Andy's voice is suave and silky (ha, not). He even, dare I say it, altered the train message once. All Metro-Voices are supposed to say, for example, "This is Fourteenth Street. The next stop is Forty-Second Street." Andy had the nerve to switch it. He said the next stop rather than the present stop first! I was beside myself. Yet he won last year, which is unjust if you ask me.

If you have ever gotten a voice that seems to be always laughing, or telling obnoxious jokes, or making gas-releasing noises, I am sorry to say that you were with our classic clown, Oliver (he likes to be called "Ollie", but that is unprofessional. I just refer to him as Oliver). Oliver consistently tells jokes and messes up the train stops on purpose. "This is Fourteenth Street. Ha, no it's not! Gotcha! It's actually Thirty-Fourth Street. Run, you little wiener with the briefcase, run for your train!" Yes, I know that almost all of you have complained about him and I have been intent on having him fired. Unfortunately, our boss thinks that he is a "real hoot."

We admit that there have been some terrible mishaps with the train voices. Rector Street has been deemed Times Square, people have stormed out of the train, and hollered at the intercom. All of this can be blamed on Howie, the klutz of the group. He has a shaky, blubbery voice that is very hard to distinguish over the static intercom. He tries his best, though. It's that bumbling fool Oliver's fault. He is always terrifying poor Howie through his jokes. Once, he told Howie that the entire transit system was under threat of a bomb because apparently that is so funny. Howie was petrified! He couldn't even stutter "Hello" for his passengers. Everyone went the entire day missing their stops, getting on the wrong trains, and becoming severely depressed after listening to Howie sobbing over the intercom.

Finally, we have our foreign member, Rosario. Rosario speaks the three romance languages: French, Spanish, and Italian. The sweetness of his language and the ruggedness of his voice seem to appeal to many of the lady passengers. At first, we were going to fire Rosario because no one could understand him. However, passengers complained that they needed his voice for their lonely single lives. Being on the train and listening to Rosario made them feel like they had a handsome someone to listen to. I thought that this was preposterous at first, but then I listened to him. Even though I am a male, my knees went weak.

We hope this letter will help you feel more comfortable on your train ride. If you have any questions, or would like to contact any of us, see the number below. Thank you all for reading this. We hope that you have a pleasant train ride!

Sincerely,
The Metro-Voices of the New York City Transit System

Saturday Morning

By Mitzi Sanchez

Welcome to Jackson Heights, a place where the short houses feel intimidated by my gigantic concrete building. Eight a.m. on a Saturday morning, the sound of the alarm irritates me. My mom yells from across the room.

"Mitzi, wake up."

"Come on, Ma, let me sleep." I'm already annoyed.

My cozy bed doesn't want to let me go. But wait a minute, the buttery, salty, and savory smell of bacon, egg, and cheese travels across my room and I just can't wait to taste it. I feel the food already in my mouth.

"Mitzi, go to the Laundromat, and buy me a phone card."

She made me eat so fast, I'm stuffed. Still that breakfast was banging.

Suddenly, I hear the grumpy old Colombian lady yelling at the garbage man for no reason. She thinks I stalk her. Seriously. She gets me so frustrated.

The Clorox is nowhere to be found. Doing the laundry pisses me off because I have to wash my sister's and my mom's clothes *and* mine.

"Don't forget about the phone card," Mama screams as if I'm deaf.

The elevator is not working again. This blue cart is too heavy; I have to bump it down the stairs. I try to be calm, but the cart is almost the same height as me. I feel like I'm dragging my sister.

As I pull the door, I see the super with his marine blue shirt and those circular glasses he's always wearing. He's sweeping up. With his husky voice he greets in Spanish. "Buenos dias." I smile and keep pulling the cart out the door.

I see those bald Chinese men again. I turned around and the old Chinese ladies are coming outside, holding big cans of rice and meat, and wearing those hideous polka-dot pajamas. I wonder if they are lining up to get food. They must be homeless or maybe they are relatives. Look at how they smile at each other. Wow, that's amazing. I wonder to myself if they do that in China. That's generous of them. No one else gives out food in Jackson Heights.

It's windy today. I am trying to roll this cart and it got stuck. How I hate this bumpy street. I have four more blocks to walk. I wonder if this cart's going to get stuck again. I hope not—it's embarrassing. Everybody's going to stare at me and make fun of me.

I hope there are no people at the Laundromat, especially those nosy and loud Indian women. They're always there gossiping about everything. Surprise, four of them are here wearing those fancy, glittering dresses. They won't stop talking. Nice, now I have to listen to them. Why are they laughing and looking at me? They must be talking about me. I shake my head and try to ignore them, which is easy since they speak another language I don't even understand. Still, they give me a headache.

Great, my mom didn't give me any money for the laundry. I have to use mine. These quarter machines better be working.

This is taking forever. Finally, forty-five minutes later I fold my clothes and my sister's, and my mom's. Why did my sister stay home? She should be here helping me with the laundry. Damn, she's so lazy.

I grab the cart and head back home.

WAIT! My mom's phone card. There are two grocery stores; on the left and the right.

Which one should I go to?

Umm, on the right corner, the owner is from Poland. He's a really nice man. He always smiles at me when I go, but he barely understands me. On the left, the owner is Dominican. Every time I go there, he gives me this mean, dirty look, and it makes me feel uncomfortable. But he understands my language. I'll go with the nice Polish man.

My mom never told me what phone card she wanted.

Which one should I get? There are so many. Should I get her the $2, the $5, or the $10 one? It's my money; I'll buy her the $2 one.

I'm thirsty, and I need something to wake me up. I should buy me something. Perhaps a little treat, a Monster drink; I love those drinks.

I'm done with the laundry. You know what? I'm going to sit on that old concrete bench and enjoy my drink.

Look who's there. My sister came to help me pull the cart. She brought me an orange juice. Maybe she's not so bad after all.

How to Watch a Sunset in Wolftown
By Jess Pastore

The panorama of the Blue Ridge is spangled out in all its glory when viewed from the front porch swing of the yellow house on the hill at sunset. Golden broom sedge gives way to dark, silhouetted cedars and blends with rising ridges of blue, gray, and lavender that have been marched over by time and Confederate soldiers and every thunderhead the county ever saw. The old swing creaks out its objections as you gaze sideways at the view, and chips of dusty white paint flake off the chain into your glass of tea to bitterly stick to the back of your throat. Don't shift too quickly at the staccato gunshots of target practice echoing off the mountains and up the valley toward you, or the old swing's planks will slip splinters into your bare thighs. Ignore the yells and engine revs and barks of chained hunting dogs which waver and float upstream from the hollow, wrapped in a lazily intense coating of smoke from a grill. Or a trash fire. Focus only on the bruised blue of dusk as it rises from the tree line, and listen for the resident cicadas as they chorus their voices slowly together, ignorant of anything but the fading light. Notice how your neighbors have noticed the coming night, and be glad your house is on a hill, where the sun lingers longer before slipping into West Virginia.

Sway heel-toe and gaze
at ridges designed to be
rednecks' distractions.

Push Tape to Signal for Stop
By Emely Paulino

On Tuesday, January 11, John Valdez crosses the busy intersection of Main Street and Roosevelt Avenue without looking both ways. Before making it to the other side of the street, he contemplates whether or not today is a show day. *Oh god look at that line, I can only imagine what it's going to be like inside.* Without slipping on the remaining ice from the recent snowstorm, he briskly sweeps in front of the first person on the lengthy line for the Q65 bus.

They're watching, he thinks to himself while trying to keep a straight face. *Stop!* His brain shrieks. John sighs heavily, takes a step back as the Q65 opens its doors and lets the passengers out. *I better make this face quick,* John decides. He purses his lips and scrunches up his face as if he took a whiff of something unpleasant. *Popeyes, McDonald's, Burger King, Tai Pan?* "All on the same block," he announces to himself.

"Excuse m—" the woman who was originally first in line begins to say.

"Hmph!" John scowls as he steps in front of her and pays his fare. All the seats on the bus are taken. Shuffling down the tight aisle, John cringes. It bothers him to look at the obscenities keyed into the bright blue plastic where so many people sit. For some time he keeps his head bent down, *Table 2, Table 6, and Table 5 need refills, quick!* until he remembers where he is again. *All of these people are disgusting; I don't know how I've been putting up with this since high school.* Holding on to the top rail, John jerks his left arm. The woman next to him scoffs and shifts away. *That'll teach you. Stay off the bus if you have more than two bags with ya,* he thinks as he relaxes his left arm. Trying to contain a smile, he glares at the man to his right as the bus swerves, nearly causing him to lose balance.

"Do you have a problem, sir?" the man asks John as he checks his watch. Next to him, a senior coughs into his sleeve. John continues to glare, *Kelsey, Sam, August 2006… When would I see them again? This bus always smells like piss, maybe if I twitch like this, ha!* and grunts back into the present. *I'm a pro, pro, produce, professor, Prozac… I don't need that,* shoots his brain. "Sir," the man repeats; but John refuses to speak. Instead he resumes doing what he's been doing for eighteen years. Once in a while, John takes a cab, but that's only when the tips at his job are good. He works as a caterer for a restaurant in Manhattan, and is sick of it. He never eats French food or drinks wine. *Care for another glass, red or white, anything I can help you with? I'm sorry, that won't happen again… red, white, glass, pass, grass, and these people drive me crazy!* Another thing that drives him crazy is the bus.

"Would you like a seat, mister?" offers a girl who looks about sixteen. John looks at her hands, covered in crumbs from the chips she was just eating, and clenches his fists. *Would you like a napkin, Kelsey? When is my stop going to come, for god's sake!* Stiffly he sits down, analyzing the bulky sweaters and stained coats that the people around him are wearing. Looking down, he sees their wet shoes, a result of the slush that has seeped its way onto the floor of the Q65. He crosses his arms and begins to mouth words to himself. *Ha, this will get them to move for sure! Why can't everyone in the bus just leave, leave me alone!*

"Mom, let's sit there!" exclaims a boy, tugging on his mother's jacket. She takes one step forward and hesitates.

"Not there, sweetie, that man is not normal," she murmurs loud enough for John to hear as she ushers her boy to another seat. For a second, he pauses. His thoughts cease to bubble as he blinks at the passengers. "Did they hear that too?" he says aloud. *Not normal, what is she talking about? I am normal, I am… right?*

My Pet
By Emma Straub

My pet, my dearest creature, my fox, my beauty. If you liked, you could run away, scurrying along the baseboards and hurrying out the door, open only a crack, but you don't! My love! It is only the two of us in this big, old house, and when the stairs creak in the middle of the night, I imagine it's you, once again come to life and protecting me from the darkness. When you arrived, your glass eyes still green and clear, I set you on the mantle, where all my visitors could see you. It was only recently—so many years later—that I heard you ask to be taken down, your dusty feet tired after standing for so long. Since then, you've slept in my bed, as you should have from the start. My pet! My sweetest fox! When I close my eyes at night, you begin to howl and bark, your jaw opening wide. I let you close your teeth around my wrist, and when I wake in the morning, I swear that you've left marks on my skin. Someday, I won't wake up at all, and the whole house will be yours.

My Brother's Keeper: Chapter 1 of *Crime and Punishment*

By Ashley Richmond

Brooklyn, 1968

"Bobby! Bobby!" Ma called out to me but I never answered, I was too tired and sore from the night before. I came home at one in the morning. I didn't want to go to school today. I knew that all the kids in Lafayette High knew about last night. It was only a matter of time before one of them opened up their big mouth. If I got caught I would be forced to live with my uncle Curtis, his wife, and my three cousins on a farm in Alabama. If that happened I was going to run away from home, because I wasn't going to stay with my crazy ass uncle and his wife. They were nice people, but they never finished school; all of their boys smelled after they finished working with the animals in the barn, and the most disgusting part about staying there was watching the things they ate. Name anything you could think of really. They ate lizards, squirrels, and turtles! I'm sure there hasn't been anything that they haven't thought about eating. There is no way in hell I'm staying with them, uh-uh.

"BOBBY WILLS!" Ma shouted as she came into my room. I grunted as I pulled the sheets over my head. She took the sheets off of me and jumped when she realized that I had a cut on my forehead and also that I only had on my briefs. I pulled the covers back over me quickly.

"Bobby, what in god's name happened to your face? And why are you in your briefs? Where are the pajamas I gave you?"

"Ma, those were Richie's, I can't…" I said.

She sighed, and then sat on the tip of my bed. "He would've wanted you to have them."

I turned away from her, I couldn't face her eyes. She turned my face to hers.

"Bobby, I know that things haven't been the same for you since Richie died; it's been hard for Sheila, Gina, and me too, but we can't dwell on the past. We have to learn to move on."

"So you expect me to forget about my brother just like that? I can't, I won't. The person who killed my brother is still out there," I said.

"Life isn't fair, Bobby, it never is. But that doesn't explain what happened to your face."

"I fell down on the steps last night when I was taking out the garbage. And my pajamas are in the drawer. Mom, it's too hot in here; when are you going to get someone to fix the air conditioner?" I asked.

"As soon as I get the money to fix it I will, but if you're not going to wear clothes at least lock the door. I don't want one of your sisters to accidentally come in here and see you like that. As for that cut, let me take a look at it."

"Okay Ma, now that I know not to sleep like this, can I please go back to sleep? My head is killing me from this cut. Oww," I said in a sarcastic tone.

"Nice try Bobby, I know you heard me calling you from downstairs and you didn't answer. The next time you do that you're grounded. Now get up, get ready and come downstairs and eat your breakfast. Your sisters are already waiting for you."

After I got ready, I ran down the steps and saw the twins sitting down at the table. Sheila was doing her homework, while Gina was reading the newspaper. Sheila and Gina are my half sisters. We have the same dad, different moms. But I didn't meet them until I was nine years old. Before my dad died we all learned that he had another family with their mother, Debra. She also used to live with me, my mom, Richie, and the twins. We all thought that she was finally happy, but we were wrong. She ran away from us in the middle of the night one day and that was the last time we heard from her, three years ago. Richie's dead now, too. I guess my family just isn't lucky.

"Bobby, you're making us late for school and we're not going to spend another day in detention, because of you." Sheila said.

They were fourteen years old. I didn't know why they just didn't take the bus.

Detroit and the Dominican Republic

By Idamaris Perez and Demetria Irwin

Hey. What are you doing here in the airport?

I just got back from visiting home, the Dominican Republic.

Cool! I just got back from visiting home, too. Detroit.

I didn't even say hi! Hola!

I'll greet you in my native tongue, too. What up, doe? So, what's up in the D.R.? What folks go there
     for?

The tropical beaches, Caribeño breeze that makes you feel at ease
The sun's powerful, welcoming rays kissing your skin
Sapphire waters rising and falling like lovers in the night
A group of men sonand sus guiras, beating their D.R.ums, shaking their
maracas, creating the traditional music of a Dominican beach
Monstrous cotton candy clouds dancing on the sky

In Detroit, our abandoned buildings wobble in the wind
The unseen force travels through empty car factories
Turning fields of knee-high brown grass into graceful hula dancers
Stinging the cheeks of those who stay with its icy kiss
Coney dogs for everyone
We even have a mini-Rockefeller Center called Campus Martius
But what Detroit is really known for is the–

MUSIC

Wait till you swoon to Aventura's romantico, sensual lyrics
"Quitate la ropa lentamente hoy quireo amanecer contigo…"
Sway your hips, move those slender arms to the ritmo of bachata
Groove your feet to the un, dos, tres pa
Let your body keep up with Fernandito Villalona's fast-paced merengue
You gotta—

HUSTLE

If you can't do it and you're from the D
You might as well turn in your Motown card, dog
From the smooth crooning of Marvin Gaye to the head-noddin' Slum Village
beats
To the scatting and riffs of jazz and soul greats who have yet to be
discovered
This is the sound of Detroit

The sound of the D.R. can be like a carnival, full of joy and laughter
A celebration where time's presence does not affect us
Life there can be suave, easygoing
It's like lying in a hammock with your hands beneath your shoulders
But it can also be tough living…

You know, when I think of the Dominican Republic
I think of hair

Chica,
If you want your hair to whip back and forth, you have to go to the Dominican *hair salon*
The thrust of their hands and their magical blowouts
Can have anybody's hair silky straight

I mostly stay in the Big Hair, Don't Care Club
But Detroit divas stay with their "hair did"
In colorful sky-high configurations that require
The skill of an engineer or architect
Not to be outdone, the fellas dumb out too
Pinstriped pastor/pimp suits
With coattails that practically touch their alligator shoes
In every color of the rainbow from Easter pastels to—

LOUD

Spanish barrios, full of obnoxious curses and yelling,
Cars blasting reggaeton songs to their fullest volume
Haitian vendors chiming their bell
"Esquilmalitos, Esquilmalitos!"
Luring squealing chamaquitos with their packs of icies

In my neighborhood, our ice cream truck had gold rims
And it played hip-hop instead of "Pop Goes the Weasel"
Go into any grandmother's house
And it smells like mothballs, cherry blend Black and Milds and greens
You might slip on toys, empty condom wrappers, or old lady pantyhose
The product of grandmothers raising their grands and great-grands
Solid brick homes paid for with auto plant checks
Lawn maintenance and utilities paid for with that side gig
Detroiters are nothing if not—

HUSTLAS

I know some hustlas in the D.R. and not the good kind
Government that needs men with tight pants
Not pants to the ground showing their pitiful, useless shames
Stupid, taunting discriminations against Haitians. Injustice. Mass
deportations of Haitians. Why can't we be good neighbors?
Never-ending blackouts that earned an anthem song called "Se Fue La Luz"

"Pa ra papan se fue la luz. Pa ra papan se fue la luz."
Broken wings, broken D.R.eams because of the country's contaminated education
Excellent education will break down the heavy chains of ignorance and
poverty in D.R.

Detroit politicians tend to suffer from a poverty of integrity
Looking at you, Kwame
Public schools that are little more than gigantic, deteriorating baby-sitters
How can we expect our chilD.R.en to do better
Call the police and it takes four hours if they come at all
My city deserves better
But even with all of that, I love my hometown

I know you what you mean
We have pride in our tricolor roots
The colorful mixture of AFRICAN, SPANISH and TAINO blood!
Our patriotic hearts never stop beating hasta la muerte*!*

Shooot, Detroit all day till the day I die
Detroiters are always the coolest mofos in the room
You know a Detroit playa when you see one
People say hello on the street
And the creative energy in Detroit is immeasurable–

I love the D...*R*

Freedom
By ChanTareya Paredes

It was the breeze that held me captive. As ghost-like tendrils of wind wrapped their arms around my body, I could taste freedom in the air. It was as if God stood over New York and sprayed it with a bottle of perfume called "Be Free." I felt alive on the six-story rooftop of my *abuela's* Harlem apartment building. It was summer and though there was no sun, I felt the night seeping through my pores, igniting wave after wave of pure heat through my bones. The rich texture of the Dominican language from the streets below like an angel's harp to my ears. The blasting of *bachata* from the adjacent building causing vibrations to mix a new life inside of my very skin, expanding my vibrant mocha to a caramel brown.

I remember spreading open my arms, stretching high into the sky, my fingers reaching for anything, everything. I was transforming into the wind, I could feel the soul of New York morphing into a figure, merging with me. I felt it burrow itself deep inside of my heart, nesting itself within the deepest confines of my soul, allowing me to absorb its energy. I felt freedom for the first time in my short eleven years of life. It was as if New York had become a piece of chocolate and I had tried it for the first time, a buttery cream exploding on my tongue. I felt like a New Yorker.

But living in New York and visiting it are two different things, and New York doesn't always embrace the shadows of the darkness allowing the lights of the city to illuminate unspoken dreams. In the morning, harsh realities are exposed in the light, and New York's enchanting night is replaced with life.

VI. IDENTITY

"Dear Diary, It's my seventeenth birthday."

Growing up may be the process of figuring out our identity, who we are—but being grown doesn't mean we've solved the puzzle. This chapter is a collection of poems, memoirs, and works of fiction about the process both girls and women go through to determine who we are, who we want to be, and how to be comfortable in our own skin. The pieces in this chapter shine light on our individual and collective journeys of transformation and discovery. The authors capture the identities we all share—and battle with: who we are proud to be, who we wish we weren't, who we were but are no longer, who we are but won't admit we are, and who others want us to be.

The girls and women in this chapter offer their personal diaries, their advice to others, and their fantastical imagined stories. They ask us and themselves: How do we know who we are? How much do our parents dictate our identity? Do our insecurities define us? Does what we do—or what others do to us—make us who we are? Do we have to act like a girl to be one? Is it our bodies that make us who we are—the crease of our eyelids or the curve our hips? Or is it our mind, our heart, or our spirit that give us real definition?

It is clear that, no matter our age, we all have to remind ourselves of our beauty and our worth sometimes.

—Nora Gross, mentor

Pressure Makes Rough Stones into Diamonds: A Letter to a Young Stone
By Nehanda Thom

Tsk. Tsk. Tsk.

You've gotta be more confident, Nehanda. You could have had these friends a while ago. You were an alley cat longing for their Fancy Feast lifestyles but you realized they didn't prance about like you thought. Maybe it's against the rules to disclose the details of your future to you but…you ended up with the most unexpected person. You finally got that first kiss, from the jock with the never-ending supply of USC T-shirts and Precious Moments cherub eyes that sadden and warm you at the same time.

You don't make the best listener, and that doesn't change much between your time zone and mine. Just hear me when I say: *slow down*. Maturity is not a timed video game with levels of mastery and prizes as you progress.

Be comfortable in your skin. Don't worry about being caught interpreting the imaginary musical score. Read your quirky literature. Wet your hair in thunderstorms. Be proud of your music collection. Have a party and leave Britney at the front door.

Don't hide behind those plastic frames; they don't hide who you are. Don't block the sun out of those stained-glass windows into your Sistine Chapel of a soul.

Don't clip the wings of your voice, regardless of who is listening. Make tangible your melodies and hum with your tight-lipped pout. Leave them in awe of your beautiful angst.

Stop using those heart-peaked lips as armor. Expose your Dentyne smile and let it blind the enemy. It is your deadliest weapon!

Most importantly: Don't let pressure break the diamond. Let it polish it.

Love you more than ever,
Neh

For Me at Sixteen
By Marisa Crawford

Run and don't stop running. Run deeper and deeper into yourself and your body and don't ever, ever turn back.

Do you want a guy with long blond hair past his shoulders who's in a band and loves the Grateful Dead, or do you want a boy with short brown hair and crystal green eyes and poetic tattoos and piercings? You don't have to decide. You don't have to decide now or ever. You will grow up. You will, I promise.

Do you want to wallow in the heavy misery of the entire world that you feel around you if you just let yourself feel, or do you want to leap headfirst into the colors that you find if you ignore the feeling? You don't have to choose.

Stay home. Or, go to the party. Tell the boys with the coffee eyes and the ponytails and the Star Wars sheets and the baseball caps that you have a giant treasure chest filled with candy under your tongue. And they can't have any. Go into your room and close the door. Light a candle for yourself.

This Poem Is About Me

By Yolandri Vargas

Her body was fulfilled with too many wishes,
Developed by too many mistakes,
She may not be the prettiest girl but she hopes to be the type of imperfect you're looking for.
She lives for the moments where she can laugh her nightmares away.
She was beautiful
And she was cool because she herself believed it,
But only in mornings,
Alone in the bathroom.
She, herself, and her
Never I.
She's searching for the goddess in herself
For the young girl she used to be,
For the inner thoughts,
The secret poems in her dreams,
For the beast she's due to be.
She's waiting.
This poem is not about me.

She believes she was born angry.
She once told me,
I am angry,
That a man has the balls to ejaculate through any woman's fallopian tubes,
Achieve physical attraction to her egg
Without truly knowing her,
Without discovering her true value,
Without finding her G-spot.
And he still earns nineteen more cents than her.
She recently began believing in destiny.
But she always believed in the beauty of feminism
She believes in the ground beneath her feet,
That Gandhi is a true G,
Swaraj and *swadeshi*.
She believes you should have Thanksgiving dinner with all your fears.
She is a believer
This poem is not about me.

She barely pays attention to her cell phone,
But she wishes that you would have called her back.
But I'm glad you didn't,
I'm lying.
She waited for your call once,
And again.
She's been meaning to write you a letter.
About absolutely nothing

Just to keep contact
So that you both know that you know that she exists,
Using phrases that don't make sense
Is because she left the bond,
The connection and the Ethernet cable behind on the cheesebus.
She walked away from a boy who sends his promises out to the horizon in empty King's Label
    bottles
She doesn't bother to look that far.
This poem is not about me.

Her vagina likes to be approached in certain ways
It is vulnerable sometimes.
Her vagina is comfortable in its own skin.
It doesn't have a first name, nickname, or last name,
Just a suffix.
There is no guarantee that it will have an interest in you.
It doesn't plan on performing a piece for you,
It doesn't even plan on writing about you,
Ever.
I'm lying.
It already did.
Her vagina has ninety-nine problems but an STI or vaginal infection isn't one.

This poem is not about me,
This poem is not about me
This poem will never be about me
Because I will never admit this.
But I promise to embrace this,
Even if this poem is not about me.

"A whimper escaped from her lips as her knees fell."
—Monica Chin, mentee

A Slight Misunderstanding

By Joy Smith

I wasn't doing anything out of the ordinary. I was just being Joy, being ten at a restaurant and heading to the bathroom. Normally my twin sister, Cherish, would have gone with me because we were always told "go with your sister," but for some reason I went alone.

I dressed how I felt comfortable, in what was my favorite thing at the time. Some girls wore jewelry or tutus. I was in love with my Sprewell jersey and Lee jeans. They were loose and fit in with what the boys were wearing. I was a baller, and to complete my outfit I topped it off with my fitted hat that covered my zigzag braids, and headed for the bathroom.

What was I thinking? Nothing, it was a bathroom, of course other women would be in there, it was no big deal. Despite my attire, I was a girl, and I had full access. As soon as I stepped one foot in the bathroom a lady held her wet hands out as if to stop me and said, "Papi, you're in the wrong bathroom!"

"Huh?" I said.

Suddenly, I was confused and angry and of course embarrassed because, well, people were now looking at me. I was naïve, I realize now. I was at that age where boys and girls were at the same height and my secondary characteristics hadn't developed yet, so it was easy to mistake me as a boy.

Still, a boy was the last thing I was. I didn't think I looked like a boy; besides, I had two earrings in my ear. Duh, boys don't wear two earrings, I thought to myself. As I sat back at the table upset and slightly embarrassed, I whined to my godmother that the lady thought I was a boy and Spanish. She told me it was just a mistake, but I was furious. This lady needed her eyes checked but then Cherish said, "You did it to yourself, Joy. STOP dressing like a boy and no one will think you're a boy. You're not a boy, Joy," she said angrily at me.

I wasn't the one she should be angry at. I was glaring at her. I wanted to burn a hole in her face. The lady already hurt my feelings; I didn't need her hurting mine too. Didn't anyone get that my feelings were bruised? This was a serious situation for me and no one was getting it or trying to make it better. And my own twin at that! She should be on my side. But this was a common statement with her. She always had something to say about my clothing. "Are you really going to wear that jersey again?" Or, "Take that hat off."

From then on I slowly stopped wearing my baller hoodies, fitted hats, and my prized jersey. I would never be mistaken again. Before my transformation was complete I was playing basketball with a group of boys, killing them of course, when a boy asked:

"Are you a boy or a girl?"

I swooshed in a three before telling him, "I'm a girl."

I was never mistaken again.

Glitter

By Tammy Chan

Kid

"When are you going to throw away all those science boards? They're taking up space!" my mom would ask me every time she took out the garbage. I never could quite answer her because a part of me didn't ever want to let them go. It was a collection of four boards, each decorated with construction paper and glitter. They were three years' worth of my brilliantly-and-geniusly-put-together science projects.

Third grade: *Float or Sink.* "Oh this pencil case is definitely gonna sink!" I said. "Yeah right, I bet it floats!" my partner, Kayla said. It sank. I was pretty genius, I'd say.

Fourth grade: *Which Bean Grows the Fastest.* The Lima bean, of course! I was right. Like I said, genius.

Fifth grade: *Do Plants Grow More in the Dark or the Light.* Light, of course! Need I say? Genius.

I was proud of my projects, always boasting about them when I'd have to carry the large tri-board to school the morning of the science fair. It was HUGE, much bigger than my small stature could handle while walking the three long blocks to school. My mom walked beside me, holding my book bag so that I could be a big girl for those few minutes, lugging the board to school all by myself. By the time I'd get to school, there'd be creases near the bottom two corners from the poster dragging along the ground as I walked. But what really mattered—the colors, the glitter, the fact that my guess had been proven—was intact. Bringing them home was just as bad, but what choice did I have? I couldn't just let the teacher throw them away—not after all that effort.

Now

I should have thrown the science boards away at the school, like all the other kids. I'd watch them after the science fair, laughing as they demolished their projects by kicking them, throwing them, and sliding on them across the gymnasium floor. But not me. Three years I did it. Three years in a row I stayed up late decorating the board, adding those last touches of glitter and drawing the final squiggly lines.

Third grade: The classic float-or-sink experiment (or, to sound fancy, "measuring an object's buoyancy"), in which we threw random objects into the tub filled with water and ended up having a mini-water fight in the bathroom.

Fourth grade: Which bean grows the fastest, employing the bootleg method of growing them in a ziplock bag with a square of paper towel and staples to support the beans' roots?

Fifth grade: Do plants grow more in the dark or light? Are you kidding me?

The three classics of science-fair experiments, the ones every kid in the school did. Did they measure my intelligence? Not at all.

I would kill to have projects like those again for school. In high school, there's no more need for crayons, colored pencils, markers, construction paper—and especially not glitter. I miss those days when the hardest assignment you had was a science-fair project. Now it's just papers —black print on a white background. BORING! I used to have time, time to kill—staying up until, at the latest, NINE O'CLOCK! I even daringly stayed up to 9:30 p.m. once, JUST once because I ran out of glue and had to rummage all over the house to find something sticky.

Nothing could have stopped me before, but now—everything could. Time. Work. School. College. Parents. Boyfriend. Friends. Hunger. Coldness. Hotness. Crazy weather. Snow after 70-degree warmth. Nothing to watch on TV. Tiredness. iPhone dying. Forgot my headphones. Annoying buskers on the train—the untalented ones. Wrong-number calls. Wrong-number calls at 4:30 in the morning. No gum in my bag. Broken nail. Bad hair days. Hair not cooperating. No more money on Metrocard. Spending a big chunk of my paycheck on a new Metrocard. Unnecessary random bag frisks in the train station during the morning rush hour AND afternoon rush hour. Fat policemen in their cars blocking the bus stop. No buses in the morning. The twenty-minute walk to the train. Crowded trains. Morning commutes. Tourists. Crappy coffee. Drama. Drama. Drama. Drama queens. Drama kings. Just drama.

Some days it's hard to tell if I'll sink or float.

I Wanna Know
By Mariah Teresa Aviles

I wanna know why,
Why you would do those things just to get by.
It's disgusting how teen girls keep your mind satisfied.
You lick your lips and stare, but why?

Hey, you!
Do you realize what you do?
Scaring little girls?
I mean, yes, we're pearls,
But get a girl your own age;
Someone on the same page.
Calling me out like that makes me feel caged.
Walking through the streets,
Only attractive to creeps,
Just like you.
I mean, it's nothing new,
But this isn't something I should be used to.
I'm just a girl trying to find my place on this earth…
Do you talk like this to the lady who gave birth
To you?
Take a step back and think, or shall you continue?
When a friend calls me in the street,
I can't even look back,
'Cause I'm afraid to get attacked
Or even verbally abused.
After seeing one like you,
My head's all confused.
A woman's worth is like no other.
Think of what it means to see an older man hollering at your sister or mother.

Oh, so now it's a different story?
Something to keep you thinking,
Now your heart's sinking.
Men older than you, seeing your family as prey,
Waiting to come out so they could have something else to say.

It probably happens every day,
But where are you?
'Cause you don't have a clue.
You're here doing the same.
Everything you're doing is fine, yet you really live in shame.
Words do hurt,
And only some brush 'em off like dirt.

Girls, don't let men's words characterize who you are,
Don't let 'em get too far;
Just remember you're a shining star.
The next time a man approaches you,
Don't let him get the best of you.
Walk away,
Don't entertain it or think about what to say.
That's only wasting your time,
Everything will be fine.
Girls, you are beautiful both inside and out,
Let your confidence rise and let no one doubt.
Don't let men's words characterize who you are,
Don't let 'em get too far.

My Voice
By Cindy Caban*

My evil voice sings to you at night; ravaging the beast inside you, awakening your soul, and making you scream and shrill in your bedsheets. Yet when the sun begins to bloom, it becomes tied with innocence, sacred to the bone. Its lovely harmony makes you smile and you follow its melody day after day, wondering if it's real. And as you try to figure it out, my voice begins to shut down as I'm afraid that the dungeons in my world are trying to escape. It slithers across your shoulder making your heart beat faster. Everyone else is afraid, but you ask for more. You look deeper within the black caves and dust. You become wrapped inside my throat and your bacteria starts to engulf me, weaken me. My voice fights back; it lunges you across the walls, spits blood on the surface of your eyes. You begin to reach closer, past my voice and into my mind, where every enclosed thought is written.

There are no barriers to protect myself any longer. You have reached what I've tried so long to keep from the world. You try to understand, try to decode the message that I breathe into my lungs each second but you fail, like everyone else you fail. I am the hidden language beneath your tongue. Read me in Braille, you won't see. Read me in Morse code, you won't see. I am the water that tempts you to jump in, fleeing from reality. As you try to become a part of me, and remain a memory, your desire is filtered back out into the world like a baby with no place to go. My memories try to build up, but they remain stiff, stuck in a times stance. The past is what contains me, sealed in a jar. My memories transcend themselves back and forth, not letting new ones blossom. And even if I can't have them all I'd rather have the ones I began with, to replay the moments that make me not want to escape but relive them. If they were all gone, I'd be nothing, because who are we without our memories but a lost voice looking for an identity?

* Cindy's mentor's piece on the following page shares this title.

My Voice

By Juliet Packer *

My voice is taking a vacation and it didn't leave me an itinerary. I'd like to think my voice is on an island in the Caribbean. There it snorkels among the coral and swims with young seals. There my voice is having a hot romance with another traveling voice. A soothing baritone whose voice is like honey or old single malt scotch. Nothing harsh. A voice like an angel, not a wispy angel, but a male angel with a wide, wide wingspan. His words are like soft sea waves caressing me.

But what if my voice hasn't journeyed to a tropical island? What if it's being held captive by dark forces that want to step on my windpipe and crush it so I can only make gurgling sounds? What if these demons want to sever my fingers so I cannot write? What if they are slimy word-hating creatures that want to invade my imagination and act like idea-eating worms? What if these parasites want to poison my every creative thought so it bleeds mediocrity? How do I cripple them? How do I lure them away?

What if none of this is true? What if my voice is neither on vacation, nor being held captive, but is lying dormant like a volcano gearing up to erupt. A snarl of anger—fingernails on a blackboard. A yowl of destruction—the cries of drowning puppies. What if there is the built-up bile of a lifetime that would scorch those I love, turning them to ash? How can I tame my voice—making it angel-song and not devil-speak? Or does it need to be both—only if cacophony comes first can the notes transmute to a waltz.

Beauties Line

By Ayodele Temple

The ebony of your complexion shows no imperfection
Correction
The contour lines of your face
Show how beautiful is your race
With every blemish
Replenishes
Your cocky demeanor
No reason to frown at that picture
Because
You have such a beautiful
Figure
How I figure
Why don't you just look in the mirror?
Isn't beauty in the eye of the beholder?
Well you are beauty real good with them pretty eyes of yours.

* Juliet's mentee's piece on the previous page shares this title.

The Power of Seeing the Future

By Alicia Maldonado

Vicky always thought she was normal, no different from any other person she knew. As she laid her head down onto her soft, marshmallow-like pillow, her mind just suddenly took off as if it was a car racing 100 mph on the highway. Suddenly it stopped and Vicky was welcomed into a world of sadness and lack of sunlight. She became frightened and worried but then she saw a familiar face. It was her mother, Laura, who she only saw in pictures because she had passed away giving birth to Vicky. She ran toward her screaming, "Mom, it's me Vicky!!! Mommy!" Laura just disappeared and left Vicky in a state of shock. Then her mind started to race again through time. She saw her birth, her first steps, and then she saw herself as a mother with her husband sitting by the fire. Vicky knew that she couldn't have dreamt or imagined this. It was too realistic for her, so it was at this very moment that she understood that she was able to see the past, present, and future.

Vicky promised herself that she would not abuse her power, no matter what. She became curious about her future, even though she wondered whether looking into the future was abusing her power.

She closed her eyes and saw herself in an amazing white dress with lace and flowers all over it. She also saw her father walking her down the aisle, to the priest, and before her was her future husband, Aaron, a boy she had known all her life.

As Vicky heard the priest say, "I now pronounce you man and wife," the vision stopped. Someone interrupted her vision and she didn't know who it was. "Why would someone want to mess with me, I haven't done anything wrong?" she thought. Then all of a sudden she was racing into the past again. Vicky stared at a monument of a man who was famous for his powers of seeing the future. Vicky read the small writing on the bottom. It said: "This man was punished because he abused his power."

Vicky then saw a man with beaming red eyes and an evil smirk. "I am Lawrence," he said. "I am the man who gave you these powers. I am giving you two choices: either you give up these powers or you give up the ones you love."

"What have I done?" she thought to herself. She didn't want to give up her powers, but neither did she want to give up the people she loved. Vicky wanted to ask her mother to help her, to give her a sign showing that no matter what she decided everything was going to be okay and that her mother would always be her guardian angel.

A week passed by as she spent every second, minute, and hour deciding what she was going to do. Then she heard her mom's voice in the distance. "Mom," she said as she turned around trying to find the source of this. Suddenly she was face to face with her mother that she had never met. Vicky began to cry and hugged her mother as Laura said, "Vicky, I love you and no matter what choice you make I will always be here with you in your heart."

"Thank you, Mom," Vicky said as her mother disappeared for the last time.

Vicky became strong and powerful and said, "Lawrence, I will give up my powers for the ones I love." As she stood on a cliff waiting for him to take her powers away, another vision came to her. It was a scene of her and Aaron, her husband, becoming old together looking over the horizon and holding one another, and she knew everything would be all right.

Genevieve

By Erica Dolland

It is at the darkest hour where breath and memory coincide as one—irrespective of its inhabiter. Bystanders menace in preoccupation with the whereabouts of the day's lost soul now sheathed in disguises. Just before the candlelight surrenders in resolve and the songstress murmurs her final note, the moonlight snakes in secrecy along the ceramic floor and crawls the first step on the spiraling banister. Her bare toe extends the glassed sole; its blackness scratches the pavement.

"Genevieve, we've been waiting," whispers a faint voice.

She turns with a swift twist of her neck only to be greeted by the lemony mint that kissed the air before its departure.

"Only in the presence of others."

Her crow's beak cleared the walkway to the center of the dance floor. Eyes shifted toward her long extended crow's beak that dismissed scornful glances. The evening's assembly of Versailles High School classmates' costumes tiptoed on the obscure but tripped in comparison to Genevieve.

"There's only one song left," her older sister Alexandria whispered in her ear.

"So!"

"So, you are late! The masquerade ball started an hour ago. Where have you been?"

"I… I…"

"You nothing. Let me see your hands."

Genevieve tried to brush her fingers against the velvety black-draped dress that bulged and contoured her slim waist. She stretched her long-nailed fingers and placed them in front of her sister's face in surrender.

"So what if I did," she replied. "All animals want liberation. It's my job to set them free. I hear the tigress purring in you. Why don't you scream and let her out?"

Genevieve let out a loud hollow that punctured the sound of the milky cello that belted in the background.

"Freak is your name," Alexandria said walking away.

She shifted the weight of her silver satchel to her front and reached for her red lipstick. Its moistness stretched to the corner of her full lips. They twitched in excitement in anticipation of the game that awaited.

The cackle of girls retreated in foolish gossip and sly whispers. Genevieve's ears dismissed their penetrative pursuits. The sound of the music led her to a dark corner where she waited as a predator does to stalk its prey.

Memory Loss

By Amanda Berlin

I'm not going to say I've lost my entire memory. There are some things I remember:

I remember Andrea writing "I hate you" in the dust on my dad's car when we were little and in a fight. And how her dad used to cut their lawn really short so we could see where their dog pooped and avoid it.

I remember kissing my uncle Sidney on the cheek, after avoiding his juicy smooches for years and realizing how squishy his cheeks were and how much that kiss probably meant to him.

I remember how cold the rec room was and how I used to wear a backward button-down shirt as a smock to keep the paint off my clothes.

I won't say I've lost my memory entirely, because I remember these things, and I know it's not because they were captured on film or co-opted from an episode of *The Cosby Show*. But there still seems to be an entire swath of my memory missing.

A whole collection of memories has been replaced, not with blankness, but with memories I am not sure are my own.

I have an image of myself in our old house. It's empty. We're moving. And I am sitting in front of my dollhouse. It wasn't a grand do-it-yourself dollhouse with shingles and wainscoting. It was a pre-fab, two-bedroom that I took to decorating with those little tables they stick in your pizza box to prevent the cardboard from collapsing onto the cheese. In this memory, I am playing with my dollhouse until I am told it is time to go. I get up, take one last mournful look, and leave. This feels like my memory. But more likely it's the series finale of some sitcom masquerading as something that happened in my past. Memories like this have woven their way into a swatch of my life that I can't even be sure was my own.

For something to exist, you need someone to bear witness. So, while this time in my life, before I had siblings, was more my very own than any time thereafter, its existence is questionable because there's no peer with whom to reminisce. There's no one to share containment duty. No one to reflect the image of the collective experience back at you.

I remember sitting under a tree at a little snack table with my friend who I think was called Michael. But I know there's a picture of that. He's wearing stripes and I have pigtails.

I remember my mother's junior high school math student coming to visit us. We sat in the back-yard. But because I can see her feathered hair and high-top Reeboks, I am pretty sure those details were recalled from Kodachrome.

When we moved, I was six, my sister was one-and-a-half, and my brother was an infant. And the only things I can remember for sure from before are those captured on film.

When I Cry
By Massange Kamara

I cry because I need to
I cry because my heart is torn apart
I cry to free my heart from insanity
I cry because it's hard to survive
I cry because depression has reigned over my life
And I can't move on
I cry because I'm hurt in and out
I cry because I'm in a battle with myself
That I'm not winning
I cry because I'm on my own
I cry because I feel desperate
I cry because every single drop of my tears carries a message of
Sorrow, relief, and forgiveness
I cry because I'm pissed off
I cry because something is eating me up
I cry because I don't feel safe
I cry because I'm annoyed
I cry because I hate to cry
But I need to

Rainbows and Fire
By Mariah Fuller

Rushing up the hill
To see the rainbow in the sky
And witness the clouds floating on by.
But it all comes to an end.
This fantasy isn't real.
I hear explosions
Booming again and again in the empty field.
Look at the flowers
Swaying in the air
Heat begins to shower
And then they suddenly flare.
The scent of sweet
Has gone away
Smoke circles from the ground beneath my feet
And I perish under the sun's ray.
Ashes are what remain
In this world of desire.
With reality in vain
Through rainbows and fire.

Red Control
By Ashley Simons

Dear Diary,

   It's my seventeenth birthday. My grandmother gave you to me a couple of days ago. It's weird because I've never had a diary before. I snuck up to my room for a while to write in you.

   I want to tell you about myself. I am an African-American girl with jet-black hair. I was also born with ruby red eyes, which is peculiar since NO ONE in my family has them. My parents say that it makes me special. You would have thought that I would be a social outcast with my uncommon eyes, but no, I'm the most popular girl in school. I live in a small town where everybody knows everybody. But I've got to admit, it gets pretty boring in this town most of the time.

   I've had a strange pain in my eyes for the past week, but when I went to the doctor, he said there was nothing wrong with them. Then today, the funniest thing happened. The pain just went away, like magic. I feel like this is a special birthday…

Love,
Andrea

■ ■ ■

   "Make a wish, honey," Andrea's mom said as she snapped a picture. Andrea looked around, seeing the smiling faces of her closest friends and parents, all gathered for her small party. She knew exactly what to wish for. *I wish for an exciting year*. Andrea took a deep breath and blew out the candles. Everyone cheered.

"Happy birthday, Andrea!" her best friends, Serena and Jackie, said.

"Thanks, you guys!" After the cake, Serena and Jackie went home. After all, it was the first day of school tomorrow and they had to look amazing.

■ ■ ■

"Wake up, Andrea!" her mom shouted from the bottom of the steps the next morning.

"Mmmmm," Andrea moaned sleepily and rolled over on her stomach in the bed. Suddenly, cold water splashed on her head. Andrea bolted up soaking wet and saw her mother standing over her with a bucket in her hands.

"Mom!" Andrea shouted.

"I told you to get up twenty minutes ago. I thought that this year would be different and that I wouldn't have to pour water on you. Now hurry up or you'll be late for school."

"Stop pouring water on me! And leave me alone so that I can get dressed." Normally, Andrea would have been punished for talking that way to her mom, but instead she turned around and walked out of the room.

Andrea got dressed in blue jeans and a light-blue top. To finish off the look she put the silver, heart-shaped locket that her parents gave her for her birthday around her neck. Inside the locket was a picture of her parents on one side and one of her, Serena, and Jackie on the other. She checked her reflection in the mirror one more time before going downstairs.

"Are you going to eat breakfast?" Andrea's dad asked.

"I'll just take a muffin to go." She grabbed a chocolate chip muffin, got into her car, and drove to John McKindle High School. When she arrived, she was immediately surrounded by other students asking her how her summer was and showering her with compliments on her outfit. People were always surrounding Andrea, wanting to be able to say that they knew her, or touched her, or talked to her. She politely asked them how their summers were and made small talk. As more and more people started coming over, she began to feel restricted. She'd always been claustrophobic.

"I need to go," Andrea said. She was through with politeness, she just wanted to get out. "Get out of my way," Andrea told the two boys in front of her. The boys parted, making a small opening. "Move, move!" she kept telling people until she finally broke out. She immediately saw Serena and Jackie and bolted over to them. She told them about how hysterical she got when she was in the crowd. They both hooked their arms in hers.

"Let's go get our schedules," Jackie said calmly. They walked into the school and went straight to the table by the by the main office.

"Andrea Jennings, Serena Banner, and Jacqueline Richards," Serena told the lady in charge of the table. The lady gave the girls their schedules, and they quickly huddled together to compare them.

"We have almost every class together except Math and English," Jackie said. The girls gave each other a disappointed look. Suddenly a boy with black hair, a black jacket, and sunglasses stepped up to the desk.

"My name is Jeremy Lansing." The lady gave him his schedule. He looked up and saw the three girls looking at him, then turned and walked away.

"He is really hot," Serena said fanning herself with her schedule.

"And obviously new," Jackie added. "I've never seen him before."

"Mmhmm," Serena and Andrea agreed.

He was very cute, Andrea thought, but for some reason she couldn't shake the idea that there was something off about him. She was very curious about this new stranger.

(To be continued…)

Tik Tok

By Kirthana Ramisetti

The newspapers got it wrong. I'm not crazy, and it wasn't random.

It started on Sunday, when I stopped in at H&M to return a neon-pink dress that looked beautiful on the hanger and abysmal on my skin tone. Then the Ke$ha song "Tik Tok" came on, taunting and insistent, like a nursery rhyme gone slutty. Unfortunately, the cashier line was stretched to the back of the room, and I had lost my iPod earbuds the week before, so I was trapped listening to it.

On Monday, guess what began playing as soon as I got into a taxi? In vain, I pressed the "off" button on the screen, but the video just kept going, the grating, sing-song voice this time accompanied by a montage of models walking down runways.

"Can't you turn this off?" I said, banging on the window.

The driver just shrugged, so I had to endure it again. As a result, I couldn't get the freaking song from tick-tocking in my brain the rest of the night.

On Tuesday, that YouTube video of Betty White singing "Tik Tok" went viral, and it was everywhere, from *Good Morning America* to *Late Night with Jimmy Fallon*. Co-workers watched it in their cubicles. My mom even forwarded me the link, with the subject line "Have you seen this? You will LOL."

Have you heard of tinnitus? When people can't stop hearing ringing in their ears? Mine was Auto-Tuned. What once felt like an unhappy coincidence now felt like a war being raged against me by a pop star destined for *Celebrity Rehab*.

So by the time I got to the subway on Wednesday, I was in a frazzled state. I was running late for work, and thinking up excuses that would fly with my boss, when my phone rang. I picked it up and heard: *Wake up in the morning feeling like P Diddy/Grab my glasses, I'm out the door, I'm gonna hit this city*

In that moment, I thought I was dreaming. Ke$ha had turned into my boogeyman, infiltrating my dreams, and I had to wake up. I ran up the steps and out of the subway. I spun around in a daze, wondering what would wake me up, when I fell back into someone.

"Watch where you're going, loser." I turned around and there before me stood Ke$ha, wearing a silver lamé bodysuit, green eyelashes, and a smug smile. I screamed. I felt like I was experiencing some kind of *Nightmare on Elm Street* dream terror, and the only way to escape was to take down my Freddy Krueger. I'm told I landed a punch on her left ear. I really don't remember this—I think I blocked out everything after I saw the ghastly eyelashes.

So no, it wasn't a random act of violence by a crazy woman. I mean, you can see how I was driven to the edge. You've heard the song, right? You understand.

"I wasn't doing anything out of the ordinary. I was just being Joy..."
—Joy Smith, mentee

Id

By Vani Kannan

When I first read about the id
it came to me that night, a neon purple
ring around a mug inside my skull,
daring me to drink but never teaching me to stop

and as I saw it then, there were three ways to go:

to dance along the edge, and to
ignore the place where purple
fades to porcelain; to

cup your hands and hope
the burning liquid warms them up
without your even trying; or

to plunge in and retrieve it,
dripping blood like raw steak
on a clean plate that you've
never liked the pattern of. But

you said, simply run a tongue
along the edge. Learn to stop
relying on what others'
tastebuds tell you.

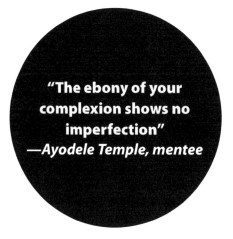

"The ebony of your
complexion shows no
imperfection"
—Ayodele Temple, mentee

Why Do I Have to Choose...
By Yvonne Ndiaye

You wasted fifteen years of my life moving me around neighborhood to neighborhood, country to country, continent to continent. I don't think you know how it hurts to not have a longtime relationship with anyone, knowing that you will leave without saying good-bye.

I don't think you understand that I'm nineteen and still in high school because of you. I don't think you understand that I need a life with people and joy in order to get by. I don't think you know what it feels like to grow up away from your parents in the middle of somewhere you don't belong. You have to listen: I don't hate you or your family but I'm not accustomed to your beliefs. It is not to embarrass you but I think I have the right to choose what I want and need.

Why do I have to choose between Mohamed and Jesus?
Why do I have to choose between Hallelujah and Alhamdoulilah?
Why do I have to choose?

What is the difference?
At the end of the day you still believe in God.
Either way, Islam or Christianity, we all are going to be judged the same way.

Why do I have to choose between Mummy and Daddy?
I'll choose Mummy anyway
But why can't I have both?

I'll pray with both religions. I'll celebrate both religions.
Because I think I don't have to choose.

I believe anyhow God will love me
I believe anyhow people will love
I believe anyhow people can't tell that I have to choose

They can't tell
They can't tell if I'm Muslim or Christian
They can't tell what I am
Who I am
Only God can.

But I chose a mother, education, and freedom.

Chinese Food on My Chapped Lips

By Lucy Tan

The hollow space below my soles set my feet free and my sandals hung off my ankles by their Velcro straps. I was little, I thought. My legs swung back and forth aimlessly, hoping but not wanting to reach something unknown in the void below the round table. I flailed my loose bare arms around and placed them on the shoulders of the two people next to me. On the left was my father, with his elbows resting on the edge of the table and on the right, my mother, devouring the food that streamed toward us with the help of waiters running like worker ants.

I didn't want to eat the mysterious food put upon the table. I stared at the china saucer before me; for such a small dish, it held blotches of a venomous substance—bright yellow, shocking red, sickly green clumps of what could possibly be mistaken for the piercing eyes of poison tree frogs. Nanny leaned her elbows upon the edge of the table and Cousin Andy played with the tablecloth. There came a rumble and bump, as the dishes wobbled in place. Murky puddles of soy sauce trembled in place around pieces of roasted duck the same way I trembled from the uneven bursts of icy restaurant air conditioning.

I'm ungrateful, too ungrateful. "The Lightning God will strike you one day," my grandmother professes. There is no such thing as the Lightning God. "Disobedient child!" I swallow the soggy mushrooms and the nights pass, as they always do, with the stars above as witness to what ill acts I've committed.

I placed these things in my stomach mindlessly. It was a duty to please my mother, my father, and my grandmother due to the hard work and perspiration my grandmother expends for two hours every night, mixing and matching various groceries from the refrigerator, feeling the rising steam on her carved face. I was little and the world ended at the edges of my daily routines. I did not have plans; I was dependent and always at the command of others.

The reluctance of obeying duties gradually began to strike me. It lived in my gut and every time I seemed to enjoy the food I was devouring, a part of me knew that eating was not pleasurable.

Eighth grade, the year before high school started, was the last year I had any spare rooms in me. Slowly, but surely, all the rooms became inundated by visitors, some staying longer than others, but all in constant demand for some part of me. They rented my taste buds, my throat, my stomach, and eventually when they needed every square inch, the only guest they allowed in was wind for airing out their rooms.

Now, looking at myself in storefront windows, I see someone running from one place to another, always too busy, too wary of wasting minutes of my time on unnecessary ventures. Food, whenever eaten, is often distasteful and seems to only be a means of comforting grumbles; the air rushing into my stomach from my fast-paced life, burning my esophagus, is often enough.

With Chinese food on my chapped lips, I rush out of my house to greet the world.

Once Obedient Now She Makes Trouble

By Tamiko Beyer

When finally she learned that pure order does not make happiness she went out into a lightning storm.

The chance of being struck was so small and so spectacular. Full tilt, she inscribed chaotic patterns on the sky's wettest night. Already, she could smell the heady mix of electricity and flesh.

::

A new hat no longer kept her satisfied for days. Searching for a new position, a different way to say. She fashioned a voice from steel and river mud, and soon it was the largest course of pleasure at the back of her throat.

::

Her privilege started to hairline crack—fine tiny sores—and she decided to form complete sentences with invisible clauses, without suffocation.

Nationality indicates position, she said. To question one's place on the grid is to tip the scale, if only a little. What if we all formed our mouths into questions marks, she asked... and wondered who was listening.

She dreamed catastrophe: a mountainside devouring the highway—mouth of mire, boulders, split trees.

::

The weak winter sun—useless drapery. Caught by her sweet tooth, her insatiable need, she turned this way and that. It tore her.

Used to adoration, she wanted now her lovers' nails down her back. Scalpels cut precisely.

Lip to tongue curled. Her back arched into other bodies and she made unpolished sounds. Not beautifully, her sternum vibrated all the way down to the most concentrated place of her hunger.

::

The seasons were skewing. She glanced at her serious watch, the one that looked like the landscape of winter progression. Counting birds that fell from the sky.

Hands against spring snow, she thought about the hot, dry summer to come. If only she knew how to plant potatoes or leafy greens. Her year away from cities had been a failure. To prepare for the end, she bought a hammer and a bucket.

She raised her arms puffed in down and stop-rip fabric and a new lover stepped into them.

::

A sparrow perched on the stoplight. It sang and she could hear it as well up close as from very far away. This was in the city where the trees are not spectacular, but it was strangely quiet just then. No bodies.

::

The pattern proves to be the key, she said, the connecting force, a form repeating itself in cells, in the organism's body, and then in society. Everyone in the cities bending down to touch their knees and toes.

When she flew her kite the string tangled in wires and the mayor made stern words at her. She slid a soup tureen across the floor at the ten-grand-a-plate fundraiser. Security couldn't say how she got in.

She had sashayed and was lovely in cuffs.

::

She cut her lip because of the dryness in the air. Then came the tornados. All the pieces were there, not there. Her family of lovers surrounded her in their own mud house. She knew what they were was impossible.

Healing
By Monica Chin

There was a buzzing noise coming from within her. It seemed to get louder as she neared the dusty radio on the counter next to the cash register. The roaring din gave off vibrations through her whole body, and she heard clicks and shrieks coming from the speakers. She looked around, wondering what was going on. Bags of chips were sitting on the shelves; milk and drinks were in the refrigerators; everything seemed to be normal. The subtle vibrations lapping against her skin soon became sharp, invading her fingers and toes. The other customers continued to shop, minding their own business. But she spotted the cashier staring at her, alarmed.

Does she hear it too? she thought. She walked over with a gallon of milk, expecting the cashier to tell her it was all a joke.

Sternly the cashier asked, "Can I help you with something else, honey?"

Laura choked out a "no" and retrieved a crumpled $5 bill from her pocket. She staggered out of the store, leaving the change and milk on the counter. The sizzling heat made beads of sweat run down her forehead. Dragging her feet to the steps of her front door, she felt dizzy and confused, as if she were in a trance.

What was that buzzing noise? she thought. The soft jingle of keys snapped her back into reality. When she opened the door, the blast of air was like a cool drink to her lips. Wiping away sweat, Laura suddenly remembered the milk.

"Laura! Did you buy the milk? I need it for the casserole I'm making for dinner!" her mother called from the kitchen.

"Uh, oh no, shoot! I forgot! Sorry, Ma," Laura called out, heading into the living room.

Her mother's head poked through the doorway. "What? I can't believe you! I reminded you before you went to school! Now I have to go get it. I didn't water the garden yet so make yourself useful for once!" her mother yelled while storming out.

Laura glared at the door as it banged shut, and tramped into the garden. White and purple petunias, pink lilies, yellow orchids and other beautiful plants littered the soil. Laura usually admired her mother's precious garden, but today she wanted to scream at it, to tell it it wasn't her fault for forgetting the milk. The fiery heat added to her frustration, and anger poured out of her like a tiny dam exploding from the weight of the ocean. She was never useful to her parents, never perfect like her older sister.

She lashed out at the innocent flowers, kicking and screaming. Then a gust of wind pushed her down, knocking her out of breath. Her stomach began to churn and bile worked its way up her throat. Her head was buzzing again, just like in the deli. Her body ached all over, as if it had formed bruises. Stiff and pained, Laura slowly got up and saw the mess she had made of her mother's garden. **A whimper escaped from her lips as her knees fell.*** She gently gathered the dead flowers and torn petals in her hands.

Tears sprang to her eyes as she remembered why her mother cared for these flowers so kindly. The small plaque in the center with a picture of a smiling teenage girl with light hair and light-blue eyes was her older sister, Mary. The plaque was still in its plastic casing; she had died only five months ago. Laura's tears splattered all over her summer dress. They overflowed into puddles, dripping down her chin onto the dry soil. The pain lifted away her hatred and frustration; she felt calm for the first time since the accident. Holding the limp bud of an orchid, she closed her eyes and pictured her sister watering the plants in her pink gardening gloves, smiling at her. She felt nothing but the flower resting in the palm of her hand.

Her mind went blank for a second. Then an explosion of colors and images of water, fire, wind, and earth sent her head reeling. Her fingers became warm as if someone was touching them, then burning hot. In her mind she saw the image of the sun. The simmering colors blinded her. She could feel its radiance against her skin, flooding her body with sweat. She opened her eyes and looked down at the orchid still lying in her hand. Her shoulders hunched as she kneeled despairingly.

"Laura! Did you water—Oh my god!" her mother gasped from behind her. Tearful, Laura glanced back to say she was sorry. But the look on her mother's face was not anger or bewilderment but jubilation. Her eyes, too, were watery and she was covering her gaping mouth. Laura snapped her head the other way and saw the garden. The flowers were so vivid and bright it was like they were newly born. All had their petals and leaves; they stood up tall with their buds facing the sky. The soil was dark brown and damp, as if Laura had watered it.

Healing
By Elaine Stuart-Shah

A whimper escaped from her lips as her knees fell.* With pain shooting up her left leg, she collapsed onto the floor. Blood rushed to her head as she clutched her ankle; she feared she might faint. The concave groove between her lower calf and heel grew soft and gummy in her hands. She watched it inflate like a balloon.

Other dancers began to gather around her—a scuffle of footsteps, a swirl of short, chiffon skirts. Their muffled voices blended with the chords of classical music playing in the studio. Fingers trembling, she unlaced the pink satin ribbons of her pointe shoe and slowly pulled it off. The elastic band stretched over the swollen patch of skin.

* Monica and Elaine, mentee-mentor pair, shared this line.

She couldn't possibly have heard the crack. But the sound was echoing over and over again in her mind: a clear, sharp snap. Everything else around her seemed distant, fallen into relief. She stared at the ankle that had been bothering her in technique class and rehearsals for months. The doctors had lectured her about the danger of repeated cortisone shots to an inflamed area—how the medication could mask the body's warning signs and lead to a far more serious injury. But she was on the brink of a professional ballet career, so close to realizing her childhood dream. She had just turned eighteen.

The next morning she learned the extent of the damage. The stress fracture would require surgery to remove the small piece of bone that had chipped clean off. There was irony in the location where it had lodged: her Achilles heel.

They told her about the long, slow process of recovery. A summer spent in bed, then on crutches, in a cast, in an orthopedic boot, in daily physical therapy. She wanted to know when she could dance again. They said after she relearned to walk.

When she awoke from the operation her foot felt foreign, numb. Hollow.

Today a sliver of a scar remains, a faint crescent-moon tattoo commemorating the moment her life changed. *This is the way the world ends. Not with a bang but a whimper.*

Repentance... An Excerpt From *The Details We Fall For*
By Michaela Burns

This piece details how a family in 14th century Europe takes desperate measures to fight off infection from the Black plague. Setting is the outskirts of London, September 1348.

"Psalms 106:29: Thus they provoked [him] to anger with their inventions: and the plague brake in upon them."

The leather whip brutally shreds the already purple bruised skin on his back into wispy ribbons. He had been resistant at first to what his father had labeled the "necessary" mortifying of the flesh, but in the end he had hesitantly consented, if only for the family's universal safety from the plague. His stripped prostrate body sags against the otherwise bare stone tiling as the punishment in God's name continues.

Yet, unlike the old days when his mother would have been concerned about preserving the sanitation of the household, the staining of the floor raises no horrified response from her. Instead, she preoccupies herself with quoting passages from the Bible in tandem with the strikes of the scourge, lest her temperamental husband turn the whip on her again. She leans heavily against her eldest and sturdiest son, who also drones Bible verses, her starved and gaunt body too weak to support itself on her own. Both persons had forgone their clothes and now stood in the chilly air with nothing more than shapeless sackcloths covering their abused bodies. Their swaying figures, silhouetted by the room's lone candle, resemble the movement of grass blades when blown by the force of the wind.

Rivulets of crimson blood leak in torrents from the numerous gashes that decorate the surface of his physical body, but also seep through his pressed lips and down his chin, pooling at the place where his forehead meets the floor. For, in an effort to contain his screams, his chattering teeth had bitten right through his tongue.

As the night wore on, and the strap raked mercilessly at every inch of visible flesh, his screams grew audible. The sound first gurgled with the swallowed blood in the base of his throat, before building in crescendo, and finally echoing from cracked lips into the cramped living space. Louder in tempo than it would usually be, perhaps because of the lack of furnishings that remained. Its high pitch clashes harshly with the soft murmuring of biblical text.

This breach of established discipline causes the father, previously fixated on his arduous task, to pause. He adjusts the leather strap in hands heavily calloused from work in the fields slowly, careful not to agitate his own marked flesh. With a flex of his beefy left arm he resumes his task. It is clear to the observing party that the next slash of the whip is fueled with malicious intent.

"YOU ARE NO SON OF MINE… You ungrateful wretch! God has given us a chance to repent and you protest?"

The incessant chanting halts at the screech of his voice, neither observing individual willing to change the course of his relentless rage.

Whish… Crack… Whish… Crack… Whish… Crack…

"I should leave you to rot like the rest of the town. Or do you think to save yourself with the advice from that lying priest?" His hysterical voice ricochets against the stone walls. The oldest son, whose eyes had long turned from the pitiful and bloody sight of his brother to flick around aimlessly, flinches at his father's shouts. He speculated that the earsplitting bellows could probably be heard throughout the entire village. That is if anyone in the plague-infected town had the ear to hear misery besides his or her own anymore.

The mother watches in silent horror. The internal struggle of whether to help her son or protect herself is mirrored on her face. In the end, self-preservation wins out. She reasons that sooner rather than later her youngest and frailest son will probably die of the Plague anyway. However, even with this rationalization, her wide eyes continue to spill tears, and her bottom lip faces the assault of stained chattering teeth. She tightens her grip on her oldest child's arm; shaking fingers grasping desperately at the sinewy unclothed limb.

"Foolish child," he snaps scornfully. "God sends us the Plague because of our sinning. Prayer alone is too simple. To stop the plague we must mortify our physical bodies."

Whish… Crack… Whish… Crack…

"No possession or bodily need is greater than the necessity of preserving the soul. Yet perhaps I waste my time on one such as you, who was born a corrupted being. God has already condemned you with lack of strength and idleness of mind. Perhaps even the actions I take are not enough to fully purify you and protect you from the Black Plague."

Whish… Crack… Whish… Crack…

The sharp copper stench of spilled blood pollutes every pocket of air in the room and wafts into the nostrils of its inhabitants. The full immersion of such a repugnant smell causes the mother and oldest son to hastily shrink away from the source. But the father doubly renews his effort to mortify his son's flesh and expel any sign of weakness. He continues the whipping in harmony with his son's discordant screams.

Whish… Crack…
Whish… Crack…
Whish… Crack…

Teacher vs. Student

By Nora Gross

I fight my soul to defeat its unkindness…*

Lately, this has been happening every morning.
As I awake leisurely whenever my body decides it's ready,
I argue with myself: does my day still have purpose?
Will I do something important today?
Am I becoming just plain lazy?

Just one year ago, my mornings were quite different.
I would be jolted awake to my alarm, five a.m.,
I willed myself into readiness for twelve hours of teenagers:
Twelve hours of teaching and learning, praising and disciplining,
Following a student into the hallway to catch her tears,
Stealing off to the bathroom for a moment of quiet.
I would come home…exhausted, but rewarded.
Stay up til all hours planning lessons, reviewing progress, caring.
I knew it:
I   was   making   a   difference.

Now, I find myself again on the other side of the classroom.
I read endlessly, I write papers only my professors will read,
I go to conferences, share my opinions, "network,"
I observe, I think… often deeply, sometimes not,
I discuss big issues:
Like, the way poverty reproduces itself,
Why some students feel disconnected from school,
How to fix our education system.
But what am I *really* doing?
Grad school, schmad school…

Perhaps that's the problem: how can I get anything done with that attitude?
How can I think and talk about the big ideas when part of me is always saying:
This is not important,
        It's not meaningful,
        You should never have left the *real* work you were doing.
How can I possibly expect to find answers or solutions if I'm always questioning myself?
Who is to say I am not   making   some   kind   of   difference   right   now…

So for now, I'll continue to fight my soul each morning,
In the hopes that I can defeat its unkindness and make this *kind of difference, whatever it is…*

---

*   Nora's mentee's piece on page 52 shares this line.

Spanish Woman

By Brittany Barker

This is for the Latina woman with the shattered hands
For the days when the morning's peak isn't too far from beautiful
And her palms are just the way you've left them

She is the most assuring woman to wake up to
She chases the nights away
Raises sons

Scientists still wonder what keeps the stars apart
Women wonder why the stars never fall in their direction
Why the men cannot unravel themselves into something equal

When it comes to identity and independence
There is no such thing as equilibrium
Its Misogyny
Sexism
Marginalism
Virgin or Whore

What ever happened to recognition—
For the mother who has enough testosterone to show her three sons how to be real men
Respect
For the strong-backed woman with the broad shoulders
Carrier of burdens
Carrier of the world
Carrier of the suns
Woman, tell these men that they are your sons

When a girl is in the budding stages of her youth
She is delicate and open
Touch her and watch how she squirms

According to the colonial Latino mind
A woman's role is to be three things:
Attractive
Submissive
Inferior
Let that man bend your pride and your spine into transparency
Do what he tells you
Mumble when you speak
Let him look down to you
Act like his mother:
Cook for him
Clean for him
Wash his drawers

Wipe his face
Make him feel like a young kid again

It's hard enough being a woman
Its hard enough knowing that there is something we have to prove
Wear your skin like a lady should
Don't slouch
Walk with a swish
Smile when he calls you sexy
Let him undress you with his eyes and tell you all the things he would love to do to you—
While you walk to work
Virgin or Whore?

The next man who asks you that question
Tell him to read a book on how to talk to women
Tell him that you are beautiful—not sexy—because you wear the color of your womanhood
        correctly
Tell him to approach you correctly

This is for the Latina woman with the shattered hands
The broken souls
The broken chastity belts

You are next
Men, your daughters are next
Woman, never give a man more than what you want him to leave with
Keep your breath in your chest
Your heart is best kept where it's always been
Usted es una mujer ("You are a woman")
Do not cringe when he says, "Virgin or Whore?"

For the "Whore"
A man's label doesn't define who you are
So what if you have a wild libido
Your sexuality is beautiful

For the "Virgin"
Who holds her chastity like a gift box
You hold that key
And make yourself autodidactic
There are locksmiths who think they can teach you better than you can teach yourself

Recuerde ("Remember")
Somos Mujeres

Monolid Monologue

By Becky Chao

Mommie says that I'm very *lang lui*.

Beautiful girl.

I don't believe it. If she really thought I was beautiful, she wouldn't be constantly bemoaning my monolids.

But you may not know what a monolid is. I didn't either, until a few years ago.

Microsoft Word doesn't even think that "monolid" is a word. You type it in, and you get that angry, jagged red scribble. When you spell-check, the software suggests that maybe you meant "moonlit," or "monolith," or "moonblind"—is *moonblind* even a word?

A quick Google search will tell you that a monolid is "an eyelid without a crease, common to many ethnic Asians"—like me!

Ever since I was little, my mother has gone on and on about how she has no clue where my eyelids came from.

"Everybody in the family has that eyelid fold," she says. "I don't understand where yours went!"

Um. Yeah, Mom, sorry my eyelid fold decided to walk itself off my face. I don't know, maybe it just thought I should look even more like an "ethnic Asian."

It's a bit ironic, since I'm definitely not the most enthusiastic Asian out there. I'm not big on Chinese culture at all. I don't know any of those boy bands who all look and sound the same, like Super Junior? Fahrenheit? Say what?

I can't even speak the language. It's a little sad. My Cantonese is all over the place. I mispronounce syllables. My pitch is all wrong. And don't even get me started on those idioms.

All those holidays? Mooncake day? I don't even know the meaning behind it—I just like the mooncakes.

So why am I the one stuck with the monolids here?

Over the years, my mother never made me feel any better about it. Somehow, she worked the subject of my monolids into every phone call, family dinner, and reunion. It became something that we joked about: "Oh, haha, Becky's weird—she's got a monolid that came from who knows where!"

But I like to entertain the fantasy that maybe I got mixed up at birth.

It makes sense!

'Cause, you know, monolids are all in the genetics. And monolids are nowhere else to be found in the Chao family.

There was a time in eighth grade when Danny, this kid in my class, called me out on being a fake Chinese. I was "too white" to be Chinese, he said. I had to be Japanese!

That would explain my short fling with anime in the summer after sixth grade. I was crazy about it: Black Cat, Inuyasha—I watched almost all of them.

And it would explain why I suck so much at speaking Chinese—because I'm not meant to speak it!

Okay, so maybe I'm exaggerating a little. To be honest, I suck at *all* languages. English, Becky? Man, do you even *listen* to yourself?

But it doesn't really matter if I'm Japanese or Chinese, because I'm still gonna have my monolids.

And the truth is, at this point, I've learned to take my mom's jokes about my monolids in stride.

She says that I'm very *lang lui*.

Beautiful girl.

I guess I should be fine with that.

VII. WRITING

"I began writing in the womb."

To be a writer means to confront the blank page on a daily basis, and always realize you have something to say. As writers of Girls Write Now we have this fearlessness. No matter our form of personal expression, our heartbeats can be heard in every word. This is because we do not just think of ourselves as writers, we know ourselves so.

—Kirthana Ramisetti, mentor

My Written Word

By Erika Marte and Maura Kutner

By Erika

I began writing...
In the womb
Literally
I sat on my mother's water bed
Twirled my umbilical cord
And wrote my first story
Words that I no longer remember but
that have developed as I grow

Writing is...
Pistachio ice cream dripping down the side of a vanilla wafer
On a too hot summer afternoon
Satisfying
It's not knowing what to say but
Knowing exactly what to write about
Writing is singing along to my favorite song
My favorite Taylor Lautner movie
The way we communicate
Life

Writing looks...
Different through each pair of eyes
Some covered with prescription glasses lenses
Each hand is naturally designed for holding a pen
Each butt fits into its own unique chair
Some writers are covered in blankets of crumbled papers
Others are surrounded by the music of computer keyboards being pressed
Writing looks different for everyone
It's another layer of skin
Unique

By Maura

I began writing...
When I was seven
On a pink journal with a princess on the cover.
The ink stained my bedspread
Pink flowers turned purple.
Blank pages were stained with thoughts:
I hate my curly hair
And Questions:
Why can't it be straight?
Sometimes I wound a strand around a number two pencil
That got caught in my rat's nest, afro, frizz ball.
I am blank pages.

Writing is...

An essay on John Steinbeck
An "exploration of the American Dream."
What is my American dream?
Writing is making my hair blonde, soft
Writing is escaping to New York City
Free of lockers full of textbooks and insecurities
Because it doesn't matter how many people tell you
You're pretty
You're thin
I want to hold your hand.
You write your own world
To forget the girl you were.

Writing looks...

Self-conscious.
But self-aware.
Writing looks like a girl who knows there is a pretty one deep inside.
She is silent, but she is brave.
She will blossom, she will bloom
Glued to her truths and confident in her talents.
Writing looks like frizzy hair and purple flowers
Number two pencils and dreams of New York
Writing looks like a child who is open to her future.
She is ready.
She is free.

Cupcake of Evil
By Gina DiFrisco

3 mutant crab eggs
2 cups troll blood
1 cup powdered dragon flesh
¼ teaspoon lion spit
¼ bar of tarantula gut-butter
1 cup powdered human eyeballs
1 live rat

Crack mutant crab eggs into large skull and mix 2 minutes. Add ½ cup powdered dragon flesh, mix 30 seconds. Blend in rest of dragon flesh. While mixing, slowly pour in troll blood. Once concoction is smooth, sprinkle in powdered human eyes and teaspoon of lion spit. Melt tarantula gut-butter for 30 seconds over heated cauldron. Then add to skull. Slice stomach of live rat and dip intestines in concoction for flavor. Pour into desired bat carcass cupcake tray and place in dragon's mouth for 30 minutes or until it reaches a scarlet color.

Serve to your worst enemy.

Evil Cupcake
By Tamiko Beyer

2 cups sugar (must be plantation-harvested)
½ cup rancid butter
3 cups of flour full of stones
2 tablespoons ash
1 teaspoon red sea salt
1 devil(ed) egg
1 cup milk (from a mad cow)
1 teaspoon extract of baby tears

In a large bowl, cream butter and sugar together until you begin to weep. Add in egg, milk, and baby tears while whispering splendid curses.

Sift flour, ash, and salt separately. Mix into the rest of the ingredients, slowly, until everything is well blended and the smell is almost unbearable. When the batter has the consistency of raw sewage, pour into cupcake tins; fill to 2/3rds from the top. Bake it at a temperature that makes everything in the kitchen sweat and groan. Cupcakes are done after the tops are glowing, but before they get too charred.

Let cool to room temperature.

Serve to your worst enemy.

Origin Theories
By Aria Sloss

I learned a long time ago that to be a writer is to ask the question, "why?" I chose to write fiction, I think, mostly because it meant I only had to ask that question of myself. It's always been a tricky business for me, asking other people the hard questions, the tough ones. Something to do with having been the kind of kid who'd rather bury herself in a book, or maybe it's just pure laziness. But if I could build an alternate me in an alternate universe, I'd make myself into a hard-core journalist and investigate my family's past. For instance: How did my great-great-grandfather make it over from Bavaria? How long did it take him to get clear over to San Francisco? Why exactly did he leave? And what was it like for the woman he married, Sarah, my great-great-grandmother? How did she feel about the clubbing of the seals? The canned salmon? The older I get, the less interested I am in where I find myself in the here and now. I'd rather learn about all the beforehands, the hows—and yes, the whys—of who and what got me here at all.

A Mentor's Mentor

By Christina Brosman

Dear Ashley,

In August 2001, when I was right about where you are now, I walked into an Arizona high school classroom. Freshman English. Well, "World Studies," which was English-slash-History back-to-back with the same teacher for both, Mz. Winget. (Really, she insisted we spell "Ms." that way. I'd be remiss not to continue to do so now.) In a time when functional eccentricity as a life choice was only recently familiar to me via the TV show *Gilmore Girls*, here was a teacher who had a minimum of four colors in her hair and an eyebrow piercing that would (and probably did) make my parents cringe. She also warned that she was going to make us work incredibly hard.

She had us at a crucial moment in our lives, and wanted to change us for the better. And not in a standing on our desks, "O Captain! My Captain!" sort of way. Her intentions came from a place of utter sincerity. And she wasn't out to change *what* we all thought, but instead wanted to influence *how*. To that end, Winget was also a veritable mantra machine, telling us to "Filter!" what we saw on the news that September and beyond, "Problem solve a solution to that!" when something was wrong, and "Move like you've got a purpose!" to keep up with her insanely brisk pace.

As promised, we were put to work. She taught us, quite painstakingly, to think about all of the mechanical aspects of the novels we read by assigning each element a different colored pen for writing notes in the margins. Breaking a harrowingly classic piece of literature down into nuts, bolts, and scrap metal to see how it worked. Watching (and occasionally napping through—I'm not proud of it) what seemed like hours upon hours of Joseph Campbell's *The Power of Myth*. Winget held each of us to the same rigorous standards. She graded our papers in green ink, fearing that putting THAT much red on the page seemed harsh. Somehow the scribbles of near-illegible green ink were easier to accept.

Now, as a "nine-year survivor" (to borrow her term for former students), I've been lucky enough to have had a few more amazing mentors of all shapes, sizes, and levels of awareness regarding said mentor status. However, I can't help but think that she opened that door first.

What I want you to take away from this is an openness that will allow you to be shaped by these people who come into your life, and to watch their role as mentors evolve. The same person to critique my thesis until I was nearly in tears also told me, in a moment of vocational crisis, my now-favorite story of hilarious things he did to a miserable boss so that he didn't go insane. Let your passions guide you to people who were passionate about the same things first. They'll shape you more than you can imagine.

All the very best (and then some),
Christina

By Chandra Hughes and Claudia Parsons

By Chandra

As the silence crept upon Kisa, she thought about her past with Koji. They had been childhood friends since middle school. In fact, he was born as her protector. Smiling sadly, she let her memories consume her.

"Kisa," Queen Akane said, slightly opening the door to Kisa's room.

"Yes, Mother," Kisa replied.

"I brought a visitor," Akane responded. She pushed a boy in front of her. Kisa stared at the boy with intense eyes.

"Hi…umm," the boy said stuttering. "My name is um…Koji. I'm in the, erm…sixth grade. N-nice to meet you, Princess Kisa."

"Nice to meet you," she replied, clearly confused.

"Koji is from the Saito family. He will be your personal protector," Akane said, smiling.

"Huh?" Kisa said, annoyed.

"Well, I'll be going then," Akane said and closed the door, leaving Kisa alone with Koji.

"Um," Koji said, kneeling to her. "I'm Koji Saito. My family grew up learning the fight to protect your family. From now on until you become an adult, I will be by your side to protect you from any evil that may occur. I know you are Juu, specialized in all the elements; however I am Hachi, specialized in fire, water, and earth, which is why I can protect you, Princess."

Kisa sighed.

"Princess?"

"Koji, you could drop the label; please just call me by my name," Kisa said in a dignified tone.

"As you wish, Kisa," Koji said, smiling at her.

Kisa stared at him in shock. It was the first time she saw someone actually smile at her. A real smile. She was so used to people putting on fake smiles just to be friends with her. That's why she didn't need friends or guys. Because all they wanted were her powers and status. And adults just smiled because they were supposed to greet the princess that way. But Koji, he smiled at her with such kindness that it surprised her.

■ ■ ■

Kisa looked up at a bunch of men peering down at her. She was tied up, and a magic field surrounded her that made her powers useless. "What do you want to do with me?" she asked.

"I wonder how much money we could get," the boss said, grinning. Kisa gritted her teeth. She was afraid, but she hated to admit it. She just sat silent, afraid to do anything. But she knew no one would save her. She knew that her father would just pay up the money they asked for. No one would go out of their way to save someone like her. She closed her eyes, sadly realizing the truth. Just then a loud noise came from across the room. A figure appeared in front of them.

"Who are you?" the boss said. The figure smiled and stepped forward. Kisa couldn't make out who it was but she could tell it was a boy.

"*Vieni avanti, e crea un drago d'acqua!*" the boy said creating a dragon of water. He grinned and said, "*Vieni avanti, e crea un drago de fuoco!*" which created a dragon of fire. He put his hands in front of him and shouted, "*Vite mie, vi commando de legare e miei draghi!*" A bunch of vines appeared, wrapping themselves around the two dragons.

"What do you want with us!" the boss said, stammering. The boy grinned.

"My name is Koji Saito! I am here to bring you the bribe price you asked for. I hope you don't mind a fire and water dragon instead of money," he said, still grinning. His dragons attacked the men, who were unprepared to fight back. Running to Kisa, Koji picked her up and ran out of the room where she had been tied up.

"Why did you save me?" she asked breathlessly.

"Why not?" Koji said, smiling. Kisa stood there staring at him. She was shocked by the immense power he had. She still couldn't understand why he saved her and risked his life instead of just paying a price. Her body trembled as she collapsed to the floor, realizing the fear she felt.

"You know," Koji said, looking at her but not comforting her, "if you're sad or scared, you can cry." He looked away. "I'll always be there for you," he said, facing her. "So show me your true feelings, Kisa. Please don't make me worry about you so much." Kisa stared at him and nodded. Dashing into his arms she sobbed countless tears. The tears she held back out of fear and loneliness. The tears when she felt like she hated her life, wishing she was never a princess when she wanted to be treated normally. Koji hugged her tightly and whispered, "I'll always be by your side. I'll never leave you, so don't worry."

Kisa shook her head, clearing her thoughts. She looked at the path ahead of her but she could only see a blur of brown. Realizing that she was about to cry, she shut her eyes quickly and wiped her tears. *It's been a while since I last cried,* she thought. She smiled a sad smile.

By Claudia

In which Cate—a New York journalist who finds herself in a strange world with monsters, princesses and flying eagles—starts to think this fantasy may not be so strange after all.

As they flew, Cate couldn't help thinking there was something she wasn't remembering about the past. She had felt an odd sensation as she hurtled through the forest with Kisa, and again as she was flying on the eagle, that she had been there before. It was almost as if she had dreamed it once, long ago.

She racked her brains, trying to dredge up the memory that she could feel just out of reach. What was it that had struck a chord with her and seemed so familiar? Maybe it was the feel of the wind and the branches whipping against her face as they flew, or the terror in the forest followed by the sweet relief when they were all safe. She realized she didn't often feel such strong emotions in her daily life in New York.

In a flash, she remembered that she used to keep a journal of her dreams. Her mother had suggested it almost as soon as Cate could write, and even before then her mother would ask her to draw pictures of her dreams. Her mother never tired of hearing Cate's fantastical stories of dreams in other worlds. Cate hadn't thought about it for years, and she couldn't remember where the journal might be. Probably at her mother's house—her mother kept everything in her room, just as it had been when Cate left home to go to university.

As she concentrated on the journal, she remembered bits and pieces of what she had written. There was one recurring dream that she used to have frequently, about finding herself without her shoes at school or out shopping. She was sure it must mean something, and she still occasionally dreamed that she was going to a job interview or an important assignment without her shoes.

But more often, she would dream of magical worlds filled with monsters and heroes. There were dreams where she could fly.

"Kyo," she said eventually. "I have the strangest feeling that I might have been here before."

For the complete version of An Illuminating Road *visit:*
www.wix.com/girlswritenowcnc/anilluminatingroad

Why They Don't Have Readings for Journalists

By Tammy Chan and Samantha Henig

You know, they don't have readings for journalists.
Readings are for "poets," slam or otherwise.
People   who   time their words?
So they soooouuuuund like music.

Journalists can time their words, too.
Introductions like ditties that rattle in your head.
I'm Renee Montagne. I'm Linda Wertheimer.
This is the BBC News Hour.

So what are you saying? An article is like a poem?

Why not? Both are concise. Careful. Structured.
A/B/A/B. Lede, nutgraf, body, kicker.
The rhythm of the news cycle like a meter. Da-daaa, da-daaa, da-daaa, da-daaa.
Headlines like haikus, crisp and cryptic.

But an article is most definitely not a poem.

Poems are a joke.
Poets—anyone can be one.
Watch—
     "Hope is alive"
Looky there, I guess I'm a poet now.
Poetry, a slab of random words
Each word only seems to "fit"
With its amateur rhyme scheme
Or its syllable count,
It's nothing but ordinary words sounding good.
An article—structured, with every word actually counting
With words backed up with facts
Poetry fails to seize without articles,
And not vice versa
Articles are a first rough draft of history,
Poetry is most definitely not.

Wait, did I just recite a free verse poem?

You did.

Ugh, you see what I mean?

But then can't anyone be a reporter, too? "We are on stage." There, I reported the latest news.

No. Reporting is more than just observing—the thing poets claim to do.

It's not enough to recount.

You have to dig.

Yes, we are on stage, but why?

Who are all these people watching us?

Why are my hands sweating? Anyone can write what she sees. But journalists must see as themselves *and* as everyone else, all at once, and mesh all those visions into one clean narrative.

Because we are communicators,

Communicating to everyone and not just one type.

You really think just anyone can do *that*?

But what if poets have it right?

Watching the world by looking inward; knowing themselves by looking out?

Poems endure. But news expires.

*If I picked my very best article up to now and filed it away until our spring reading, would you want to
hear it?*

Would I want to read it?

Probably not. I'd rather work on the next one.

Maybe that's why they don't have readings for journalists.

Exactly.

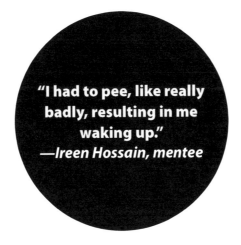

"I had to pee, like really
badly, resulting in me
waking up."
—Ireen Hossain, mentee

Why Reading? Why Not Writing?

By Dalina Jimenez

I've always been asked why I like reading so much, but never manage to give the same answer. My answer changes as time passes. Seeing my personal experiences reflected in memoirs, my hopes for the future ignited by love stories, and my thirst for cultural exploration satiated by tales framed in an international setting—all are just a few of the reasons I adore reading. My escape into the world of books reveals different things to me at different times. When I'm sad, turning to a great book offers real comfort. When I'm happy, I can relate to the giddiness of a character on the page. These ever-changing gifts from reading have motivated me and shaped me into who I am today.

My earliest memory of reading consists of hot afternoons spent in bed while my aunt watched over us. I always looked forward to these readings. It was on these afternoons that I realized a life-changing secret: I was not just a good reader, but an excellent reader. I enjoyed reading so much that I forgot about how hot and sticky it was in the room. I could escape. I could read quickly, or savor what I read slowly. I could read anything—newspapers, sci-fi, romance, poetry. I could even memorize passages that I read. No obstacle could get in the way of my reading. When my parents couldn't afford the expensive books needed for school, I'd read late into the night at the library. When the books I needed weren't available at the library, I found a way to memorize the reading from a classmate's book at school. Instead of weakening my love for books, these experiences strengthened it, proving to me that I was skilled at reading. I took pride in this.

My love for writing developed in a very different way. In fact, at first I despised writing. I wrote very little. Writing did not come naturally to me. It seemed more like a burden, and when I did write, sentences were left halfway complete, and doodles replaced words when I couldn't find the right ones. I found it difficult and at times outright tedious to place my thoughts on paper. I hated the time spent weighing what was safe to write and what things were better left unwritten, kept away from prying eyes. But, when did I start to love writing? I can't recall exactly, but the love did bloom. The transition came when I decided I needed an outlet to express my thoughts. It was a scary experience. At first, too scary. Doubt consumed my attempts again and again. I was still a newbie at the world of words; I didn't know how to work with them, how to transform my writing into an honest expression of the thoughts in my head. But with practice and patience, the fear vanished. I was free and experimented with every form of writing I could: different tones, moods, and settings I found appealing, interesting, or daring. I'd fallen in love *twice*.

Just Like You

By Jessica Greer

"Would you like this one for your birthday?" my mother asks. "It's up to you." I stare at a midnight-blue felt journal on the extravagant display of personal journals at our local bookstore. Blown-up pictures of Anne Frank and Sylvia Plath reign over the display table as the icons or goddesses of personal release through writing. Hundreds if not thousands of minute blue and yellow beads are sewn onto the felt-covered journal that I pick out with my gaze. Different shades of blue and yellow make up a swooping, star-filled sky on the face of this blank booklet. Vast seas in the sky. This is exactly where I want my thoughts to reside. The pathways of my mind will be more beautiful if I can put them in a beautiful place.

On the morning of my birthday, my new, visually stunning journal awaits me. I'm fifteen. I sit in a room alone, marveling over my gift's intricacies. My mind drifts to figures throughout history who have used their writing as an escape, a release. An image of a girl on a windowsill baring her soul while scribbling in her journal surfaces in my mind. I wish to find my escape as she has found hers. I sit down to write, to have my own experience, but each sentence that begins my journey is met with the bold, dark line of my pen, censoring and censuring what's been shared. At the half-page mark, no progress has been made—there's just a dark array of vertical, horizontal, diagonal, and zigzagged lines all working together to cover the words that lie beneath them, and the writer above them who believes they're not worth being read. I keep thinking what people will say among peers, in classrooms, in book clubs, in Internet chat rooms, and in their own minds, hundreds of years from now, after what I've written has been discovered, published widely, and exposed completely. Will they speak of my strengths or my weaknesses? Or of my fatal inability to grasp truth? I place my journal in the *farthest* corner of my closet, behind the worn-out shoes, under forgotten stuffed animals, books, and gloves with missing pairs from winters past, and tuck this attempt away.

Fantasy is what we want, but reality is what we need. I think of what freedom means and how freedom is so much like writing. A time when it never occurs to me to think if others are watching, to be moved without expectation. A rush that overcomes and casts me out to sea, leaving behind whatever part of me that used to stand on the dock and watch.

"You know, they don't have readings for journalists. Readings are for 'poets,' slam or otherwise."
—Tammy Chan and Samantha Henig, mentee-mentor pair

Privacy

By Nancy Mercado

Julie's pink and blue Hello Kitty diary sat on the desk, its cheap lock open and dangling from the clasp. I picked it up and made a joke about reading it, and when Julie didn't immediately object, I opened it to the very first page in slow-motion exaggeration to show her that I was taking my threat one step further. Except, instead of seeing Julie's scratchy script exposing her deepest, darkest secrets . . . I saw my own neat bubble print.

"Um, Jule, what is my diary doing here?" I asked, my feet curling into the plush blue carpet that stretched out across her room.

"Oh, I totally took it home with me by accident the other day. I forgot to tell you," she said, looking not the slightest bit culpable.

It wasn't *totally* unbelievable. We owned identical diaries and we had placed no stickers on the covers to distinguish/tarnish them. And, since the Hello Kitty franchise wasn't exactly preparing for the possibility that two best friends who lived next door to each other would one day decide to own the same diary, I'm pretty sure that our locks and keys were identical. Her key opened my diary, it was that simple.

"But you must have realized it was mine at some point! Did you read it?" I asked. But I already knew the answer.

"Yeah, a little," she said.

"That's so not okay!" I said. I channeled some righteous indignation. Really though, I was the worst kind of hypocrite. By the age of nine, I'd already broken into my siblings' diaries, read my parents' love letters, and raided my brother's porn collection. I was a born snoop, through and through. So I knew what it was like to want to know what was behind what people projected on the surface, and I even understand the impulse to search that information out. It was what Julie said next that was so baffling.

"I know, but Nan, why didn't you tell me that your brother's going to rehab?"

She was mad at me. For something that she'd read in my diary! Even at the height of my snoopdom, I knew enough not to confront people with what I'd uncovered. But since I wasn't yet savvy enough to know the ways in which a person could completely deflect an accusation and turn it around, I said, "I'm really sorry I didn't tell you, Jule."

Twenty-six years later, I think that I probably could have predicted that it would be my own diary staring back at me if I'd thought about it long enough. Julie was an open book. She was then, and still is. It was me who had secrets. It was me who guarded my feelings and my details with a tight-fisted privacy that must have driven Julie crazy. And you know, maybe it was this event, or the fact that I'd breached the privacy of so many others . . . but even today my journals are written with the self-conscious knowledge that someone might read them.

Career Day at the Charter School

By Nancy Shapiro

Volunteered to tell fifth graders
how I got my jobs, lived my life.
Perhaps I *am* the pro they seek—the oldest,
I believe, of anyone at the school,
including faculty, staff, and other volunteers.
I watch one fifth-grade teacher prepare
his students for the day with a PowerPoint presentation
on the computer, projected on the classroom's white board.
This is New York City's largest charter school,
located in a renovated ribbon factory.
So what can I relate to the hundred kids
who come in classes of twenty-five with a teacher
to shush and monitor them?
Some specifics are necessary—the name
of the nonprofit I directed for thirty years—
Teachers & Writers Collaborative.
What does "collaborate" mean?
It's a "nonprofit"—what is this?—and
in every class, the first answer is: "You don't get paid."
No, and I take a stab at "profit" vs. "nonprofit,"
but move on quickly (another volunteer is here
from Goldman Sachs—let her handle that one).
We talk about their school, the local hospitals,
their churches, synagogues, mosques, about the arts,
about wanting to help others, build a community.
Some of the kids have a list of questions—generic
queries for all the careerists, such as the dog trainer.
What is the hardest thing you had to do?
What hurdles did you face? What did you love the most?
If you could change anything, what would it be?
I loved the people, and I would have given them
more—more money, more benefits, more time together
around the lunch table talking movies and books.
Only one boy knows just want he wants to be:
a bus driver for New Jersey Transit.
I am thinking about my own fifth-grade teacher—Miss Klang—
and how all of us were in love with her in 1958.
It is, I say, the life you are living *now*
that will shape your future—the books you read, the way you
work together in groups, how you treat your friends.
I tell them Willa Cather's quote:
"Most of the basic material a writer works with is acquired before the age of fifteen."
And since it's the last day of National Poetry Month,
I hand out note cards so they can make a poem for their pockets,

asking them to write three lines beginning with "I remember,"
and, for their teacher, mentioning Joe Brainard's book
toting up his childhood memories.
Hands go up all over the room to share their lines.
We talk about expanding to capture the details.
Not just "I remember the first time I played football"
but "I remember the first time I played tackle football,
and Jimenez threw a 'hail Mary' pass that I caught five
yards from the goal and ran in for a touchdown."
Though sometimes we just listen—
"I remember when they told me my grandmother died"—
because as he reads, the young boy's eyes fill with tears
and here's the point, a moment to mold through the years.

What's Twenty Percent of Forty-Eight?
By Ireen Hossain

I had to pee, like really badly, resulting in me waking up. It was dark, and I looked at the bright digital clock, which said 1:32 a.m. I got up and headed for the bathroom. The bathroom light was on, meaning someone was in there. I knocked on the door.

The familiar voice of my dad said, "I'm in here."

"Hurry up, Baba! I need to pee!"

"Okay, hold on." In a matter of minutes, my dad came out and I rushed in, before my bladder exploded.

After I came back out, I saw my dad in the kitchen, looking through the refrigerator.

"There's nothing to eat in here. What did your mom make for dinner?" my dad asked.

"Fried chicken. Why are you home so early?" My dad's a yellow-cab driver, and he worked the night shifts, coming home at dawn.

"There's no business tonight. Ugh, I'm so hungry," my dad groaned. He walked toward the door. "Go back to bed, I'm going to eat out and then come home."

"I want to eat something too!" I exclaimed.

"Shhh!" my dad shushed me. "You're going to wake your sister up. And no, go to bed, Ireen."

"Please, Baba! I want to go with you!"

My dad rolled his eyes and said, "Fine. But you have to be quiet!"

I nodded insanely like a bobble-head doll. My dad ushered me out of our small apartment. We went down the eight million stairs from the fourth floor to the first floor and headed outside toward our bluish Toyota van. My dad unlocked the car, and I sat up front next to him. "Where are we going, Baba?"

"You'll see," he said with a smile, and started the car.

We head toward Manhattan from Queens, and then I asked again, "Where are we going?" My dad ignored me. For about fifteen minutes we just hung out in the car, listening to the radio. I was singing along to a song when my dad started to slow down the car. I looked out the window and saw a *long* line of people standing. "Baba, what are they doing?"

My dad proudly said, "They're waiting on line to eat one of the best halal chicken and rice platters of New York!" I looked at him a bit confused. "You'll understand when you eat it. Now get out of the car and wait on line. I'm going to park the car."

I did as I was told, and waited on the longest line in history. I had been standing patiently for about ten minutes when my dad finally came and stood next to me. "This is ridiculous, Baba," I told him.

He shook his head. "No, Ireen, the taste of this food is ridiculously good!"

I rolled my eyes; he was being so dramatic.

"So, how was school today?" my dad asked, trying to make small talk.

"I got the highest grade in my class for English," I bragged.

"What about math and science?"

I glared at him. "Who cares about those classes? I'm going to become a famous writer."

"Life requires math and science! What's twenty percent of forty-eight?"

"Ugh," I groaned. "I don't know!"

"What do you mean you don't know? Its basic knowledge!" my dad exclaimed. "I'm a dump, and now you're being a dump."

"Baba, it's *dumb*."

"Don't correct me! I've been in this country for over ten years, I know my English!"

"Then use it properly!" I exclaimed.

"Don't be smart with me!"

My god, my dad's such a drama king. "I'm not being smart with you, Baba. I'm just telling you that the word is dumb, not dump."

"Ireen," my dad started off his rant, "even though I dropped out of school, I studied English in Bangladesh, and I got the highest grades."

"Okay, that's great," I told him sarcastically.

"If I went to college, then I could have been a doctor or a businessman. But I didn't listen to my parents. Math and science are very important, and I realized it too late. I don't want you to end up like me."

"Oh my god," I said, and sighed. "I'm sorry, Baba, but you've been stuck with a daughter who's illiterate in math and science."

"What meat do you want?" the gyro man asked. Wow, I didn't even realize we had gotten to the front.

"A mix of beef and chicken please," my dad said. I watched the gyro man as he prepared the rice platter. The smell was *so* good!

My dad paid the gyro man, and we headed to our car. The moment we got into the car, my dad and I dived into the food. My dad was right; the food was ridiculously good!

The rice mixed with the little pieces of beef and chicken tasted great together. I took out the small container filled with white sauce and put it all over my rice. I combined the rice, meat and the creamy white sauce. Oh god, the taste was *sensational*.

As my dad was eating he said to me, "If you're going to be a writer then you will be a fantastic writer! Even though you are a dump at math."

I shook my head and grinned. "You mean dumb."

"Don't start with me, Ireen."

VIII. PAIR SNAPSHOTS

"That was our moment."

As Pair Support Co-Chair for the last three years, I'm often asked what it is, exactly, that I do. And, one night while watching Tina Fey on "30 Rock," I found the perfect answer: "I support women. I'm like a human bra." In this case, "women" includes the high school girls we nurture in our program, as well as the amazing mentors who help them navigate through the murky waters that are the teenage years.

This chapter is exactly what it's called—a snapshot—but in the following pages, you'll learn more about what makes the pair relationship so special. You'll witness the discovery of new cuisines; a shared love of Madonna and the Bee Gees; the bonding over "nerdy grammar questions"; and the realization for one mentor that her teen heartthrob is merely an aging actor to her mentee.

The pair relationship takes patience, dedication, and time to cultivate. From our "speed-dating" event and weekly pair meetings to our monthly workshops and the end-of-year readings, each milestone in the program is a step forward for our pairs. Sometimes the start is rocky and the engine sputters before taking off, but once pairs find speed, it's hard to slow them down.

Pairs often spend their time together writing, and flipping through a mentee's portfolio is evidence that she's grown over the season, not only as a writer but as a young woman. As one mentee notes in this chapter, she learned not only to take chances as a writer, but in life. But don't think that mentees are the only ones to benefit from the program; mentors learn more about themselves and what they do than they ever imagined, and it's no stretch to say that every woman who participates in the program is inspired by the young woman who looks to her for guidance.

I hope that as you read through these personal reflections by our pairs, you'll feel the same warmth and inspiration we all feel being part of the program. Because, like Jeffrey Campbell shoes and skull earrings, everything is better in pairs.

—Anuja Madar, Pair Support Co-Chair

Tatyana Alexander was born and raised in Brooklyn and is a sophomore at the Academy for Conservation and the Environment. Her mentor, **Jessica Benjamin**, is a grant writer for New Leaders for New Schools and has also worked for StoryCorps, The Arc of Minnesota Southwest, and the Greater Mankato Area Diversity Council. This is Tatyana and Jessica's first year with Girls Write Now.

Says Tatyana:

Professional. Humorous. Coming in from work. Same height. On my level. She told me she doesn't know how to spell. I laughed. She told me she's bad at transportation, too. I felt good. She played basketball. Me too. We both love when people are so happy they sing. She forgets how old I am, talking to me the way she talks to her friends. I have to say, "Jessica, I don't know what that word means." I smile. She understands my work and asks questions that bring out the best of my writing. She also understands my situations and tries to help in the best way possible. She loves her work and takes it seriously. I couldn't see myself having any other woman for a mentor.

Says Jessica:

My favorite moments with Tatyana are after we've packed up our notebooks and pens. We walk to the subway together, placing bets on whose train will pull into the station first (almost *always* mine!) and talking about the most random things, like how funny men look in running tights. During these walks, I'm not worrying about us meeting a deadline, or wondering if I've helped her enough with her story, or how we'll find time to meet next week. I enjoy those walks most because in those moments, Tatyana is my friend—one I feel lucky to have.

Lashanda Anakwah is a junior at the Marble Hill School for International Studies and resides in Mosholu in the Bronx. **Rachel Cohen**, her mentor, joined the Associated Press at its New York City headquarters in 2007 as a general assignment sports reporter. This is Lashanda and Rachel's first year with Girls Write Now.

Says Lashanda:

We agreed that submitting an entry to the Scholastic Art & Writing Awards wasn't just to win. It was for the experience. But winning would be nice, too. We decided easily the genre would be poetry—my strong suit. Rachel sat by me when the words were thick and thin, always having something encouraging to say and adding helpful input. "So, how's it going to end?" Rachel asked one day while we were diligently working. At that moment I realized what GWN was all about. Here was this brilliant sports writer from the Associated Press totally immersed in my poem. We both shared a love of writing and that's why we were there.

Says Rachel:

We usually meet at a Barnes & Noble, where finding two empty chairs is always a minor miracle. That means we're crammed in inches from other people who can clearly hear our conversations about everything from poetry imagery to debate team topics. One day a woman sitting across from us asked what we were working on. Turns out she publishes children's books. We talked about her authors and, for some reason, the royal wedding. That took up most of our session, but that was OK. It felt great to share our love for writing and our projects outside our pair. And we left giggling with a story to tell.

Diamond Arriola lives in the Bronx and is a senior at the School for Excellence. This spring, Diamond was featured in the *New York Post*. Her mentor, **Ingrid Skjong**, is executive online editor of Niche Media, publisher of *Gotham*, *Hamptons*, and other lifestyle magazines, and also writes for the fitness page for *Gotham*. This is Diamond and Ingrid's second year with Girls Write Now.

Says Diamond:

"No way! Your favorite singer is Madonna?" Ingrid was fond of my unique sense of music genres over dinner at Café Mogador, not too far from Astor Place. It was a charming place to learn about one another and share our favorite hits from the legendary Madonna: "Live to Tell," "Justify My Love," "Vogue," etc. Most importantly, I found a role model I can depend on and learn from. She has guided me through good times, tough times, and baffling moments of being an adolescent. I am forever grateful for my mentor.

Says Ingrid:

For a weekly meeting, Diamond and I went out to dinner at a restaurant called Café Mogador on St. Marks Place. It serves Moroccan food—a cuisine she had never tasted. We ordered couscous (new to her), hummus, pita bread, shrimp (which she loved), and lamb (which she sort of loved).

We laughed and chatted, and I learned she loves new things and has a spectacularly deep knowledge of music (Madonna! Journey! Prince!). The glint in her eye was delightful and reminded me what a smart, interesting young lady she is. Next dinner? Ethiopian.

Mariah Teresa Aviles resides in the Bronx and attends the Young Women's Leadership School of East Harlem where she is a sophomore. **Allison Adair Alberts**, her mentor, is a fourth-year PhD candidate at Fordham University. This is Mariah and Allison's first year with Girls Write Now.

Says Mariah:

Walking into Starbucks, I look forward to Allie's updates about how things are going with her, her family, and school; that's how we always start our pair sessions, about each other. There's usually one thing that sparks our attention and as we think of ideas that flow together, the encouragement follows. I truly appreciate the relationship my mentor and I have, because we can express ourselves clearly without hurting one another's feelings. It has been a blessing to work together.

Says Allison:

Shivering, I clutched my paper cup of black tea with milk (my usual) as I sat on the cold metal bench. Our usual Starbucks was overflowing, so Riah and I retreated to a nearby park beneath the 2/5 train to rehearse her CHAPTERS reading. Despite the freezing temperature—and the fact that I had forgotten to wear socks—we forged on, alternately giggling and rehearsing, as Riah transformed her poem into a powerful spoken word performance. The slanting winter sun set quickly behind us: two writers, enveloped in the crisp Bronx afternoon.

Brittany Barker has lived in Harlem her whole life. She is a senior at Hostos Lincoln Academy of Science in the Bronx. Next fall, Brittany will attend Dickinson College with a full scholarship from the Posse Foundation as well as a scholarship from the Knicks Poetry Slam. This year, Brittany competed in the finals of the Knicks Poetry Slam at the New Amsterdam Theater on Broadway. **Josleen Wilson**, her mentor, is author of more than thirty nonfiction books and has her own consulting firm, Sparks Fly Up Creative Solutions. She also serves as Readings Co-Chair on the GWN Program Advisory Committee. This is Brittany and Josleen's third year with Girls Write Now.

Says Brittany:

"Honey, you are going to win this," she said. The night before my final Posse deadline, we worked at Josleen's house really late—well, she worked, like it was her future that was at stake. The way she paced back and forth, printing out, making copies of all of my documents, making sure my poetry portfolio was perfect, showed me how much she cared about this for me. In retrospect, I believe that night was the perfect testament of our relationship over the last three years, always working hard for what "we" wanted to accomplish.

Says Josleen:

It was her first all-nighter, certainly wouldn't be her last. "This is what writers do," I said.

"Why?" she asked. I laughed, but I don't think she was trying to be funny. Her eyes were drooping. We had started at three that afternoon and it was now after midnight. We were almost finished. Except that each time we printed out the final essay in her scholarship application, we always saw something that could be better. "Hang in, kid, you're going to win this, you deserve it. Do you believe me?" "Yes," she said. And we took another crack at it.

Evelyn Berrones was born in Guayaquil, Ecuador, and came to the Bronx, New York, in 2005. She is a junior at Hostos Lincoln Academy of Science. This year, Evelyn won a Regional Gold Key from the Scholastic Art & Writing Awards. **Nancy Shapiro**, her mentor, was director of Teachers & Writers Collaborative (T&W) for almost thirty years, and she currently serves as co-chair of T&W's board. This is Evelyn's first year and Nancy's fourth year with Girls Write Now.

Says Evelyn:

After Nancy and I first met, she helped me work on my memoir about my childhood in Ecuador and moving to New York City. The memoir I wrote won a Regional Gold Key Award from the Scholastic Art & Writing Awards. Though I mostly like writing fiction, I've liked exploring all genres at GWN and at Nancy's dining-room table.

Says Nancy:

I love Evelyn's imagination. Even before we started writing together, she had written several stories that explore the complex lives of teenagers trying to figure out how to balance desire and commitment when those two forces pull in opposite directions. We like to write at my dining-room table, sharing juice, tea, and fruit or cookies and talking about big issues and tiny grammatical nuances.

Michaela Burns lives in Manhattan and is a senior at the Calhoun School. Her mentor, **Erica Dolland**, is a fourth-grade math teacher at the Bronx Lighthouse Charter School. This year, Erica traveled to Ghana, West Africa, where she worked with the International Foundation for Education and Self-Help as a trainer-of-teachers. This is Michaela's second year and Erica's third year with Girls Write Now.

Says Michaela:

Faint afternoon rays drizzle through my frayed bangs as I approach the Starbucks on the corner of 103rd Street. I wrinkle my nose as the familiar tangy whiff of brewing coffee tickles the inside of my nostrils. Typically, during our one-hour-a-week session, my mentor and I settle in seats closest to the window, where we can watch the fast-moving city over the brim of our lattes and ponder possible writing subjects. Today is no different; my mentor waves to me from her chosen place in front of the window, writing utensil in hand and notebook in sight. I join her in our space of writing.

Says Erica:

My compliments are to the curry. Who knew Indian food and crafting creative prose would go hand-in-hand on a Wednesday night meet-up session, especially with stained

fingers marking lined paper. In between pulling naan and continuous gulps of cold water to cool the ravaging peppers, we talk, or at least try to, about character development ideas, journal muses and, of course, as always, politics. I realize how extraordinary this young woman really is: so fluid and intelligent in articulating her opinions on domestic policy, witty and whimsical in her ideation of a recent sci-fi piece, yet whose innocence is even more subdued by the coconut milk sauce dripping from her chin. She is a rare gem! I realize our writing becomes a canvas where all that is said between us lives, and all still yet to be learned begins to breathe.

Cindy Caban lives in Williamsburg, Brooklyn, and is a sophomore at Millennium High School. Her mentor, **Juliet Packer**, is an Emmy-nominated professional television writer whose credits include *Falconcrest*, *The Waltons*, *Palmerstown USA*, *As the World Turns*, and *All My Children*. This is Cindy and Juliet's first year with Girls Write Now.

Says Cindy:

At our first meeting, I was nervous that my mentor wouldn't like me or that I'd be too awkward and not much would be said. But once we broke the ice, I knew I didn't have anything to worry about. Juliet and I learn from each other and she helps me grow as a writer. I enjoy her company, and I love that we visit different museums, watch films, and talk about what books we're reading. Now, during our workshops, I rush down the steps to make the 2 train, excited to talk to Juliet about my week and my writing.

Says Juliet:

Cindy and I got off to a late start. We met for the first time on January 13, 2011. Cindy was so open and engaging that I felt comfortable right away. But on February 24, there was a real "click." We were having our regular pair session at GWN; we'd done some writing and editing, and I was trying to come up with a prompt. I told Cindy about one in the GWN Handbook: "What if Harry Potter never went to a magical school?" Cindy and I both drew a blank. We couldn't imagine Harry without Hogwarts. Then Cindy said, what if Harry Potter ended up in *The Hunger Games*? We were off and writing. When we finished and shared, we discovered we'd come up with wildly different scenarios, but both made us laugh. And I felt closer to Cindy and her inner Katniss than I ever had before.

Olivia Carew lives in NYC and currently attends the James Baldwin School as a senior. Her mentor, **Tasha Gordon-Solmon**, is a featured entertainment blogger for The Huffington Post, the literary associate at Women's Expressive Theater, and a proud member of the Ars Nova Play Group. This is Olivia's first year and Tasha's second year with Girls Write Now.

Says Olivia:

In the small apartment I live in with four of my relatives, I learned long ago that there are not many ways to find that moment of peace I need as a writer. While I've learned to fight the noise with my iPod, the time I spend with my mentor, Tasha, always provided me the free space to flow. Tasha and I got to work on everything from a letter to the editor to screenplays to a monologue. Plus, she was able to break down every single one of my poems and that allowed us to have meaningful discussions on my message as a writer. I love the hour that I get to spend with Tasha because it is always productive and peaceful.

Says Tasha:

One week, I asked Olivia which piece of writing she would like to submit for an upcoming GWN deadline. I assumed she would pick something from one of the workshops or our previous pair sessions. She pulled out three brand-new poems she'd written that week: one was fierce and political, one light and joyful, one emotionally raw and poignant—all of them layered, lyrical, and bounding off the page. Even at times when she feels like she is struggling, I am constantly amazed at how prolific and talented Olivia is.

Tammy Chan lives in Forest Hills, Queens, and is a senior at Talent Unlimited High School for instrumental music. This year, Tammy won a regional Gold Key and a national Silver Medal from the Scholastic Art & Writing Awards for her nonfiction writing portfolio. **Samatha Henig**, her mentor, is the digital news editor at *The New Yorker* and has also worked at *Newsweek* and DoubleX by Slate. This is Tammy's second year and Samantha's first year with Girls Write Now.

Says Tammy:

Reluctantly sliding my articles across the yellow table into Samantha's hands made me realize something—why wouldn't I want an actual journalist to read and critique my work? It was then that our love for journalism came alive. Our passion merged as we invested in editing my pieces for the Scholastic Art & Writing Awards. It was the first time she had read my clips. My heart pounding, hands trembling as she flipped the pages, marking up the pages until the definite type-print font had handwritten words all around it, arrows pointing, brackets placed. Our communication about communication started right there and then.

Says Samantha:

When we were looking through some articles Tammy had written over the summer, she asked me about when to use an em dash versus a semicolon. It was the sort of nerdy grammar question that would only come from someone who really cares about writing—doing it well, doing it correctly—and the sort of question that gets me excited. I did my best to answer, and, in the course of things, also told her about [sic], which she thought seemed "mean." We had connected on a personal level early on, but now we were connecting as writers.

Says Becky:

I step off the elevator of the The New York Times building, our usual meeting place, and find Jen waiting. I'd sent her a draft of a new piece the night before, and I'm still a little iffy about sharing something so personal. But we start going over it together, pausing every once in a while to exchange stories about growing up, how it felt to be so "un-Asian" in our Asian families, our relationships with our mothers, writing love notes to boys and everything else—and I wonder why I was so worried in the first place.

Says Jennifer:

"What kind of feedback are you looking for?" At our first meeting, I asked Becky a flurry of getting-to-know-you questions, but that one was especially crucial. It would guide the way we approached her work, our relationship as writers and readers. I was ready to go easy on her—to tackle the big, amorphous things (voice! inspiration!) while letting some of the little things slide. But Becky laid it down right away: "I want to go over everything, line by line," she said. "I want you to be tough." *Awesome*, I thought. *Girl after my own heart.*

Becky Chao has lived in New York all her life and currently resides in Brooklyn. She is a senior at Stuyvesant High School. This year, Becky won Regional Gold and Silver Keys from the Scholastic Art & Writing Awards. This fall Becky will be attending Duke University. Her mentor, **Jennifer McDonald**, is an editor at *The New York Times Book Review*, where she works with both fiction and nonfiction. This is Becky and Jennifer's first year with Girls Write Now.

Monica Chin has lived in Manhattan all her life. She is a sophomore at Baruch College Campus High School. This year, Monica won a Regional Silver Key from the Scholastic Art & Writing Awards. **Elaine Stuart-Shah**, her mentor, is a Brooklyn-based freelance writer and graduate student at NYU's Arthur L. Carter Journalism Institute. She was previously the senior associate features and travel editor at *Modern Bride*. This is Monica and Elaine's first year with Girls Write Now.

Says Monica:

"Please let me pay for this!" I gasp, furiously shoving money toward the cashier at the Barnes & Noble Café. My mentor laughs and says, "Oh no, it's my treat, really! DON'T PAY!" She smiles and pushes my hand aside. From the first moment I met Elaine, I knew I had made the right choice. "Speed dating" was a bit intimidating. I was nervous opening up to such intelligent, witty, professional writers. But after pairing up with Elaine at our first workshop, I was excited. Writing with Elaine is nothing but encouragement, giggles, and compliments. She, being a nonfiction writer, and I, fiction, are the perfect match.

Says Elaine:

Monica and I have shared so many meaningful moments over the past six months that it's hard to pinpoint one specific time our bond sealed. There was the session we spotted Jon Stewart two tables over and spent the hour stealing glances at him. At another meeting we described our childhood bedrooms; I confessed that at Monica's age my walls were plastered with photos of Leonardo DiCaprio, to which she responded, "Isn't he really old?" We're constantly laughing and discovering how much we have in common. Like the words we shape into sentences each week, our relationship is a work in progress.

Kristasiah Daniels hails from Crown Heights, Brooklyn. She is a freshman at the Brooklyn School for Music & Theatre. Her mentor, **Michele Thomas**, is the managing editor at the French Culinary Institute in New York City and has also written several textbooks and teaching materials. This is Kristasiah's first year and Michele's fifth year with Girls Write Now.

Says Kristasiah:

I remember when I first started talking to Michele and she said she was weird. I said, "I'm weird, too." We started talking about my first workshop and I started telling her where I got the inspiration for my fantasy fiction story. I told her about my boyfriend at the time, my friends, and how they related to the characters, and she laughed at all the different identities. After a while, it started feeling easier to talk to her, and then I couldn't stop talking.

Says Michele:

Krissy's sheer creativity blows my mind. I remember those early meetings, when I was trying to be all "mentor-y" and grown-up. It didn't work out. Within a few pages of the story about Serenity and the three muses from Hera, I was hooked. I forgot about being a grown-up and we were suddenly writers together. We kept talking, she kept writing, and we forgot the time. I feel it's always like that in our pair writing sessions.

Gina DiFrisco was born and raised in the Bronx and currently attends the Urban Assembly School for Green Careers where she is a sophomore. **Tamiko Beyer**, her mentor, is author of the poetry chapbook *bough breaks*. She is also poetry editor of *Drunken Boat* and founding member of Agent 409, and leads creative writing workshops for at-risk youth and other community groups. This is Gina and Tamiko's first year with Girls Write Now.

Says Gina:

Every week we meet at the Girls Write Now main base. It's almost never the same. We talk about our week, about ourselves. We write about this and that. However, our writing is never the same. I feel that with the help of Tamiko, my writing has grown, making more sense with every paragraph, every word, and every story or poem. I also feel like with every session, I can understand a little more about Tamiko and the way she writes. The writing we do is more to me than just writing, it's a connection between two individuals.

Says Tamiko:

One gray Friday, Gina and I sat at a table in the Girls Write Now office, antique postcards scattered in front of us. We wrote for a good while, constructing stories from the postcards and their fading, handwritten messages. When we finally stopped, we both exhaled as if we had been holding our breath the whole time. As we read our pieces out loud, we marveled at the worlds we had created individually and as a pair. Sometimes, magic happens when two people write together; a different kind of communication opens up. That's exactly what happened that electric afternoon.

Sharline Dominguez was born in the Dominican Republic and came to reside in Brooklyn when she was just three years old, in 1997. This year, Sharline won a Regional Silver Key from the Scholastic Art & Writing Awards. Her mentor, **Sarv Taghavian,** is currently a writer for MTV Networks International and previously worked for Bravo. This is Sharline and Sarv's first year with Girls Write Now.

Says Sharline:

Sarv and I connected when we first met at a Starbucks in Midtown. It was extremely cold outside and I had no battery to call Sarv once I got there. We somehow met up and agreed that the editing process was difficult to undergo. When I told her that I am going to Thailand this summer and how nervous I was, she comforted me because she was going to Spain at the same time. At last, I could go home and tell my mom that I met someone who was just as weird as me, and most importantly, a woman writer.

Says Sarv:

About a month and a half into our meetings, Sharline and I tried doing a fiction prompt together. We took a line from a random page of a nearby book and used it as the opening line to a new piece from each of us. My piece turned out okay, but I was blown away by the scene Sharline was able to execute in about twenty minutes. It was vivid and beautiful, filled with sensory details and a gripping main character. I've felt so privileged to be a part of such a brilliant young writer's life this year.

Anaís Figueroa has lived in Manhattan her entire life. She is a senior at the Urban Assembly School of Business for Young Women. Her mentor, **Katherine Nero**, has written, produced, and directed numerous short films and is currently producing her first feature-length film, *For the Cause*. This is Anaís and Katherine's first year with Girls Write Now.

Says Anaís:

My mentor and I were at Dunkin' Donuts discussing the Oscar-nominated movies. We were both upset that *Inception* didn't get the recognition it deserved. Katherine was explaining how every aspect of the film was important to the main message of the movie. Every time I've seen a movie, I've never able to go into depth about the movie's plot and themes. With Katherine, I not only got to say what I thought, but I had the opportunity to expand my ideas about the film. This is an exciting, new experience that I look forward to whenever I'm with my mentor.

Says Katherine:

The other day as Anaís and I were walking on 145th Street, I wondered aloud how we ever managed without ATMs. It suddenly dawned on me that Anaís did not share my familiarity of a world that predated the existence of ATMs, cell phones, and 24-hour cable television. The bringing together of multigenerational perspectives is what I enjoy most about being a mentor for Girls Write Now. Anaís and I discuss and learn from each other's experiences, which greatly enriches our perceptions and writing, respectively.

Says Mariah:

Linda and I began to connect once we realized that as writers, we will always face criticism or have doubts about our writing. The only people that I have ever allowed to read my personal writing were my friends, my mother, and younger brother. Linda has helped me realize that what I write are my ideas and has meaning to me. I always complain about how dark it sounds or if it's garbage but she says, "So what! Who cares about what everyone else thinks! It's what you like about it!" I like to hear her opinions about my writing because they make me feel more comfortable and less self-doubting.

Says Linda:

It was a special day for me when Mariah allowed me to buy her a cup of tea. In our previous meetings, when we'd go to a pizza shop, Mariah said, "No thank you," whenever I offered her a soda, tea, a cannoli, whatever I hoped would entice her.

The day she said, "Yes," I almost had not bothered to ask, assuming she'd say, "No." But, when I went to order a tea for myself, luckily, I decided I should at least ask. Then, in her quiet way, Mariah said, "Yes." I paused to make sure I'd heard right. With sugar, no less! It felt great!

Mariah Fuller lives in the South Bronx and is a sophomore at Hostos Lincoln Academy of Science. **Linda Corman**, her mentor, writes and edits for non-profits, think tanks, managements, consulting firms, and major financial institutions and is currently working on a novel. This is Mariah and Linda's first year with Girls Write Now.

Jennifer Fuster was raised in Florida, but now lives in Manhattan. She is a senior at Jacqueline Kennedy Onassis High School. Next fall, Jennifer will be attending Pratt Institute. **Hannah Morrill**, her mentor, is the senior beauty editor at InStyle.com. Hannah has also worked at Simon & Schuster and on an organic sheep farm in Vermont's Mad River Valley. This is Jennifer and Hannah's second year with Girls Write Now.

Says Jennifer:

Hannah and I have developed a close relationship throughout the two years I've known her. And that's because she's always a great listener and adviser to me, especially when I'm in a slump. She truly cares about my success and is not only involved in our GWN duties, but has also played a very large part in helping me apply for colleges this year. She's been an important support system in my life and has witnessed growth and maturity in me that is of course from her help—from being an outstanding mentor whom I've shared many laughs with.

Says Hannah:

Jennifer is a budding artist, an effortlessly talented writer, and a lover of New York City with a Floridian's innate calm. She has a creepily dark sense of humor and an insatiable desire to learn new things, and her creative spark blows me away. I want everything for Jennifer that Jennifer wants for herself—college, success, a closetful of Jeffrey Campbell shoes, a collection of oil paints, a cute but not too pricey prom dress, an unembarrassing summer job, a non-lame boyfriend, a happy, fulfilling, and wonderful life—and I have no doubt that she'll achieve it all.

Nathalie Gomez was born in Rhode Island but raised in Queens, New York. She is a sophomore at Benjamin N. Cardozo High School in Queens. **Amanda Berlin**, her mentor, currently works in marketing and publicity as a writer and strategist and has been published on Forbes.com and in *Teen Identity* magazine. She recently launched the

webzine, The Thrivivalist. This is Nathalie and Amanda's first year with Girls Write Now.

Says Nathalie:

As I walked out of the subway onto the street, I spotted a lady with blonde hair. I didn't recognize her at first, but she looked familiar. So I started following her, but then she went into a store, and I lost her inside. I looked around, and couldn't find her. I gave up and went to the meeting spot. When I got there, I saw the lady I was stalking. I knew she looked familiar. She was my amazingly talented mentor, Amanda. Since stalkers always stalk awesome people, wouldn't it be obvious that Amanda is awesome? Yes!

Says Amanda:

The moment I met Nathalie, I knew we would be a great pair. But, despite the "love at first write" it took us a while to open lines of communication. Now that we have, the similarities between us are piling up. We both like to write, obviously; we both like fiction; we both have two siblings; and we both care deeply about the fair treatment of others. These are all things you learn relatively early on. As we open up even more, as is inevitable as we hone our craft, we've realized even more similarities. When we set our timer and started free-writing to brainstorm our anthology pieces, we both wrote about the same pivotal childhood experience—moving at a young age and the huge impact that had on our lives.

Priscilla Guo hails from Forest Hills, Queens, and is a freshman at Hunter College High School. This year, Priscilla won two Regional

Keys from the Scholastic Art & Writing Awards—one Silver and one Gold. Her mentor, **Kristen Demaline**, is a graduate student at Milano, The New School. She contributes to the GPIA/Milano Graduate Student Blog and has participated in the Women's Theatre Collaborative as a playwright and performer. This is Priscilla and Kristen's first year with Girls Write Now.

Says Priscilla:

Coffee beans grinding into our hair as we walked in through the door. It was October and the smells of pumpkin and cinnamon wisped around us. I hadn't known Kristen that long; it was our second meeting. We were sitting at a table in Starbucks. There were different glazed spots on the wooden table, hinting at spilled coffee from the day. Kristen was reading a piece I had just written when all of a sudden, music filled the café. It was the Bee Gees. I found myself moving along to the music and I looked up. Kristen was doing the same. We just laughed. She was surprised I knew who the Bee Gees were and that was only the beginning.

Says Kristen:

Priscilla and I had only been working together for a short time, but I knew we had a lot in common. We love writing in the same genres, we're passionate and dedicated students, and at first we can seem quiet and reserved. That fall afternoon, it was chilly, a hint of the long winter to come, and we were diligently, pleasurably at work. Until the Bee Gees began playing, and as I sheepishly sought an apology for my humming along with a song, I looked up to see her smiling and doing the same. I was thrilled to discover another thing we have in common that day: taste in music. We laughed together and have been doing so with ease ever since.

Larissa Heron was born in Manhattan just a few blocks from where she currently resides. She is a freshman at the School of the Future. Her mentor, **Aria Sloss**, is a 2007 graduate of the Iowa Writers' Workshop, where she was awarded a two-year Iowa Arts Foundation Fellowship. Her fiction and nonfiction have appeared or are forthcoming in *Glimmer Train*, the *Harvard Review*, *FiveChapters*, and *Edible Brooklyn*. This is Larissa and Aria's first year with Girls Write Now.

Says Larissa:

Getting to know my mentor has been an honor! From the first days of our contact, I have known her not only as my mentor but also as a valued friend. Aria would be described as a lovely, intelligent, lively, optimistic, and good-natured person! Our first meeting was at B&N (a place surrounded by references), Aria and I discovered our many commonalities right away! Both of us had lived in the Berkshires, Aria in Great Barrington and I in Becket, towns only thirty minutes away from each other! For years, we both went to the same shops, Co-op, and had surely crossed paths before. Many other similarities surfaced and our relationship fused!

Says Aria:

I hate to qualify Mark Twain, but familiarity can breed a whole lot more than contempt. For example: great conversation. From the start, Larissa and I had no trouble talking, but as time went on we started having trouble stopping. Whether it was about comparing our dogs or our days, the conversations we had across one of a dozen café tables at Barnes &

Noble were exhilarating, often hilarious, and always memorable. I'm a big believer in listening as a crucial form of learning, and I like to think we both learned bucketloads listening to each other, week after week after week.

Ireen Hossain was born in Bangladesh and moved to New York when she was just fifty-two days old. Since then, she's lived in Astoria, Queens, and is now a sophomore at the Young Women's Leadership School of Astoria. **Wendy Lee**, her mentor, also lives in Astoria, Queens. She is an assistant editor at HarperCollins Publishers and authored the novel *Happy Family*. This is Ireen and Wendy's first year with Girls Write Now.

Says Ireen:
I had talked to a few women mentors, but they were not into fiction or were living in Manhattan. I needed a Queens resident, someone who knows where I'm from. "I live in Astoria," I said to the woman in front of me, who was named Wendy. Her eyes widened. "Really? Me too." Bingo.

Says Wendy:
There I was at the Girls Write Now speed-dating event, hoping to find my mentee, the girl with whom I would be spending an hour, each week, for the rest of the school year. It was a monumental task. With a feeling of apprehension, I looked at the nametag of the girl sitting across from me. "My niece has the same name as you," I said. "But it's spelled I-R-E-N-E."

"Yeah," she said. "I think my parents meant to spell it that way but they messed up." That's when I knew Ireen was my perfect match.

Chandra Hughes was born in China and came to America when she was six months old. She now lives in Spanish Harlem in New York and is a sophomore at Millennium High School. **Claudia Parsons**, her mentor, was born in Scotland and has traveled the world as a journalist for Reuters, working in Turkey, Italy, Spain, Iraq, and now New York. This is Chandra and Claudia's first year with Girls Write Now.

Says Chandra:
I'm not one to like writing about facts. Fantasy and fiction are my style, so when I found out my mentor was a journalist I became worried. Naturally creative writing and journalism don't go hand in hand. However, the fantasy workshop inspired me to write a story and on our first meeting we began to write. "An Illuminating Road" is about two young adults meeting by fate and getting to know one another, just like Claudia and me: Cate, a journalist from New Jersey, created by Claudia's imagination, and Kisa, a princess from a magical world called Rondelia, created by me.

Says Claudia:
When Chandra asked me to be her friend on Facebook, I figured I must be doing something right. If she lets me be an observer to her digital life, I thought, it indicates some degree of trust. In fact, we found Facebook was a helpful way to write the story we are

working on together—a fantasy piece about a New York journalist and a princess in a different world. We would send each other the latest installments by Facebook messaging. I don't have many sixteen-year-olds among my Facebook friends, so it's been a great way for me to get to know Chandra better.

Kathryn Jagai lives in Brooklyn and attends Hunter College High School, where she is currently a junior. This year, Kat won both a Regional Gold Key and a national Gold Medal for her poetry from the Scholastic Art & Writing Awards. Her mentor, **Therese Cox**, is an adjunct assistant instructor of English at the City University of New York and currently writing a coming-of-age novel set in Dublin. Her fiction has appeared in *The Brooklyn Rail*. This is Kathryn's third year and Therese's first year with Girls Write Now.

Says Kathryn:

Therese's mind is a haphazard trove brimming with Irish customs, obscure music, and picturesque settings from all over the world. She imparts WWII trivia in the same breath as publishing anecdotes, relates stories about her band whilst discussing new projects, and never ceases to amaze with constant energy. Through art books, music addictions, sketches, photography, and our varied creative indulgences that always seem to come back to writing, Therese has shown me that you can always explore the world with the same relish you had when you first began. You just always have to be willing to take the risk.

Says Therese:

Fueled by a Java chip frappuccino and an iPod shuffle, Kat is tapping away at her laptop, fingers skittering so fast over the keys they've set her skull earrings swinging. A new poem. Sketches. Novel ideas. Oddball challenges we'll spend the week working into fiction. Torn-out clues from *The Guardian* cryptic crossword. Invented Texts from Last Night. 50,000 words in a month? Let's do it! Kat adds me as her NaNoWriMo writing buddy. Shadow Draconian, meet Faintly Macabre. From Kat I've learned the languages of mermaids and fashion proclivities of selkies. Her mind is pure steampunk energy; her writing soars.

Yvetha Jean was born in Haiti and four years ago she moved to Brooklyn, New York. She is a senior at International High School at Lafayette. **Nora Gross**, her mentor, is currently pursuing a master's degree in sociology of education at the NYU Steinhardt School and is also collaborating on a children's book on racial segregation. This is Yvetha and Nora's first year with Girls Write Now.

Says Yvetha:

Understanding: this is one of the words that describes my mentor. She always finds a way to understand me and respect my opinion and point of view. Having a vibrant mentor like Nora to guide me through challenges is the most wonderful thing. She is so supportive; she inspires me to become a better writer and also explore new forms of writing. She urges me to go deeper with my writing. My mentor is the key to my achievement.

Says Nora:

Yvetha's favorite subject to write about is one that scares me tremendously—love. Since our first day together, I've been gently nudging her to explore other topics, ones I thought *I* could be more helpful with. As we grew more comfortable with each other, I became more persistent and less gentle in my nudging. But my persistence was matched only by Yvetha's eager infatuation with love poetry! So the day that Yvetha came to our session with the first draft of a (non-love) poem about her home country of Haiti, she just about made my day.

Dalina Jimenez was born in the Dominican Republic. She moved to New York in 2003 and now lives in Washington Heights. She attends the High School for Health Professions and Human Services, where she is a junior. **Jessica Greer**, her mentor, works at Ballantine Bantam Dell, an imprint of the Random House Publishing Group, and has been published on hellobeautiful.com. This is Dalina's second year and Jessica's first year with Girls Write Now.

Says Dalina:

My stream of consciousness upon our first meeting: warm smile. Comforting voice. Not afraid to laugh with me. Happy to be with her already.

Says Jessica:

At our first meeting we were squished together in tightly placed fold-out chairs at a Girls Write Now workshop. We were awkwardly attempting to balance paper plates holding bagels and rolling carrots on our knees (not an easy feat!). Dalina seemed quiet and curious. I was eager to know what thoughts were churning in her mind. When the writing exercises began, Dalina dove right in, either writing furiously or lost in a train of thought contemplating her next literary move. Her writing floored me. It was so different from the quiet persona I thought I was sitting next to. She was bold, brave, and creative. I was hooked.

Massange Kamara moved to the United States in 2004 from Guinea in West Africa. She now resides in the Bronx and is a senior at Bronx International High School. This year, Massange won a Regional Gold Key from the Scholastic Art & Writing Awards. Her mentor, **Jenny Sherman**, is a freelance writer whose work has appeared in magazines such as *Men's Journal*, *Blackenterprise.com*, and *Jewish Living*. This is Massange's second year and Jenny's third year with Girls Write Now.

Says Massange:

Crossing the Washington Bridge is the one thing I look forward to after a long week in school. We always plan to meet at the Starbucks in Washington Heights where either all the good seats are always taken or there is no place for us to sit at all. After wandering around we finally sit in a restaurant. It goes like this. Jenny: "Are you hungry? Do you want something to eat?" Me: "Hmm, not really." Jenny: "Really? Are you sure? How about a drink?" Me: "OK, maybe a hot cocoa." We then spend an hour talking about college applications and annoying parents. From there we move on to small moments in our lives. Like Jenny's trip to Ghana, how she used to watch her host mother sweep the compound every morning, and how I grew up doing the same thing in Guinea. These conversations would soon become our inspirations for a new poem.

Says Jenny:

You drive. You steer along a slippery country road. It is nighttime, and the snow-covered fields are blue in the way they are when lit by a winter moon. The words come. Driving makes them flow, makes them run through a dark ditch of space between you, makes them pour from the mouth so thick and heavy you must pull to the shoulder, set the gear in park, stare straight ahead as you let the tongue thaw. You drive into dark places, still buckled in the seats. The car is warm. The map underfoot. You're lost, but not really.

Xiaoyu Li is a senior at International High School at Lafayette in Brooklyn. She was born in Guang Dong, China, and moved to Brooklyn in 2008. Xiaoyu won a Regional Silver Key from the Scholastic Art & Writing Awards for a piece of persuasive writing. **Katherine Jacobs**, her mentor, is an associate editor at Roaring Brook Press where she edits young adult novels, nonfiction, and picture books. This is Xiaoyu and Katherine's first year with Girls Write Now.

Says Xiaoyu:

It has been an incredible year! I remember our first chapter began with Kate's enthusiastic encouragement, "We are going to discover what you like to write about," in Starbucks. We explored more awesome places as we continued our writing adventure: The Tea

Lounge, Gorilla Café, and Flying Saucer. No matter where we met, we always started with the ritual embrace, coffee, and casual conversation. As we promised each other to explore interesting writing, we would start with a free write. Fortunately, we always ended our date nicely with a big smile from Kate when I said, "I like writing about this."

Says Katherine:

I was shocked when Xiao confessed to me at our first meeting that she didn't really like writing. The GWN staff had prepared me for lots of challenges but this was not one of them! So we took it one step at a time, trying out different writing exercises, getting inspiration from the monthly workshops. And we discovered that Xiao is a gifted and lyrical poet. That she doesn't enjoy imagining fantastical characters, but she loves listening to other people tell their stories and recording them with sensitivity and emotion. Her perspective is a constant inspiration to me as a writer and a friend.

Joanne Lin lives in Manhattan's Chinatown neighborhood. She attends Millennium High School, where she is a sophomore. **LaToya Jordan**, her mentor, works as the assistant director of communications and PR manager for New York Law School. Her poetry has appeared on the literary sites The November 3rd Club and the Splinter Generation, among others. This is Joanne and LaToya's first year with Girls Write Now.

Says Joanne:

I remember the screams from children, the laughter, and scent of coffee surrounding us every Sunday. I'll always think about the cozy feeling of books stacked in every bookcase. At times we would talk about anything, mostly about family because we both hold our families close to our hearts. I would tell her snippets of my life, often leading to us throwing back our heads and laughing. Sometimes she fascinates me with her writing; it makes me admire her skills. Sometimes, though, it's not the writing but having someone to talk to. It's the feeling of being comfortable with an adult while sharing common interests. I love the sound of us making remarks on strangers and the silence that invades when we're both scribbling away.

Says LaToya:

It was our first meeting and we were both nervous. Joanne and I broke the ice by each sharing a little about ourselves. We were amazed to find out how much we have in common, such as writing about our families and a love of blogging. We both are the oldest child to parents that are younger in age than the rest of our friends' parents. And we both hate it when people think our moms are our sisters! There were lots of laughs during that first meeting and we continue to find new connections at our Sunday sessions.

Daelina Lockhart lives in Staten Island. She is a senior at the College of Staten Island High School for International Studies. This fall, Daelina will attend Manhattanville College with a Manhattanville Presidential Scholarship. Her mentor, **Heather Graham**, is a senior editor at iVillage and has written for web sites like Papermag.com, NYMag.com, and Mediabistro.com. This is Daelina's second year and Heather's first year with Girls Write Now.

Says Daelina:

Heather and I met for a brief time at GWN, where we were introduced after losing our original mentor and mentee in the middle of the year. Even though our first meeting was short, I sensed that she was cool. My sense was correct because during our second meeting, Heather and I made a connection as we discussed our lives and hobbies. We realized that we both enjoy cooking and eating ice cream. I believe that Heather is an excellent mentor and I also don't know how my college process would have been without her prepping me for college interviews and helping me with my personal statement.

Says Heather:

In the beginning, Daelina and I were working in different pairs. We found ourselves without our counterparts around the same time and GWN put us together. We planned our first meeting to practice for Daelina's upcoming college interview. I immediately saw her forward-thinking ambition and impressive self-awareness. She nailed that interview, so we concentrated on her writing. Poetic and well-crafted, Daelina's talent and creativity inspired me to write a poem, a genre I abandoned long ago. I've been so honored to work with her in these months—she taught me that all I have to do to write, is write.

Octavia Lowrie was born and raised in the South Bronx. She is a senior at the School for Excellence, also located in the Bronx.

Julie Polk, her mentor, works as a writer at the branding firm Siegel + Gale. Her solo show, *Red White Black & Blue*, was named a Hidden Gem of the 2002 NY Fringe Festival by NYTheatre.com, and she has an MFA in nonfiction from the New School. This is Octavia and Julie's second year with Girls Write Now.

Says Octavia:

The relationship I have with Julie is amazing. She taught me how to write from different perspectives, use different tones of voice, and turn my creativity into a masterpiece. She helped me with grammar and spelling, and with my lateness. She supported me when I had a difficult personal problem, and she never judged me. And we had fun! A couple of Saturdays we went to movies and just had a good time. Although this is my last year in GWN, it's not my last year seeing my favorite mentor. We plan to still keep in contact, and I thank GWN for this opportunity.

Says Julie:

Tavy and I missed connecting one weekend. We started our make-up phone session talking about how to avoid that happening again. Then we started talking about fun stuff, like the poem she was working on, and the book I was working on—and which teachers drove her nuts—and our families—and our families' pets—and an hour later I was lying on the couch chatting and laughing like I do with all my girlfriends. And that's the moment when it hit me how much more than a mentor-mentee relationship we have. We have a friendship that's become important to both of us.

Alicia Maldonado lives in the Lower East Side of Manhattan. She is a junior at NYC iSchool. **Temma Ehrenfeld**, her mentor, has received two journalism awards as well as a scholarship to the Breadloaf Writer's Conference. Her literary essays and short stories have appeared in the *Hudson Review*, *Prism International*, and *Michigan Quarterly Review*. This is Alicia and Temma's first year with Girls Write Now.

Says Alicia:

A time when the lines of communication opened up between my mentor and me was when we went to Barnes & Noble. Temma and I usually spent our weekly meetings at Girls Write Now. One day we decided to venture out and go to the place where some writers basically live, Barnes & Noble. We rode the escalators like we were riding roller coasters at an amusement park, trying to find the perfect spot to sit and talk. Finally we found a spot where the store had chairs lined up so people could sit. We sat there for about an hour and a half talking about our feelings.

Says Temma:

I'd lost my watch: a simple one with a beige leather band, a round face, big numbers and a second hand. In the Swatch store, Alicia and I giggled over watches with polka dots and stripes. I pointed out my old watch. Beside it a watch with a lovely silvery-blue face glimmered. Alicia stood beside me, as I tried it on. She was in no rush. "The other one is easier to read," she said, reading my mind. "You're right," I said. That night, I found the lost watch, so I now have two of the same, reminding me of my supportive—and sensible—mentee.

Erika Marte was born in the Dominican Republic and came to live in the Bronx, New York, when she was two years old. She is a senior at the Bronx School for Law, Government, and Justice and was her class valedictorian. She will attend Hamilton College next fall as a Bill and Melinda Gates Millennium Scholar and also received a scholarship from Los Padres Foundation. Her mentor, **Maura Kutner**, is the associate features editor of *Harper's Bazaar*. Her writing has appeared in *Town & Country*, *Marie Claire*, *Travel,* and *Weddings*, and the blog New York Insider. This is Erika's fourth year and Maura's third year with Girls Write Now.

Says Erika:

I finished the last sentence of my poem and braced myself for the wave of cheers and applause. I immediately turned to my right for comfort and support, and lips covered in red lipstick, shaped into a wide smile, exceeded my expectations. Maura rubbed my arm, and that's how our second year together began. Together we laughed, had misunderstandings, disagreed, enjoyed meals, and wrote stories. Together we had a friendship.

Says Maura:

Erika and I have been working together for three years. Over that time, she has blossomed, both as a writer and a woman. This year, more than any other, has been a huge growing experience for both of us. We learned the importance of communication, honesty, and friendship. The shy fourteen-year-old I met years ago is now the valedictorian of her class, and I could not be

more proud of her. Her presence in my life has been a gift, one I know will carry on as she spreads her wings in college.

Meghan McCullough resides in Forest Hills, Queens, where she has spent her entire life. She is a senior at the Baccalaureate School for Global Education. This year, Meghan won a Regional Silver Key from the Scholastic Art & Writing Awards, and, this fall, will be attending Amherst College in Massachusetts. **Heather Kristin**, her mentor, is currently working on a memoir. Her first novel, *Brooklyn to Bombay*, was a finalist for the Amazon Breakthrough Novel Award. This is Meghan and Heather's fourth year with Girls Write Now.

Says Meghan:

Seven p.m. in Williamsburg is not a good time to review college essays. After getting kicked out of three restaurants for using a laptop, Heather and I found ourselves in a dark café, squinting into my laptop screen. "I need to get into this college," I said. "This essay needs to be perfect!" We read my essays in the haze of the café until the grumbling of our stomachs drowned out the words. "You'll get in, Meghan," Heather said as we got up to leave. Against my better judgment, my heart did a flip, because I trusted her, and I believed her.

Says Heather:

"I'm gonna throw up," Meghan said. We were an hour into watching the James Franco film *127 Hours*, and I too felt sick. Franco plunged the dull knife into his flesh. "He almost got the vein," I said, barely able to watch. After Franco broke his arm and became free, I realized the film was a metaphor for writing. Meghan and I met four years ago and began the process of digging deep, hitting the bone, and finding our voice. Sometimes the writing was difficult, but most of the time it hit a vein that went straight to the heart.

Shyanne Melendez was born and raised in New York City. She lives in lower Manhattan and is a junior at Millennium High School in the financial district. Her mentor, **Amy Feldman**, is an award-wining journalist who has been published in *Time, Forbes, Inc.*, and *The New York Times*. She has edited for *World Policy Journal* and taught nonfiction for Gotham Writers' Workshop. This is Shyanne and Amy's first year with Girls Write Now.

Says Shyanne:

I had never been to a bookstore dedicated to one genre of books before. So when Amy suggested a mystery bookstore I just had to say yes, being that one of my favorite genres is mystery. This was new for us both and we spent an hour finding books we wanted. This came along with our laughter, as we discovered new things about each other. I found one of my favorite books to this date in that store and it was all thanks to Amy, my mentor.

Says Amy:

The waiters who work at the Washington Square Diner have gotten to know us, and give us the same table each week. We sit across from each other, our black journals open on the pale pink Formica, and talk and write—fiction and poetry for Shyanne, nonfiction for me. Though the forms we choose are different, our approaches to topics are often similar. After going to the mystery bookstore one day, we wrote a short story together, trading the notebook every few sentences, ending only when we'd killed off the characters. It's been an amazing year so far, and I'm grateful to have gotten to share it with Shyanne.

Deiona Monroe hails from Harlem, New York. She is a senior at the Beacon School, and will attend Temple University this fall. **Ilana Manaster**, her mentor, is pursing an MFA in writing from Columbia University, concentrating in fiction and translation. As the winner of the Gilda's Club of Northern New Jersey annual Laugh Off, she is also working on a novel about stand-up comedians. This is Deiona's second year and Ilana's first year with Girls Write Now.

Says Deiona:

The strangest thing is that before our first pair session, I had never met Ilana; it seemed as though fate had put us together. Before encountering her, I didn't truly know what to expect and hoped that Girls Write Now had made the right decision of placing together people who didn't even know each other. Luckily, a perfect match was made. Ilana was just as bubbly as I was, always ready to take on the day while making sure nothing got boring or overwhelming. We laughed, connected, and even realized that we had much more in common than we thought.

Says Ilana:

I like to wait for Deiona. I wait for her in a café at Columbia University. Graduate students swarm around, stressing, flirting, and I sit at a little table with my coffee—Deiona doesn't drink coffee—looking through the glass doors, waiting for her to arrive. When I see Deiona approach, with her headphones and upright posture, I think: this is just the beginning for you, girl. She waves, and sits down at the table I've saved, and I can see the long and exciting life ahead of her.

Yvonne Ndiaye is a senior at Brooklyn International High School. She was born in the Bronx, moved to Senegal, West Africa, when she was seven, and returned to New York City in 2008. This year, Yvonne won a Regional Gold Key from the Scholastic Art & Writing Awards and read her original work at Fordham University's Poets Out Loud at Lincoln Center reading series. **Naima Coster**, her mentor, is pursuing an MA in English with a writing concentration at Fordham University. This is Yvonne and Naima's second year with Girls Write Now.

Says Yvonne:

A moment when I really felt connected with Naima was when we were sharing ideas about relationships and love, the positive and negative parts of them. I think then we learned something from each other and got to know a part of each other that never came out before. We ended up writing a poem about it that what we submitted for the CHAPTERS reading. It came out to be a very nice piece that teaches others the same way it taught us.

Says Naima:

Yvonne and I connect over many things—our love of poetry, funny stories, and life in New York. This year we also connected as young women writers with many different languages present in our lives. We read interlingual poems by Gloria Anzaldúa and Harryette Mullen and then wrote our own: me in English and Spanish, Yvonne in English, French, and Wolof. We were able to share stories of our families, the sounds and qualities of our different languages, and the practice of writing together about the topics most central to our hearts and identities.

Ariana Nicoletta lives in Staten Island and is a senior at LaGuardia High School of the Performing Arts. This spring, Ariana won Honorable Mention in the category of long teen plays in Writopia Lab's 2011 Bestival Playwriting Competition. Her mentor, **Anita Perala**, spent several years working for Perseus Books Group and is currently working on a historical novel. This is Ariana's second year and Anita's first year with Girls Write Now.

Says Ariana:

I was a mess when I first met Anita. I had a large pile of SAT vocabulary cards, a long list of colleges, and an empty Common Application sheet. Anita was my refuge from all of this. She calmed me down, treated me to a Starbucks coffee, and helped me to write a myriad of supplementary essays. After all of the craziness had passed, we treated ourselves to a night out at P&J's Restaurant and a play. It was a memorable night, spent sharing stories while splitting spicy french fries. Through the thick and thin, I had made a true friend.

Says Anita:

It was almost winter break, and after weeks of working with Ariana on revising, editing, and polishing college application essays, both she and I were in need of a break (and a respite from too-familiar Starbucks at Sixty-sixth and Columbus). The plan: dinner and a performance of *Hairspray* at her high school. My expectations were high—after all, wasn't this LaGuardia, the *Fame* school? The performance was terrific, but what was even more fun was getting to see Ariana in her element and to meet her family, a fitting way to celebrate the end of the year.

Marlyn Palomino was born in Miami, Florida, raised in Bogota, Colombia, and currently lives in Queens, New York. She is a senior at the Flushing International High School in Queens. In April, she read her original work at Fordham University's Poets Out Loud at Lincoln Center reading series. **Nancy Hooper**, her mentor, is a science writer whose work has appeared in a wide range of publications, including *Discover*, *People*, and *LIFE* magazine. This is Marlyn and Nancy's first year with Girls Write Now.

Says Marlyn:

"Now, that guy is cute ... okay let's write." Nancita and I shared a great connection from the start. We love to laugh—laugh to amuse, laugh to support, and laugh to hope. A "mentor" meant little to me, until the day I met her; she gave it a meaning—becoming a powerful figure in my life. "Cut and paste, and remember to show don't tell," she would always say. I

did just that, enjoying every moment working with her. Nancita is a down-to-earth woman ...very admirable and inspiring. Her personality is great! It is so easy for us to click. We're always ourselves around each other and our conversations are long, interesting, and very amusing. We are not just mentor and mentee now, but older and younger sisters as well. *Tu Lunita te quiere*, Nancita!

Says Nancy:

Go nuts! Get crazy! Give me juicy words! Those were my orders—requests!—and Marlyn delivered the goods. We had a blast working together this year. We discovered we have a lot in common: We're both Librans, we both lost our mothers—Marlyn's to cancer, mine to mental illness—and most of all, we love to laugh! I nicknamed her Lunita, in honor of Luna, a kitten she rescued one cold night by the light of the moon. She calls me Nancita. We text every day, and say I love you—often! We, the Libran soul sisters, bow to each other with gratitude for the time we've shared together.

ChanTareya Paredes, or TT, was born in Okinawa, Japan, but grew up in Charlotte, North Carolina. She moved to Brooklyn in 2008 and is currently a junior at Millennium High School in Manhattan. This spring, TT read her original work at Fordham University's Poets Out Loud at Lincoln Center reading series. Her mentor, **Alissa Riccardelli**, works at the NYC Teaching Fellows program and has studied at the Chenago Valley Writers' Workshop and the Tin House Summer Writing Workshop. This is ChanTareya and Alissa's first year with Girls Write Now.

Says ChanTareya:
There should be a law that kids in high school shouldn't have to get up before 12:00 p.m. on Saturdays. I was standing in Starbucks on a Saturday morning waiting for my mentor, holding a seat. Okay, I should rephrase that earlier statement: there should be a law that kids in high school shouldn't have to get up before 12:00 p.m. on Saturdays UNLESS their destination is a Starbucks. I didn't mind exchanging my oxygen for the rich scent of coffee beans. And when Alissa walked in, I knew I was going to be perfectly fine. It takes me a lot to sit patiently and have my work edited. Funny thing, I didn't realize that two hours had passed until my mother called and asked me where I was.

Says Alissa:
When I think of TT, I think of mochas, sticks of gum, mechanical pencils, little notebooks, and laughter. She's someone who stands out, is constantly energized, and always makes me laugh. On the day we met, we sat next to each other at the Poetry Workshop and couldn't exactly communicate, though I was so anxious to. She blew me away with her confidence and love of words. On the walk to the train later that night, we talked about jewelry and neighborhoods and writing, the two of us going a mile a minute. We were completely excited for the year ahead and all that we would learn about each other.

Emely Paulino lives in Queens and is a sophomore at the Young Women's Leadership School of Astoria. This year, Emely won a Regional Silver Key from the Scholastic Art & Writing Awards. **Jess Pastore**, her mentor, works as a fundraising coordinator for the American Civil Liberties Union. This is Emely and Jess' second year with Girls Write Now.

Says Emely:
Whether we're meeting in our usual spot or venturing to other locations, my meetings with Jess are always enjoyable. We begin by debriefing about our week, its ups, downs, and interesting moments. At most of our meetings, there's a soundtrack provided by the café that's included in our weekly commentary about art, books, or events. Through these conversations we've found inspiration and tips to help each other with our writing. After working together, we noticed that our styles are on different ends of the spectrum, but complement each other in a way that leaves us both happy and eager to write.

Says Jess:
Since our first meeting in a Bosnian café in Astoria, where Celine Dion songs blared on a seemingly endless loop, Emely and I have been eagerly comparing notes on music, movies, books, and art. We have so many opinions to discuss that it often takes an hour to get down to the brass tacks of our weekly meetings: our own writing. But when we do, I'm always surprised and thrilled all over again. Emely's patience and clear, concise voice are the perfect foil to my own attachment to detail, and I love watching the history between us grow as we share and write the stories of our lives, to the tune of Astoria's myriad café soundtracks.

Idamaris Perez lives in Washington Heights and goes to school at St. Jean Baptist, where she is a junior. Her mentor, **Demetria Irwin**, is the senior editor at MadameNoire.com and has been published in the *New York Amsterdam News*, *City Limits*, *Clutch* and the *The Boston Globe*. She is currently at work on the draft of her first novel. This May, Demetria and Idamaris were featured on USA Today's Kindess blog. This is Idamaris and Demetria's first year with Girls Write Now.

Says Idamaris:

Our first meeting was unforgettable. It was when Mother Nature was in her best of moods. She allowed Demetria and me to have a special first moment. Strolling my way to the Starbucks at Seventy-Eighth and Lexington while people swiftly walked past by me like at rush hour, I felt eager. It was my first time meeting Demetria. I waited for her outside of Starbucks. She came and we casually greeted each other. We entered Starbucks and decided to have a snack. She surprisingly treated me to a yummy dessert and hot chocolate. From that moment, I knew that my mentor was going to take care of me like a little sister.

Says Demetria:

We clicked from day one. We initially met up at Starbucks, but since it was a relatively warm fall day, we ended up sitting on those rocks in Central Park that are reminders of New York City's glacial past. We found out we had a lot in common, like parents with high expectations and a love of people watching. You'd be surprised how many people look just like their dogs in Central Park! We didn't write

on that first day, but we did recognize each other as writers and we agreed to support one another. We've stuck to that.

Anna Poon lives in Brooklyn and is a senior at Hunter College High School. This year, Anna won eight Gold and Silver Keys from the Scholastic Art & Writing Awards, including a Gold Key for her senior writing portfolio. She will attend Brown University this fall. **Nancy Mercado**, her mentor, is an executive editor at Roaring Brook Press working on middle grade and young adult novels. This is Anna's third year and Nancy's second year with Girls Write Now.

Says Anna:

Every time we meet we always manage to find something to talk about until our meetings run overtime and become more parts conversation than writing. But whether our conversations are about literature, old friends, boys, or music, I like to think of it as fodder for our writing and our writing minds. One time we both connected over how spectacularly good our brothers are at butchering our parents' native tongues, Chinese and Spanish. Because we are perfectionists, like all good writers are, and they just like to run their mouths. Then again, we do our fair share of that, too.

Says Nancy:

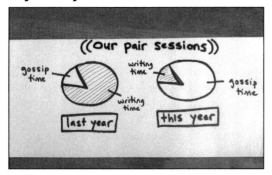

This is my unscientific grid of the amount of time spent in my pair sessions with Anna on writing and chatting this year vs. last year. I'm quite proud of these stats and the dwindling writing time, which is perhaps an odd thing to admit since Girls Write Now is a writing and mentoring program, emphasis on the writing. But to my mind the more we share in the chatting/gossiping section, the better our writing, the more I understand how to offer suggestions, and the more inspiration we get for our writing. I need to hear about the guy at school that Anna is interested in and Anna needs to hear about my trip to the South by Southwest music festival. This is essential to the writing process!

Ashley Richmond is a senior at Dr. Susan McKinney Secondary School of the Arts and she lives in Brooklyn. This fall, she will attend Nyack College. **Christina Morgan**, her mentor, works at Houghton Mifflin Harcourt in the trade adult editorial department. This is Ashley's second year and Christina's third year with Girls Write Now.

Says Ashley:

Funny, dependable, down to earth, and creative: these words describe Christina's personality as both a writer and a mentor. When I look back at my writing pieces from two years ago to now, I smile because my writing has improved a lot, thanks to her. She is the one main person who has both read and edited my work without making me change my writing style or my thoughts. Instead, she has helped me to advance them by teaching me many different writing tricks. She has taught me that the best writers always express themselves to the fullest, and I'm going to miss working with her when I graduate from Girls Write Now.

Says Christina:

The door was locked. Not simply closed, but surrounded by an intimidating iron gate, bolted shut with a heavy, rusty chain. The Jamaica Bay branch library was not open anymore on the weekends. I realized I would have to come up with a new place to meet Ashley on Saturday mornings in Carnarsie, Brooklyn. But where to go? The McDonald's in the strip mall across the way from the library proved our savior. It is there that we've plowed through college applications, GWN assignments, and occasional celebrity gossip. I think McDonald's will miss us next year.

Mitzi Sanchez is currently a senior at Flushing International High School and lives in Jackson Heights, Queens. Mitzi moved to New York from Mexico just over five years ago. She will be going to Lehman College in New York City this fall. Her mentor, **Rhonda Zangwill**, works at Barnard College as the senior associate director for institutional support. She has published work in *Hoi Polloi*, *Calyx*, and *Gotham Gazette*, among others. This is Mitzi and Rhonda's first year with Girls Write Now.

Says Mitzi:

I'd never heard of Barnes & Noble before Rhonda asked me to meet there. Big, old bookstore on Union Square. Our first session was on a rainy day. I was rushing to get there on time. We usually meet on Wednesday or Friday. It's never the same. Second floor on the cafeteria, crowded and loud. There was nowhere to sit. Luckily, we found a brown wooden table. Two chairs, one table, and two stories to share. With tears running down our cheeks, a special feeling developed, and it made me feel that she'll be there for me no matter what. Rhonda gently reminded me of the importance of being a writer, and not to think too much but just put my feelings on paper. Writing was already a friend of mine, but now we share a friendship that will last. It's been a great year so far. I'm looking forward to more mysterious writing adventures, and coffee.

Says Rhonda:

Not long into our first meeting, the clamor of the bookstore café evaporated. I heard only Mitzi telling me, trusting me enough to share a remarkably personal family story. Soon we were both sniffling, but also smiling. Pablo Neruda says that things remembered often blur in the recall. Did we share a pack of Kleenex at that moment, or the remains of a blueberry muffin? Who knows? What I do know is that we shared something more important and lasting: a connection, a bond suffused with trust-honesty-empathy and even a little bit of laughter. Come to think of it, not a bad prescription for the writing life.

Emily Sarita has lived in Brooklyn and Queens her whole life. She currently resides in Williamsburg, Brooklyn and attends NYC iSchool in Manhattan, where she is a junior. **Jana Branson**, her mentor, is a culinary publicist at John Wiley & Sons. This is Emily and Jana's second year with Girls Write Now.

Says Emily:

Starbucks was the local spot that Jana and I spent our time talking and writing at. The smell of the coffee and the music playing in the background was so comfortable that I wondered about exploring more coffee shops. Jana and I would explore different cafés like Amy's Bread and Cocoa Bar. Somehow, we always ended up in a Starbucks. It's nice to know how a coffee shop can really bring two people together. I'm glad I have Jana as a mentor. She makes me want to be a better person and writer.

Says Jana:

Our meetings each week have become such a constant in our lives—amidst the snow, the rain, SAT's, school, work, college tours, and family and friends—we can always count on our weekly pair sessions. One week, as we sat down to chocolate twists and coffee (it's amazing how much can happen in one week), we decided to write about our weeks and read to each other instead of telling each other. We didn't put down our pens for twenty minutes, and what we both wrote was surprising and wonderful.

I: (*thinks hard*) The laundry.

R: So maybe you can write a piece called "Laundry Sucks."

I: Could I call it just "The Laundry"?

R: Right on!

Ilana Schiller-Weiss was born in Xiemen, China, and moved to New York when she four. She lives in Manhattan and is a freshman at the School of the Future. Her mentor, **Rollie Hochstein**, has published two novels and three dozen short stories. Her work has been anthologized in O. Henry Prize and Pushcart Prize collections and she recently won first prize in a *Glimmer Train* competition. This is Ilana's first year and Rollie's sixth year with Girls Write Now.

Says Ilana:

I don't even really want to be a writer when I'm older. I count myself more as a practicing writer. The first time I met Rollie, I was not expecting an older mentor. But Rollie helps me to find my writing voice and to just let things out. The time Rollie and I fully clicked was when we started to work on the writing.

Says Rollie:

Rollie: So, Ilana, what do you want to accomplish this year with GWN?

Ilana: Well, uh, I thought maybe I'd like to get a, well, a stronger writing voice?

R: OK. We can try for that. You've brought in some writing. It's about an elf in a park. You have a fine vocabulary, good command of language, and a humorous style.

I: Thank you. (smiles)

R: Maybe you should write something you have strong feelings about. You're so agreeable. Maybe you should write about something you hate. What do you like to do least?

Syeda Showkat was born in Bangladesh and immigrated to New York at four years old. She has lived in the Bronx for the past thirteen years and is a senior at the Nightingale-Bamford School. This year, Syeda won a Regional Gold Key from the Scholastic Art & Writing Awards and had her original play directed and performed by theater professionals at the off-Broadway June Havoc Theatre as part of Bestival 2011. Next fall, she will attend Kenyon College. **Kirthana Ramisetti**, her mentor, is managing editor at Snackable Media and writes a blog focused on media and entertainment. She also serves as Co-Editor of this Anthology, and as Communications Co-Chair on the GWN Program Advisory Committee. This is Syeda and Kirthana's second year with Girls Write Now.

Says Syeda:

I had my first meeting with Kirthana in the fall of my junior year. We bonded quickly over our love of pop culture and the hot guys on *Glee*! It was a great start and, as time flew by, our Starbucks meetings (incidentally caffeine free) extended from the world of television shows and writing to our daily lives, habits, likes and dislikes. Kirthana and I have learned so much about each other that we have become more than just a mentor-mentee pair. I can proudly say that I've not only found an amazing mentor but, more importantly, a great friend.

Says Kirthana:

When Syeda and I were paired together, we immediately bonded over *Glee*. While we had a lot of fun conversations about the show, I think what deepened our relationship was when we compared our Thanksgiving experiences. Since we're both South Asian, we talked about how our turkey day meals are an interesting (and often funny) fusion of South Asian dishes and spices. In exchanging these stories, I was first introduced to Syeda's amazing gift for storytelling. It's been a true honor to be her mentor, and I'm so excited to see what the future holds for her.

among other things. After seven months, our experiences and memories are still growing. Maybe there will be even better ones next year.

Says Christina:

For geographical convenience, we met at the Borders by Penn Station. Like going off to war, the battle for a table was a bonding experience in itself. But despite the consistent location, the shape of our meetings was never the same. I attribute that to Ashley. One week she'd bring in a poem, the next her first-ever short screenplay. She pushed me out of my comfort zone and into genres I would rarely read, let alone attempt to write. It's been a phenomenal year, and I can't wait to see what the next one brings.

Ashley Simons was born and raised in Cambria Heights, Queens. She is a freshman at St. Francis Prep in Fresh Meadows, Queens. Her mentor, **Christina Brosman**, works at NBC Entertainment on the publicity teams for shows such as *30 Rock* and *SNL*. This is Ashley and Christina's first year with Girls Write Now.

Says Ashley:

I was nervous about meeting Christina for the first time since we found out we'd be working together. I got off the dirty E train with my mom and walked to Borders on Seventh Avenue and Thirty-Fourth Street. "Here we go," I said, as I opened the doors. That first day was an interesting experience. We talked and got to know each other. We found out each other's likes, dislikes, and favorite books and genres,

Cherish Smith lives in Arverne, Queens. She is a senior at Brooklyn Community Arts and Media High School. Next fall, she will attend SUNY Oswego. **Vani Kannan**, her mentor, is the associate managing editor of psychotherapy titles at W.W. Norton & Company. This is Cherish and Vani's third year with Girls Write Now.

Says Cherish:

I would say there was an instant click between Vani and me before we were officially paired. Even now it blows my mind how we managed to request one another. I'm always quick to remind Vani whenever we share the story of GWN origins that I thought her name was Bonnie for a while. Silly, I know. As every year passed it's gotten better and better. Vani and I have inside jokes that my TWIN doesn't even know about, and that's how I know our relationship is nonrefundable.

Says Vani:
Cherish is young with an old soul and I'm old with a young soul and we meet somewhere in the middle. We sit on her bed and write songs and laugh like kids at a sleepover, and sip hot drinks across a table from each other talking about the harder stuff the way I imagine "grown-ups" do. One day, maybe when she is thirty and I am forty, we'll meet in the middle somewhere.

Joy Smith lives in Arverne, Queens, and is a senior at Brooklyn Community Arts and Media High School. She will attend SUNY Oswego this fall. Her mentor, **Emma Straub**, released a collection of short stories, *Other People We Married*, in January and her debut novel is forthcoming. This is Joy's third year and Emma's second year with Girls Write Now.

Says Joy:
When I think about ways in which Emma and I fused, to be honest, I don't remember. In general, whenever we meet our time is full of laughs and maybe that's why I can't remember. I just laugh off all the specifics of our relationship. But if there is one thing I can remember: it's when we both realized that we didn't remember how we came up with our reading piece. But it doesn't matter because I can recall the times when she asks how my day is or what happened in school, and gives me advice on my teenage life. That's what I'll always remember.

Says Emma:
Joy is a sly one. What I love most about our pair sessions is when she surprises me with a precise zinger of an observation. She is the queen of deadpan delivery. Sometimes we write during our meetings, sometimes we snack, sometimes we spend the whole hour talking. Whatever we do, it's always entertaining.

Shannon Talley was born in Manhattan and raised in the Bronx. She is a senior at Celia Cruz Bronx High School of Music and, next fall, she will attend Plattsburgh State College. **Jen McFann**, her mentor, is a recruiter for a government volunteer agency. She won a 2002 Scholastic Art & Writing Award for novel writing and also served in the Peace Corps in Georgia. This is Shannon and Jen's second year with Girls Write Now.

Says Shannon:
It's hard to pick out a moment when you connect with someone that you have so much in common with. With discussions of fantasy and sci-fi, history and writing, every conversation between Jen and me seems like one where we connect. However, I think that we connected the most this year when we were pondering ideas for our reading piece and it hit us…this is our last year at Girls Write Now! That gave us a stronger connection and the inspiration for our reading piece came from that—the fact that we would be leaving this life behind and starting a new one really soon.

Says Jen:
Shannon and I usually ricochet through a few cafés on Seventh Avenue before we find one

with an open table. The longer we search, the greater my sense of failure as a planner. I'd felt the same rising remorse for inadequate preparation as I waited in front of sixty girls and women for a reader at our first workshop. Just then, Shannon—never one to seek the limelight—raised her hand and read, quietly keeping our boat afloat like she does every Tuesday when she elbows her way through the Penn Station commuter crowds, improvising with me all the while.

Lucy Tan is a junior at Stuyvesant High School and lives in Brooklyn, where she's lived her whole life. This year, Lucy won a Regional Silver Key from the Scholastic Art & Writing Awards. Her mentor, **Lee Clifford**, is the founder of Altruette, a charitable company that designs products for nonprofits. She previously spent ten years as a writer and editor at *Fortune* magazine. This is Lucy's first year and Lee's second year with Girls Write Now.

Says Lucy:

I find Lee to be a very good conversationalist, always able to make some fun out of my stressful schooldays whenever we meet. She brings me out of my reserved and stressed frame of mind for an hour every week, which is a comparatively short but priceless time. Schoolwork often pushes me into a metaphorical hermit shell, otherwise known as the desk I sit at many hours a night, and I inevitably lose track of the outside world and the greater me. Our weekly meetings, though, are valuable and reflective, allowing me to walk out onto the street at the end of every hour feeling new and refreshed from the things we've talked about and the words we've written.

However frazzled my student life may be, I would not trade the time spent with Lee for an extra hour of studying every week.

Says Lee:

Lucy is one of the most goal-oriented people I've ever met. But she doesn't always come right out and say what's on her mind. For our first few meetings we talked a bit, did some random writing exercises, and got to know each other. But at about our fourth meeting, I felt like it would be a good idea to dig a bit deeper and figure out if Lucy had any specific ideas about what she wanted to get out of GWN. I expected some vague responses about becoming a better writer, but instead it turned out that Lucy had three very specific goals, which she immediately laid out. First, explore writing in "other" voices; second, complete a long fiction piece; third, submit her poetry to competitions. It surprised me (in a really good way) that she had such a firm grasp of what she wanted to accomplish, and her direction has focused our pair sessions ever since.

Ayodele Temple lives in Brooklyn and is a senior at the Urban Assembly School for Law and Justice. She will attend Hampton University in Virginia this fall. Her mentor, **Sacha Phillip**, is a freelance copyeditor and an editor at *Honey* magazine. She is currently drafting her first novel. This is Ayodele's second year and Sacha's third year with Girls Write Now.

Says Ayodele:

The past two seasons felt like a lifetime, and over this time I've gained a best friend. Sacha has come to ALL my shows, either as part of the crowd of the people who came to support me or as the only one. She also helped me throughout my college process and helped me get into my first choice school. I'm thankful for having her in my life and I hope she will be there for me for years to come.

Says Sacha:

Over the past two seasons of Girls Write Now, Ayodele and I have shared an inspired journey—through literary genres, poetry slams, and the college application process. I watched proudly as she blossomed from an introverted, though passionate, sophomore poet to a college-bound stage-commanding performer of her own one woman show. I can't wait to see what she achieves in her next "stanza."

Nehanda Thom lives in Brooklyn and is a senior at Brooklyn Collegiate. Next fall, Nehanda will attend St. John's University in New York with a Ladder for Leaders Mayoral Scholarship. **Marisa Crawford**, her mentor, is a senior editor at Small Desk Press and the author of *The Haunted House*, a poetry collection which won the 2008 Gatewood Prize. This is Nehanda and Marisa's first year with Girls Write Now.

Says Nehanda:

She sat next to me for the first twenty minutes of the workshop. She wore large glasses, and had straight brown hair and brown leather oxfords. Her morning salutations were complemented by what seemed to be a genuine smile, so I knew I'd be comfortable with her for the next three hours. We talked to each other more than necessary, shared our desire to be paired with someone "cool,"

as if being assigned a middle school science project partner. When our names were called together, I looked everywhere but to my left side where she sat. That was our moment.

Says Marisa:

At the first GWN workshop, I sat down next to a young woman with big brown eyes and a stylish purple outfit, and we started chatting instantly. We were both a little jittery and nervous to learn who we were paired with. When my name was called, I scanned the entire room, until I realized Nehanda was standing right next to me. We laughed and hugged. She was eating a blueberry bagel, and as the day went on we joked about how well her breakfast matched her purple outfit. I knew it was going to be a good year.

Yolandri Vargas lives in Inwood Heights, Queens, and is a senior at the New Design High School. This year, she won a Regional Silver Key from the Scholastic Art & Writing Awards. Yolandri earned a Ladders for Leaders Mayoral Scholarship and will attend SUNY Purchase next fall. Her mentor, **Robin Henig**, has written eight books and is a contributing writer for *The New York Times Magazine*. She received a 2010 Guggenheim Foundation fellowship and was a finalist for a National Book Critics Circle Award. This is Yolandri and Robin's second year with Girls Write Now.

Says Yolandri:

I was stressing out about visiting the campus of SUNY Purchase on my own for the first time. Robin told me that planning out my trip, just like she does before her trips, would make me less nervous. Maybe Robin doesn't know this, but with the schedules and maps of the Metro-North and Beeline 12 bus, she taught me how to get to Purchase and also that getting lost was okay. Eventually, somehow, I would be able to find my way to wherever I am going. And if my destination changes mid-trip, that is also okay. Mistakes and taking chances are essential to life. Robin has encouraged me to take chances with traveling, calling a boy I like first, and getting lost in my life to figure myself out.

Says Robin:

The first time Yolandri was supposed to visit SUNY Purchase she cancelled "because it was raining." I was upset; would all her hard work be undone by her fear of traveling solo? I understood that fear, so we plotted her trip carefully. Yolandri went to a Metro-North station the day before to buy her ticket. But on the appointed day, she ended up at the wrong station! Luckily, she phoned me and with the help of a guy on the platform, we figured out how to get to the right station. I knew then that I'd been a help to Yolandri. She now has the inner strength to head out on her own toward the rest of her life.

Quanasia Wheeler lives in Harlem and is a senior at Bronx School for Law, Government, and Justice. She will attend Agnes Scott College in Georgia this fall with an Honors Scholarship. Her mentor, **Cynara Charles-Pierre**, is the creative director of internal communications for News Corporation. This is Quanasia's fourth year and Cynara's second year with Girls Write Now.

Says Quanasia:

The moment that really set up our relationship this year was when Cynara and I were in McDonald's during our trip to Georgia. We were there with her mother and her nieces and I learned she isn't intimidating only to me. She was giving her nieces the same kind of interrogations that she gives me during our meetings, and I found it to be very funny.

Says Cynara:

A moment that gave me a little more insight into Quanasia was when I was picking her up from the airport in Atlanta and the first thing she told me (with a sigh) was that she loved boys with accents. I then knew why she was interested in attending college in the South. I assumed her interest in Spelman was about the sisterhood when, ironically, it was all about the boys. I had no idea what a little flirt she was until then. I thought it was so adorable, and very much something a seventeen-year-old girl would care about.

Samantha Young Chan lives in the Lower East Side of Manhattan and is a sophomore at Baruch College Campus High School. **Kristin Vuković**, her mentor, is a freelance reporter and researcher at *InStyle* and was also a reporter for *Condé Nast Traveler's* Gold List 2011. This is Samantha's first year and Kristin's second year with Girls Write Now.

Says Samantha:

I was sitting by a table at the GWN headquarters when I heard footsteps approaching. Glancing up, I watched as Kristin walked into the room. I hadn't met her yet and, as this was my first time, was very excited. Once she sat down, we began to chat. At first, we only answered the icebreaker questions, but then we started to talk about our lives and learn lots more about each other. As we left the building later and stepped out onto the cool, breezy streets, I definitely knew I couldn't wait until the next time we met.

Says Kristin:

When I first met Samantha at GWN, I remember thinking we'd be a great match. There were many sessions where we focused on editing her pieces at Starbucks and Artichoke Café near GWN—it was amazing to see her rapid improvement in such a short time. But the real moment of connection came when we did a sensory exercise through Chelsea Market and the High Line. We used all five senses, including tasting gelato, and recorded our impressions in our journals afterward. I was thrilled when Samantha told me she'd never done anything like that before.

Mentoring the Next Generation of Women Writers Since 1998

Girls Write Now is the first organization in the United States to combine mentoring and writing instruction within the context of all-girl programming. We match bright, creative teenage girls from New York City's underserved public high schools with professional women writers as their personal mentors. With mentoring at its core, Girls Write Now offers an immersive experience that fully engages the participating girls through one-to-one weekly sessions with their mentors, monthly genre-based collaborative workshops, a public reading series, college preparation, free therapeutic support, and countless opportunities for scholarship and publication. **While half of New York City's youth fail to complete high school, 100 percent of GWN's seniors graduate and move on to college—bringing with them awards, scholarships, a new sense of confidence, and new skills.** At Girls Write Now, our mission is to help these girls realize their writing potential and to provide a safe and supportive environment where they can expand their talent, develop independent creative voices, and gain the confidence to make healthy school, career, and life choices.

To join or support Girls Write Now, visit us online at www.girlswritenow.org.

Letter From the Executive Director...

Seventy-five years ago, Virginia Woolf argued that a woman who wants to write should have a room of her own. To create that space for the hundreds of young girls we serve each year, we leased a full office suite. In September 2010, Girls Write Now moved into raw loft space overlooking Manhattan's bustling Garment District. Nestled between Port Authority and Penn Station, surrounded by views of water towers, rooftops, and a silhouette of the midtown skyline, the women of Girls Write Now had tickets to any destination imaginations could conjure. Among the sewing machines and fashion wholesalers, we added our dreams and our stories to the neighborhood fabric. After twelve years of sharing a workplace, we finally had a home of our own.

Friends and supporters donated desks, chairs, and office supplies; our hardworking staff designed an open plan for collaborative work; and writers filled the shelves with their books. With pens, notebooks, and a bank of computers, our new class of talented young women, and more than two hundred volunteers and mentors, set up shop. On any given day, this room of our own on the Eighteenth Floor might host an intergenerational memoir writing workshop, a poetry curriculum planning meeting, an Anthology Committee roundtable, drop-in hours with a pro bono therapist or college prep advisor, and as always, one-to-one editing sessions.

Just nine months after settling in, our accomplishments were recognized with an invitation from the President's Committee on the Arts and the Humanities to the White House–our second visit there in less than two years! The East Room almost felt like home when our First Lady welcomed us, and literary idols shared their fears and pleasures of being a writer. On the local scene, Girls Write Now was admitted into the prestigious MacArthur Foundation network of nonprofit organizations. Along with partners like the Museum of Modern Art and the Brooklyn Public Library, we have begun to explore innovative ways for young women writers to acquire the writing skills necessary to meet the challenges of twenty-first century media.

Girls Write Now is home to an ever-growing community, building from our core of mentors and mentees, to an intricate network of volunteers, as well as to the more than 7,000 alumnae who have been enriched by our programming. At the conclusion of our thirteenth season, we stand poised to mentor the next generation of women at a time when the digital potential of their words transcends not only the borders of New York City, but also the psychological and socio-economic boundaries that historically have kept women from writing. We are committed to refining our enterprise of communal writing for a new era.

With deep gratitude for everyone in the Girls Write Now family who contributes to making our ambitions possible.

Sincerely,

Maya Nussbaum
Founder & Executive Director

HIGHLIGHTS FROM 2010-2011

Our Girls:

- Continued Girls Write Now's impressive 100 percent college acceptance rate. Graduating mentees will attend schools including Brown University, Kenyon College, Duke University, Hamilton College, Mount Holyoke College, Dickinson College, Agnes Scott College, Temple University, and St. John's University in the fall of 2011.

- Were awarded 25 Gold and Silver Keys plus two National Medals from the Scholastic Art & Writing Awards. Additionally, Girls Write Now was invited to participate in the 2011 National Scholastic Art & Writing Awards Exhibition at the World Financial Center.

- Read with Marie Howe at Fordham University's Poets Out Loud at Lincoln Center reading series.

- Earned impressive honors and awards, including a graduating mentee who was selected as a Posse Scholar and was a finalist in the Urban Word Knicks Poetry Slam. Two girls were recognized by Bestival, a production of forty-five award-winning plays by teen playwrights—one received an Honorable Mention and another saw her play directed and performed by theater professionals Off-Broadway.

- Received a prestigious array of scholarships, including the Bill and Melinda Gates Millennium Scholarship, the 125th Anniversary Women's Scholarship from Bryn Mawr, Ladders for Leaders Mayoral Scholarship, Knicks Poetry Slam Scholarship, Dean's Scholarships, and the Pace Incentive Award.

- Maintained our successful student retention rates, with 82 percent of eligible mentees returning from previous years and 94 percent of girls who entered the program staying through the full 2010–11 year.

- Celebrated American poetry and prose at the White House with President Barack Obama and First Lady Michelle Obama at a May gathering of poets and cultural luminaries that included Elizabeth Alexander, Rita Dove, Billy Collins, Steve Martin, Jill Scott, Common, and Aimee Mann. Ten poets from our Mentoring Program attended an afternoon poetry workshop hosted by the First Lady. Girls Write Now was one of seven organizations from around the nation invited to participate.

Our Mentors & Leaders:

- Published numerous books and stories, including Emma Straub's *Other People We Married* (FiveChapters Press, 2011); Tayari Jones's *Silver Sparrow* (Algonquin Books, 2011); Maggie Pouncey's *A Perfect Reader: A Novel* (Pantheon, 2010); Renée Watson's *A Place Where Hurricanes Happen* (Random House, 2010) and *What Momma Left Me* (Bloomsbury, 2010); Léna Roy's *Edges (*Farrar, Straus and Giroux, 2010); Ruiyan Xu's *The Lost and Forgotten Languages of Shanghai: A Novel* (St Martin's, 2010); and Nana Brew-Hammond's *Powder Necklace* (Washington Square Press, 2010).

- Achieved an ever-increasing year-to-year mentor retention rate, this year at nearly 60 percent, with four of our mentor alumnae moving on to leadership positions on our Program Advisory Committee or Board of Directors.

Girls Write Now:

- Served 120 combined women and girls through our mentoring program—a record number and an increase of 10 percent from last year, more than a 70 percent increase over the past three years.

- Accepted more than 90 percent "high-need" girls, as we targeted six low-performing public schools in five boroughs for special outreach, along with our 50-plus regular partner schools.

- Developed additional support systems to meet our mentees' needs: a volunteer Therapy Panel of 11 licensed therapists for consultations and individual counseling sessions with mentees, and a volunteer College Prep Advisor with open office hours and individual sessions by appointment.

- Expanded the Girls College Bound program by 70 percent, from 150 to 250 participants.

- Launched our Youth Board, composed of Girls Write Now active and alumnae mentees, who helped lead workshops and trainings, interviewed guest authors, emceed public readings, and were instrumental in designing our growth and digital media plans.

- Held our first major fundraising benefit, featuring an exclusive performance of *Carson McCullers Talks About Love*, written and performed by Suzanne Vega. The evening raised funds for our Mentoring Program while expanding our audience and reminding guests of the potential inherent in our girls (McCullers published her first piece at nineteen).

- Saw the largest crowds ever in attendance at our spring reading series, CHAPTERS, hosted at the historic John Street Church in lower Manhattan, featuring a line-up of guest authors curated by literary blogger Maud Newton.

- Received significant press coverage, including a *Wall Street Journal* profile and articles in *New York* magazine, *Time Out New York*, and *Metro New York*, as well as online coverage through Tonic, Flavorwire, The Rumpus, and USA Today's Kindness blog.

- Was one of 11 non-profits invited to be 2011 partners in the MacArthur Foundation-funded New Youth City Learning Network for NYC-based organizations that use digital media to educate high-school students.

- Veteran community leaders were accepted to present at an AWP Panel for the second consecutive year, sharing Girls Write Now's teaching practices with writers from around the nation.

- Continued to expand our fundraising efforts between 2009 and 2010, marking a 35% increase of foundation, corporate, individual, and government contributions. Our goals for 2011 reflect a 71% increase of nearly $200,000 in just two years to fund mentoring enhancement, curriculum extension, and program expansion.

- Cheered as our Founder and Executive Director, Maya Nussbaum, was named by the Feminist Press as one of their "40 Under 40" marking the future of feminism.

GIRLS WRITE NOW LEADERSHIP

Girls Write Now's largely volunteer-driven operation is fueled by a talented brain trust of professionals whose tireless service to our ever-growing community is a gift beyond measure. With pride, we celebrate our esteemed network.

BOARD OF DIRECTORS

Andrea Juncos, Board Chair

Lisa Chai, Treasurer

Keisha DePaz, Secretary

Marjorie Coismain

Julie K. Kohler

Nancy K. Miller

Maya Nussbaum

Kamy Wicoff

Linda Winston

Finance & Audit Committee

Lisa Chai, Finance & Audit Chair

Marjorie Coismain

Julie Kohler

Yanelly Molina

Maya Nussbaum

Joanne Sepetjian

Fundraising Committee

Marjorie Coismain, Fundraising Chair

Jana Branson

Paige Cerand

Ashley Howard

Maya Nussbaum

Erica Silberman

Elaine Stuart-Shah

STAFF

Maya Nussbaum, Founder & Executive Director
Meghan McNamara, Program Director
Jessica Jorge, Program Coordinator
Emily Grotheer, Communications Coordinator
Jessica Wells-Hasan, Director of Development & External Affairs
Marek Waldorf, Development Manager (through April 2011)

Consultants

Maria Romano, Curriculum Consultant
Jennifer Hou, Technology Consultant
Tamiko Beyer, Teaching Artist
Susanna Horng, Teaching Artist
Mary Roma, Teaching Artist
Erica Silberman, Teaching Artist
Hope Pordy, Attorney
Alan Stricoff, CPA, Controller
Gabriel Gutierrez, Bookkeeper

Interns

Samantha Diaz	Amalie Kwassman
Caitlin Hamrin	Giovanna Montepaone
Avital Isaacs	Natalie Thomas
Marlee Kimmick	

College Preparatory Volunteers

Moira Taylor, College Prep Advisor
Thomas Rabbit, Consultant

Audio/Visual Volunteers

Jennifer Chu	Nabil Rahman
Caitlin Curran	Ann Marie Reilly
Kei Haynes	Julia Smith

213

PROGRAM ADVISORY COMMITTEE

Morgan Baden, Program Advisory Committee Chair
Kirthana Ramisetti, Communications Co-Chair
Nicole Summer, Communications Co-Chair
Maya Frank-Levine, Curriculum Co-Chair
Mary Roma, Curriculum Co-Chair
Andrea Gabbidon-Levene, Enrollment Co-Chair
Heather Smith, Enrollment Co-Chair
Erin Baer, Pair Support Co-Chair
Anuja Madar, Pair Support Co-Chair
Erica Silberman, Readings Co-Chair
Josleen Wilson, Readings Co-Chair

Workshop Teams

Fiction
Allison Adair Alberts
Kate Jacobs
Jen McFann
Nancy Mercado
Aria Sloss

Poetry
Tamiko Beyer
Mayuri Amuluru Chandra
Marisa Crawford
Jessica Greer
LaToya Jordan
Nancy Shapiro

Journalism
Linda Corman
Amy Feldman
Robin Henig
Nancy Hooper
Claudia Parsons
Jenny Sherman
Ingrid Skjong

Memoir
Jessica Benjamin
Samantha Henig
Rollie Hochstein
Demetria Irwin
Heather Kristin
Wendy Lee

Screenwriting
Christina Brosman
Cynara Charles-Pierre
Therese Cox
Temma Ehrenfeld
Katherine Nero
Sarv Taghavian

Sketch Comedy
Jana Branson
Erica Dolland
Tasha Gordon-Solmon
Ilana Manaster
Julie Polk
Michele Thomas

Readings Committee

Amanda Berlin
Heather Graham
Maura Kutner
Hannah Morrill
Jess Pastore

Juliet Packer
Anita Perala
Sacha Phillip
Emma Straub
Kristin Vuković

Anthology Committee

Kirthana Ramisetti, Co-Editor
Léna Roy, Co-Editor
Karen Schader, Copy Editor
Lee Clifford
Rachel Cohen
Naima Coster
Kristen Demaline

Nora Gross
Vani Kannan
Jennifer McDonald
Christina Morgan
Elaine Stuart-Shah
Rhonda Zangwill

ADVISORY BOARD

Caroline Berger
Lisa Bowden
Tara Bracco
Paige Cerand
Celesti Colds Fechter
Jenny Comita
Kathryn Daneman
Dimitra DeFotis
Allison Devers
Sandra Fathi
Anne Fernald
Jennifer Fondiller
Rigoberto Gonazlez
Catherine Greenman
Catherine Hardee
Allison Hellegers
Susanna Horng
Gloria Jacobs
Tayari Jones
Min Jin Lee

Elizabeth MacCrellish
Courtney E. Martin
Julie May
Bruce Morrow
Maud (Rebecca) Newton
Cindy Pound
Sara Reistad-Long
Lyla Rose
Margaret Leigh Schmidt
Nancy Shapiro
David Shuff
Kathleen Sweeney
Leslie Taylor
Moira Taylor
Michele Thomas
Timothy Travaglini
Christina Wang
Renée Watson
Tiffany Winbush
Cindy Yang

Youth Board

Rocio Cuervas	Amalie Kwassman
Samantha Diaz	Carmen Li
Shira Engel	Yolandri Vargas
Emma Fiske-Dobell	Samantha White
Tina Gao	

Therapy Panel

Kristin Long, Co-Chair	Cora Golfarb
Julie May, Co-Chair	Judi Levy
Betty Bederson	Nancy Long
Jason Conover	Stephanie Vanden Bos
Barbara Draimin	Sarah Zahnstecher
Judi Evans	

GIRLS WRITE NOW SUPPORTERS

Girls Write Now would like to thank Amazon.com, which provided the charitable contribution that made possible this year's anthology, *Opening Lines*.

We are grateful to the countless institutions and individuals for their generous donations at all levels. While space restricts the number of donors we can recognize here, each and every gift has allowed our organization to grow and thrive. Thank you.

Government

National Endowment for the Arts

New York State Council on the Arts

New York City Department of Cultural Affairs, in partnership with the City Council

Manhattan Borough President's Office

Foundations & Corporations ($10,000+)

Amazon.com
Brooklyn Community Foundation
William T. Grant Foundation
The Hyde & Watson Foundation
The Rona Jaffe Foundation
New Youth City Learning Network Fund at The New York Community Trust
No Longer the Island of the Day Before Foundation Fund of RSF Social Finance
The Pinkerton Foundation
Union Square Awards, a project of the Tides Center

Foundations & Corporation ($1,000 to $9,999)

Adco Foundation
Assurant Foundation
Baird Foundation, Inc.
The Bay & Paul Foundations, Inc.
Colgate-Palmolive Company
Crosswicks Foundation, Ltd.
EILEEN FISHER
Ferris Greeney Family Foundation
The New York Community Trust
Palisade Capital Management
Patrina Foundation
Ruth Asset Management Co., LLC
Significant Objects
The South Wind Foundation

Foundations & Corporations ($250 to $999)

American Express Charitable Fund
ATE Logistics, Inc.
Glassybaby, LLC
The Leon Levy Foundation
Protégé Partners, LLC
Snackable Media LLC
Susquehanna International Group, LLP
Time Warner
Tinderbox Arts
United Way of New York City
Vicky Dry Cleaning, Inc.

Individuals ($1,000+)

Maurice & Sophie Biriotti

Lisa Chai

Lee Clifford

Keisha DePaz

Catherine Greenman

Edward P. Krugman and Ethel Klein

Nancy Mercado

Anne T. Pelletier

Léna Roy

Charles and Karen Schader

David W. Selden

Kamy Wicoff

Individuals ($500 to $999)

Janet Jeppson Asimov

Marya Cohn

Marjorie Coismain

Catherine Hardee

Allison Hellegers

Andrea Juncos

Julie K. Kohler

Oksana Kukurudza

Michelle T. Laraia, Ph.D.

Nancy Long

Thomas E. McCullough

Nancy K. Miller

Bernard J. Picchi

Margaret Leigh Schmidt

Steven R. Shapiro

Nomi R. Silverman

H. Michael Summer

Linda Winston

Individuals ($250 to $499)

Jami Attenberg

Nina Berg

Leo J. Cox

Brian Cumberland

Kathryn Daneman

Kathryn Edwards

Amy Feldman

Maura Frank, M.D.

Dr. Helen Ghiradella

Rigoberto Gonzalez

Kyle Good

Linda Gui

Akir Gutierrez

Michael J. Hirschhorn

Gloria Jacobs

Courtney E. Martin

Frank Michnoff

Julia Monteith

Ashley Phillips

Julie Polk

Hope Pordy

Janine Poreba

Todd Pulerwitz

G. Michael Royal

Dr. Sanjay N. Shah

Ardath K. Solsrud

Susan Straub

Maureen E. Strazdon

J. Courtney Sullivan

Elisabeth Summer

Jay Suresh

John H. and Maria A. Taylor

Eric C. Tone

Margaret Waller

James S. Wicoff, M.D., P.A.

Suzanne Woolley

In-Kind Consultation Services

Shena R. Ashley & Paul D. Hirsch, Maxwell School of Syracuse University

Cause Effective

M+E/Michael Fusco Design

Megan Henry

She Writes

Karen Schader, KAS Editing

Joanne Sepetijan

David Shuff

Siegel + Gale

Kathleen Sweeney, Video-Text

Deb Tremper, Six Penny Graphics

Youth, I.N.C.

Youth Development Institute, a program of The Tides Center

In Kind

4 Cats Press

Algonquin Books

Alliance for Young Artists & Writers

Altruette

Avon

Morgan Baden

Belathee Photography

Jamie Cat Callan

Lisa Chai

Constant Contact

CRAVE nyc

Dean & Deluca

Delta Fiction

FiveChapters Books

Graywolf Press

Stuart Griffin

H&H Bagels

HarperCollins

David Hart

Henry Holt Books for Young Readers

Holt Paperbacks

Jennifer Hou

Institute for Expressive Analysis

InStyle Magazine

The Jagai family

John Street Church

Knopf Doubleday

Little, Brown and Company

Edna and Donald McNamara

Suzan Merrit

Nicole Miller

Norma J. Niehoff-Emerson

Juliet Packer

Nicholas William Parsons

Penguin Group

Poets Out Loud at Lincoln Center

Daniel Posner, Grapes The Wine Company

Devoynne Prophet

Random House, Inc.

Roaring Book Press

Scholastic, Inc.

Scholastic Books

Simon & Schuster

Spivak Lipton, LLP

Sunday Salon

Gail Stuart

Sarv Taghavian

Tiffany & Co.

TLCommunications, LLC

Wiley & Sons Publishing

Willow Books

Josleen Wilson

Linda Winston

Writer's House

Young to Publishing Group